Blackwell, Elise, 1964 –
Grub /

Brooklyn Branch
Jackson District Library

WITHDRAWN

# Grub

Elise Blackwell

The Toby Press

*Grub*
First Edition 2007

*The* Toby Press LLC
POB 8531, New Milford, CT 06776-8531, USA &
POB 2455, London WIA 5WY, England
www.tobypress.com

© Elise Blackwell 2006

The right of Elise Blackwell to be identified as the author
of this work has been asserted by her in accordance
with the Copyright, Designs & Patents Act 1988

All rights reserved. No part of this publication may be reproduced,
stored in a retrieval system, or transmitted in any form or by
any means, electronic, mechanical, photocopying or otherwise,
without the prior permission of the publisher, except in the case
of brief quotations embodied in critical articles or reviews.

This is a work of fiction. The characters, incidents, and
dialogues are products of the author's imagination and are
not to be construed as real. Any resemblance to actual events
or persons, living or dead, is entirely coincidental.

ISBN 978 1 59264 199 4, *hardcover*

A CIP catalogue record for this title is
available from the British Library

Printed and bound in the United States
by Thomson-Shore Inc., Michigan

Blackwell, Elise, 1964 –
Grub /

Brooklyn Branch
Jackson District Library                    11/05/07

*This contemporary retelling of George Gissing's*
New Grub Street *is dedicated to every*
*writer with an unpublished novel*

# Chapter one

It had been casual, the remark that changed Jackson Miller's understanding of what his life would be. The caterer had just rolled out his three-decker birthday cake: a replica of the historic luxury liner docked in Charleston Bay. Peculiar calliope music trickled from the wall-mounted patio speakers as Jackson breathed in the smell of spun sugar.

Some other kid's mother had whispered *rich boy* as the cake was presented. "My son's *parents* may be rich," his father drawled in response, "but that says nothing about Jackson. I plan to spend our money before he inherits a penny of it." His father's laugh had pierced the tinny music as Jackson waited in line with his guests, squinting against the sun, to see if the frosting tasted like it smelled.

That's all it had taken to alter his course. That's all it had taken, because he already loathed the man who never let him take a chess piece without retribution, who lined up his sailing trophies across the breakfast table every time his son failed to touch home plate, who told his son that reading too many books would divide him from useful society.

Had Jackson's decision to triumph alone in the world come

later than his ninth birthday, he might have chosen a more sensible career. He'd been good at things from the day he learned to walk, and he might have succeeded at any number of them. So he'd been told by his mother and then by the teachers whose thresholds he'd crossed. If Jackson had postponed his decision to rise on his own merits until the age of thirteen or fourteen, he might have made money in law and followed with a political career. He might have battened down and accomplished something in science or medicine. If he'd waited out high school—those were the years that brightened his complexion and delivered his height—he might have had a real shot at the stage or screen.

Timing is decisive, though. On his ninth birthday, Jackson had just read *My Side of the Mountain*, the first book he'd truly loved. And so as he watched the yacht-cake sag in the summer heat, he decided to succeed as a writer. In the years that followed, he wrote very little. But he read every novel he could grab and studied the biographies of Hemingway, Fitzgerald, and later Henry Miller. He practiced his lines on college girlfriends, told his father to go to hell and stay there, and spent a precarious year in France, where he wrote a story a month. Admitted to a good graduate school, he revised those same dozen stories until they were really pretty good. Now, fifteen years after that decisive birthday, his stories had landed Jackson on the patio of the Outlook Bar on the last night of the Blue Ridge Writers' Conference. Grasping the rail installed to keep inebriated patrons from slipping down the mountain, he surveyed the view. The sun had just set, and the mountains curved against the pink, darkening sky. Jackson photographed the image with a blink and considered metaphors to capture its essence. He tried to picture whales swimming, but the color of the sky didn't suggest the ocean. He considered elephants, planets in orbit, giant shadows. The only satisfying idea he had was that of ink on paper. That's not bad, he thought: the writer seeing the world as script.

Still, he was certain he would think of something much better when he was not drinking his third gin. He believed what Norman Mailer claimed: the only difference between an experienced writer and an inexperienced one is the ability to work on a bad day. From the father who had cut him off, Jackson inherited confidence as well as the height that had made him sixth man on the only team his college ever sent to the NCAA tournament. He had talent, enough of it, and the impoverished-gentry charm supplied by what remained of his Charleston accent. He would provide the rest himself; he planned to start a writing regimen as soon as he was back in New York. No one was going to write his first book for him.

Exhilarated by altitude, expansive vista, and intended new rigor, he determined that he would return to the Blue Ridge Writers' Conference—as paid guest rather than paying participant. He told himself he would arrive as the author of largest reputation and bank account. Five years, he gave himself. He gave himself until the end of his twenties.

He had reason for optimism. The week had gone well. The members of his workshop group had admired his short story about the ambitious young gentile dating the daughter of a rabbi. Leading his workshop was Andrew Yarborough, who had noted Jackson's subtle wit and praised several turns of phrase. "The woman's terrific, too," the venerable editor said. "You do good women."

Jackson had also captured Yarborough's attention while discussing the other story up for analysis that day: a beginner's piece in which a man on death row wakes to find that his situation was a bad dream. Jackson had been the one to explain that the ending was a gimmick, and a clichéd one at that. Worse, the writer had missed the only intriguing idea in her story. "Imagine," Jackson had said, "imagine the glory of the condemned man when he realizes that he has brought society to its last resort. What a thrill that must be. At any rate, there's no other reason to write this story, and no reason to read it as it is now."

As Jackson finished his speech, he saw the writer's chin tremble and realized he'd gone too far. "But the descriptions are first rate, quite original, particularly of the chaplain," he added, wondering if he was turning into as big a prick as his father.

"Most of the physical description is pretty good," Yarborough had agreed. "But have you ever noticed that almost no one has gray eyes in real life?"

As they made their way out of the building and into the summer's full humidity, Jackson watched the young woman who'd written the story stride quickly across the parking lot, her arms folding the marked-up copies of her manuscript tight to her chest.

Yarborough clapped him on the back and whispered, "They're dumb as shoes, aren't they?"

Jackson had known that his fantasies of being approached by an agent keen on selling his stories wouldn't materialize, so this seemed like a real gift: a nod from a man who had launched many a literary career. He felt bad about the other writer, but he believed that blunt criticism was the greater kindness in the long run. She would avoid her mistakes next time and improve her writing, or else she'd move on to something she had more talent for and be the happier for it. He decided to count the week a general success, as the beginning of something bigger.

Giving up on the mountains, he turned back to the conversation heating between his friend Eddie Renfros and two other one-book writers: a young woman named Jennifer Reiner, who'd published a novel detailing the bed-hopping antics of twenty-somethings considerably less pudgy than she was, and Henry Baffler. Jackson and Eddie had met Henry at the conference, adopting him as a sidekick and reminding him when meals were served. Henry was the author of *The Quotidian World* and champion, in the form of passionate essays published in obscure periodicals, of something he called The New Realism.

"No, no, no," Eddie said in a bourbon-assisted staccato. "You shouldn't even have a notion of plot until at least your third draft." He ran his free hand through the reddish hair that always looked overdue for a cut and shook his head, clearly exasperated with the idea that anyone might write using an outline.

*Sea Miss*, Eddie's first novel, had been published four years earlier to real acclaim. The critic who had named it to the Book Critics' Circle of *The Times* had praised it for its intensity of language, gemlike images, and refusal to sacrifice character to plot. It was precisely this hailed unobstrusiveness of plot, Jackson was convinced, that accounted for the book's paltry sales and the rejection of Eddie's second novel, *Vapor*, by every major publishing house in New York. This serial rejection was, in turn, the cause of the writer's block that Eddie referenced at the slightest inquiry into the status of novel number three, as yet untitled.

"He spends more time writing desperate query letters to tiny presses that publish only two books a year than he does on his new work," Eddie's wife had confided to Jackson.

Jackson knew that his friend was about to tell one of his most well-worn stories. Eddie was about to explain that it was while he was working on the third draft of *Sea Miss* that the idea of the young woman came to him—*emerged from the images themselves*, he would certainly say, *from the language*—leading him to what plot the book did contain and resulting in the change of title from *Sea Mist*.

Eddie had been his best friend since the first day of their first Iowa workshop, but Jackson was convinced he couldn't hear the story repeated again without hurling himself over the protective gate and off the mountain top. He scoured the crowd on the patio for a less dramatic means of escape. He could excuse himself to the bar to purchase the next round of drinks, but a mental count of the contents of his billfold ruled out that option. He had just enough for two more of his own drinks, provided he had sufficient authorization left on one of his credit cards to cover the tank of gas back to New York.

"Look," he said. "Look casually," he emphasized. "Over your left shoulder, Eddie, just glance. That's Andrew Yarborough."

"Everyone says the Lannan Foundation and the Isherwood Foundation both call him for names. He got that experimental novelist who claims to write inside-out—whatever the hell that means—a grant for ten grand," said Jennifer.

"Inside out?" Henry's scrawniness made his head seem large, and when he tilted it Jackson almost expected it to fall off his neck. "I wonder if he means his process is inside out—how he goes about writing—or if he means the book itself. Interesting idea."

"The guy thought it was a joke when they called," Jennifer continued. "Thought one of his friends was playing a prank. They told him they had their ear to the ground and found out about his work. But it was Andrew Yarborough who passed along his name."

"Ten grand," Jackson repeated, thinking that was just the amount he needed to even his debts. "Based on what that guy writes and where he publishes, I assume that was considerably larger than his last advance. Now he probably thinks he has some sort of proletariat credibility, while it was really Andrew Yarborough."

"I heard he introduced Nancy Sloan to his agent, and she got Nancy a six-figure advance for a collection. A collection set in Kansas, for godsakes." Gesturing with her hands as though she wasn't holding a mug, Jennifer sloshed beer on her pointed shoes.

Jackson handed her his napkin and smiled. "For the damsel in distress."

"As I was saying," Eddie commandeered the conversation. "It was while writing the third draft of my book, while reworking a description of morning fog over the ocean, that I realized that I was using, using without intending to, decidedly feminine language."

He annunciated *using without intending to* slowly, with practiced emphasis, again raking his hair.

Jackson grabbed his escape. "There's nothing I'd rather hear again than the story of the miss from the sea's mist, but I'm just liquored up enough to seize the day. I'm going to throw my up-and-coming self in the path of Herr Yarborough. I hear he's starting a new journal now that *The Monthly* has passed over to Chuck Fadge, so he may be in need of an assistant editor who shares his tastes in literature." He set his empty glass on one of the knotty pine picnic benches. "Whatever those may be."

Feeling his adrenalin rise, Jackson composed his pitch in the twenty steps it took to navigate the patio. He grasped Yarborough's fleshy hand in greeting and then spoke quickly, tasting the fumes of his last gin. "I may be just the man you're looking for, but I'm going to say straight out and right up front that I do not see any room for poetry in your new journal. None at all. Not now and not later. We—and I use the plural pronoun only speculatively, only as an act of optimism—we want to build a new kind a readership, a new circulation. Cultured but not old. Select but not small. Well-read but not poor." And then, to make sure that Yarborough considered him in the right context and with proper affection, he added: "Wearing good shoes, not as dumb as shoes."

The middle-aged woman who had been talking to Yarborough was not unattractive, but she flashed all the accessories of a neglected resort-town wife: crystal pendant, wide silver rings and bangles, and a fringed summer sweater dyed the precise blue of her eyes.

She moved her wine glass to her left hand and accepted Jackson's handshake. "It's such a pleasure to meet so many writers." She squinted in an imitation of merriment. "I mean, this is what it's all about, isn't it? The camaraderie of a community of writers. The support, the feedback. How fabulous to feel as though one is normal, as though expressing oneself in words is a worthy thing to do. Noble even, or at least no worse than any other occupation."

Jackson tasted the word *noble* in his mouth, then repeated it aloud. Impressing Yarborough was the most important move he could make in his career, he calculated, at least until he had actually written a book of his own. He looked steadily at the woman, feeling the old basketball-court thrill. "Let me guess. This is your first writers' conference. You use journal as a verb. You call what you write creative nonfiction, but it's really more a case of uncreative non-writing." He pictured his smile as it looked in the mirror and produced it, his voice gaining volume. "I dare you to tell me I'm wrong."

The crinkles that fanned from the corners of her eyes held for several seconds, but her mouth fell out of its smile immediately.

Jackson turned to Yarborough. "I guess they let in anyone who pays, but it really is time to outlaw people who have led uninteresting lives from writing memoirs."

"Your name, young man. Remind me of your name."

Forgiving Yarborough for not remembering his name, Jackson congratulated himself for taking a risk.

"Jackson Miller," he said, "author of 'Old Waldman', the story from yesterday's workshop. If things go my way, and I have every hope they will, you'll be hearing my name a good deal in the next few years."

"Not if I can help it, but, Jackson Miller, I guarantee you that I won't ever forget your name again. And for your information, my wife is one of this country's finest poets." Yarborough took the blue-eyed woman's elbow. "She's won prizes you've never even heard of."

Jackson cursed himself aloud as he pushed through the absurdly narrow doorway and into the crowded bar, seeking the only person who could restore his confidence after so serious a misstep.

He found Amanda Renfros at the bar, surrounded by a buzzing semicircle—men trying to catch her attention with louder voices, sharper or merely raunchier jokes, larger bills appearing to buy more rounds of drinks.

"Make room," he heard her say. "Our next most important writer has arrived. Make room."

He heard a male voice parse the double meaning of *next most important*. Emotionally winded from the encounter with the Yarboroughs, he was relieved to have such weak competition.

He shouldered through, and Amanda popped up, patted the stool. "Take my seat while I lengthen my legs. I need to stand." And there she was on full display. She had the long blonde hair and green eyes of the it-girls of his teenage years, impeccable posture, and a waist curve that gave Jackson an uncomfortable misty feeling that he preferred not to examine. Doreen, his ex-girlfriend and current roommate, always said Amanda had perfect bone structure, but Jackson saw in her face an endearing asymmetry. Her smile reached a little further on one side, and her nose, while straight, pointed just slightly to the left. A modern girl, he thought, though there was something regal about her that transcended contemporary style. He couldn't quite see her as an ancient Greek beauty or a Victorian aristocrat, but he could easily imagine her cast as one. Someone should write her a screenplay, he thought, wondering if her beauty would translate into two dimensions.

"Bartender, get this man some gin." Amanda leaned over him to place the order, pressed her hand on his shoulder, let him smell her hair—grapefruit clean despite the visible smoke in the bar. "Throw in a twist while you're at it."

"I could use a double," he said to her ear. "Do you think I'm turning into an asshole?"

"Turning *into* one?"

"Aren't you the wit. But seriously, I think I made two women cry today. In any event, I've gone from 'next-most-important' to 'most-likely-to-be-blacklisted.' *And* I'm a fraud. I can't even think of a new way to describe those mountains outside."

"Of course you can, Jack." Her voice was bright as she swirled the ice cubes in her glass. "If anyone can think of a new way, you're that guy. You may not have timeless beauty and profound themes and unobtrusiveness of plot going your way, but you're nothing at all if you're not a man of your day."

# Chapter two

Eddie Renfros awoke feeling as though his forehead was wrapped in rubber bands. It was going to be one of the major hangovers of his life. Top ten, he thought, perhaps even top five. He opened one eye, closed it, then reluctantly opened both, wincing from the already full light. Lying on his side, he took in the brown acrylic blanket, the cabin's glossy faux stucco walls, the artwork painted by someone untrained in perspective, the white resin table holding last night's final empty bottle. This is what it's going to be like, he thought, once we lose the apartment.

He'd suspected, even at twenty-three, that his early success was a jinx. Still in Iowa, his MFA a semester away from completion, he'd been granted an advance that sounded like the beginning of wealth and prompted him to propose to Amanda, whom he'd always figured would wind up with Jackson if she didn't abandon them both to marry a rich guy.

Now, indulging in a little hangover-earned self-pity, he resented his early fortune. It would have been better to have had his first novel go unpublished, to have placed *Vapor* modestly but with a good house, and to be on the eve of his breakout book. That's how it used to happen for writers, how it's supposed to happen. If Eddie couldn't finish and sell his new book soon, they'd lose the Murray Hill apartment where Amanda said she could live happily until they really made it. She had already worked in a publishing office a year longer than the year they'd agreed upon, and Eddie knew all too well that Amanda wasn't the kind of person who could work indefinitely for a boss who wasn't as smart as she was. He contemplated what it would take to keep her if they had to move somewhere cheaper, but that was too dreadful to consider even when he was feeling well. He could barely admit to himself and certainly had not admitted to Amanda that he had nothing of a third novel beyond a thrice reworked thirty pages.

He turned to reach for his wife. He would pledge undying love, show remorse, beg her to find the vending machine and buy him a coke. "I'm ready to get home and really write. Tomorrow I go back on a schedule," he rehearsed. "Once we're back in the city, things will be better than normal. I'll finish my book by winter. I'm not even going to revise the first chapter again."

His fingers grasped only cool, thin sheet, and he turned over to find himself alone in a room that smelled like mold. Sometimes when he awoke to find Amanda already up and about, he feared that she was really gone, that she hadn't even stuck around to make sure that he would indeed become the failure he seemed capable of being.

When Jackson had asked him if it was wise to marry someone ambitious, Eddie put it down to jealousy. Yet he'd also taken the question seriously; it was something he'd weighed. The simplest answer was that he loved Amanda. He loved her looks, of course, but he also loved her because she was funny and interested in the world. He admired the strength of imagination and the determination with which she had reinvented herself at the age of eighteen. He thought, even, that she could lend him some of what he lacked, that perhaps he could write while she managed his career. And feeling like a success with a book under contract, he hoped he would satisfy her desire to rise in the world.

Now, wretched, he fell back into sleep.

When the creak of the opening door wakened him, he was

both grateful and aroused to see his wife, coke can and ice bucket in hand.

"I don't deserve you. You're perfect. You're stunning." He could barely speak through the headache squeezing the width of his forehead.

She poured the coke expertly. The fizz rose through the ice just to the rim of the glass and subsided before she topped it off. "Drink some cold caffeine and find the courage for a shower. The reading is in an hour, and then we need to hit the road."

The reading was held inside the faux-chalet Outlook Bar, the sight of which brought back embarrassing memories from the previous night. Eddie could be obnoxious when he mixed liquors. Now he remembered ranting about the drafting of his first novel, telling Henry Baffler about the blurb from Jonathan Warbury that had arrived too late to go on the jacket, and letting Jackson know he'd had sex with Amanda that morning. He vowed that in the future he would stick to the same cocktail all night, alternate drinks with glasses of water, and keep his big mouth shut.

The beer-on-carpet smell unsettled his stomach, and his headache hadn't let up. He'd only been able to get down about half the coke. His goal now was to not vomit on stage. They took a side-front table, and he concentrated on the view of the mountains through the wall-sized plate-glass windows as the room filled with hundreds of people.

"This will be the most people you've ever read to," whispered Amanda, her hand comforting on his thigh.

The reading of published past participants was the final event of the week-long Blue Ridge Writers' Conference. Eddie was slated to read third, following a woman who'd written a novel about the yearnings and losses of the members of a book club and Jeffrey Whelpdale, a basically amiable fellow forging a literary career in the absence of evident talent.

Whelpdale had not gone so far as to self-publish, but he hadn't received an advance for his book. It had been printed by a West Coast house whose publisher was an old chum of his, and the son of a man with a wad of expendable capital. Whelpdale had generated sales by placing each of the stories in the book of interconnected short stories—he called it a novel in stories—in assorted youth and other writer-targeted magazines such as *Swanky*. He'd also sold thousands of copies to writers themselves through his "writers' resource website," whose features included "hot agent of the month" and "creating a literary prize." It could only be a matter of months before he penned a how-to book about writing and publishing.

Jackson and Amanda loathed Whelpdale, but Eddie liked him despite himself. Whelpdale was so frank, so utterly honest about what he was doing and why, that you couldn't fault him for ulterior motives. And his happiness at the success of other writers seemed genuine. Whelpdale seemed to think he was doing what he was doing for all of them. Besides, he was one of those big guys who actually *is* jovial, and Eddie generally enjoyed talking to him.

Jackson, looking incredibly fresh and as annoyingly tall as ever, approached and took a seat at their table. "Great crowd. Capital." He looked around. "They serving coffee?"

"Downright uncivilized, isn't it?" Amanda swung her hair over her shoulder. "Who are you looking for?"

"Have you seen Andrew Yarborough here?"

"Nope," Eddie said, wondering if Amanda's rearranging of her hair signified a change in mood.

The conference host—an elderly, spry woman with sterling silver hair and a reputation as a master of the short story—stepped on stage and welcomed the crowd.

"This is both the saddest and happiest day of every year. Saddest, because our fabulous week is over. Happiest, because this reading is the proof in the pudding that our hard work and effort, not to mention our faith—yes, our faith—can and will be rewarded." She punched her fist into the air.

Amanda and Jackson snickered a little. Eddie feared that Amanda would be stricken with the giggles. In Iowa, they'd once had to leave a poetry reading because she couldn't stop laughing and the poet had hated them both ever after, even though Amanda had tried to apologize, tried to explain that it wasn't the poems but an association they triggered that had caused her laughing fit.

"Does she think she's preparing troops to march to their death to save Paris?" Jackson whispered.

The woman at the microphone continued. "Not only that, but our work will reward the world with more great writing to lift the human spirit." And with that, she introduced the author of *The Book Club*.

Amanda snickered again, and Jackson coughed into his hand.

The writer ascending the stage was a woman Eddie had heard earlier in the week telling a group of young admirers, "Now that I've done the novel thing, I'm not sure what I'm going to try next. Some kind of catering business, maybe, or perhaps just a screenplay. And I've always wanted to paint."

Eddie figured she deserved the disdain of his wife and best friend. He hated the idea of writing as midlife hobby, the idea that writing isn't a lifelong commitment to an art form but just one more skill to acquire, one more activity to check off your list. Still, he glanced left and right to silence Amanda and Jackson, and the three alumnae of the country's most prestigious writing program braced themselves to hear the paisley-wrapped novelist read about the small loves and large disappointments of the members of a women's book club.

"She's brilliant, really," Amanda said when it was over, no longer bothering to whisper. "Write about your target audience, and they will buy."

Whelpdale took the stage next with a swaying gait that moved his formidable body from side to side. He tucked his hair behind his ears, adjusted the microphone with confidence, and cleared his throat into it. What followed was characteristic Whelpdale: slews of sentences containing "as though" and "as if" in which the two parts were identical rather than analogous. "He walked quickly into the room, as though he wished to move fast," he read in a lilting voice. "The house's owner had hung a Mets cap and an original Picasso, as though he believed the two belonged at the same level."

Jackson snorted.

"She put on her sweater, as if she were cold," sent Amanda back to giggling.

Even so, all would have been fine, except that Whelpdale read for fifty minutes. The entire session was supposed to have lasted an hour—twenty minutes per writer. People were leaving. At first only those in the back slipped away. Then around the room whole tables rose noisily and left.

Whelpdale read on. "He found her appearance simpatico, as though she were agreeable and sympathetic to him."

"Get off the fucking stage," Jackson finally hissed, his southern accent leaking.

Whelpdale looked as though he'd been struck across the face and finished with haste.

Eddie stood quickly and read for seven minutes to those who remained. Amanda had pleaded with him to read from the second book or the new one—there were often agents and editors present at these things—but Eddie was more comfortable reading from a published book than from a manuscript and in his condition he wanted to read something familiar. Avoiding eye contact with his wife, he read the emergence scene from *Sea Miss*. The room was well over half empty when he shut the book with a soft clap.

Amanda cursed Whelpdale for the first hour of their trip home. "I'm so angry on your behalf!" She drummed the dashboard of the rental car with both fists, holding the steering wheel straight with her knees.

"I don't deserve you, Amanda. To defend me when everything is my own fault. If I could be more disciplined, I'd be out on my own book tour now instead of third billing at some conference for would-be writers."

"You just need to get back home and on a schedule. Maybe a timer would help."

"I wish I was good at something else, or had a family business I could go into. Then I could give you more. It's stupid to try to write for a living. I'm an idiot for doing it."

"Don't be dramatic," she said. "Writing is as good a business as any. But since we aren't independently wealthy, you might try a little harder to think of your work as your business. You could do good work *and* work that would sell if you could only look at it a little more practically. I know we always make fun of Jack, but he's not altogether wrong. I won't be surprised if he sits down and writes a bestseller someday."

"Well, I'm not Jack. He's naturally optimistic, and I'm not. I know you're probably right, but that doesn't mean I can actually do what you suggest." He watched the blur of trees through the passenger-side window. "I need your sympathy more than your advice."

"Eddie, it's just that romantic poverty sounds good when you're young, when it seems noble to write beautiful, obscure work. But it gets old fast. I liked reading your reviews, hearing you on the radio, having people recognize us at the bookstore. And now I know what good things cost. I don't want to go back to living like I did as a kid. That's not why I got the hell out of Wilkes-Barre on my eighteenth birthday. If I had to choose between literary reputation and contemptible popularity, I think I might take the bestseller."

"No you wouldn't, Amanda. You're not like that."

"But you're so talented, Eddie, I want you to have the audience you deserve. Wouldn't you rather be read by more people than less? Don't you want people to hear what you have to say?"

"What I have to say, yes. Not what they want me to say. Not at the price of writing crap. Have you tried to read some of the books that are out there?"

"But you write beautifully. Your book wouldn't be crap. It would just be more accessible, more the sort of book you can't put down because you want to find out what will happen." Amanda always used her hands when she talked, and now, even as she used one hand to drive, her right hand fluttered. "This is what I propose. Take a week and plot out a short book—one with a good story to it. Then write it out, but with the classic Renfros style. You'll see that you can tell a good story and write well."

"Don't forget that it takes a particular talent to write that sort of story," Eddie continued. "Plot has always been the hardest but also the least important thing to me."

"We need gas." Amanda, both hands back on the wheel, veered the car onto a billboard-lined exit. "Look, just pick something straightforward, something that the book clubs will eat up. A love story. A dead child. An animal with supernatural empathy. A narrator with some rare affliction or who's already dead."

"I'm going to assume you're joking. You know that's against everything I believe in, everything you believe in," he said as they pulled into a brightly painted station. Before stepping out to pump the gas, he muttered, "Or used to believe in."

After the tank was filled, they found a diner, where Eddie treated his hangover with grease, eavesdropped on the local dialect for future use in a story, and watched his svelte wife eat two pieces of coconut cream pie instead of lunch.

"It's the only thing edible in these sorts of places," she said, explaining as she always did why she would eat only pie in a diner.

"You don't really want me to write a novel about a supernatural animal?" asked Eddie, putting more pepper on his hash browns.

"Of course, not, Eddie. But I do want you to think more about what you write before you start writing it. I bet you could write a really interesting historical novel."

Back in the car, now behind the wheel, Eddie suggested that they might cut down on expenses as an alternative to making more money. "We could move across the tunnel. There are some really good apartments in Jersey City. A lot of artists and bands are moving over there. It's becoming a place to be."

"I don't care how much 'there is there'. If you think I'd live in New Jersey for even a day, you don't know me at all."

Eddie smiled at the Gertrude Stein reference. He looked at his wife's pretty cheekbone, the shape of her ribcage, the profile of her breasts, and began to rack his still sore brain for interesting situations and a plot that someone would turn pages for. Perhaps it wasn't a bad idea to consider a novel set in the past, to comment on the present by depicting another moment in time. Maybe he could discover something about human behavior in a time of war or famine while using a historical plot as a framework.

# Chapter three

Jackson Miller had spent his final ten dollars on two overpriced drinks at the Outlook Bar on faith that he had enough plastic credit for a tank of gas. Now he found himself hundreds of miles from New York, standing in the animal heat and insect hum of tiny Wattleborough, North Carolina, inserting every credit and debit card he possessed into a heartless gas pump. Each effort produced the same effect: dot-matrix orange letters proclaiming "authorization denied."

He pondered his options, which were few. His family was out of the question. His mother had secretly wired him a little money when he was living in France, but his father had found out. Jackson had promised himself that he would never ask again, and he knew that was a promise he'd keep. He could phone Doreen, his ex-girlfriend and current roommate, and convince her to give the clerk a credit-card number over the phone. Given the large amount of money he already owed Doreen in rent, and given the fact that she worked hard as a waitress to cover her own expenses and save for culinary school tuition, she would be furious with him. Possibly so furious that she would laugh at the idea of him penniless in Wattleborough, North Carolina, and show no mercy. If he didn't call Doreen, that left begging from strangers, like the red-eyed men back in New York who insisted they were neither homeless nor substance addicted and couldn't believe what had happened but needed to borrow seven dollars to get some diapers and a bus ticket to Queens, where a niece or a daughter awaited them. Jackson vowed to cough up the seven bucks the next time he was creatively panhandled.

He inventoried the three other cars at the pumps. A fairly young man wearing belted shorts was filling up an SUV in which sat a woman and two fat children. No doubt the man would ask himself what Jesus would do and conclude that his savior did not want him handing over his hard-earned money to itinerant writers with empty gas tanks. Jackson really couldn't blame him.

There was an older woman gassing up a new sedan and a young woman climbing out of an old, sunburned Honda. Figuring that the older woman might lock herself in her car if he approached, that people with crappy cars are more sympathetic to states of poverty, and that what Doreen called his wholesome good looks might be used to greater effect on the younger woman, he headed for the Honda.

Despite an anemic complexion and loose clothes, she was cute, with short, very curly dark hair, large brown eyes, and skinny hips. He couldn't place where, but he was sure that he'd seen her before.

"You were at the conference, right?" he said, relieved to have some connection, an in.

"Yes," she said. "But that's not where you know me from. I didn't even see you this week. I didn't see anyone, hardly, and probably shouldn't have come. I was holed up with my laptop."

"Working on a book?"

"I'm not sure I'm ready to admit to myself that it's a book, but, yeah, I'm working on something. I don't really like workshops, you know, having people read my stuff." She shook the gas nozzle ferociously, but it was getting the better of her.

"Let me get that for you." Jackson lifted the bottom of the nozzle, which then slid easily out of its locked position. "If you'll pop your gas cap, I'd be happy to do the honors."

"Thanks. I'm really useless with some things." She rubbed her arms as if cold in the near hundred-degree weather.

The smell of gasoline bloomed around Jackson as he considered how to time his request. "If I didn't see you at the conference, where have I seen you?"

"At 'The Valley of the Shadow of the Books.' I work there."

"Of course." Jackson placed her in context now, saw her in her 1950s thrift-store dresses and keds, squatting over a stack of books, reading one that she was supposed to shelve. "My roommate works across the street, at Grub."

He wanted to ask her name but was worried that she'd already told him and would be hurt that he didn't remember. Perhaps he could get it from the bookstore, or maybe she wore a nametag at work.

"I'm going to have to find a new job soon. I guess you've heard the store is closing down. Can't compete with the chains is part of it, but also the owners are just tired."

"I don't want to sound unsympathetic, because it's a great book-store and all. But it's not exactly shocking that a place called 'The Valley of the Shadow of Books' wouldn't make it. Quite a mouthful, and not what you'd call cheerful."

"I think it's a great name, but, you're right, it doesn't exactly roll off the tongue."

The pump clicked, and Jackson returned the nozzle to its holster, twisted on the gas cap, and slammed shut the little door. A drop of sweat ran down his neck, and his shirt was beginning to stick to his back. "This is embarrassing," he said. "But I have to admit that I'm really glad to have run into you. I mean, I'm glad to have run into you just to see you, but also because my bank seems to be down. My debit card won't authorize and I stupidly left my credit cards in New York. I really hate to ask this, especially since you're about to be out of a job, but could you buy me a tank of gas and a sandwich? I'll pay you back as soon as I get home. I could bring the money to you at work." He paused to smile at her. "It would give me a good excuse to see you again."

She returned his smile, and Jackson realized that he did indeed like the look of her. Her pale skin looked cool and fresh, fine pored and slightly watery, like the inside of a radish. And there was a slight goofiness to her facial expressions and the way she tipped her head from side to side when she talked that he found endearing. She looked smart and sweet at the same time, which was an increasingly rare combination among the women Jackson encountered. Simpatico, that's what that jackass Whelpdale would say about her.

She insisted that Jackson get some chips and a drink with his sandwich and that he take a twenty-dollar bill in case he needed more gas later. "It's fine," she said. "Just pay me back." She swiped her card in the pump and waited while he filled his tank.

"Tell me something," he said. "If you don't want anyone to read your work, what do you write it for?"

She shrugged and tilted her head sideways. "It's just what I do. I started writing stories when I was five."

He found it so peculiarly charming when she shook his hand that he didn't register the significance of her name until she was gone.

"Margot Yarborough," she had said.

She must be Andrew Yarborough's daughter. Jackson cursed his idiocy and vowed to develop a more diplomatic character. Once, when Amanda had asked him about his family and why he never set foot in Charleston, he'd told her, "I haven't burned many bridges in my life, but when I do burn one I use kerosene and fan the flames." He hadn't merely taken a risk with Andrew Yarborough; he'd been downright foolish. It might well hurt his career when he would least expect it, and it had probably cost him a chance with a really great girl.

Still, two hundred miles later, eating a slightly stale pimiento-cheese sandwich while stopped at a railroad crossing, he cheered considerably. It was a freight train that whooshed by, disappearing around a bend in the tracks well before its sound faded, but it nonetheless reminded him of the train he'd first taken to New York. He hadn't napped or read on the trip but sat straight, full of conviction that he was one of the men who succeed in life.

He drained the bottle of sweetened tea and crossed the tracks, accelerating hard, eager to get home and get to work.

# Chapter four

Andrew Yarborough had built an old-fashioned literary career and was one of the few people at the conference who had found some success as both writer and editor, though considerably more as an editor. He'd spent most of his career at a single publishing house. He knew he was no Max Perkins—he couldn't claim a Fitzgerald of his own—but he had been a real friend to his writers and a truly fine editor. He had discovered and published many young writers, ushering them through the thrill of literary debut, nursing them through a disappointing second novel, nurturing their ascendance into a sturdy career as a mid-list writer or, on occasion, celebrity.

After decades of good work, he'd been squeezed out following a merger. He'd tried a few stints at other houses, but was always asked to leave or left on his own accord after a few months or perhaps two years. It wasn't so much that he'd lost his taste for his work but that the work itself had spoiled. In his last position at a major house he had been called a list-builder, and his work had been defined not as editing but as acquisition. There was little good will there toward talent that didn't sell well, small tolerance for the sophomore slump, no willingness to risk a quiet novel that might prove a sleeper.

What bothered him most was the shift to decision-by-committee. No doubt it prevented some truly horrible books from being published, but it was clear that it overemphasized market concerns and selected for lowest common denominators. He'd had to write rejection letters for several brilliant but peculiar novels he'd badly wanted to publish. Those letters had eroded him, but he always wrote them himself, always took the time to provide a good reading of the work and suggest someone else who might find a way to publish it.

He couldn't say whether he'd quit or been fired, but he remembered the shaking anger with which he'd argued with one publisher over a nine-hundred-page labor novel that was as dazzling and important as it was desperate for substantive editing. "It's the writer's job to have the book ready for the copyeditor," was the line that had infuriated him and started the fight that ended in unemployment.

After that, Andrew had managed to survive as a critic and the nearest thing to a pundit that literature would take notice of. Though he had punctuated his editing career by writing novels that were kindly, albeit sometimes lukewarmly, reviewed, he couldn't find another novel in himself, and he no longer had the patience he once had. He planned to return to fiction eventually, but meanwhile he reviewed books widely—for a while as editor of *The Monthly*—and made himself felt among the overlapping circles frequented by writers. Even though he was no longer populating the literary landscape with his own discoveries, he at least felt like he was, as he put it, fighting the good fight. He championed worthy books, called attention to new talent, and spoke out against trends that diminished literature. And so his professional life continued to offer an anodyne for—or at least an alternative to—his miserable home life.

While it was true that his wife had written some good poems early in her career and also that he defended her to strangers, it was decidedly not the case that he liked her. He was embarrassed by her ridiculous pursuits, and what he felt for her crossed into disdain. After a health scare that proved to be hypochondria and after discovering and putting an end to her husband's only prolonged extramarital affair, Janelle Yarborough had embarked on a long, shallow spiritual journey whose stops included Tarot cards, sweat lodge ceremonies, and the local Buddhist temple. If it was indigenous anything or if the hawker of the religion du jour used the word *healing*, she was a firm believer.

This would have been horrible enough in itself, but she doubled the punishment inflicted on her husband by allowing her sage-scented mumbo jumbo into her poetry. First there had been the book of poems exploring Jungian archetypes. Next came the creation-myth poem cycle, and things just got worse. Now she led personality-based writing workshops in their home and accepted poetry prizes given not by literary foundations but by women's centers and environmental groups. The phone rang for her all day, making it hard for Andrew to get his own work done now that he had to work out of the house.

What he didn't know was whether all this nonsense was the product of an irritating but blameless stupidity or rather a calculated form of vengeance made more cruel by its subtlety and longevity. His uncertainty on this point, together with her family money, his own Catholic guilt, and their shared experience as Margot's parents, accounted for the duration of a marriage that most men would have run from, alimony costs be damned. Instead of seeking a separation, Andrew resigned himself to his fate—penance for marrying and then cheating on a younger, not particularly intelligent woman who happened to have perfectly blue eyes.

After cutting out of the reading at the Blue Ridge Writers' Con-ference—the book-club woman had been abominable and then the fat kid had droned on and on in prose that could only be described as, well, prosaic—Andrew allowed his wife to take the wheel. Janelle insisted that she was the superior highway driver and, furthermore, that he needed to take a nap because he was grumpy. He let her drive to quiet her, regretting it when she put on some horrible cassette of chanting and water sounds. At his insistence, they had agreed long ago that the driver always picked the music, so he had no recourse. She aggravated her crime by jerking the car faster then slower then faster in ways seemingly designed to flare his chronic neck pain.

Still, he was happy. Today was the day that Chuck Fadge's new book would receive the most negative review in the recent history of *The Times*. Since taking over the editorship of *The Monthly* from Andrew, Fadge had spent two years praising the runniest dreck and writing nasty reviews of the finest novels being published. If it was pretentious, Fadge called it *innovative*; if it was solid and well crafted, he called it *too quiet*. Now Fadge had had the nerve to publish the cynically motivated *Exhaustive Compendium of Literary Knowledge*. Fadge had rushed his book to press, knowing that Andrew was working on a similar but more serious and considered work on the same general topic.

Now he was going to pay. Andrew had been contacted about writing the review himself, but he knew, as did the editor who'd contacted him, that it could only hurt his reputation to get into an ugly public fight with Chuck Fadge. The story the reading public would digest was that Yarborough was angry over losing his editorship of *The Monthly* to Fadge. People wouldn't understand that Andrew could have kept the job if he'd thought it was still worth having. And so they might think him merely vindictive and fail to understand the validity of his criticisms of all things Fadge. Andrew knew that he was ill-tempered and hard to get along with, but his commitment to good books and to writers was life-long and genuine. He hated Fadge for the simple reason that Fadge was an enemy of literature.

What he had said to the editor who phoned had been carefully couched: "I'm afraid I could not be as impartial as a *Times* reviewer is expected to be. Besides, you couldn't pay me enough to read that book." He omitted the fact that he had already read the galley and made a few alterations to his own book after doing so. "Quarmbey's your man," he had said. "He'll do the book justice, write just the kind of review I suspect you're looking for."

Though he had been tempted to inquire about content and progress, Andrew had studiously avoided his querulous friend since passing along his name. He didn't want one of his characteristic anti-Fadge phrases to make its way into the review; he wanted no appearance of involvement. Now, after weeks of waiting, the day had arrived.

"Stop in the next city of any size," he boomed at his wife.

"That's still a dictatorial tone," she said, "but at least you're not as ill-humored as you were."

"I hope that means you'll stop trying to put hot stones on my stomach while I'm sleeping."

"Like your stomach's flat enough!" She turned on her shrill laugh.

Andrew was in such a fine mood that he let it go. "There," he pointed. "Take the next exit."

The absurd town had a single main street, and it wasn't hard to locate the combination coffee shop and newsstand. The place smelled like sausage and eggs and yesterday's ashtrays. Small groups of old men and a few middle-aged couples talked. Andrew assumed their conversations centered on the latest in hog-farming technology, local sports, and who was fooling around with whom. He asked the teenaged girl presiding over the counter display of cigarettes and gum whether she carried *The Times*.

"Sure do," she said. "We get three copies every single week."

When he saw the empty rack, Andrew almost lost his temper.

"We get three copies, because we can sell three copies," the girl said. "But unless you're one of those what needs an untouched paper, you can probably find one lying around."

Andrew moved from table to table, grabbing papers and looking over shoulders at mastheads.

"Mister, you need to relax and just ask for what you want," said an old man scrunched under a baseball cap. "I'm betting by that shirt you've got on that you're looking for a copy of *The Times*." With that and a grin, he stacked the paper's sections and handed the mess to Andrew.

"Thank you," was all that Andrew could muster.

"Now remember what I said, and relax. I'm sure your stocks are on the rise or will be plenty soon."

Back in the car with the pieces of *The Times* and a cup of coffee, Andrew found the book section.

"I don't suppose you brought me anything." Janelle started the car, which reignited the godawful crap that she called music.

"Trust me on this one: they don't sell herbal tea in this town."

Back on the highway, Andrew read morsels of the review to his wife, laughing out loud. He wished he had a better audience, but not even Janelle's disapproving twist of her nose could dampen his glee.

"He actually calls Fadge a nincompoop! I haven't ever seen that word in *The Times* before. Never. He calls him a moron, a fool, a dullard, and—this is the best—an ingénue. Says the book has no redeeming qualities. Ha! Takes him to task for having such an East Coast bias that he includes Tama Jamowitz but not Willa Cather and that absurd Saffron boy trying to write about nine-eleven after reading Günther Grass for the first time, but not William Faulkner. Rick Moody but not Sherwood Anderson. As if Faulkner hadn't passed the test of time. And this is in an 'exhaustive compendium of literary knowledge'. Ha!"

"It seems a bit cruel in tone." His wife returned to humming along with the noise coming from the dashboard speakers.

"Fadge got off light. He should thank his lucky stars."

Andrew smiled. Janelle was right; the review was vicious.

"Darling, I know that Fadge was awful to you. I know he stole your job, but, really, other people's failures aren't our successes."

"Don't even breathe another word of that self-help crap to me. My feelings toward Fadge aren't personal. It's nothing less than this: he represents everything I am against, everything that is wrong with publishing. I've got no problem with low-brow trash, you know that. But we're in real trouble when we start confusing middle-brow pretenders with literature just because other fools are willing to pay money for their books. Fadge is loathsome, moronic, and evil. He's out to kill literature and culture and everything that's good. All Quarmbey did was tell the rest of the world, and the world should thank him."

"Oh darling, you always exaggerate so."

After Andrew spent his laughter, he hit the eject button and popped in Warren Zevon. "Pull over. I'm driving the rest of the way home."

# Chapter five

Jackson Miller slept deeply after the long drive and awoke in time to make the coffee before Doreen got up. The small galley kitchen was the only clean room in the apartment. Neither Jackson nor Doreen owned a vacuum cleaner, so the living-room carpet wore a coat of dust and crumbs too small to pick up by hand. The room was dormitory-like, furnished with boards and concrete blocks, upside-down plastic crates, a foam sofa with stretched seams, a bean bag chair, an old portable CD player, discs stacked in random order. The bathroom had neither vent nor window. The roommates kept it from becoming a site of pest infestation with occasional wipe downs using a threadbare towel, but the room never gleamed.

The kitchen, on the other hand, smelled mineral clean and was stocked with Doreen's good equipment: copper pots, small appliances manufactured in Germany, thick cake pans, expensive knives and whisks. Jackson was no cook, but he liked the sturdiness of well-made objects, as well as standing in a room that was both clean and cleaned by someone else.

Doreen thanked him when he poured her coffee, kissed his cheek, and welcomed him home.

"Master of the small gesture, that's me. I'll even make you an omelet. You must be tired of handling food after last night."

"And I have to work lunch today, so that'd be great."

Noticeably pretty on first glance, Doreen was one of the few women he knew who looked good in bangs. The rest of her light brown hair was long and straight, and her face was lightly sprinkled with freckles undisguised by makeup. Unless dressed for work, she wore only faded jeans and white tee-shirts. She looked like someone who had done little but ride horses until she was an adult, despite the fact she was from Manhattan and had never owned a pet. Most of all, Jackson admired the line of her back, the way the small of it curved in, leaving a slight gap between her jeans and her skin and revealing the color of her panties, which, in contrast to her tomboyish outer clothes, were always lacey, shiny, silky, or otherwise tempting.

He would have very much liked to win back her romantic affections, but had for months now been assigned to the twin categories of entertaining-but-perplexing friend and money-owing roommate. He knew that any effort on his part to loosen the belt of her turquoise robe and lure her back into bed would be greeted with amusement at best and more likely with irritation. Jackson sighed and cracked the eggs into a bowl. He added a splash of milk and whisked the mixture the way she'd taught him. He buttered a skillet and lit the gas burner with the disposable lighter they kept next to the stove.

Doreen poured orange juice and set the table with cloth napkins, reflecting her commitment not to dining elegance but to frugality. She was a practical young woman, a trait Jackson respected even as it exasperated him.

"You know, Eddie Renfros should have married either an heiress or a girl like you. I don't think Amanda is going to be satisfied with a modest life." Jackson divided the omelet between two plates and carried them to the table.

"Things aren't going well for them?"

Jackson took a large bite. "Eddie still can't publish his second book. He's supposed to be well into another one, but I don't think he's gotten very far with it. He's just the kind of guy to end it all with a bottle of vodka and pills."

"That's a terrible thing to say, Jack. All the more so because you sound like you enjoy the prospect."

"Of course not. I will admit that I was jealous that he conned the prettiest girl at Iowa into taking a chance on him, but he's still my best friend. It's frustrating to see him squander his talent. And her life. He's just not the kind of person who can make it without a job."

"As opposed to you?" Doreen's tone bordered on scornful.

"At most Eddie's going to write a competent, modest seller every three years." Jackson drank his whole glass of juice. "As for me, I've got a plan to make some decent money. Then maybe I'll marry a rich woman."

Doreen laughed. "I thought you were going to wait until you were old enough to marry a woman half your age. You'll need your own money for that."

"Doreen, you should write a book. One of those cat mysteries or maybe a children's book. What you need to do is get together half a dozen examples of the kind of book you want to write. Study their conventions. Think of something new to add—an attractive twist, something that will get you a bit of attention—and then go to work methodically."

"Like you?"

"I'm serious. Forget the muse and just write a certain number of pages every day. Five pages a day, and you'll have a whole novel in two months. Clean it up, query forty agents at once, and you've got a career." Jackson noticed that Doreen was surreptitiously reading the front page of *The Times*, but he continued, undeterred by her lack of interest. "That's what Eddie doesn't understand. He thinks he's Homer or Shakespeare. He thinks I'm a hack, which of course I do aspire to be in a way. If you want to make a living writing, you've got to give the people what they want. You can't tell them what they should be reading. We're not geniuses—just smart guys who should be supplying the public with the food it likes."

"Like I'm supplying the food you like?" Doreen stood, cinched her belt, and cleared the dishes. "I'm guessing that you'll need a patron, or at least an indulgent roommate, to be able to enact your scheme."

Jackson was glad he hadn't phoned her for money from North Carolina. "If I had it in me, I'd write the trashiest of trashy novels."

"Under a pseudonym, I suppose?" she said, rinsing the dishes in the kitchen sink.

"Absolutely not. I'd sign my name proudly. But I'm not claiming that it's easy. To please the vulgar, you must somehow embody the genius of vulgarity. I doubt I have that specialized talent, but I know that I can write for the college-educated dolt. I think I could write the books that doctors and lawyers read on planes—or at least buy at the airport to hold while they nap. Or the kind of books that people just out of college talk about with each other. What they want is to feel that what they are reading is special and clever, even though they can't distinguish between fine pastry and supermarket birthday cake, to use an analogy from your world." He paused for a breath. "I'm gearing up to write a vapid book that appears to be smart."

"Please don't rock the chair back like that. The slats are getting loose." Doreen leaned against the kitchen counter, the sun wrapping her shoulders. She gnawed at the fingernails of her left hand—her single unattractive habit.

"And," Jackson finished, "I'll get laid left and right. What was the name of that guy who joined The Band because someone told him he'd get more pussy than Frank Sinatra?" He'd said it to get a reaction from her—she hated crudeness—but she was already headed for the shower, and didn't hear.

Jackson showered after she was done, then dressed in his last clean shirt and pocketed the two emergency twenty-dollar bills he kept hidden in an empty CD case.

When Doreen emerged from her room, pretty and neat in her white blouse and short black skirt, Jackson said, "I'll walk you to work. I've got to talk to a girl who works at the bookstore."

"The cute short-haired one?"

"Curly hair? Skinny?"

Doreen nodded.

"How do you know her?"

"I've talked to her a few times at the store or when she picks up takeout for the owners. She's a nice person. Not your type at all. How did she have the misfortune to meet you?"

"At the conference, sort of."

"It's a small world, I guess is the thing to say."

"See, you could write for the masses."

"You know what else they say: New York is a big city of small neighborhoods."

"Exactly," Jackson said, bounding down the stairs. Out on Ninth Street the late summer sun warmed the stacks of garbage bags and the air smelled like overripe bananas, coffee grounds, and something less pleasant.

As they walked, Jackson asked himself if he believed his own arguments and the answer was equivocal. He didn't really want to write trash, but neither did he want to waste years of his life writing things that no one would read much less pay for.

A block later, he asked: "Doreen, why do you say she's not my type?"

Doreen just laughed and shook her head.

"Doreen, I really am going to pay you back." He put his arm around her shoulder as they strode toward midtown.

# Chapter six

When Margot Yarborough encountered Jackson Miller at a North Carolina gas station, she'd been on the cusp of two realizations. The first was that she was writing a novel—possibly a fine one. As the daughter of Andrew Yarborough and the filer of new fiction at a large, failing bookstore, she suspected that the last thing the world needed was another novel. Particularly one by someone like her: young, lacking in real-world experience, and sometimes more interested in words than in people. But it was precisely her love of words that made the realization pleasing. She was making the thing she most valued: a lovely novel.

Her second realization was less pleasant. She was on the verge of losing the only non-disagreeable job she'd been able to obtain—without her father's help, which she had refused—with nothing but an NYU literature degree. She would have to return to her parents' bicker-filled house on the Hudson until she could make a better plan for her life.

As distressing as this situation was, at least it would give her more time to write. What she felt every morning and every evening as she neared her computer could be described only as pleasure. All day the store was filled with writers shopping instead of writing, writers complaining of writers' block, writers lecturing each other about the agony of creation or the fickleness of their muse, writers browsing the shelves and griping that they had no time to write. Her days were filled with writers not writing, and she had told more than one of them go home and write.

"No one's making you be a writer," she'd told a regular one afternoon, "You shouldn't do it if you don't enjoy it."

Many of her happiest hours were spent alone with sentences, trying them out in different forms, leapfrogging words and phrases across each other, finding combinations of adjectives and nouns never before placed in proximity. She knew that she mystified her friends whenever she turned down an invitation to a party or out to hear music, but, well, she was who she was.

She reminded herself that her room at her parents' house—which she would have to reclaim from her father, who had been banished there for snoring—offered a serene view of the Hudson. She'd set up her computer before the window and finish the work on her book. Then she could figure out how to make her way in the world.

Margot finished shelving ten copies of a new novel about a group of women in a sewing club, each, according the flap copy, coping with her own threads of tragedy. It was time for her break when she finished, and she stepped out to get a little sun on her face.

It was still summer, still hot, but the mugginess had subsided, and Margot could feel and smell fall in the drier air. She sipped a cup of tart lemonade from the bookstore café as she walked the block to a courtyard where she liked to sit.

"Miss Yarborough!" a man called out as she was about to slip through the iron gate.

Margot turned but saw only a swarm of indistinct bodies and faces.

"Miss Yarborough, I'm glad to run into you."

Now Margot recognized the voice. She found it charming that Jackson Miller called her "Miss Yarborough" as though she were a character in a Victorian novel. He was accompanied by the pretty girl who worked at the restaurant across the street and sometimes stopped by to browse the cooking magazines.

"My roommate, Doreen Maud." Jackson swept his hand from Doreen to Margot and back. "And my agreeable and most kind new acquaintance, Margot Yarborough."

After they had exchanged greetings, Doreen excused herself to get to work. "You people of books must wonder how I exist in a world of dishes and food," she laughed.

"On the contrary," Margot answered. "I kind of envy you."

Doreen stretched her mouth into a long line, then said, "Because of all the agents and editors who 'lunch' at Grub?"

"I didn't mean that. I envy you because you seem to live a real life among real people."

"If you can call waiting tables real life and Grub's patrons real people, you may have a point. But that's all debatable."

"I'm telling you, Doreen, you could be a writer."

Jackson's comment finalized Doreen's departure.

"Funny you should envy her for not writing," he said to Margot, "because I've been trying to convince her to try her hand at it."

"Would that be easier for her than waiting tables?"

"Likely harder, wouldn't you say?"

He held the gate wide and ushered her into the courtyard. She chose a shady bench, and they sat, Jackson moving closer to her as they talked.

Margot drained her lemonade and set the cup beside her feet. She brushed her shoes lightly over the moss that grew between the bricks, then leaned over to touch its velvety texture. "It depends, I suppose, on several things."

"Of course," Jackson said. "And I'm not claiming that Doreen has any particular inclination to write. But I'm not sure she's got any for cooking either, and there might be more money in writing if she went about it the right way, wrote the right kind of thing."

Jackson's gestures were large and easy, and he touched her arm frequently, but in a way that seemed natural. Margot appreciated the way that he gave momentum to the conversation, not seeming to mind that she was soft-spoken. The trait had annoyed her last boyfriend, who'd told her that he was tired of asking her to repeat herself. He'd said that during their break-up fight in the bar where she worked, where his band played, and where they'd met. She'd started to suggest that maybe all the feedback had damaged his hearing, but she let it go. She'd already accepted the job at the bookstore and was happy to leave that particular boyfriend behind with the bar.

"And, well, money matters, doesn't it? I should know, because I haven't got any to speak of, though I do have this for you." He proffered the two twenties.

"Was it this much?"

"Well, maybe if you have a five in change…but, no, keep it. You were kind to have saved me from the Wattleborough debtors' prison."

Margot folded the bills into eighths and pushed them into her dress pocket. "I do like a man who pays his debts promptly, but is money still so very important, in this day and age?"

"Without it, you spend most of your life working for the first rung of the ladder. It's increasingly important to start a writing career with money. Otherwise you wind up teaching five composition courses and never writing a word."

"I suppose." Margot leaned over her knees again, this time scraping at the moss with her fingernail. "But don't you think that really good work will eventually gain attention? Even in this day and age?"

"Later rather than sooner, I'd argue. The quantity of books being written makes it impossible for all but the luckiest and most heavily marketed to get any attention. Take Jonathan Warbury. He isn't a friend of yours, is he?"

She sat up and looked at the bright green under her nail, saying somewhat absently, "I don't mix in those kinds of circles."

"Well, I wasn't going to run him down, but my question is this: is there anything that makes his work any better than that of twenty other similar writers I could name? Not at all. He's reasonably clever, yes, and he's certainly prolific. But so are plenty of others. The reason we've heard of his name—the reason you think of him mixing in circles you don't mix in—is because he started with money and moneyed friends. He went to Harvard, and his father is tied in with the editor of *The City* and all kinds of people who have pull."

Margot noticed that he'd woven her comment into his words, that as much as he loved to talk, he was also listening to her. Her voice registered with him.

"Warbury's first book was reviewed before anyone had read it. No one cared what was in the thing."

"Is that true?"

"I *am* a blowhard, but it's true. My prediction is this: soon writers won't publish books to make a name for themselves; they'll make names for themselves so they can publish their books. I've got a friend named Eddie Renfros—"

Recognizing the name, she interrupted. "I loved *Sea Miss*."

"Well, Eddie can't get his second novel published to save his life, and it's certainly no worse than *Sea Miss*. But the first one didn't sell as well as it was supposed to, so he's history. If Warbury had written *Sea Miss*, it would've won the National Novel Award or some PEN prize, and they'd be lining up the Pulitzer for the second book that poor Eddie can't even get published by the University Press of Southern Alabama or Alaska or whatever it is. Instead, *Sea Miss* was lost in a flood of that year's books. With computers, anyone who can type three hundred pages can claim to have written a book."

A pigeon landed a few feet from them and scooted from brick to brick, scrabbling but finding no trace of the stale bread crumbs sometimes tossed out by old men with dogs and children minded by nannies.

"Eddie couldn't help being born into an obscure Wisconsin family, of course, but he made a mistake in not marrying money. Then he compounded his agony by marrying a woman who loves success. Poverty and failure are disasters for any writer, but all the more so to him."

Margot resisted the urge to bend down and feel the coolness of the moss again. She looked at Jackson. "And what about you? Do you need to be rich and successful to be happy?"

"Well, Margot, I don't plan to find out if I'd be unhappy poor."

Margot tilted her head from side to side, shrugging her shoulders to work out a kink.

He massaged the back of her neck and upper back with his large hand, and she closed her eyes. He was good at touch, strong and unhesitant but not too hard. She slumped a little, relaxing, feeling lines of energy move down her back. Finally she pulled away and stood up, knowing it was time to get back to work.

"I'll toss that for you." Jackson pointed to her empty cup, but he looked across the courtyard. "I think I know that guy, you see the skinny one in the brown tee-shirt? I think that's Henry Baffler. He's a writer, too. Everyone's a writer, it seems."

She raised her cup with two fingers, comparing their hands—hers small and white and unmarked, his large and tan and dotted with freckles and moles—as he took it from her. They both looked up at the same time. He opened his mouth and then closed it without speaking, and it seemed like a full minute before they broke their gaze. He crumpled her cup and threw it to the trashcan, making it easily though it seemed far away to Margot.

"I won't be looking to marry money. I plan to make my own so that I don't have to." He walked away, then turned back, hands stuck in his front pockets. "I haven't ridden the Staten Island ferry in months and months. Want to go sometime?"

Margot smiled and nodded, wondering why she was attracted to someone even more jaded about the literary life than her father was. Perhaps it was simply because he was tall and good-looking and it had been a while since she'd broken up with the guitar player. But she knew there was more to it. She liked his fluid voice, his abundance of self-assurance, the way he folded her opinions into his own. Anyway, it was just a ride on the ferry and she was fated to head up the Hudson soon enough.

She looked at her hand, the moss now a thin green crescent like an ordinary dirty fingernail. She thought about the chapter she would work on that night, in which she would describe a bayou through the eyes of her protagonist.

Back inside the store, she found a book of black-and-white

photographs of southern Louisiana and imagined how they would look in color, trying to evoke the exact hues of brown and green.

# Chapter seven

Eddie Renfros did not launch his new writing schedule the day after he and Amanda returned from the Blue Ridge Writers' Conference. Yet within a week, he found himself regularly at work on an entirely new book, ticking off his three or four pages every twenty-four hours. For the first time, he had, as Amanda suggested, outlined the plot of the novel before he started. He told himself to think of it as an experiment. It might even be fun, he'd decided, to make his characters do what he needed them to do. It was a form of power he mostly lacked in the unimagined world he inhabited. He found, too, that knowing what was coming—both what scene he'd face the next day and how the story would end—eased the floating anxiety he felt whenever he was writing something long. His chest didn't feel as tight, and it was easier to moderate his drinking. Thinking of the next morning's work, more often than not he was able to stop after a couple. And sometimes he avoided the booze altogether by going to bed early. There were those nights that he sipped late and too much, but these seemed to serve the writing. He'd read back over those late-night paragraphs the next day and, despite the lurking typos, be relieved to find good writing.

Amanda's suggestion of a historical novel had appeal—something he might make a name for himself with—and he planned to write one next, when he had more time. But it was too late for that now; the research necessary to write a fine literary novel with a historical setting would take months. Instead he conceived a novel about music. The book centered on a viola player in a string quartet: a married woman with two small children whose lover—a famous conductor—dies in a plane crash. If he'd started writing it a year earlier, he might have spent most of his time spinning images of grief and crafting evocative descriptions of the musical pieces he mentioned. Instead, he tried hard to write a plot of human interaction. He gave his protagonist a deaf daughter eligible for a surgical implant that mimics hearing, as well as a promiscuous best friend who may or may not be sleeping with most of the other characters, including the violist's husband. About midway through the book, Eddie planned to bring in the lover's widow to blackmail the narrator into working on the dead man's compositions, resulting in a strained friendship between the romantic foes and an unhealthy fascination with the conductor's son, who happens to look just like his father. In short, Eddie had almost more plot than he knew what to do with.

He admitted to himself that he was writing for a particular demographic. He was writing to predetermined plot rather than discovering the story via hundreds of deleted paragraphs and pages. Yet the book was by no means a potboiler, and his sentences were careful. He played with the interesting motifs of sound and its absence, and found the novel addressing serious themes of artistic as well as marital fidelity, including the negotiations that artists make with their audiences and the costs they impose on art. He wasn't selling out, he told himself, but rather examining the idea of what it means to sell out.

It would be a short book, written in the first person Eddie found most natural. In late September, with sixty usable pages, he calculated that he could compile a full draft by mid-December if he did not take a day off and did not overthink matters. He could polish the manuscript across the holidays and deliver it to his agent in January, just as the editors were returning from vacation.

Yet this calculation gave him less encouragement than he needed. The New Year sounded absurdly far away. And while he felt that his prose itself was as capable as ever, he carried no great passion for the book as a whole. On many a morning, the novel struck him as simultaneously too domestic and too melodramatic. While it was the sort of book that might make the rounds of a few women's reading circles, the advance it could garner would not be sufficient to clear all of their debt.

Besides, Eddie knew himself well enough to foresee that he would not work away for months without a day off. Of course, if he wrote six pages one day, then he could afford a Saturday off. Perhaps he'd do that next week, or even this week, and take Amanda to the park and to see some art. She always glowed in the presence of great paintings, holding his arm and talking about ideas instead of things.

After laboring over two paragraphs on Tuesday afternoon, Eddie rose to make another pot of coffee with the new machine that Amanda had, as threatened, purchased. He wondered how much it had cost, but he knew that asking would invite discord. Their financial worries had nibbled at his sleep, and he'd been able to rest no more than four or five broken hours for several nights running. He'd learned to mark the small hours by the sounds of the city's nocturnal necessities: the one o'clock grocery delivery truck with the grinding brakes, the two-thirty sidewalk construction crew, the three o'clock street cleaning machine, the five o'clock building garbage trolley.

Throughout this painful nightly roll of the clock numbers, Amanda slept soundly by his side. Her even breathing and the warmth from her limbs saturated him with dread. He could not believe that she loved him with the old love, and he feared that only the greatest of publishing luck would be sufficient to hold onto her. Soon, he thought, she won't even sleep with me. And it was that terrible idea that prompted him to rise on the roughest mornings—those mornings when he was most exhausted—and face the inscrutable computer screen.

He tried to convince himself that sleep deprivation was good for his creative process—being closer to the dream space and all that crap. But he knew that fatigue was not conducive to a book-length work, and he often found himself fundamentally stumped by such logistics as getting two characters from house to car or moving an object out of his protagonist's left hand and into her right. Unintentional rhymes slipped into sentences that were becoming tortured: "A revision of her decision would have made her an object of derision." He wanded whole paragraphs for deletion and endured a gnawing anxiety when he imagined other people reading his most deplorable lines. The reviewers would ignore him if he was lucky, but excoriate him if they noticed. It would have been better if they had not loved *Sea Miss*. They might go easier on him now, refrain from using that damning word: disappointment.

The writing went better, generally, in the evening, when Eddie managed to remember and take encouragement from the fortunate years when his fine writing style had come as easily as typing itself and Amanda had loved him without restraint. Still, even late in the day, the elaborate description of a setting that was thematically meaningful or the subtle revelation of character motivation often seemed beyond his powers as a writer. He stuck to as much dialogue as he thought he could get away with. Dialogue had been all but missing from *Sea Miss*, a tale in which the characters seldom encountered one another and rarely spoke when they did. Now Eddie found that dialogue filled up pages quickly. And when he didn't know how to round out a necessary scene, he could always have his characters discuss something or other. On this Tuesday afternoon, with the newly brewed coffee boosting his keyboard speed, the viola player and her promiscuous violin-playing friend were conversing about deaf culture. Their dialogue was stilted, he knew, but he could fix it later.

He called for Amanda to come into the study they had separated from the living room with a pale blue shoji screen, pretending that the long, narrow space was indeed another room.

"I'm busy," she answered.

He waited. "Come when you're done?"

"I'll be there in ten minutes."

When she appeared twelve minutes later, her face—cautious

eyes but clamped jaw—looked apprehensive but hard. "I hope you haven't called me in here to tell me how badly your work is going. You used to agree with me that writer's block is just mental laziness."

He flinched, visibly he feared; this was not the mood he'd hoped for. "I just wanted to tell you that I'm a third of the way through. I just wrote the hundredth page." The exaggeration approximated truth, and Eddie nearly believed his words.

"Thank goodness. That's really good, Eddie." She smiled at him for what felt like the first time in days, her mouth pulling slightly wider on one side. "Are you going to write some more tonight?"

"I wasn't planning to, not if you'll come sit with me. We don't talk enough these days."

"I'm kind of in the middle of something. In awhile, though, okay?"

Eddie followed her around the screen, resisting his desire to still her slightly swiveling hips between his hands. Instead he veered into the galley kitchen attached to the living room that also served as dining room. Amanda liked to say, "We'll know we've made it when every room has only one purpose."

He poured himself two fingers of bourbon and pressed his novel from his mind. Leaning against the counter despite its uncomfortable metal edge, he sipped his drink and watched his wife at the dinner table, which she had covered with stiff foam. She was cutting mats for two drawings she'd bought at a gallery across town.

"I know we can't afford works by artists who have already made it big," she'd said, "but I hate bare walls and I'm certainly not going to hang posters like a college student."

Not wanting to anger her, Eddie had refrained from asking the price of the original drawings. He'd let the table she was working on go unmentioned, too. Right after they moved into their Murray Hill apartment, she'd convinced him that they could furnish it better and more cheaply by scouring the local flea markets than they could by ordering through catalogues as did most of the people they knew. Amanda soon developed an eye for quality, age, and authenticity. Now their apartment sat impeccably furnished, and they had the credit card bills as evidence.

She drew a line with a pencil and then followed with the Exacto knife.

Eddie refilled his whiskey before scanning the living room bookcase. *Madame Bovary*—now that's a book with fine style and a juicy plot, he thought. It was also a novel that was not written under a daily quota system, not written with a timer ticking in a writer's ear. He pulled it from the shelf, wondering whether he could restructure his new book into a contemporary retelling of Flaubert's quotidian tragedy.

Amanda rose from her precise work, poured herself a drink, and sat back down at the table.

"Remember when we read this for 'Form and Theory'?" He scooted to the end of the long sofa so that her back would not be fully to him.

"I remember it well enough." Her voice reminded Eddie of a string of beads, an impression he found soothing. She laughed, shook her head. "Poor Jackson barely got through that course."

"I suppose," he said, "that the study of Flaubert isn't going to help me now. Sometimes I worry that I've read myself into paralysis. Maybe I could write something decent if I stopped reading altogether. Or maybe I'm reading the wrong sorts of things. Maybe I should read only books completely unlike what I'm working on. Or perhaps just poetry. Maybe I should quit reading all prose until I'm done with the book. Or maybe just stop reading fiction?"

"Eddie, you passed the hundred-page mark, and here we are having a nice time. So naturally you have to turn morbid."

He wanted her to turn to him, to celebrate his small triumph of page count. More: he wanted to know that she loved him no matter what he wrote, or how little. He watched the changing angle of her elbow as she followed her pencil line with the tilted blade of the exacto knife. Her slices were precise, and when she lifted the mat, the rectangle she'd cut from its center fell out clean, making the smallest plop as it hit the table. When she turned to him from this victory, her hair slinked across her back, revealing her profile, chin slightly lifted.

"I'm sorry," he said, feeling the whiskey stubbornness solidify, "but you knew when you married me that sanguine isn't my basic nature."

"Fair enough, but you weren't in full gloom all the time either. It's like you think my only job in the world is to cheer you up through one existential crisis after another. I hate to say this, Eddie, but it's time you developed a little stoicism if nothing else. You should feel good. You're a third of the way through the new book and starting to work at a real clip. And you have an outline. This time you actually know where you're going. That should give you some hope."

He wanted to stop, to spin the conversation from the bad direction it was headed. He could almost come up with the words to save the evening, but something perverse—not anger but some smaller, rarer animal—took him over. "Hope? Don't delude yourself about the size of the advance I'll be getting even if I manage to place the thing."

"No more depressing talk tonight, Eddie." She used his name as though it belonged to a child. "It's tedious. Just finish the new book, and let's see what happens. Why don't you read something to me like you used to? Read some *Madame Bovary*." She sat on the other end of the sofa, twisting her drink audibly on her open hand.

So he read, his voice tight as he controlled his windpipe and esophagus, afraid of the thing that would fly out if he opened wide. Amanda listened, her smile serene, like a person who faced no difficulties in life whatsoever.

Eddie read the agricultural speech and then Flaubert's exquisite description of Emma Bovary's variegated eyes before sliding the book back into its slot between *Tender is the Night* and *The Good Soldier.* "Amanda?" he asked, his voice gaining volume across the few syllables of her name. "Do you still love me a little?"

"Much more than a little."

With her answer, his throat relaxed a little, the Adam's apple softening. "Even though I've sunk to painting by numbers? To writing some rush-job, plot-driven book?"

"Is it so bad as all that?" She crossed her legs and leaned forward, the body language of interest—real or feigned.

The book that had earlier seemed like it was going reasonably well now turned horrid in his mind—an embarrassment. He wanted her to understand, to console him, to love him anyway. "Confoundedly bad," he said. "I don't even want to put my name to it."

"Eddie, why? Why?"

"It's the best I can do right now. Don't you love me enough for that to be okay?"

"If I didn't love you that might be okay. But it's terrible to think of the reviews. You're Eddie Renfros, author of *Sea Miss*. I married a man of talent."

"Fuck the reviews!" Eddie headed for the bourbon, which Amanda had left out on the kitchen counter. He suspected her of leaving it in view because she wanted him to fail, wanted him to be weak. The bottle taunted him with imaginary spousal recriminations: *Go ahead and give me a good excuse to leave you. Better yet, drink yourself to death and make quick work of it.*

His voice trembled when he said, "Promise me right now, I insist, that you won't read a single review. Not one. Not ever. Promise."

"Sure, fine, but other people will be reading them."

"Fuck other people. It's your opinion I care about. I don't want you to loathe me just because I'm not in top form just now. If I can get this book finished and out, I'll develop a really good idea, something I can feel passionate about. Then I'll write my big book, one that you can be proud of, one that will make the reviewers swoon and secure a permanent reputation. Then I'll be able to work steadily but without some ridiculous, arbitrary quota in my head."

"Maybe you should stop this book. I'm not sure you should be writing at all if you aren't writing well."

"Jesus, Amanda! Have you forgotten whose idea this book was?"

In the early days of their marriage, such harsh words from him would have made her cry and he would have apologized and comforted her. The argument would have ended in bed, first with tender affection and then raucous sex.

Now, though, Amanda sat stonily, her face set and her eyes dry. "I'm going to ask for a raise, and I'll look into getting a new card so that we can move over the other debt to a lower interest rate. Maybe I can sell a painting." She gestured to a framed piece hanging across from the bookcase. "That guy just got a one-man show at that new gallery in Chelsea. I'm sure I can sell it for more than we paid for it, and that'll tide us over so you can take a little more time with the book, make it better."

Eddie watched her from the living room as she washed her glass. Her body twisting left and right with the motion of her hands, shaking only with the movement and not from any deep emotion. He wondered what they had left, if he couldn't even wound her anymore.

Before walking into the bedroom, she said, "Keep in mind that Flaubert plotted that novel to the half page before he wrote it. To the half page, Eddie."

# Chapter eight

For several days after their harsh words, Amanda Renfros avoided her husband as much as she could, ducking quietly around the apartment and declining to join him on walks. She did not want to distract him from his work—that was part of it. It was urgent that he finish the book. Then they could see what would happen, and she could decide what she needed to do.

Amanda had grown up in Wilkes-Barre, Pennsylvania, among brothers who would have become coal miners if they'd had any work ethic, but who chose instead an existence of knock-off Steelers merchandise and part-time bartending. Her mother hadn't been able to scrape together enough to buy Amanda a thesaurus or a prom dress, but she always found the down payment for yet another cheap stereo, video player, or microwave oven. Her mother, often as not, couldn't figure out how to hook them up or program them and just assumed they didn't work.

"Cheap buys cheap," the young Amanda warned her, knowing that in mere weeks the discount warehouse would advertise another electronics sale. Awake in the middle of the night, Amanda's stomach would clench as she thought of the drawer full of warranty and rebate cards that had never been filled out and mailed in. She visited home her first Christmas in college because her dorm closed for the holiday, but she had not returned to Pennsylvania since.

Now she wanted to enjoy her apartment as much as she could. She and Eddie had done well to find the place, and Amanda had spent long mornings walking from flea market to flea market, store to store, to fill it up. It wasn't easy to put on the façade of a success-ful couple of letters on the kind of money they had, but she'd done it. The apartment was a walk-up, but Amanda reasoned that the four flights of stairs were the only reason her increasingly sedentary hus-band hadn't packed on more than the ten pounds he'd gained since their wedding. The building was an old tenement, but no one could flinch at the address. A well-known stage actor lived in the building, as did a songwriter who'd been briefly famous in the seventies and was now experiencing a cult revival. Plus, it could properly be cat-egorized as a real apartment and not a studio or loft. The rectangle of kitchen was fully visible from the living room, yet it was clearly a separate room, with tile flooring instead of the wood of the rest of the place. The living room served as dining room and study, but comfortably so, and the bedroom was removed by a small hallway past a bathroom stocked with plush towels.

It was increasingly obvious, though, that they weren't making it. When they'd married, Eddie's advance for *Sea Miss* had seemed like real wealth, and neither of them doubted that royalties and another book contract would follow soon enough. With the advance petering out two years into their marriage, Amanda had offered to work for a year. Eddie had resisted at first, telling her that she should write a book and that he'd get a job. "I don't want you to get a job," she'd told him. "I married a critically acclaimed novelist. Besides, I have nothing to say and I'm getting bored at home." She'd found a job as an assistant to an acquisitions editor at a textbook publisher, and Eddie had agreed to let her work for exactly one year. "If I don't have a new advance by then, it'll be my turn to work while you write." But one year had become two, and Amanda now held the job of the man she used to work for. The publisher had found out she could do the same work for two-thirds of the salary. It certainly wasn't enough money for them to live on in the manner she already considered slumming. Now that the advance was long gone, the credit-card debt was mounting.

The idea that they might have to move not to one of the brownstones on the now-gated Sniffen Court or to an address further up the East Side but to something that represented a step down in prestige twisted into resentment as it grew. Amanda could not quite forgive Eddie for suggesting that they move to Jersey City. It was as inconceivable that she should ever say "New Jersey" when detailing her address as it was that she would move back to Wilkes-Barre and ask for a job in the bar where her brothers worked off their tabs. She had always believed in destiny—and that hers was fairy-tale golden. But now, as when she was a child looking up at the cracked plaster ceiling that dropped paint flecks on her favorite stuffed animals, she worried that she'd somehow been switched, that someone else was living the good life that had been marked for her.

On Sunday afternoon, she declined Eddie's invitation to walk in the park. "It's a beautiful day," he offered. "Hints of fall in the air. We could stop at the Pierpont Morgan on the way and wind up at the Met?"

She insisted that she had tasks to complete, but that was a lie. The apartment gleamed, she'd finished the shopping, and their paperwork was up to date. "Besides," she said, "you know I hate to go to museums on pay-what-you-want-day. They fill up with all kinds of people."

"The Met is always pay what you want."

"I know, but it's Sunday. People with boring jobs like mine will be there."

After Eddie sulked out, she sat on the sofa and tried to read a novel that had been favorably reviewed in *The Times*, but she had no real interest in the book. Indeed, her interest in reading fiction had become almost exclusively practical: what was selling, what was new or old, in or out, what was being noticed. She put the book down and rounded the shoji screen to check its Amazon ranking and used-copy value. While she was on the website, she checked the numbers on *Sea Miss* and then on the books of every writer she knew. A woman that she, Eddie, and Jackson had been in graduate school with had written a memoir about living with an epileptic child. Amanda felt the old, anxious tightening of her stomach when she saw that the book had a considerably higher sales ranking than Eddie's. Any *Sea Miss* royalties would be paltry next time. She vowed to call his agent, see if she couldn't drum up some more foreign-rights interest. The Spanish and Dutch rights had been sold early on, but French and Japanese would be better, worth maybe several thousand dollars.

She silently cursed Eddie for not thinking to make the call himself. She hadn't minded working more than the year they'd agreed upon, but she certainly couldn't go on forever working for the idiot who was her boss—a man who expected her to drum up publicity and reviews for four textbooks all titled *Literature*. When she'd begged him to let her give the anthology she'd acquired a more interesting title, he told her not to mess with the formula. He didn't even seem to understand that all their anthologies were competing with each other for market space.

She realized more fully than before that she was going to have to take charge of things, take charge of her own life, at least, if she wasn't going to wind up an underpaid under-editor and the wife of a penniless man whose only claim to fame was that he once wrote a pretty good book that a thousand people read some number of years ago.

Eddie was from a nice middle-class family, neither rich nor poor. They were midwesterners who never bought anything they couldn't pay for in cash. He didn't understand what she knew: poverty is a learned meagerness of spirit as much as it is a number on a ledger. Eddie didn't know what it was to clean coffee grounds off the floor every week because another off-brand trash bag had split at the seams. While his parents read *Consumer Reports* before purchasing a television that would work well for years, her mother spent twice as much making lay-away payments on several cheap sets that never showed clear pictures. Amanda remembered the smell of her mother's house as the smell of petty aspirations, failure, and emotional stinginess. Because Eddie didn't understand what she was afraid of, he couldn't save her from it. He had no conception of how far they could fall.

When the obvious solution struck Amanda, it came with the energy to enact it. Instead of badgering Eddie about his excuse of a career without any indication that he himself was interested in that career—and against evidence that he thought she actually enjoyed nagging him—she should launch her own. After all, she'd been one of the best writers in the workshop.

Unlike Eddie, Amanda had not spent her childhood imagining other lives and scribbling stories and fantasizing about the writing life. She'd read what was necessary to be a good student, knowing that a scholarship was her one-way ticket the hell out of Wilkes-Barre. She'd planned, from an early age, to attend law school, marry a fellow student, and practice law part-time while running a perfect household filled with quality things that worked like they were supposed to and were under warranty in case they did not.

After a torrid affair with the English professor who helped her pronounce her 'G's—and motivated partly by anger that he'd heard her drop them in the first place—Amanda had started a novel about a beautiful twenty-year-old woman having a torrid affair with her Henry-Higgins-like history professor. For reasons Amanda could no longer reconstruct, she'd sent off thirty pages of *He Should Have Listened*, together with the application form to the Iowa MFA program, while she was studying for her LSATs. When she'd opened the letter offering her the program's most prestigious fellowship, she'd laughed out loud.

She had performed well enough in workshop, mainly because she was a sharp critic and possibly also—she knew this—because her professors were male. When Amanda looked in the mirror, she saw the tall and crooked girl she'd been at Wilkes-Barre Junior High School. But she knew that men saw something else; repeated experience had allowed her to trust the fact that she was beautiful even though she couldn't see it herself.

In Iowa, she'd set aside her misguided novel to write her thesis: a series of short stories about attractive young women and the men they dated. She'd flirted with both Eddie and Jackson, but she'd been strict with herself. Until word broke about the sale of Eddie's novel, she'd carefully followed her most important Iowa rule: never date a writer. Then, caught up in the excitement of her friend's success, she'd wavered. She was young enough that she thought it meant something that they were both left-handed and gazed at the world with green eyes.

They'd graduated, married modestly in the backyard where Eddie had made mud pies and learned to catch, moved to New York, basked in the glowing reviews. She clapped louder than anyone when Eddie read at the CIA bar with none other than Jonathan Warbury.

One of her mistakes, she realized now, was that she had trusted Eddie's talent over her own. She'd quit writing not because she wasn't good at it but because she thought she had little to say and that a writer needed something to say. Eddie had never discouraged this decision. Now that she had decided to write again, she still didn't have much to say to the world. But she no longer believed that having something to say was necessary.

And so that Sunday, alone in the apartment she feared losing, she found herself pondering what she could write that people might want to read. Nothing too light or vapid—this was, after all, the post 9/11 world—but nothing too complicated either. From studying bestseller lists and reading the book reviews in women's magazines, she knew that the most popular trends were telepathic or at least empathetic animals, themes of loss and emotional restoration, and novels about people in paintings or the painters who painted them. These waves were heading back to sea, she understood, and would be replaced by the next thing. But there was still time to ride one, particularly if she could come up with a new twist and work quickly.

Thinking that she might write a book blending all three motifs, she sat down with a postcard of the painting of dogs playing poker. Jack had sent it to them from Charleston, where he'd spent a month between Iowa and moving to New York—a stretch of time he'd begged them not to ask about. Amanda smiled at the bad art and typed, centered and in italics, *Bad Dog Séance*.

The going was harder than she'd imagined. For twenty minutes, she couldn't figure out who had died. Yet four hours later, she'd written an entire story. She read through it, the piece's two central problems glaring at her. First, the tone was unabashedly sarcastic, and you can't sell books to the masses without playing it straight. And second, there was the length: only twenty-two pages long. Nevertheless, she saved it to her USB drive while vowing to get to a museum to find a more appropriate painting on which to base her book.

She was singing to herself and trying to roll sushi with a bamboo mat when she heard Eddie's footsteps ascending. Her spirits grew higher when he walked through the door with Jackson Miller and Henry Baffler.

"Look what the cat drug home," Jackson said cheerfully and gave her cheek a loud kiss. He handed her a bottle of bourbon. "For the cause."

Though they weren't as tight as they were supposed to be, Amanda sliced the sushi rolls and plated them with wasabi paste and pickled ginger. She emptied trays of pineapple-shaped ice into the nifty copper ice bucket she'd found in a retro housewares store. She set out glasses and a pitcher of water together with the bourbon, gesturing to the table with a stack of napkins. "Help yourself."

Jackson popped a roll in his mouth and plunked two cubes of ice in a glass. "I've started a novel," he announced. "I'm filling it with stuff that the book-club and college crowds will eat up. Different typescripts, the occasional blank page, a hodgepodge of diary pages and letters."

"That sounds awful," Henry said absently.

"The idea is to make the reader feel clever, as though any chimpanzee or eighth-grader couldn't figure out what I'm up to."

"That's a one-of-a-kind plan," said Eddie, quickly following Jackson in the cocktail mixing. "How far along are you?"

Jackson laughed. "You're on to me. I'm on page seven. But, really, this is the book. It will be in stores in eighteen months tops."

Henry Baffler said, "You should try the snowflake method." His dingy shirt, washed so many times that Amanda couldn't discern its original colors, hung from his rectangle of a torso

"Henry, do get something to eat and sit down. You're so skinny you make me nervous." Amanda handed him a napkin.

Eyes on the floor, streaks of red climbing his neck, Henry accepted the napkin and helped himself to some food. "I saw it on-line. Some guy who writes Christian sci-fi or some such. He tells you exactly how many plot turns and character reversals you need and on what pages to put them. Claims you can draft a book in a month."

"That jackass Whelpdale wishes he'd thought of it first, no doubt," Jackson said.

Now Henry looked directly at Amanda. "It's everything that New Realism opposes. It's plot over character, the fake over the real."

Enjoying the opportunity to play hostess and amused by her effect on Henry Baffler, Amanda waved everyone to bring their drinks into the living room.

"I feel quite guilty," she said, "for pushing Eddie toward a more plotted novel. I think it's what he needs, but, well, I hate to think of him rushing through something just because I chided him for writing too fastidiously. It would be fatal to his career, I think, for him to hurry through something and have it be weaker than his last book."

"Do you mean *Vapor* or *Sea Miss*?" Jackson asked.

Unsure whether the absent-minded tone in which he murmured this question was real or feigned, Amanda backtracked: "I only meant that *Sea Miss* will be hard to top with a stronger book. He's such a great talent and all." She reached for her drink and sipped it, barely opening her lips.

"By the way," Jackson asked, "did you all read Quarmbey's review of Fadge in *The Times*?"

Though he'd spaced out the words 'you' and 'all', Amanda could still hear the accent that Jackson had carried to and all but abandoned in Iowa.

"Harshest review I ever read," said Eddie.

"Delicious, wasn't it?" Amanda spun out. "When I heard about it, I thought it was too good to be true until I read it myself."

"Still," Jackson said, "I suspect that Fadge is more of the future than Quarmbey and his ilk. I met him recently—Fadge, I mean—at a party, and we had a pretty decent chat. But he's the funniest-looking guy you can imagine. Huge head on a short body. He asked me to send him something for *The Monthly*—preferably an essay on some aspect of the writing life or a profile of a writer, that sort of thing."

Amanda looked at Eddie to see if he was bothering to look interested. A profile in *The Monthly* could generate a little interest in his work, but he just didn't think that way. Eddie popped a roll into his mouth and ate it whole. In his ballooning cheeks, she could see what he might look like if he really let himself go to rubber.

"I sent him a piece ten months ago and am still waiting to hear," Henry said quietly. "On the New Realism."

"He only reads the solicited stuff. It's a waste of time to submit over the transom there."

"Then it hardly seems fair, does it," Henry mumbled, "to say that they accept unsolicited manuscripts and to forbid simultaneous submissions. They've tied up my essay for almost a year."

"I certainly hope you don't abide by that simultaneous-submission thing," Jackson said, sounding truly alarmed. "You should have every story and essay you've ever written out to twenty places at once. You can even hire someone to do it for you so you don't have to face all the rejection slips." He drained his glass and allowed Amanda to take it for a refill. "Oh, get this. I was checking out the publication, and who do you think had an ad in the back? He's selling 'services for writers', including submissions like I was just saying and of course manuscript triage. Any guesses?"

"Don't tell me it's Whelpdale!" Amanda handed Jackson the new drink.

"None other. He'll even be your 'nag'. For a fee, he'll phone you weekly or monthly—or daily if you pay enough—and scold you into writing. You have to pay extra for the 'overbearing mother' version of the service."

"And to think," Amanda said, "that I could have been charging Eddie for my services all along."

"But what would that make you?" Eddie said quickly, not meeting her eyes and instead turning to Jackson. "I suppose you're right about Whelpdale. He sounds shameless."

"It's the 'manuscript doctor' that gets me. A man who didn't get a penny for his book and hasn't written another one, trying to make a living by telling other people what to write. He claims that he recommends the books he likes, post-improvement no doubt, to agents."

"I suppose anyone can recommend anything to anyone— whether he knows him or not." Amanda smiled at Henry, whose neck blushed again.

"It's a swindle," Eddie said. "I suppose that's what it's coming to. Soon we'll need an agent to get an agent."

The men finished the food quickly, leaving only a green smear of wasabi paste and a few pieces of pickled ginger on the plate.

"I would have made more if I'd known there'd be four of us," Amanda said. She returned to the kitchen, where she fanned crackers and cheese onto a white serving platter. Slicing an apple, she said over her shoulder, "Seems as though we all have new prospects of one sort or another. I did some writing myself today. I'm thinking of a whole book now."

"That's capital!" Jackson said. "Though I might add that this news is long overdue. You should have three books out by now. You were probably the best writer in workshop."

Eddie grabbed a cracker as soon as Amanda set the plate on the coffee table. Through bites, he said, "Now I have to defend Amanda's right to not-write. Should we be writing just to be writing? I always thought Amanda's decision not to write until she had something to say was an honorable position."

Measuring her words and looking at Jackson and Henry but not her husband, she said, "Maybe I have something to say now."

Jackson rose to pour himself more of the whiskey he'd brought. "Hell, I'd defend her right to write about nothing at all. We would all do well to write about nothing whatsoever."

"Besides," Eddie said tentatively, "Amanda has all the makings of a great editor."

Amanda felt her temper quake but kept it underground and still spoke quietly. "Quit talking about me in the third person. You need a Harvard degree or a daddy on a Fortune 500 board to get hired as anything better than a sub-editor these days. I have all the editorial smarts in the world, but I could sit on my lovely derriere in that office for another year and I'll still be working for people who aren't as smart as I am."

"Lovely indeed," Jackson whispered loud enough for Eddie to hear.

Eddie stared at Jackson before turning to Henry. "So tell us what you think about writing about nothing. What are you working on these days—a new article for *(A)Musing Aloud*?"

"No, they've totally sold out to the mainstream. Actually, I'm onto a novel as well." Henry looked out the window, then around the room, while the others waited for him to expand.

Finally, Jackson said, "What's it about? Something more than nothing?"

"An objectionable question. Better to ask the writer: 'What's the reality?'"

Jackson grinned at Amanda, then said, "Very well then, what is the reality?"

"The reality is that I've started observing a bailiff who eats lunch in the park where I sometimes sit, down from that bookstore that's closing down. He's a talkative guy who loves to go on and on about the people who come into court. He's developed a typology, one that works for both the people he encounters and, he claims, the pigeons he feeds his sandwich crusts to."

"A courtroom novel. Capital." Jackson slid a slice of apple between his white teeth.

"No, no. Anyway, it's small-claims court. My book is simply going to tell the bailiff's true story. He's dating now, and you should see the woman. Large and squinty, about ten years older than him," Henry said, sounding nearly in awe. "So the book will follow his lunch hours and theories and courtship. It will be plotted not by me but by the choices my real-life character makes."

"The ultimate in character-driven fiction," Amanda said dramatically, imitating the voice-over on so many movie trailers.

"It will be the prime example of New Realism. Everyone will finally understand what I'm advocating. It'll be a great book." So excited that he forgot his shyness, Henry stood and paced the apartment. "It will encompass the decently ignoble—nothing bestial, mind you. I figure it will take me at least a year. I want the writing to be loving, slow, careful, but also blunt and true to the quotidian world."

Amanda and Eddie exchanged a stare.

"And don't you think this is a great title? *Bailiff.* Simple, clear, not deceptive."

Now it was Amanda and Jackson who traded looks.

"I envy you," Eddie said after an extended silence. "You have real enthusiasm in your voice."

"I can't imagine a man with a wife like yours envying the likes of me. Even my bailiff is luckier in love than I am."

"Well, Henry, maybe someday soon you'll find your own large, squinty woman. Better yet, steal the bailiff's and spice up your novel."

"That would be authorial interference," Henry said, serious as stone.

Jackson cocked his head at their peculiar friend. "Speaking of courtship, I need to take off. I have a date tomorrow."

"Good for you!" Amanda and Eddie said at once, Eddie's voice given volume by what Amanda interpreted as relief.

"I'm worried, though. I've been thinking altogether too much about this girl, and I'm not sure that's good. I suspect she's close to flat broke, which is the last thing I need. She's got family publishing connections, but I doubt they'd be available to me. A foot-in-mouth error I'm trying not to repeat. Anyway, even if her family did welcome me, her father's connections are a bit obsolete. It's not the same scene as it was even five years ago. Fadge'll tell you that."

"Then why her?" Amanda asked. "Surely there's other talent afoot."

"Of course, and I haven't closed my eyes to the world of attractive women." He paused. "She's an odd girl, for sure. She reads enough for six people, I suspect. I don't know how to explain it except to say that she's the kind of girl that gets into your head. She makes me want to be a better person."

# Chapter nine

In his house on the hill overlooking one of the widest stretches of the Hudson River, Andrew Yarborough toiled on his critical overview of fiction. On his strongest days, he could admit to himself that, as a fiction writer, he would never shake the detested designation of "mid-list writer." It was a phrase his editor and his agent liked to toss about, sometimes aiming to cajole him into writing something different. "If you can't be Philip Roth, think younger," his agent had said as he began his last novel. At other times, the blasted term was used to prepare him for a lower-than-expected advance. "Think Martin Bland," his editor had said when making the weak offer on his last novel.

More painful, though, were the signs—increasingly hard to shrug away—that he wasn't as important an arbiter of taste as he had been. Evidence was mounting that the literary world was trying to sidestep him. Two years earlier, the Lannan Foundation had called him, as usual, for names of promising young writers. But the Foundation had given its award to someone not on his list, to a writer he hadn't even read. Last year, the call from the Foundation hadn't come at all. The real blow, of course, had been the coup that led to his replacement, by the odious and unctuous Chuck Fadge, as the editor of *The Monthly*. His mutinous subordinates and the treacherous publisher agreed, they claimed, that the magazine needed a new look and a new vision. They accused Andrew of fossilized literary tastes, said he was stuck in some muddy past. Now, under Fadge, *The Monthly* reviewed every goddamn book that called itself a collage and included extended masturbation scenes.

Andrew was willing to admit that he was quarrelsome, prone to bad moods, and more likely to reach for anger than any other emotion. It was, after all, the emotion that had best served him, that had driven his best work. He could even admit that the failure of the world to give his talent its full due frustrated him, and he cringed a little whenever he read a letter to the editor written by some old crank wanting to be recognized for some accomplishment that no one cared about. Braggarts, he'd noticed, are people whose talents aren't trumpeted by others. Perhaps there was even some merit in his agent's admonitions that he stop making enemies, stop alienating editors, stop running down popular writers in reviews—at least while they retained their popularity.

He could hardly stand to talk to her anymore, though. She'd begged him to come with her when she left the large agency where he'd started his career, pilfering an impressive roster of talented authors. It had been over antipasti, at the outdoor café across from Lincoln Center, where the waiters sing almost as well as the performers on the stages across the street. "Almost," Andrew had told her, "is a crucial word in the sorting of talents." She'd said she had what it took to make him really rich and really famous.

It had been a mistake, of course, to sleep with her—all the more so because she wasn't his type: absurd leather pants, limp carrot-colored hair and ironic glasses that made her look like a cub reporter out of DC Comics. He would never have made a pass at her, but he wasn't a man to turn down an offer. She'd spent an eternity calculating the tip, over-tipping the attractive waiter by about as much as she generally under-tipped good-looking young women. "I want you to screw me," she'd said as she signed her name, looking up with an expression picked up from a movie.

He'd laughed and said, "You sure do have a way of asking that's hard to turn down."

What had followed were a handful of assignations at a Lexington Avenue boutique hotel, each a more disappointing version of the previous. The day Jonathan Warbury came over to her agency, Andrew knew she would end the affair she'd asked him to start. She still phoned him occasionally, pumping him for inside news, until he told her that sex was the price he charged for information. "I've already got a wife," he said, "and at least she'll cook for me."

He should have found a new agent, but inertia—or something he couldn't quite define—had taken hold of him. And truthfully, he hated the other agents he'd met, and he hated most of their loathsome clients. Chuck Fadge was the worst of them all. In Andrew's mind, Chuck Fadge stood for them all.

In a horrible journal called *The Balance*—the name itself was a joke—Fadge had published two reviews of Andrew's second most recent novel, one positive and one negative. The positive review had damned with faint praise, while the negative review had been biting, smart, funny, and vicious. Andrew suspected that Fadge himself had penned both reviews, which had been published under the ridiculously pseudonymous bylines Gabriel Schlipper and Cormandy Page. And a suspicion held long enough functions as certain knowledge.

Andrew was convinced that his new work, his critical overview of fiction, could raise his stature. At the least, it should ensure sales of all his books on college campuses for the next decade. If he could get the editor to handle it right, the book could return him to prominence. It had been a misfortune that Fadge had published his similar book first, but surely at least college professors and old-school editors would prefer Andrew's more learned offering. There was no chapter on Brett Easton Ellis; there were twelve pages devoted to Ralph Ellison. He'd omitted that snot-nosed Yalie who'd ripped off the finest literary ideas to have emerged from the shambles of postwar Germany, but he was including thoughtful analyses of Günter Grass and the exquisite W. G. Sebald. Now Quarmbey's review of Fadge offered the possibility that even the hoi polloi might half understand why these choices mattered.

Andrew was man enough to acknowledge that Fadge had a style considered attractive by many, though it continued to shock him that glib and acrobatic were so often conflated with well-written these days. He'd once overheard Quarmbey calling his own prose bloodless, though certainly professional jealousy, the large snout-full of booze Quarmbey could be counted on to drink, and the fact that the confirmed old bachelor no longer had much success with young ladies were at least partially responsible for the nasty adjective slung at his friend. Though Andrew was certain that his prose was not at all bloodless, he was aware that some graceful editing of a kind once but no longer performed by an actual editor might be in order.

So he received the news of Margot's imminent return home with even greater joy than parental affection alone might have accounted for. Her careful pen had improved more than one of her father's reviews and articles. She'd joked the last time she lent him an edit that even a graduate-school professor would have to credit her as co-author for the amount of work she'd done—that's how good-natured she was. She was a fine daughter, always helpful. She was humble and kind and naturally intelligent, in short, everything that her absurd mother was not.

Andrew held one worry about Margot's return home: Janelle might infect the bright child with her worsening nonsense. He vowed to separate them as much as possible and to keep Margot so busy with the copyediting of his manuscript that she'd have no time for any of her mother's mush-headed archetype workshops. He planned to complete the book draft before Margot returned home at the end of the month.

When the doorbell chimed one Wednesday morning, Andrew had long since put down his pen in order to indulge his usual forms of creative procrastination: de-alphabetizing his CDs to arrange them by genre and year; moving correspondence from pile to pile; sneaking quick looks at a mildly pornographic website before deleting his browsing history. "Goddamnit!" he shouted. "How am I expected to get any work done, ever, with these constant interruptions?!"

He waited for his wife to answer the door, but instead the doorbell rang again.

"See what I mean? I can't win." He shoved his chair back in a great drama of exasperation, as though he actually had an audience, and walked heavily through the house. He paused at the living room, where his wife stood before a dozen middle-aged, middle-weight, shockingly unattractive women, who apparently thought it was beneath their intellectual dignity to make any effort whatsoever to doll themselves up. The cloying smell of vanilla candles seeped from the room. Andrew was positive he'd have a headache inside five minutes.

"What I want you to think about next," Janelle said in her false-honey voice, "is your inner warrioress. She is who I want to feel on the page."

"I'm going to be ill," Andrew said. "I'm actually going to vomit." He swung open the door and was relieved to see a man standing there. "Quarmbey. Thank God. Come on in if you can manage to ignore that nauseating scene." He gestured to the living room as they passed and led Quarmbey out to the back deck, stopping off in the kitchen for a bottle of vodka and two tumblers.

"What's the redhead's name?" his friend asked, awaiting his host's pour.

"Trust me, you don't want anything to do with any of them. Big underwear on all of them except Janelle, and, in her case, who the hell cares."

After Quarmbey downed two quick shots, he said, "Andrew, I've been set up, and I need to hear it wasn't you."

"Of course it wasn't me. What the hell are you talking about?"

While sipping his third and fourth shots of vodka, Quarmbey told Andrew the bad news. "Normally an aggrieved author's only recourse is to write a letter to the editor, but those assholes, those traitors at *The Times*, are giving Fadge an entire page to respond to my review. Not in the letters section. A real page."

"That's an abomination." Andrew refilled both their glasses. "Clearly Fadge used his connections, pulled some strings, made some calls. Believe me when I say that nothing is beneath him. He has no pride."

"I thought *The Times* was the one paper left free of that sort of back-scratching, log-rolling crap. Apparently it's fallen into the gutter with everyone else."

"I wonder if they planned this all along—set us up—or whether Fadge marshaled his forces after the fact." Andrew remembered that he'd been asked to write the review himself and was proud of himself for not snapping the bait. He searched his memory for everyone he knew who still worked at *The Times*. "I'm going to make some calls of my own," he said.

His workday completely screwed, he allowed himself to get tipsy before calling his old friend a taxi.

"Really," Quarmbey said, "ask Janelle if that redhead is single."

"You drink too much." Andrew slammed the door and waved on the car.

Back in his study, he pulled the novels he'd written from the shelf, stacked them on the floor, and stood next to them. "Knee high," he said. "My career is knee high." With a sudden panic, he realized that he couldn't remember the title of his second novel. *High Sorghum*? He chewed the words. No, that was the title of his third novel. *High Sorghum* had been his weakest novel, but the second one—that was a great book. As he tried to recall the words of its title, he realized that he did not even remember where the book was set in place or time.

He stood for ten minutes before bending over, hands gripping his thighs for balance, to read from the spine, *Wintergreen: A Novel of the Frontier*.

# Chapter ten

Despite her height, or lack thereof, Margot was easy to spot among the sparse herd waiting for the ferry. She wore a slim, orange tank dress, sandals in place of her usual canvas sneakers, and an armful of wire-thin silver bangles. Next to her, the other women in the crowd looked coarse and vulgar; the men, grotesque.

"You look beautiful," Jackson said. He kissed the side of her head and breathed in her smell: unscented soap and baby powder.

The midday crowd was light—tourists and couples and old people and one or two down-and-outers, instead of commuters bumping shoulders. Jackson and Margot found a place on a bench.

Margot looked at her lap, where her hands neatly gripped a brown paper bag, then away. "I figured I'd bring lunch," she said to the air on her left as Jackson, seated to her right, strained to hear. She handed him a sandwich. "Is pimiento cheese okay? It's kind of kitsch, if nothing else."

"Pimiento cheese is perfect," he said, and it was. He ate the sandwich and the crisp apple Margot offered next. "That's the second pimiento sandwich you've given me. I'll never forget either of them."

He unfurled his height, wiping his hands on his jeans. "I'll get us something to drink, and we can go out on deck."

Summer had lingered into fall and the day was warm. The movement of the boat generated a perfect breeze. Jackson and Margot gazed at the Manhattan skyline, glanced at each other, then looked back at the city's squares and rectangles, the buildings with flat roofs and those with pointed hats. The sun glanced off the water, making the rising scene look two-dimensional—a façade or stage set rather than a place where people lived out real lives.

"A free ride and less than two dollars for a German beer. Best cheap date in New York City."

"Date?" Margot asked, then swallowed a small, quick gulp of her beer, her hand oddly high on the neck of the green bottle, her bangles tinkling as they slid up and down her arm with its movements.

"Not that you don't deserve the most expensive date in Paris." Jackson, knowing that he was speaking into the wind, spoke loudly.

"Paris?"

"Look at that skyline. Isn't it wonderful to see what the city looks like when you're still in it but not quite?"

Neither of them mentioned what was missing from the skyline, and Jackson was relieved that enough years had passed to render that conversation optional. He wanted to keep things light with Margot. She was a serious girl—he admired that—but he wanted her to have a good time. A good time with him.

"So have you finally admitted that what you're writing is a book?" he asked.

"I'm afraid so, afraid that it is a novel."

Margot tipped her head from side to side in a manner that Jackson found at once goofy and thoroughly disarming. She was serious, but there was nothing pretentious about her, nothing practiced. This was a girl who had never smiled for the mirror, whose facial expressions were natural and unlearned. He wanted to wrap her up in his arms, throw himself between her and anyone or anything that meant her harm.

"That's fantastic," he said. "It's terrific that you're writing a book. I won't ask you what it's about—isn't that the worst question always?—but I will ask you how it's going."

She smiled a girl's smile. "I don't know how I'll ever finish. I'm only through my second draft."

"You have an entire second draft?"

Her nod was barely perceptible, and now it was her shoulders moving in awkward jerks.

"Spell-check it and send it out."

"Oh, no, it's not ready." She sipped from the beer as though just remembering that she held it. "This is good. Nice and cold. You tell me about your writing."

"I'm aiming to write a big book, you know, splashy. I plan for my first novel to be my break-out book. It's not the literature that I'm sure you write. I'm moving around attractive stockbrokers, cocaine, gigolos, a dash of deviant sex." Noticing that Margot was again glancing away, Jackson paused. "But it's really kind of a morality play," he continued. "A pinch of *Macbeth* in the mix."

"Sounds ambitious." She touched the tip of her nose with her finger and quickly lowered it, sending the bangles sliding down her forearm in a musical collision.

"According to one definition of the word, yes, it is ambitious."

Together they watched the Statue of Liberty approach as though it and not they were moving. Jackson felt the momentary coolness of its shadow.

"Not a lovely face on her at all."

"You're not the first to so say," Margot replied.

Jackson winced at the accusation of unoriginality, but, when he replayed Margot's comment, detected no rebuke in her tone. "I once knew a fellow," he said, "named Chuck Wood. By the time he was ten, he'd heard the woodchuck tongue twister so many times that he'd just grin this huge grin and say 'never heard that one before.'"

"I suppose it's fitting that the symbol of independence wouldn't be soft or pretty in an easy way. But I do think she's rather handsome."

"There's only one face I can see right now." He cupped her cheek, her face small in his large hand, then retreated. "So, anyway, what will you do now that The Shadow of the Valley of Books is closing? You taught once, right? Do you have an MFA?"

Margot twirled one of her short curls with her middle finger. "An MA in literature. I wrote a thesis on the destiny of coincidence in Thomas Hardy, mostly in *Far from the Madding Crowd* and *Return of the Native* but I touched on *Jude* also. A lot of people have written about destiny and coincidence in Hardy, but I've searched everywhere and I think I'm actually the first person—I know, it's hard to believe—to address the destiny of coincidence in his work."

"I knew you were a more original thinker than I am. Say, Margot, you could probably still get a teaching job. The Metropolis Workshop thing is always hiring. There's lots of online stuff now too, the low-residency writing programs and all that. I don't mean become a teacher—I think so much more highly of you than that—just something to do for awhile. Of course, if you liked teaching, you could pick up an MFA."

"Oh, no," she said, shaking her head very slowly but with great emphasis, like a little kid resisting vegetables. "I could never show my writing like that. I hear it's like baring your veins to wolves."

"It's not so awful, really," Jackson said, even as he recalled some of his harsher workshop statements and the time he'd told a first-year student that workshop was a blood sport and to high-tail it back to Florida if she couldn't take it. "Besides, you'll be baring your work for reviewers." The word 'baring' seemed almost lewd said in proximity to her exposed arms, whose perfect creamy tone made Jackson want to both run his hands down them and leave them unsullied by his coarse touch.

"If it ever comes to that, which I doubt, I suppose you're right. But that's different. At least you're not in the same room. You can read your reviews or not. Or read them when you feel up to it." She gripped her almost-empty bottle in a way that resembled the wringing of hands, then added, "Maybe I'll use a pen name if I ever publish."

Jackson sucked the fresh breeze. "Margot, I realize it's no coincidence that your last name is Yarborough. I should think your father could get you an agent, of course, but he could also help you get a job in publishing, a good one that would pay quite a bit better than a bookstore. An editorship or a staff position as a reviewer or something. I think the publishing world would really benefit from the views of someone like you."

"I would never do that. I want to make my own way in the world, get whatever I get on my own merit."

"Margot, no one does that any more. If they ever did."

As the boat sounded its horn and closed the distance to Battery Park, Jackson wished he could slow its progress, make the first half of their ride last forever. Margot wasn't the prettiest girl he'd spent time with, but her sweet earnestness pulled at him. He loved her mix of unpracticed elegance and childlike gestures.

"Let's ride straight back," he said. "I don't want to get off the boat. Ever. Maybe we'll ride back and forth all day. I know this will sound silly, but I feel like we'll both be okay if we just never leave this boat. We'll stay on the boat forever, and no one will know where to look for us."

Margot smiled as the ferry docked on the Staten Island side. "I like that, but I'm pretty sure they make you get off. But we'll be back on in just a few minutes."

While they waited to re-board, Jackson noticed the line of Margot's slender thigh under the thin fabric of her dress and felt disproportionately happy when she leaned against his arm for a moment. This must be what falling in love feels like, he told himself. They said little until they were back on the ferry's deck, again in motion, this time heading back to the city of books and papers.

Margot turned to face him straight on, balancing with only her hip on the boat's rail. "Jackson, can I ask you something?"

"Anything at all. Anything."

"Do you really think of this as a date?"

"I was hoping that it was a date, that you were thinking of it that way. I hope that it is a date, that it counts that way to you. We're so different—my God I have a foot of height on you—but I really like you, Margot. I like you a lot."

Margot tilted her head toward her shoulder. Her chest and throat blushed pink against the pretty orange dress.

"The thing about me, Margot, is that I *would* use any connections I had in a second. You need to understand what kind of person I am. I'm not so good a person as you are."

"I think you're a fine person, Jackson." She said his name tentatively, as though trying it out, imitating the way he used her name when he talked to her. "A very fine person."

"Really?" The sun soaked his head as they neared the Statue of Liberty on the return pass, this time missing its shadow.

Margot nodded vigorously. "That's what makes this all the more awful. I'm moving at the end of the month, up to my folks' place in Annandale-on-Hudson. I'll get to the city once in a while, but I'm a homebody, I really am, that's something you should know about me. And besides, I want to finish my book, make it something perfect and beautiful. But you could visit. It's a nice place, really, a very good place. And you can get there on the train."

"Oh, Margot," was all Jackson could muster for the moment. After a long swig of imported beer, he inhaled sharply and told her, in edited form, about his unfortunate encounter with her parents.

"That's terrible," she whispered when he'd finished. "It really is terrible."

She let him draw her into a hug, her hands trapped between them. He squeezed as tight as he could trust himself to, afraid of crushing her. When they pulled away, he saw that the plastic button on his shirt pocket had left an imprint on her cheek: a red circle on her small, pretty face.

"We'll figure something out," he said to himself as well as to her. "I promise that we'll figure something out."

Margot cocked her head. "Hey," she said, "did you hear the one about the writer who died?"

"Tell me," he said, thinking her downright brave.

"St. Peter offers him the option of heaven or hell and the writer asks to see each one before deciding. As they descend into the fires of hell, the writer sees row upon row of writers, all chained to their steaming-hot desks and being whipped by demons. 'Show me heaven,' the writer says. They ascend to heaven and there's row upon row of writers chained to steaming-hot desks and being whipped by demons.

'But it's just as bad as hell,' the writer says. St. Peter shakes his head, and says, 'No, because in heaven your work gets published.'"

Jackson reached out and softly pulled one of her short curls. "Margot, I really do promise that we'll figure something out."

She smiled and nodded, her head still tilted.

# Chapter eleven

The impromptu party at the Renfros apartment had provided Henry Baffler with more minutes of companionship than he'd had since returning from the Blue Ridge Writers' Conference. It had left him both hopeful and lonely. Amanda wasn't his type—he'd always preferred beauty that was flawed and names with soft centers—but being around her made him long to live with a woman. At the same time, that Eddie Renfros, a struggling novelist, could claim the affection of such a wife as Amanda suggested that the starving artist's life need not be dismal and solitary.

Henry did not romanticize writers' poverty, nor did he feel as though he had chosen it. If anything, his role had picked him, or, perhaps more accurate, it was simply what he was. Though he'd grown up in a middle-class home with three televisions and no bookcase, he'd forever been the kid lurching around the playground—walking because sitting was not allowed at recess—trying to read Samuel Beckett or Diderot without tripping. He'd been too peculiar for even the least powerful bullies to bother with and indeed would have avoided socialization altogether had not a few poetically minded girls noticed that unusually lush eyelashes fringed his large, gentle eyes.

He remembered each of them, those girls who'd sent him lines from Keats and Shelley on pages torn from notebooks and who had offered him his sexual education in a series of kind acts. These girls with soft names were, he realized, the sort who in another time would have carried care packages to consumptives at the sanitarium. He wanted a female in his life again, but this time, he thought, he'd like a girlfriend with a bit more blade and a little less charitableness.

And so it was that the following week found him examining his clothes with a more critical eye than usual. Every stitch fit easily into a single bureau drawer in the efficiency apartment leased by his absentee roommate: a wealthy NYU student who didn't want his Mississippi Baptist parents to know that he really lived with his girlfriend. In exchange for his cut-rate rent, Henry had only to relay messages from Mississippi across town and learn to parrot phrases such as, "Sorry, you just missed him" and "He's at the library again—always studying so hard." Though he was ultimately willing to excuse these fibs as one of the costs of his survival as a writer, Henry despised lies and never told them to anyone other than the disembodied drawls on the other end of his phone line.

In fact, his general refusal to lie was in part responsible for his economic predicament. If he'd articulated any interest in selling dinette sets, he'd have inherited some money. Instead his family's small wealth was given in its entirety to his older brother, who had feigned an interest in running the family furniture store in Bakersfield. The brother promptly sold the business and bought the condominium in which he snorted away the rest of the Baffler assets in the form of powdered cocaine. Everyone in the family admitted that Henry was the one who had imagination.

Henry wished there was some money to tap. He didn't need much and was happy enough without even a computer. It was just as well that he had no email at home and so could limit his experience of electronic rejection to his twice-weekly visit to the bank of free computers at the public library. The written rejections—often a single sentence on a small square of paper—found him easily enough.

He knew he should take Jackson Miller's advice and submit each of his stories simultaneously to a dozen journals and magazines.

But even with the cheap box of envelopes he found at a thrift store, submissions were precious; each required at least the cost of copying the pages, the better part of two dollars to mail the story, and thirty-seven cents for the stamp on the self-addressed envelope that would carry the rejection note. That was the true indignity: to have to pay to transport your own rejection.

Often the spurning editors repeated what he had been told by former teachers and classmates: his scrupulous honesty hindered his storytelling, swamping his plots with too many details from real life, some of them implausible on the page. But that's what he knew how to do: to record.

When he turned his Realist's eye on his wardrobe, he found a bleak situation. Both pairs of jeans and the khaki pants had been patched multiple times by Henry's uneven hand sewing. By this point one pair of jeans had split beyond repair through the crotch and down the inseam, and Henry kept them only as a source of patching material for the other pair. He owned three tee-shirts, all of them washed thin. He had two shirts with collars, one of them wool, plus a corduroy jacket that was mostly too warm in the fall and not warm enough in the winter. He also owned a single glove, one pair of socks that he wore only in cool weather, and a pair of disintegrating brown shoes. He would soon have to visit the thrift store for new shoes and fresh tee-shirts. His best hope was to attract a girlfriend who lacked sartorial sense. It wasn't a good idea, he suspected, to hook up with another fiction writer, but sometimes, late at night, he imagined a vague-faced poet or painter or musician; a girl composing music in a minor key, thin fingers poised to strike a chord.

Though he was broke and lonely, Henry was not unhappy. He had placed two new articles advocating his version of New Realism. It was true that one had appeared in the final issue of *(A)Musing Aloud*, a now-defunct journal with minimal circulation edited by a former instructor. But the other piece was being published in the new issue of *Swanky*, and people actually read *Swanky*. Henry viewed today's work as the experiment that could tie his ideas together and prove with finality that his literary theory worked at the practical level: he planned to stalk the bailiff during his lunch hour.

Excited by this scheduled adventure in eavesdropping, Henry put on his wearable pair of jeans, one of the flimsy shirts, and his shoes. At the apartment's single sink, spaced midway between the faucetless kitchen and bathroom, he brushed his teeth and wet down his hair. It was already close to noon, so he rushed down the stairs. As he stepped onto the street, he was comforted as always by the bright light and fresh air that never penetrated the interior-facing room where he slowly constructed his paragraphs.

Though his studio flat was dark and cramped and smelled of dust and mold and things he didn't care to register, Henry reveled in his neighborhood. It was the setting of a real writer; it kept him in touch with real people. Henry loved his perennially unfashionable block, which the Irish gangs of decades past had abandoned to the Dominican families who were now Henry's neighbors. The only evidence Henry could see of the Gaelic thugs who had once ruled Hell's Kitchen were the large, friendly cops who smoked cigarettes and ogled attractive women in front of their tiny brick-front station. This was a part of Hell's Kitchen too charmless to have succumbed to gentrification, and the stores that Henry passed were functional places. These were businesses not dependent on walk-in traffic but stores that certain sets of people had to visit, once a year or so, from other parts of the city: vacuum repair, saltwater aquarium paraphernalia, dry-cleaning supplies, industrial kitchen wares. The only places of note were the Hit Factory, where in one great rock-and-roll week, David Bowie and Lou Reed had both recorded iconic albums, and the peculiar plaza that was the area's one futile effort to lure the theater crowd further west. The plaza now boasted little more than a wholesale pet-food store, empty store fronts, and a mediocre movie theater where shooting occasionally broke out. Henry's favorite local spot was a comical French restaurant decorated with varnished jigsaw puzzles of the Eiffel Tower and Edith Piaff, staffed by laconic old women, and known for having boiled celery on the menu. He'd eaten there only once, a seal-the-deal meal paid for by the roommate he hadn't seen since. He touched the restaurant's wrought-iron window box, which held only dry dirt and a few straw-colored weeds, as he trotted past it toward the courthouse.

He'd long argued the superiority of character-driven fiction over the tyranny of plot, though Eddie Renfros's amorphous plots were not, he was convinced, the right way to go. Though exquisitely written—all the editors who rejected it said so—*Vapor* was basically unreadable. You could read the same page over and over like a lovely poem, but there was no reason whatsoever to turn to the next page. What Eddie had gotten away with in his first book, he'd taken too far in his second. Even Eddie himself seemed to realize this now, and the poor chap was now trying to develop iron-handed plot.

Henry was formulating an alternative. Plots exist. Plots are real-life. People do things, and things happen, and those things result in still other events. The trouble comes when the writer forces plot onto character like, depending on your world view, God or fate or the randomly cruel universe. Jackson Miller was wrong with all his talk of life and fiction as one big farce to which the individual can respond with no weapon save mocking laughter. Henry's idea was to treat life and the destiny of individual lives with absolute impartiality and respect. He would not be the omnipotent author but rather the chronicler who sets it down. He would spread his hands and say, "Look, this is the kind of thing that happens." He was going to let his protagonist determine his own plot.

As he rounded the corner, he slowed, keeping close to the storefronts he passed. He stalled entirely when he spotted his bailiff eating lunch with his outsized lady friend in a small shaded park. Henry crept his way behind them, choosing a bench where he was partly hidden by a spindly ash but could hear the conversation that would be his novel's dialogue.

Henry told himself that he would never have to write a big dramatic scene. Real drama happens so rarely in life, and, even when it does, real-world melodrama happens in ways useless to the novelist, who must, at the least, strip it from its circumstances and render it convincing. His prescription for fiction was a return to ordinary events and people: the head-cold that interrupts the would-be love scene, the pretty girl's prom night ruined by a large pimple, all the numerous repulsive features of common decent life—presented coldly, with great seriousness and no hint of the facetious.

Grub

"Take that pigeon," his bailiff was saying. "It just takes what it wants. I see his kind—in human form, mind you—all day long." He paused and then huffed out, "Sure do. All day long."

Henry tuned out all the jangling sounds of the small park, concentrating on the surprisingly high pitched voice of his protagonist as the man told his squinting girlfriend about a landlord seeking damages from a tenant who failed to replace a light bulb. "More gall than a gall bladder," the voice scraped.

Henry touched the fingertips of both hands to his cheekbones. The muscles of his face lifted against his fingers as he pictured himself putting quotation marks around the bailiff's lines. Yes, his character was going to provide him with all he needed.

# Chapter twelve

Amanda Renfros was more dispirited than her husband when the final rejection of his novel *Vapor*—a form letter from a tiny press—arrived early in the week's mail. She had enjoyed being married to a man of distinction. "My name is Amanda Renfros," she'd tell clerks. "I see you have several copies of my husband's book, but after last week's review in *The Times*, you might want to consider a table display."

Now that *Sea Miss* was out of print and the laudations were cold, Amanda was as likely as not to offer what she considered to be her more interesting maiden name: Amanda Yule. Her worry that Eddie had lost his talent had developed into an anxiety that gnawed her stomach like her childhood fears. Above all, she was angry with herself. She knew that she should have been more circumspect, thought more carefully about the future and what it meant to grow older before committing to, of all things, marriage to a writer. Perhaps it wouldn't be so terrible if Eddie was at least fighting back, but it seemed as though he didn't much care if one or both of them wound up working in an office for the rest of their ordinary lives. The worst thing she could imagine was leading an uninteresting life, working the same hours as all the other drones. Every month she felt the doors to her future narrowing.

It was with such thoughts running through her mind that Amanda, on a whim, called in sick. The call was easy; she'd always been a good liar, knowing, as most fiction writers know, the precise amount of detail with which to decorate the untruth. After she hung up, she deleted the name "Amanda Renfros" from her silly first attempt at a popular book. She replaced it with "Amanda Yule" and then, for no real reason, with "Clarice Aames". She sent the file containing "Bad Dog Séance" to *Swanky*, one of the magazines that both accepted electronic submissions and had a circulation worth counting.

After showering and drying her hair shiny straight, she dusted herself with verbena powder and dressed in good underwear, slinky gray pants, and an interesting shirt. She couldn't be running around the city looking like she wasn't even trying. She admitted this: if Eddie refused to do what was necessary to make things work out for them, she'd need to look her best wherever she went. "What women should do," she told herself, "is choose a man after he's old enough for it to be clear whether he's made it for good or not."

This thought troubled her, because it suddenly made the future unpredictable. She pictured the Eddie of old—boyish in his animation over every positive review, every "best of" short list—and felt melancholy wash away whatever had sparkled inside her.

Feeling sad and newly hollow, she completed the task of packaging herself well. She put blush on her cheeks, gloss to her lips, and diamond studs in her earlobes before easing her feet into pumps that made her six-feet tall. When she looked in the mirror, she saw again the awkward girl with the off-center mouth, but when she softened her frown and centered her lips, she glimpsed what she was after: the woman most men found beautiful.

Thus readied, she struck out for the Frick to find a painting begging for its own novel. She rode her high heels well, walking quickly past the old firehouse. Looking up at the inexplicable relief of a bulldog's head that crowned the building, she wondered if that had planted the subliminal idea for "Bad Dog Séance" and vowed that her future literary choices would be conscious. At Third Avenue, she rounded the corner where Carmen Gigante had been shot, everyone said by Gotti, fifty years after Gigante murdered the editor of *Il Progresso* just down the street. She walked down 36th Street, slowing to look at the much-coveted apartments of Sniffen Court—now gated and fully gentrified and looking much cleaner than it did on that Doors album cover that her brothers probably still listened to.

She walked uptown on Lexington, away from what she considered her neighborhood's most dispiriting landmarks—the former Rutledge Inn where the Tylenol killer once stayed and the silly bar that had finally taken down its "first baseball game played here" plaque under threat of lawsuit from civic boosters one river and eight miles away. Now she strolled by anachronisms she found charming: the weird little police outpost that had guarded the Cuban embassy since Castro's platform-shoe-era visit and the subterranean pool hall still called the 'Soldiers, Sailors, and Airmen Club.' Maybe she'd put them in a book someday.

Not many women could walk much of Manhattan's length in the shoes Amanda wore, but her stride was unchanged as she approached the Frick. After paying fifteen dollars, she flipped open her notebook and moved methodically through the small museum's various rooms, reassured by the feminine click of her heels on the floors, imagining what it would be like if the Frick was a house—her house.

She'd always been calmed by the presence of great art, almost as though she knew the painters themselves and had not grown up in a house where the only art in evidence was a paint-by-numbers covered bridge and her brothers' black-light posters. The point of pain in her stomach, which had been nearly constant for weeks, disappeared.

She dismissed Corot quickly, remembering the joke: "Corot painted three thousand paintings and five thousand of them are in the United States." The Rembrandt's rich color held her rapt for several minutes, but ultimately she decided that the portrait of a single person, no matter how much narrative it implied, did not offer enough material for the two hundred fifty-six printed pages that made the ideal book-club novel.

Doubting her instincts, she wondered if she should have

gone instead to the Whitney or the MoMA. Maybe a Lichtenstein was the thing; she could mimic the comic-strip pointillism. But, no, that would be too arty, too punk, would hit the wrong audience. Its audience would be too small. She smiled at the thought that Clarice Aames could write a Lichtenstein story. For that moment, she thought of Clarice Aames as another person, a someone she might phone and offer an idea for a story.

Amanda lingered at the Hobbema pictures. They appeared to be landscapes or scenes of empty houses and sheds in landscapes, but, at the right distance and angle, it was easy to see the people the artist had hidden in window frames, behind tree stumps, huddled in tall grass. A possibility, she decided, though she was concerned that the artist was not famous enough. It seemed a shame that he had quit painting so young when he might have made a real name for himself.

Amanda forgot Hobbema as she stepped into the frothy bizarreness of the Fragonard room. Of course, she thought, she needn't have considered anything else! She must have known, in the back of her mind, that it would be the Fragonards, and that was why she'd started for the Frick rather than the Met or that godawful Dahesh shrine to ravished virgins and false exoticism.

Alone in the room, her faith in her instincts restored, Amanda smiled sideways. Fragonard was perfect: famous enough, weird enough but not too weird, historical, pretty, and—this was key—full of sexual possibility. That odd fellow heading off the canvas had to be sneaking off to do something kinky. She determined, on the spot, to title her novel *The Progress of Love*, to name her buxom heroine Libertine, and to write the book in four months.

Before leaving, she bought a copy of each of the gift shop's publications on Fragonard and also a book about Hobbema, which she paged through on what she considered a well-deserved taxi ride home. After all, she'd walked all the way up the east side in the highest of heels and this was the day she was taking her fate into her own hands.

Eddie was busy in the kitchen when she opened the door. "I'm making you a real Caesar salad," he said. "The kind the Hollywood types used to drive to Tijuana for."

"They went to Tijuana for the liquor and bull fights," she said. "The salad was secondary. But it sounds good, so long as you leave the raw egg out."

His head dropped a little. "I sort of coddled it, and I washed it first."

Amanda's mood was so light that she couldn't summon her nasty side. She kissed her husband's cheek. "All right, then, but if I get salmonella poisoning I'm filing for divorce."

"If I poison you, I'll hold your hair back while you puke."

"Don't be gross, Eddie. Particularly not if you want me to eat."

Over the chilled salad bowls, she told her husband the story of Meindert Hobbema. "You should write a novel about him. It's perfect for you. He had all this talent, but he just stopped painting in his late twenties. Just stopped. And it's apparently not because he was ill or tortured or consumptive or anything. He just up and quit and took some clerk's job like the assistant important underling of weights and measures." She paused to roll an anchovy onto her fork and bite into its saltiness. "Anyway, your mission, should you choose to accept it, is to find out why he quit painting and write a novel about it. Think tasteful but not low-budget screenplay while you're at it. You know, include enough dialogue and some cinematic scenes and images."

Eddie shoved salad into his mouth at an impolite pace.

"Slow down," she said. "Try to enjoy it. It's really very good."

She did not mention Fragonard, nor her intention to write a novel, and she most certainly did not state the small, important truth that she already had a title—or the much larger truth that she'd decided to quit her job.

# Chapter thirteen

While Margot Yarborough felt a fragment of guilt over moving her snoring father back into her mother's room and some embarrassment over her failure to make it in the city, she was happy to be back in her family home. Despite her parents' years of bickering, she thought of her childhood fondly. And perhaps because of that bickering, she had made, from an early age, a sanctuary of her room. She thought of it as spring: the wall paint reflected fresh green, the few pieces of furniture and the floor planks were whitewashed, and her linens and curtains reminded her of meadows in April. Her father had contaminated the room with cigar smoke, but several days and nights of open windows and a vase of fresh lavender restored the illusion of the world emerging from winter even as the yellow and red leaves outside the window made it obvious that winter was still to come.

Her New York apartment had been small, furnished with the basics alone, so she'd moved home with only a suitcase of clothes, a box of kitchen objects, her writing materials, and forty-seven boxes of books.

"Unpack your clothes, honey," her mother had said. "But these other things need to stay in the garage until you decide what you need at hand. Visual clutter actually inhibits mental clarity. There's been research—not that your father will hear of it. I shudder when I walk by his office."

Margot placed her clothes on hangers and in drawers. She set up her laptop, arranged her notebooks and pencils, and stacked both drafts of *The Reluctant Leper* on the antique white table at which she had made her first literary attempt at the age of six. It had been an Emily Dickinson imitation: a poem she'd called "The Long Grass Blade." She wondered if a copy still existed and whether the poem contained a salvageable line, some phrase she could weave into her novel—a sentimental joke hidden to all but her.

After her mother left to take an exercise class she called "burning pilates," which she'd begged Margot to try as soon as possible—"you need to build muscle and bone while you still can," she'd admonished—Margot slipped out to the garage. There she unpacked the forty-seven boxes of her books in order to select ten volumes she would allow herself to keep inside. Several hours later, she had moved thirty-seven books into her room and still had to go back for a dictionary. About half the books she'd pulled out were favorites. The other fifteen were those she had at the top of her to-read list. Though she had many contemporary novels and poetry collections in the repacked boxes in the garage, not one of the books she took to her room, save the dictionary, had been published after 1910.

There was rap at her door, which swung open and was filled by her father's substantial body.

"Just setting up my workspace," she said.

"I can't tell you how glad I am to hear that, Margot. Quite a coincidence that you've come home now, actually. I've been doing some thinking, and I think you're just the person to help out your dear old dad in his time of need. It's time for old dad to get some more points on the scoreboard, however late in the game."

Margot knew the conversation's blueprint: it was her turn to remind him of his many accomplishments while assuring him that he was plenty young enough to do more. She got so far as to open her mouth, but the words wouldn't come readily, as they once had.

"I'm not getting any younger," he said when he registered her silence, "and there's no use telling me otherwise because I know what I see when I look in the mirror." He brushed back his hair, resting his other hand on the stomach starting to overhang his belt. "But I've still got time to make my mark, at least with the help of my loving daughter." His tone was playful—mock sarcastic—but it seemed like a transparency overlaying something more serious, even worrisome.

Margot had made herself hungry toting books back and forth, but at this her appetite retreated and her neck felt cold. Her shoulders shuddered, a movement she tried to contain, keep small. Perhaps it was at this moment she first contemplated her father as mortal. "What did you have in mind?" she asked, risking this mistake.

"Just a bit of copyediting. My new book is finished. Finally finished!"

"Congratulations," she managed. "Has your editor seen it?"

"Just needs a bit of copyediting, you know, a fresh pair of eyes." Her father's smile was wide, his voice louder than necessary. "I'd do it myself but my eyes aren't what they used to be, and of course my time is our money. It's not like your mother pays the bills around here."

Margot rested her palm on the tall stack of her own draft pages. "Sure, Dad. I'd be glad to help out with a little proofreading, but I've got my own project to finish as well."

"Yes, that's it exactly. Proofreading. Maybe just a little fix here and there, if you see a sentence that could be more elegantly worded. Of course, there are a few spots that need a dash of filling in. You know how the process goes. Every writer leaves in a phrase here or there that's really just a marker. I mean, all I'm saying is that I may not have caught them all."

Margot nodded slowly. "When were you thinking? I'd be happy to get to it just as soon as I finish—"

"The sooner the better, really, given that your dad's not getting any younger. Plus Fadge already has his book out." He brightened, his smile transforming into something genuine. "Did you see that review in *The Times*? Got what he deserved." He stepped toward her and set an awkward hand on her shoulder, something like a pat, before retreating to the door.

That night, Margot slept fitfully, dreaming shallow nightmares in which she floundered in a sea of green ink and copyediting marks. Faulkner whispered words she couldn't discern; not another language but not quite English either. Fitzgerald laughed uproariously and pointed. James Dickey pinched her bottom. The pages of the marked-up Balzac manuscript she'd seen at the Pierpont-Morgan library flew at her like road signs in a 1950s movie. Though she was still exhausted, waking was all relief.

Abiding by Miss Manner's admonition that a robe, brushed hair, and clean teeth are the minimum requirements for a breakfast appearance, Margot arrived in the kitchen ten minutes after waking to find her father talking at her mother's back.

"Guess what!" he exclaimed, turning his entire body to follow his perpetually stiff neck. "I just received the best email I've ever started the day with. It's too good to be true." He paused for encouragement but continued without it. "Fadge has actually made things ten times worse for himself. Ordinarily an abused writer's only recourse is the letters page, but Fadge pulled his dirty little strings and was granted an entire page—in the goddamed *Times*!—to defend himself like the helpless little boy he is. Quarmbey was livid, let me tell you. But now! Now! Now the employees this was forced on got in the last trick. Fadge's response will be printed under a huge banner that says 'I'm Not Really an Idiot.' It'll be in this Sunday."

Although Janelle had purchased two electric juicers, she had since declared them too loud, saying there was too much noise pollution in the world already. Now she squeezed oranges by hand, her waist twisting with her work. Without disrupting her rhythm, she said, "It seems cruel."

"That's right! Cruel indeed." Her father laughed at full volume. "And there's nothing Fadge can do now. He'll have had his unprecedented page. They can't give him more, and he'll look babyish enough as it is. He won't even have grounds for complaint, because he actually says those words—'I'm not really an idiot'—in his response. Can you imagine writing such a thing? Knowing it was to be published with your name on it? You can just shoot me the day I ever so much as think of writing such a line. I mean, if you have to tell the world you're not really an idiot, the world is going to catch on to that one. People are stupid, but they're not that stupid."

Margot was slowly growing accustomed to eating breakfast with others after several years of doing so alone more often than not. And she felt better watching her mother wince at her father's sausage and freezer pancakes, catching her father make faces at her mother's raw oats in yogurt.

"It's like the good old days." Margot worked a spoon into her berry-laced cereal. "All of us together but different." Still at the table, she devised a schedule for alternating work on her novel with the copyediting of her father's mess of a manuscript.

And thus her days passed: after spending three morning hours on her father's book, she turned to her own work, pausing only for an afternoon snack and, if one of her parents was home to remind her, a bit of dinner. Though she was mostly happy during these weeks, she felt slight alarm whenever she thought of Jackson Miller. His emails to her were much shorter than the long paragraphs in which she elaborated on the movement of the river outside her window, on her worries about sending her book into the world, on the way the books she read changed her moods the way colors shift in a kaleidoscope. Though brief, his emails were frequent, and in them she detected fondness and possibly a good deal more. If she forgot to check her email or failed to write to him for a couple of days, she read both worry and pouting in his tone. The first time he closed a note *Love, Jack*, she wondered if it signified a new intensity in his feelings or something more ephemeral, an affection sliding sideways like a cloud's shadow.

He continued to sign his name with the term of endearment, but of course he couldn't very well stop once he'd started. Perhaps it had become a habit, even a way of limiting rather than deepening their friendship, like a kiss on the cheek or a routine hug goodbye. She remembered that he was from Charleston, and she understood that social codes were different in the south.

She remembered a visiting writer she'd chatted with during a sparsely attended signing at the bookstore. Sitting behind a large, unsold stack of his novel about baseball reenactors, he'd said, "The problem with a Yankee is that he'll tell you everything he knows in the first hour you know him." The man had spent the next hour telling her more than she wanted to know about southern ball leagues while she, northern born and disinterested in sports, had said next to nothing. He'd given her a vigorous hug when he left, as though there were old friend. And so she decided not to put too much stock in the warmth of Jackson's coda.

Despite stray thoughts about Jackson Miller, Margot thought more about writing than about any person. There were days on which she had little confidence in her novel, concluding that her self-delusion about its quality was total. In the main, though, she was smitten with *The Reluctant Leper*. It told the story of a man traveling though nineteenth-century Louisiana. After a few misadventures in The Crescent City, an encounter with a relatively plain but pure-of-heart Creole girl living in the marshes near Lake Pontchartrain inspires the protagonist to perform a good deed. He agrees to carry supplies to the leper colony at Carville, an institution that Margot had researched painstakingly. If she'd had the money, she might have flown to Louisiana, but, truth be told, she preferred to study books—representations of places, people, and things—over the things themselves. And ultimately writing was, after all, an act of imagination.

Once at the leper colony, her hero is wrongfully mistaken for a diagnosed leper and interred. After fifteen years—years that see increased understanding of leprosy as Hansen's disease—he finally proves to a doctor that he is not infected with the bacterium responsible for the disfiguring condition. Then on the eve of his release, he realizes that he has lost sensation in his fingertips: he has finally contracted leprosy from a decade and a half of living in close quarters with lepers. No one knows, so he is free to leave. Yet inspired by the memory of the virtuous Creole girl, he chooses to stay and live out his life among an eccentric cast of lepers. He dies an obscure but happy man, sustained by his outcast friends and his love for a woman he met only once, never slept with, and has not seen in years and years.

After two weeks, the novel was only a line edit away from completion—though what completion might mean or bring, Margot could not conjecture. Her father's book, on the other hand, was still not fit for consumption and was taking every bit as much time as she had expected it to. Not that his book didn't contain astute observations about the history and practice of literature—it did. But Margot was sadly unsurprised to find numerous faulty quotes, dates, and other facts. Worse, some of her father's "place markers" represented mere glimpses of undeveloped ideas. Most of the missing material pertained to women writers. One trick she needed to perform was to provide opinions on Willa Cather and Virginia Woolf in her father's voice but in such a way that would keep feminist critics from eviscerating him. The thing was to write like her father—with flare and expansiveness—only tightened and given more clarity, grace, and compassion than he generally mustered.

Margot finished her work on *The Reluctant Leper* early on a Sunday morning, which left her able at last to foresee the completion of her work on her father's crowning literary accomplishment. At breakfast, she watched her father—his mouth full of freezer-to-toaster pastry—again laughing at the enormous banner over Fadge's page-long defense of his history of literature: "I'm Not Really an Idiot."

Instead of announcing her good news, she retreated to her room and savored it privately. I just wrote a novel, she told herself. I just wrote a novel. Her misgivings gone, at least for the moment, she felt almost giddy.

When she went online and found several new messages from Jackson—all brief but increasingly pleading—she realized she'd let the rest of her life go while she completed her book. Just like a real writer. She hit reply to his latest email and typed: "I just wrote a novel. Can you celebrate?"

# Chapter fourteen

Jackson Miller ignored the pile of clothes, some clean and some dirty, sprawling on his unmade bed. He ignored the dust animals congregating in the corners of his room. He ignored the stack of unopened mail. As he had every morning since he'd started his novel, he wrote. He was two chapters from finished.

All fall he'd been living off ongoing rent extensions from Doreen and a new credit card from a bank he'd never heard of, as he typed away at his tale of greed and drugs but mostly sex on Wall Street. His working title was *Pig-Male-Ion*, though he knew he'd have to come up with a serious title soon. He routinely reminded himself: I am writing a young man's book, but I am writing it for women more than for men. They'd buy it in droves, he believed, because women want to understand men, because women do not understand that men fall into two categories: those who are inexplicable and those too dull to require explication. That's what he planned to say in the interviews—that men are either inexplicable or too dull to bother with.

Jackson wanted to appeal to young readers, to hipsters, so he played with every trick he thought he could get away with: letters written in alternative typescripts, diaries that trail off pages with the suicides of their authors, the inclusion of small illustrations and visual puzzles, the occasional blank page signifying moral bankruptcy. There would be stuff to talk about, texture to make his readers feel clever.

He'd cleaned up as he went along, so there'd be no need for a second draft. The story was the story, and, font tricks aside, it told itself. He'd worked well and quickly, and the end was within a week's reach.

He spent the afternoon crafting the query letter he planned to send to twenty agents whose names had recently appeared in the "Hot Deals" section of *Publishers Weekly* and then checked his email. Plenty of new messages, but none of them were from Margot. He'd been so sure, that day on the ferry, that she was falling for him. And once a week she sent him a long email—or sometimes an actual letter by post—detailing her life or discussing some idea she was pondering. But she often went days without contacting him, and she never mentioned missing him or suggested that they might get together. Jackson, used to being chased by women, wondered if she was playing by some old-fashioned rule book, if she'd found an etiquette book in some used book store on courting for girls fresh out of finishing school. He wanted to see her but couldn't very well knock on her father's door, and he didn't have the money to take her out. He'd have to invite her down for a night in, he decided, which would require getting Doreen out of the house.

Despite their lack of forwardness, though, Margot's letters were intimate in their own way, and unless he was a poorer judge of character than he had reason to believe, Margot wasn't playing at anything. She wasn't calculating. He sent her another email, this one containing a corny joke about a writer who comes home to find his house on fire. His wife explains that she'd been lighting the fire when his agent called and the curtains ignited. His every possession charred or consumed, the writer asks, with uncontained excitement, "My agent called?"

"I'd rather have you call me," he concluded the email, and signed *Love, Jackson*, though Margot continued to close her notes *Fondly*.

He was constructing a well-deserved sandwich when Doreen came home. "And how are the luminaries at Grub?" he asked, spreading spicy mustard on a slice of rye. "Overhear any agents wooing bestselling authors or hammering out hardcover-softcover deals?"

"I did cook for those tennis sisters and their editor."

"Editor? You mean coach."

Doreen shook her long ponytail. "Editor. They're writing a series of young adult novels."

"I keep telling you, Doreen. That's exactly what you should be doing."

"Jackson, you've said this kind of thing yourself. It's like that actor who wrote the novel about the retarded kid. Their books are being published because they're already famous. I'm not. But anyway, it doesn't matter. I don't want to be a writer."

"You like to read."

"Yes, but I don't like to write. Part of your problem is that there aren't enough readers who aren't also trying to be writers. I don't want to be a writer. I want to be a chef, have my own restaurant, and have all those editors and agents and big-time writers and tennis stars lunching on my roasted beets."

Jackson cut his sandwich in half and opened a bottle of beer. "Say, Doreen," he said, "think you could get me a discount if I have lunch at Grub in a while?"

"Not with your credit history," she laughed.

Jackson awoke the next morning with a title, which he pasted into his query letter. To save money as well as time, he emailed the letter, together with the first three chapters, to those agents who accepted electronic queries. He printed out the other queries, addressed the envelopes, and walked to the post office. In the crisp air, Jackson felt the energy of fall, of school in swing and people back to work, of productivity and success. The day was going his way. The line at the post office was short, and the clerk was young and pretty. The bagel he picked up on the way home was still warm, and that afternoon the sentences came easily. Shortly before five, he received two emails and one phone call from agents interested in representing the book now titled *Oink*.

"How about I hand you the manuscript over lunch?" he said to the agent who phoned. "I promise that if you liked the chapters I sent, you'll love the whole book."

"Hell, I don't even have to read it," she said. "How about tomorrow?"

"Tomorrow should work," Jackson answered. "Half past twelve at Grub? Can you make the reservation?"

That night, working straight through the small hours, Jackson finished writing his first novel.

# Chapter fifteen

Eddie Renfros stared at the computer screen, his knuckles locked as he faced the first page of the fifteenth chapter of *Conduct*, a page that was, after an hour of sitting, still blank. The viola player and her husband were scheduled, according to his outline, to fight over their deaf daughter's tentatively planned surgery. But Eddie could not shake the belief that these two characters were not combative. As he had grown to know the two as people, he saw that the husband's reaction to disagreement was avoidance, while the wife sought escape in excitement and pleasure. Neither of them was predisposed to direct conflict. Yet to stay on schedule and keep his plot in line, he needed to stick to his outline and force the characters into a full-blown argument. He imagined Amanda laughing at him, saying, "My God, they aren't real people."

At this moment, he felt enormous admiration for Henry Baffler—for Henry's commitment to his artistic ideas, loony though they sometimes were. Eddie also admired Henry for protecting his independence. Henry had no wife to support, no literary reputation to protect, and he didn't seem to mind living in near squalor.

Eddie took a third coffee break and reconsidered Amanda's

words on the painter Hobbema. It seemed highly peculiar that she should want him to write such a book—a novel about a talented but not especially well-known painter who quit painting in his early thirties. And then it struck him that he was in Hobbema's position, albeit removed by three centuries and one art form. Perhaps Amanda was telling him something altogether different than what her literal words said. Perhaps she had planted the idea not because she wanted him to write about Hobbema but because she wanted him to imitate the painter—to get a job at the ministry of weights and measures or whatever the hell it was that Hobbema had done. And to quit writing.

He went back to the computer and stared at the words 'Chapter Fifteen' until they blurred and then came back together distorted. He played with their letters like an anagram, came up with the word 'fatter' but no noun for it to describe. His heart fluttered, as it did when he was nervous before a public appearance, but here he was all alone with just his partially written novel. Again he tried to decode Amanda's intent. Hobbema just quit, and he could too. No one ever said he *had* to be a writer. It would be liberating to quit: no more guilt when he didn't work, no more worries about succeeding at something few people can succeed at, no more thinking about invented lives in the middle of the night.

Eddie took his mug to the dining room table, rummaged through the paper until he found the want ads, and circled every job that anyone might possibly give him. Copyediting seemed most likely, and there was a copyediting gig at one of the major house's small imprints. An editor at that imprint had been one of the first to reject *Vapor*, and Eddie had admired the directness of her letter to his agent. Where certain other editors had overextended metaphors about unfinished paintings and vague "editorial" concerns about not having fallen in love with the main character "as a man," this editor had declined on the grounds that the book "would be a modest seller at best." It was an opinion he could swallow, not the kind that tormented him with revision possibilities in the middle of the night.

He phoned the number listed and was granted an afternoon interview. He told himself that this didn't signal the end of his writing career, that he might well get more writing done under the discipline of a job schedule. He reasoned that the less time he had, the more he would appreciate it and the more wisely he would use it. He'd benefit from the variety of occupation. He would write novels precisely because he didn't have to. Writing could become a treat and a joy, or maybe he'd prove himself one of those writers who can't not write. Kafka had had a job and so had Wallace Stevens, and that wasn't even counting all the writers working as teachers. Even the great Faulkner had paused to earn a few bucks from Hollywood.

To prove his point to himself, Eddie returned to his computer and marched his characters through their confrontation and through the first six pages of chapter fifteen—twice his regular daily quota. He showered, dressed in slacks and his only fresh-looking blazer, walked up to his midtown interview, claimed his visitor's badge at the security desk, and rode the elevator to the nineteenth floor.

The man who interviewed him—and would be his superior if he landed the job—looked to be several years younger than Eddie, and worked not in an office but a cubicle. He shook hands energetically and spoke with the animation and satisfaction of a man whose income, however small, is assured.

"We're launching a new line of romances," he said, pushing bangs from his eyes to peruse Eddie's resume, which highlighted his degrees and his publications but listed little in the way of employment history. "Not exactly the literary work you might have been hoping for."

Eddie smoothed his slacks with his palms. "Doesn't matter. I enjoy copyediting. It may be my favorite part of my own process. Seriously. I'm good at it, and I want the job."

"But can we afford you?" The young man leaned forward as he asked this. His tone was difficult to parse, and Eddie couldn't discern whether it was serious, lightly joking, or downright mocking.

"I'm not as much above your figure as you might imagine." Eddie's voice was husky, his words ending with a cracked laugh. He paused. "Please give me the job." His tongue sat dry and heavy in his mouth.

"Well, it's a bit comical to have a well-reviewed author

copyediting bodice busters, but you know your own business best and no doubt you're not the only writer in this line of work. Just promise: only copyediting, no editing. The prose will appall you, but you must leave it alone. Just fix the outright errors and find the typos."

They agreed on thirty hours per week, because the publishing house would be unable to offer health insurance or the other benefits of full-time employment. Despite the paltriness of the salary named, Eddie felt good as he walked home. He was downright happy about the prospect of some regular income—at least he could pay the interest on their credit-card debt—and pleased with himself for having done something, having taken matters into his own hands. No more feebleness; he had made a decision and was on his way to acting like a responsible man. He nodded to the cops outside the Cuban embassy as he rounded the corner toward home.

When he entered the apartment, he heard the once-familiar rhythm of Amanda's fast typing on a keyboard. Whereas he could only hunt and peck, Amanda had been properly trained and could type as fast as she could think. He'd always taken pride in his slow, old-fashioned typing, imagined that it improved the quality of his word choices and cadences and put him in the company of those great writers of decades past who worked with manual typewriters. Now, though, he wasn't sure. If he could type properly, perhaps *Conduct* would already be completed and he could move on.

He waited for Amanda to finish what she was working on, pushing aside the thought that it might be a long, heartfelt email, for he knew that his wife corresponded back and forth with several friends. Sometimes she told him a joke that Jackson had emailed, and he wondered how often they communicated.

"How did the writing go today?" she asked when she walked into the living room. As always, her face made the room seem lighter, sunnier.

"Six pages, so I could even take tomorrow off if I wanted to."

She sat directly across from him, on the red leather chair facing the sofa. "But you aren't going to do that, are you?" She looked steadily at him, her gaze underscoring the tone of her comment as instructional rather than inquisitive.

"I'm not going to," Eddie assured her. "But I am going to have to tinker with my writing schedule. I've taken a job."

"A job? What job?" Amanda sat straight and smiled with only one side of her mouth.

He told her about the interview and the job he'd been offered.

"Let me go over this and see if I have it right. You applied for a job as a romance-novel copyeditor? And then you actually went to the interview?"

"It's just part-time, to supplement what you're making until I can get an advance. I'll still be working on the novel. I'll still be first and foremost a writer. But unless you're willing to move somewhere much less expensive, we've got to do something to make some money. I wish I were a rich and famous writer, but the truth is that we're broke. Flat broke."

Amanda stroked the fine hairs on her arm. After a long silence, she said in a quiet, resolute voice: "I won't allow it."

"Either I take this job or we move to New Jersey."

"To me, it makes no difference. Either option is intolerable."

Eddie's anger, pent up so long by his fear of annoying his beautiful wife, swelled into something he couldn't contain. "Amanda, are you my wife or not?"

"I am certainly not the wife of a copyeditor of romance novels. That's not why I've been working for idiots for two years."

"You were the one who told me the Hobbema story. What was I supposed to gather from that?" His rage now full blown, he was bellowing.

"Hobbema? My God. You are so thick. I wanted you to write a book about something interesting, something with a bit of human drama in it, not to abandon your talent!"

"But all that talk about how he quit painting at my age and got a job and supported his wife."

"Was it lost on you that Hobbema could have gone on to be a great painter? Instead he's a footnote about what might have been. He spent over four decades—forty fucking years—weighing bottles of imported wine that he couldn't afford to drink. He and his maid of a wife are buried in a paupers' cemetery. Is that what you want for yourself? For me?"

"I notice you didn't say 'for us.'" Eddie paused, force draining from his words even as they grew more harsh. "Whatever you think of me, you're my wife. Now you are the wife of a copyeditor as well as a novelist. If I see fit for us to move to Jersey City, you'll come with me."

Eddie saw now what he'd never noticed before: the four years they had passed together were starting to appear on his wife's face. A line marked the width of her forehead and the corners of her eyes crinkled just slightly. He couldn't call them laugh lines, though, as she glared at him with a fierceness he'd never seen.

"Do as you see fit? You're out of your fucking mind."

She'd never before said such horrible things to him, never yelled at him with profanity. He wanted to grab her arm, yank her to her feet, and then shove her back down to start the conversation over again. He held his hands in fists on his thighs, choking down anger, and felt his tears come. As Amanda looked away in scorn, Eddie wished that he *had* grabbed her, shaken her up. She would have at least recognized him as strong. She would have been the one crying instead of sitting there coolly. Finally, they both stood, facing each other across only a few feet.

"You won't move with me then?"

"If a copyeditor commuting from New Jersey is the life you offer me, then no, I think I'll pass. I've been working to support your writing. I'm certainly not going into the business of offering subventions to copyeditors."

"You would be more ashamed to share my plight than to have everyone know that you're a heartless wife?"

"Look, Eddie, you have one more chance to save us from degradation: finish your goddamn novel. Yet you refuse to do the work and instead embark on this ridiculous course of action. You want to drag me down with you. I can't and won't do it. The disgrace is all yours. Everyone I know thinks I'm a martyr, but I don't want to be a martyr just because I was unlucky enough to marry a man with no ambition, no fortitude, and certainly no regard for my feelings."

"No regard for your feelings? Everything I do is for you!"

He stepped closer to her, but he could see in her face no vulnerability to him at all.

"If you leave me," he said, "that's it. I won't take you back."

"I'm afraid that's likely." She shrugged her shoulders.

"That's what you want, isn't it? You're bored with me and looking for a reason to leave. Maybe the copyediting was a bad idea, but the absurdity of our situation made it seem plausible. Amanda, you've given me no hope. You insist on staying in this ungodly expensive apartment. And you've never given me any reason to believe that you'll stand by me if the worst happens."

"Eddie, I don't want to argue anymore. Call that publisher and tell them you don't want the job. Finish your book. Then we'll decide what to do about the apartment. And our marriage."

He yelled: "Decide what to do about our marriage?" After a few audible breaths, he continued, in a softer tone, "See, I always know that leaving me is an option for you. It kills me. It's probably the reason I can't write well anymore. If you only realized, then maybe you wouldn't be so heartless. Instead of confirming my worst fears, you could be trying to prove that I'm wrong about them."

"And you might try proving that you're willing to do your utmost to save me from humiliation."

"Humiliation is a pretty strong word. Jesus. And I *am* doing my utmost. It's hard, though, when I get so little encouragement from the woman who is supposed to love me, from the one person who is supposed to be on my side."

"Eddie, I know that you've had to work in the face of repeated rejection. I feel awful for you, I really do. But you need to work in a better way, to write smarter. Until you really give that a try, you have no right to give it all up and no right to drag me down with you. I want to lead a big life, not a pathetic one. And as for encouragement, well, what the hell have I been doing if not encouraging you by working so you can write?"

"Would it be such a disgrace to be the wife of a copyeditor? And if it became full-time, maybe you could quit your job and write that novel you were thinking about in Iowa."

"A copyeditor of romance novels? I'm ashamed all the way down that you would sink to this. You're an author. You're Eddie Renfros, author of the critically acclaimed novel *Sea Miss*."

"Amanda." Eddie choked on her name. "Maybe you could take an ad out in *The Times*, letting everyone know that you are in no way connected to my failure. Like those people who distance themselves from their spouses' debt. You could let it be known that you married a success who wound up a failure. Through no fault of your own, of course."

"Don't be a simp, Eddie. It's, well, it's repulsive." She paused, and he could see her posture relax just a bit. "Look, you're having a bad day, and that could happen to anyone. Call the place back and turn down the job. Then finish your book, and we'll go from there." Her words formed a command, yet they weren't harsh. She was all business, dutiful parent to tantrum-prone child. "But call right now so we can put this behind us and never speak of it again. Call and tell them that you couldn't dream of being a romance-novel copyeditor. Tell them you're on pain pills or sleep deprived, that it was a mistake they need to forget about. Call right now, Eddie. This moment."

Now a frantic edge entered her matter-of-fact tone, and Eddie feared that she might lose control. He feared it even as he longed to witness it.

"If I do as you bid," he said, testing, "I'll only look weaker in your eyes. And then you'll never sleep with me again. Is that your goal? To despise everything about me, to have an excuse to sleep with your back to me forever?"

"My goal here is to be your friend and save you from yourself. Call right now, and then get back to work on your book. I can see that the financial worries are making it hard for you to work, so I want you to try and forget about money for now. I'm going to demand that raise, this week, and that'll help until you finish your book. And I can cut back on some expenses, cut some corners. All you have to worry about is finishing your book."

She held out her arms to him and stroked his hair as she allowed him to rest his head on her shoulder. He leaned into her touch, breathing in the subtle citrus of her bath powder.

He should be grateful to her, he thought. Many wives would push their husbands to get a job, any job, but Amanda understood that all he'd ever wanted to be was a writer. "I'll make the call," he said, but for a moment he didn't let go.

# Chapter sixteen

Henry Baffler typed away the fall on the electric type-writer he'd received his freshman year in college—his only legacy from his entrepreneurial grandparents. One Friday in November, after several hours of work on *Bailiff*, Henry made one of his bi-weekly treks to the library, checked his bag with the woman at the security window, and sitting down in the computer area, was relieved to find his inbox empty of rejection emails. After he had deleted all the penis-enlargement and night-cream advertisements, he was left with two messages. The first was a note from a Canadian poet, an intriguing installment in their ongoing correspondence on the overlapping boundaries of fiction and poetry. The second was even better: a message from the editor of *Swanky*, which read, "Just received your first fan letter. Will publish next month and mail copy."

When he went to retrieve his bag, the woman who'd given him a square number 19 was gone. "Nineteen," he said to the stocky man who had replaced her.

The fellow had subdued his spreading body with the navy blue pants and blazer of his uniform, but his acne and the gold-plated skull hanging from his earlobe suggested that he usually wore black tee-shirts stenciled with the names of heavy metal bands. The kid pushed a leather briefcase at him.

"This isn't mine," said Henry.

"Nineteen," the kid said and lifted his chin to the person waiting in line behind Henry.

"The woman working earlier must have made a mistake. That's my bag, one up from nineteen." Henry started to explain the ease of the mistake, how it might appear that the number marked the cubbyhole above rather than below.

"We're professionals here," the kid said. "We attend a training session. We know which way the numbers go."

"Whatever the case," Henry said, perplexed more than annoyed, "That's my bag. And this is not my briefcase."

The kid folded his arms and straightened his shoulders—a no-nonsense gesture of skepticism straight from an action movie, if Henry wasn't mistaken.

"Look moron," said the girl behind him. "Why would he say that crappy bag was his if it wasn't? If he was dishonest, wouldn't he take the leather briefcase? Looks expensive."

The kid chewed his lip, his own gesture, a chip in the tough-guy persona. "Depends what's in the bags," he said, thrusting out his chin, proud of himself.

Henry observed these gestures, thinking the kid might make a more interesting character than he'd assumed on first glance.

"They may have training sessions but they clearly don't have screening tests." The girl spoke out of the side of her mouth but loud enough for anyone nearby to hear. She was a bony girl with long hair, frizzy blonde roots coming in under the black. "Anyway, the inside of the bags brings us to a solution. Why don't you just ask him what's in his bag? If it's his, he'll know what's in it."

The kid paused, his eyes moving with his thoughts, as if to prove he wasn't the sort to fall for fast tricks. "Okay," he said, patting the briefcase. "What's in here?"

"Not the briefcase, you moron. His bag."

"His alleged bag."

She poked Henry in the back. "What's in your bag, guy?"

"There's a large red comb with two teeth missing. In the out-side pocket, in with a subway map."

The kid unzipped the pocket and nodded. He re-zipped it, returned it to its cubby, and spread his hands on the counter. "Yeah? What else?"

"What else? Are you a fucking moron?" The girl jumped and slammed her boots into the tile. "A red comb with two teeth missing?"

"Those kind of combs always break."

"You so small in life you gotta find this way to feel a pathetic iota of power?"

"I can call security on you, too." The kid pointed to a sign reading NO PROFANITY.

"Profane," Henry whispered. "You are profane." He turned to gaze into the wide library, the place that held all that he most loved, the place that allowed his first novel, despite its terrible flaws, its own slot on the top row of a middle case on the second floor, as though it had been written by Dostoevsky or Diderot or Calvino. Sudden violence surged in him: an unpremeditated desire to leap on the counter and bury his thumbs in the kid's eye sockets—like Cornwall on Gloucester or like Sophocles blinding Oedipus, his own character—to take away forever his right to look upon the sacred place where he was allowed to work.

Henry inhaled as fully as he could, swallowing the surge of anger, feeling the effort of composure as pain in his temples. When he could speak calmly, he said, "Open the main compartment. You'll find a copy of last spring's issue of *Swanky* and a large manuscript titled *Bailiff*. Trust me on this: it's not worth anything to anyone else." He waited while the kid returned the bag to the counter and opened it, seeming almost surprised to find that Henry was right, as though Henry were prophetic or clairvoyant rather than the bag's rightful owner. "Give me my fucking novel right now," he hissed at the miscreant.

As Henry left with his bag, he heard the girl tell him that she read *Swanky*. Still quaking with anger as the words swirled in his ears, he only registered them later, when it was too late to ask her name.

Discomfited by the encounter over his bag and his missed opening with a girl, Henry hurried home. He was late to meet Matt Baker, a client he was tutoring for college admissions: the least disagreeable job he could find whose schedule wouldn't decimate his real work. He'd done what he could to ready the kid for the SAT and was now helping him with his application essays.

Matt Baker was waiting on his stoop, gaze cast down, avoiding eye contact with the group of amused-looking Dominican men two buildings down.

"Sorry I'm late. Come on up." Henry's stomach rumbled, and he hoped Matt's mother had remembered to send along payment for this session and the last.

The two set up at the small table. The apartment's low ceiling made it seem all the more cramped. Henry could move around with enough ease when he was home alone, but Matt was a robust kid with black hair raised 1950s style. His huge hands seemed to absorb free space.

After reading over Matt's essay draft, Henry said: "You've got to learn to write in shorter sentences, at least some of the time. The content isn't bad—not bad at all. But you've worked it all into three appalling sentences when you should have written at least a dozen. You need some elegant variation, and don't even get me started on the comma splices. The admissions committee is going to keel over from sheer fatigue."

"That's the problem exactly," Matt exclaimed, working a hand over his pomaded ducktail. "That's the problem. I know it, but I can't help it. The thoughts come in a big clump."

The sound of the doorbell surprised Henry, but he was glad when he heard a friend's voice through the intercom. He buzzed up Eddie Renfros and Jackson Miller. "Come on up, but I've got another fifteen minutes with a student."

Sitting on shabby floor cushions, Eddie and Jackson chatted over Henry's few magazines, including the issue of *Swanky* in which his essay on New Realism had appeared.

Henry moved his pen across Matt Baker's essay, breaking sentences in two, reclaiming dangling modifiers for the nouns they belonged to, banishing wrong-headed adverbial clauses, noting places where added details served to bog down the prose and other spots where specificity would bolster Matt's vague claims to collegiate worthiness.

"I see, I see," Matt murmured. "Don't worry. I don't fear revision. It's compersition that scares me silly. Know what I mean?"

"What you mean is composition," Jackson cracked from his seat on the floor.

"Indeed, I do know what you mean," Eddie chimed in. "It's the same for me. I'm misery personified until I have an entire draft."

"Personified," Matt said, "I think that's one of the words on the SAT practice test."

At the end of the lesson, Matt collected his papers and books and stood. He shifted his weight from the heels to the balls of his feet and back again. He glanced at Eddie and Jackson. At last he said, "Mr. Baffler, is a check all right? My mother sent a check this week."

Henry calculated the length of time it would take to clear the check, and the pit in his stomach enlarged. "Of course, Matt, that'll be fine. I'll see you next week and we'll get that essay ready to send out."

After Matt left, Jackson asked, "So what are that young man's chances of getting into a good school? Seems rough-edged but looks kind of smart. Or at least he would be if he washed all that rockabilly crap out of his hair and lost the loafers."

"He's really smart," Henry said. "But he can't write a sentence to save his life. He's getting better, though. I wouldn't take his money if I didn't think I could help, if I didn't think he had a chance."

"Really?" Jackson cocked his head, amused.

"I turned down another student recently. Really, that guy had no chance of anything but community college in a poor state. I could have used the money—and how—but the food would have choked me. Matt'll be okay, though. He'll get in somewhere. And it's not like he wants to be a writer or anything. He wants to program computers or work in a lab or some such—I forget exactly."

"Henry," Jackson said. "Have you considered trying to get a full-time teaching job? You seem to be good at it. And you don't look like you're eating very well."

"I don't want to talk about day jobs," Eddie said, his voice a weird mix of angry and forlorn.

Henry looked at the floorboards. "No school would hire me. I never even finished my undergraduate degree, and I don't have anything to wear to an interview." Brightening, he pointed to the *Swanky* open on Eddie's knees. "Hey, guess what. That essay just received a fan letter. It'll be published next issue, on the letters page."

"That's terrific, Henry," said Eddie. "I hope its author is a beautiful girl who goes weak at the knees for New Realists."

"I don't suppose you get paid for a fan letter?" Looking almost comfortable in his foam nest, Jackson reclined further, crossed his ankles, and put his hands behind his head.

Henry shrugged, considered the idea further, then laughed at its absurdity.

"Jackson's got some pretty good news," Eddie said.

"Yes, lunch is on me. I'd say at Grub, but I don't think they'll let us in looking like we do. But let's go somewhere good." He smiled at Henry. "Somewhere with very large portions and imported beer."

Henry was now so hungry that he had no appetite whatsoever. "What's all this about? You were almost as bad off as me last month."

"Jackson's got a big-time agent. She submitted his novel to fifteen different editors and already has two calls of interest." Eddie's delivery was hurried, cheerful but forced.

"Yes," said Jackson. "One editor said that he was a fan and not to make a move without talking to him first. The other called to ask if we'd sell world rights or just North American. It's starting to smell like a bidding war."

Henry felt a smile come on. "How terrific for all of us, Jackson, to hear that it can happen like that!"

Jackson led them the long blocks across town. Henry's appetite was still stunted by the queasiness of a long-empty stomach; he had to remind himself to push forward, maintain the pace, keep up. Half an hour later, they stood on the crowded sidewalk in front of a store-front Italian restaurant.

Jackson said, "It's a hole in the wall, but I've heard the entire Italian press corps eats here."

Unlike Henry's neighborhood, the area was one of busy people—people with jobs, people with things to see and places to go and stuff to buy. It required strength combined with a little give to stand still, and Henry was being pushed toward the restaurant behind his friends just as Jeffrey Whelpdale stepped out. Eddie greeted the coincidence with enthusiasm, but Jackson's reaction was cool.

"Glad to see you guys!" Whelpdale exclaimed. "I've got big news!" Whelpdale struck a match and held it to a cigar. He puffed at the cigar with exaggerated inflations of his jowls, yet failed to keep it lit. Though Henry had never smoked, even he could see that Whelpdale had no idea what he was doing. "I started a workshop: how to write a novel in ten easy lessons. And, well, the workshop was a bit of a wash, but I met a great girl. Very attractive, tremendously interesting. Just my type, too: dark, pale, skinny, anemic looking."

"Skinny?" Jackson said, suddenly interested in what Whelpdale was saying. "What's her name?"

"Theresa. She's from Birmingham, of all places. Great accent— the whole southern thing."

"Right," Jackson said, seeping sarcasm. "The whole southern thing."

"Anyway, she's very soft-hearted, wants to learn to write but couldn't afford the workshop. I asked her on the spot to marry me. I scared her, which is understandable, but then she softened. I told her I'd work day and night to help her write and sell her novel. I practically had to beg her to borrow a little money from me. Anyway, that's how it started, and now she's agreed to marry me. A month from today, as soon as she returns from a trip to Alabama."

"I congratulate you," Eddie said, his voice hollow. He held out his hand to Whelpdale, who dropped his cigar to shake it.

"You give hope to us all." Jackson gripped Whelpdale's hand, preventing him from rescuing his cigar before it was crushed under the foot of someone with somewhere to be.

"Great," Henry whispered, wondering if he would ever be lucky in publishing or love—and then puzzling over which he would choose if he could only have one or the other. Love, he decided; he would choose squalor with love. The words 'love' and 'squalor' invoked

Salinger for him. He realized that he hadn't read Salinger in years and really should go back to him to see how his work intersected with New Realism. Someday he hoped to write a literary history of New Realism—after it was established—and it was possible Salinger could be seen as a precursor.

Realizing that Whelpdale had gone on his way, Henry followed Jackson and Eddie into the restaurant. The smell of slow-cooking sauces warmed the room, and breathing the air inside felt almost like eating. A stooped, square-shouldered Italian man of indeterminate but advanced age led them to a table and handed them menus listing the names but not descriptions of the establishment's dishes. The other waiters congregated in the back of the rectangular dining room, near the kitchen's swinging doors, in ill-fitting black suits, looking nearly as out of place as the black-and-white zebras on the shiny red wallpaper.

"I've never before associated zebras with Rome," Jackson said, his smile relaxed.

Henry grabbed a breadstick and consumed it faster than he meant to. He took a slice of bread, stacked it high with butter, and ate that too.

When the waiter trudged over, Henry ordered last. "Bring me your largest meal, but no squid."

"Bring him a steak," Jackson said, "with a few pounds of pasta on the side."

"So what's up with the zebras?" Eddie asked. "Italian zebras?"

"I guess it's fitting," Henry said.

"And why is that?" Jackson asked, his voice louder than anyone's.

"Your book: it'll be black and white and read all over."

Jackson and Eddie winced at his joke but laughed nonetheless.

Jackson called out, for the whole place to hear, "And bring us one of those really big-ass bottles of Chianti. We've got some toasting to do."

# Chapter seventeen

The day after he took Eddie Renfros and Henry Baffler to lunch, Jackson Miller still didn't have a formal offer on his novel. He believed that good things generally happen quickly, that delay was most often ominous. Cursing all fifteen editors for stalling his advance, he paced his apartment and considered a very early drink. He was relieved to receive Amanda's invitation to meet her at the Frick.

Before heading uptown, he left a message with his agent instructing her to call him on his cell phone if the news came. "Yes, I know," he said in irritation, "I know you could have figured that out yourself, but I'm letting you know. Use the cell phone."

"The drinks are on me," Amanda had said when she called him, "to celebrate your imminent fame."

He planned his reply on the subway: "Your money will never be any good when I'm in the room." She'd go along, he was sure of it.

He found her in the Fragonard room, looking beautiful in a pale blue dress and high heels. It was so different, he thought, looking a woman eye to eye. With Margot, he had to look at the top of her head or crick his neck to meet her gaze.

"You look like you belong here, Amanda. You positively match. You're a vision of pastel."

Amanda smiled. "I suppose I'll be seeing your name in the 'Hot Deals' section of *Publishers Weekly* soon. Are you holding out for six figures?"

Jackson registered that she said *I'll be seeing* rather than *we'll be seeing*. "That's what my agent expects." He rubbed his stomach. "I love saying 'my agent.' Sounds good, doesn't it?"

Amanda gave him a hug and kissed him halfway between his cheek and mouth. "That's wonderful, Jack. I'm so happy for you."

"I just hope that it's deserved."

"You worked hard. You looked at what the market needed, and you sat down and wrote it. Of course you deserve every success. I've got a good feeling, too, about the splash you're going to make."

"Amanda, there's no reception my book could meet that would make me any happier than I am seeing the smile I see now." He delivered this line in a tone of mock charm intended to veil the truth in his words.

"Jack, I brought you here because I want to show you something." She linked her arm in his and walked him through the rooms of the museum.

Jackson was struck by the complete absence of smell, which gave him the impression of rarified air, of life in a vacuum. "I could live in a house like this," he said.

"In here. There." She pointed to a landscape of a somewhat ramshackle house in the woods.

"Not there, I mean here, in this house, the Frick house."

"I know what you mean, silly. But I want you to look at this painting. Find the people."

Jackson focused on the canvas and, sure enough, was soon able to point out several human figures that had not been apparent on first look. "The original 'Where's Waldo' game," he said.

"This is the thing," Amanda said, and she told him the story of the talented young painter who had traded art for bureaucracy.

"That's a great story," Jackson said. "A great story."

"Exactly. I tried to sell Eddie on the idea of writing a book about Hobbema, but he doesn't get it. I thought you might."

"But you're writing again. *You* should write about it."

Her hair swished across her shoulders as she shook her head. The fabric of her dress was very thin, real silk under his fingertips as he held her arm, lightly, as though it meant nothing.

"I'm fishing for different trout," she said. "I'm working on something else, going for the women's market. But this book would be just right for you. More serious than your first, but it could still be clever. And it would appeal to your audience now in a few years. Write for them as they age, and you'll have a career the rest of your life."

Jackson nodded and further studied the painting, admiring the moderate use of primary color among the woodsy tones. It was accomplished, clearly, yet there were odd glitches in perspective and the texture of the paint was sometimes smooth and sometimes bumpy. The painter hadn't got it quite right. He could have been a great, Jackson concluded, but he needed more practice. Amanda was right about everything, which had always been part of her magnetism. A beautiful woman who was practical, with instincts you could trust. Eddie had no idea what he had, none at all.

"So do spill," he said. "What's your book about?"

"I'll tell you soon enough."

"Put a dead child in it. That's what's selling now."

"True, which means that won't be selling in a year and a half, when my book will be published."

"Will be?"

Amanda nodded readily. "Will be. Speaking of dead children, do you know the awful story of the Frick child? A little girl, I think, about three or something. It was a needle or pin that got stuck in her arm or leg. Shouldn't have been a big deal, but it got infected and this was before antibiotics. She died, and her parents were naturally devastated."

"It goes to show us that money can't buy everything," Jackson said, grabbing a handy platitude.

"Exactly. It can't buy everything."

After walking a few blocks, they picked out a bar advertising its formidable line-up of martinis and stepped into pulsing florescent blue light. Jackson used his line when Amanda slipped her billfold from her purse: "Your money will never be any good when I'm in the room."

"You're such a good friend to me, Jack," she answered, her billfold quickly disappearing.

One drink later, Jackson asked her if she was sure she didn't want the Hobbema idea for herself.

"It's something I want you to have," she answered. "It's one thing I want to give you." Another drink later, she asked him about Margot. "How's the new girl? Still thinking about her too much?"

"I care a lot about what happens to her. I can say that. She's a very nice person, absolutely decent."

"Is she well suited to you? I bet she's just the sort to really shine at your publication parties—brilliant and stylish and full of tact and wit. Just like you." Amanda circled her cocktail with the little straw, bit her bottom lip, gazed back at Jackson. "That's what you deserve—and what you'll need."

"Well, that's not quite the right description for her, but I care about her tremendously." Jackson reached again for the studied charm that he hoped would mask the truth in his words and added, "After all, you're already taken."

# Chapter eighteen

**M**argot Yarborough was online looking up train schedules to New York. She'd meant to get down sooner, as soon as she'd finished her novel, but the days had slipped by. She'd spent some time investigating and selecting a reputable agent—and of course her father's book still required her ministrations—yet she still couldn't quite account for the time that had passed, not to herself or to Jackson. In his emails, Jackson continued to seem solicitous of her welfare. He asked her about her home, the name of her childhood dog, whether she'd gone to her high school prom, and, most recently, whether she ever wore high-heeled shoes. He also pressed her. "Just pick a day," he'd written most recently. "Like tomorrow." Of course he must be questioning her interest. She did like him, but the idea of having his affection at a remove was sometimes more attractive than the idea of seeing him. She knew this was crazy, just a funk or something. She had warned him she was a homebody. But still, this was the week. Tuesday, she thought. She was deleting an email in which she promised to come down on Wednesday when she heard her father yelling.

"Margot!" His voice, even from down the hall, was large.

"Telephone! Please do tell your friends never to phone here before noon. You know I can't work with these distractions."

Margot couldn't imagine who would be calling—she'd let all her school acquaintances fall away—and chided herself for hoping it was good news. On the other end of the line was the agent who had agreed to represent *The Reluctant Leper* provided she kept her expectations in check.

"The money's not great, but it's not too bad for so literary a first novel." The agent then named a senior editor at one of New York's most prestigious imprints.

Margot made her repeat the name, dug her fingernail into her fingertip to ensure that she was awake, and then said thank you nearly a dozen times. She promised to come into the city to have lunch with the agent, whom she had never met, and her new editor. Her editor! It seemed too good to be true. She would have to remember which woman was named Lane and which was Lana.

"By the way," Lana intoned as a calculated afterthought. "One thing we'll want to discuss is the title, so give it some thought. Make a little list."

Margot explained that she had made a list, that she'd thought very hard about the title and decided that *The Reluctant Leper* was exactly right.

"Just think about it," her agent said. "I'm sure Lane will have some ideas to bounce around as well. Lane's super busy, but I'll try to schedule us a lunch next month."

At the good news, her mother hugged her. "You believed in yourself, set yourself free, took real ownership, and look what happened! This belongs to you, Margot, and no one can ever take it away."

"No one can ever take it away from me? Why would you say something like that?" But Margot accepted her mother's hug and grinned.

Her father looked momentarily stricken, though she couldn't discern whether it was her news or her mother's affirmation-speak that had sickened him. His recovery was quick, and then he seemed happy for her.

"Wonderful news, my dear, wonderful. I always knew you had a real talent. Now someone else has finally noticed. Wonderful. Let's all go out tonight. Hell this news is even good enough that I don't mind eating out with your mother if we can find a restaurant that doesn't serve fois gras or milk-fed veal or swordfish or oppressed broccoli stalks or God knows whatever else your mother isn't eating these days." Despite his mini-tirade, his laugh was warm. "Say, Margot, what kind of advance did your agent mention?"

"Not bad," he said when she named the sum. "Very respectable."

Though her news was large enough to warrant a phone call, Margot, as ever, felt more comfortable expressing herself through written words. She emailed Jackson about the acceptance of her novel for publication, wrote that she was certain that his would be next—and in a much bigger, more impressive way. And she told him that she was finally coming down to New York. "I have wanted to see you," she said. "It's just been an odd stretch."

For dinner that night, Margot's parents settled on a Japanese place where her mother could have green tea and sushi and her father could order steak, pan-fried noodles, and sake. He talked Margot into a glass of wine with her dinner and then into a second one for dessert. Her thoughts had an audible buzz as she rode home in the back seat, her parents up front squabbling over whether or not the heater should be on.

Back in her room, she opened an email from Jackson. His note congratulated her heartily and thanked her for thinking of his book in her moment of triumph, mentioning that it was now in possession of a top agent.

"There's something I must be honest about," his words continued. Reading them, her chest tightened and yet she also felt giddy, flattered by his intimate tone, his seriousness of purpose. "I must tell you something, because you are one of the few people I respect. I don't know you very well, it's true, and you certainly have made yourself scarce lately. But I know quite enough to respect you, and so I feel that I have to warn you that I'm a selfish person. Not brutally selfish, and the thought that I'm at all selfish does trouble me. If I were rich,

I think I would be generous. I would be a good person. I'm civilized, if nothing else. Because I'm not rich, though, and because I *am* selfish, I'm likely to do ugly things to make some money and make a name for myself. Or at least I'm willing to do them. I tell you this in case you read my book and despise it, which you may. I cannot afford to live as I would like to, to write the literature I might aspire to if I could touch the family money or if I won the lottery. That is, simply, one of my facts."

Margot smiled, thinking that someone really living an unworthy life and writing unworthy books wouldn't declare it so plainly as Jackson had.

She read on. "I hope you really will come to see me soon. And maybe because I don't trust you to, I'm wondering if that invitation to visit up there might be possible. Perhaps enough time has elapsed since I met your father that it might now be all right if I spent an afternoon on the Hudson. I think we need to see each other. Otherwise we'll never know, and we might as well know, don't you think?"

For the next day and a half, Margot's mood alternated between elation over the sale of her novel and anxiety over broaching the subject of Jackson's visit with her father. Long possessed of the ability to work under any circumstances, she concentrated on completing her father's manuscript. Its delivery, she knew, would improve his mood. Meanwhile, her mother did little to help the atmosphere at home and had inflamed her father by advertising—in the local paper as well as the bulletin board at the health food store—a new workshop based on an ancient system of personality types. To make matters worse, the new workshop was not limited to poetry, about which Andrew cared little, but included fiction, about which Andrew cared deeply, and memoir, which Andrew actively loathed. Memoir was fifth on her father's "enemies list", a page topped by Chuck Fadge, *The Monthly*, the editor who had granted Fadge a full page to respond to Quarmbey's review, and an agent in Manhattan who had once rejected Andrew's single attempt at a postmodern novel and who now accepted only clients under the age of thirty-two.

Margot decided to approach her father about Jackson's visit when she handed him the completed and copyedited manuscript. She convinced herself that, as stubborn as her father could be, he would not be able to ignore the hard work she had donated to him. And if she could make him understand her affection for Jackson, then surely he would be happy for her. Perhaps he could even understand Jackson's ambition and grudgingly respect the success that she believed was about to come to her friend.

One of the few rules her mother had succeeded in enforcing in their home was the no-smoking rule. So when Margot finished her work on the still-untitled manuscript, late in the afternoon after working practically through the night, she was unsurprised to find her father outside, in a lawn recliner, in the midst of one of the year's first snows.

He puffed angrily at a cigar. "Damn thing's rolled too tight. They're making cigars for people who don't actually smoke them, that's what's happening."

Margot rolled a sympathetic sound from her throat and refrained from making a comment about people with real problems.

"So we should put word out about your book, line up some reviewers sympathetic to the Yarborough name."

Margot's purr caught in her throat like hair. She'd given no thought to reviews, and almost no thought to the idea that publication meant that people would read her novel. She pictured the shelves at The Shadow of the Valley of the Books, the short queue of buyers with a twenty-dollar bill or a credit card. She pictured her pretty hardcover—imagining Spanish Moss tangled with the long dark hair of the Creole girl on the cover—and realized that people would be asked to spend more than twenty dollars to read what she had written alone in her room.

"Yes, dear?" her father asked, inflating and deflating his cheeks as he worked the unsuccessful cigar.

"Your book," Margot said quietly, noticing that it was quite cold. "It's finished."

"Thank you," her father replied. "I just never feel quite right about sending a book out without a second pair of eyes on the proofreading. Glad you had a few minutes to spare for me."

"Dad?"

"Well, now, well, of course you're more of a copyeditor than a proofreader. I'll be sure to put your name in the list of people I thank on the acknowledgements page. I can't single you out, because that might ruffle other feathers, but you and I'll know you'll be the most important person in the list."

"It's not that. It's just that I want to invite a friend up for a day, for a visit. He's a writer, in fact." Margot was about to add that Jackson's book was being represented by a top agent when she realized Jackson's agent was the woman who occupied the number-four slot on her father's list of enemies.

"Oh, I see," her father was saying. "It's a he, now, this friend, A he."

"Yes, Dad, my friend is of the male persuasion. You've actually met him, though it's unlikely you'd remember."

"I have a great memory for faces and names. Never forget one. Who is your young man, my dear? I must say I'm jealous like any father would be, but I think it's high time for this sort of thing. The way you always read and avoid the sun, and even your mother knows more about a kitchen."

"I have had boyfriends, Dad. And I do cook—for myself. But here, well, you know. Between you and Mom, there's really nothing I could make." Margot stopped herself, got back to the point. "The thing of it is, Dad, the thing of it is that you met my friend and—I'm sure owing to circumstances more than anything else—you two got off on the wrong foot. But really he's a very good guy, and you have a lot in common. You'll find him good company. And he's a gentleman, he really is. A bit of southern charm."

"What father's heart doesn't warm to the term *gentleman*?"

Margot was relieved to see that her father finally was inhaling smoke from his cigar. She paused to give the nicotine time to make it into his bloodstream.

"Yes, terrific, so what's his name?"

Margot smiled. "His name is Jackson. Jackson Miller."

Giving her every hope, her father's words started quiet and slow. "Ah, Jackson Miller. A nice young gentleman with literary aspirations. I'm sure he's a top-drawer, first-class, A-list sort of chap. Ah, yes. I'm sure he's a truly fine human being. Well, that's wonderful for you, and I'm sure you will have nice visits in all sorts of houses."

"Dad?" she asked, frightened by his increasing speed and volume.

"But here's the thing of it: not one of those houses will be mine. I'm sure he's upstanding and talented and the king of all the dance cards." He worked his cigar expertly now and seemed to enjoy the crescendo of his own voice. "But I don't like him, and I don't trust him, and he will never set foot in any house I own."

Margot's shoulders stiffened.

"I'm sorry," he said, his tone back to normal. "I know I sound like an asshole. But I promise you that I'm doing you a favor. Jackson Miller is not a good guy. You can do much better, my dear. Much, much better. Hold out for a real talent—or at least a man who's a lot nicer than your father. Take a look at what I've turned your mother into."

He looked almost sad, and the uncharacteristic candor made Margot's come-backs die in her throat. She sealed her mouth, her swallow dry, and rested her hand on his shoulder.

"Now that that's out of the way, my dear, I wanted to talk to you about using your advance to best advantage. Take some time to think it through, but don't dismiss this idea: *The Hudson Review.*"

"It's freezing out here," she said, stepping toward the house.

# Chapter nineteen

Eddie Renfros surprised himself, finishing his first draft of *Conduct* ahead of schedule. When he compared the experience to the exultant day he completed *Sea Miss* or even the quiet, proud moment he typed the final word of *Vapor*, he found that his happiness was watered down, the sense of satisfaction mixed with some more common substance. He wondered whether this marked a more mature stage in his life as a writer, or whether it was simply because he'd never felt passion for this book.

Still, it was an accomplishment: two hundred ninety-seven pages sat stacked next to the computer under a title page that bore his name. And there was something to the idea of story; this book had a plot. Yet it wasn't completely inorganic. Despite his detailed outline and, under Amanda's tutelage, his strict adherence to it, there had been discoveries. He hadn't planned, after all, for the reader to suspect that the narrator's promiscuous friend was, despite her promiscuity, really in love with the cellist all along. That had been suggested by the material itself; it had come the way that writing used to come for him—from the act of writing itself.

Of course the manuscript was a mess, full of many ordinary

sentences and lines of dialogue that were mere filler for the more interesting, stylized dialogue he would weave in during revision. It needed to be curried with a very fine-toothed comb.

Though Eddie had finished the draft of *Conduct* and Amanda celebrated with him that evening, in general she seemed no happier with him. She was silent more often than not. Eddie knew that silence was reproach and that Amanda used it to conserve energy. "Just because you're unproductive," she'd once explained to him, "doesn't mean you can drag me along for company."

But now that he was productive, it seemed unfair of her to pout because his book needed revision. "Every book needs revision," he said.

She tried to explain her mood away, to blame it on the fact that she was now preoccupied with her own work. But then one day he rounded the blue shoji screen and saw that the stack of his pages was gone. He sat, his hand resting on the spot where his novel had been, until he heard the door to their home open and the tips of Amanda's heels clicking softly on the wood floor.

"Where is it?" he asked, projecting his voice over the screen but not shouting. "Where is it?"

He heard her sigh, soft and tired. "I gave it to your agent."

Amanda knew that the book wasn't ready for his agent. He had overheard her at parties and on the phone telling not just Jackson Miller but also Henry Baffler and Whelpdale, whom she loved to loathe, that her husband had written a book he would be unwilling to read. Should his agent accept the novel and then sell it—both events seemed far-fetched—everyone he knew would greet the publication date with private scoffing or a sad shake of the head.

Sitting there, his hand still where his pages had been, he imagined for the first time what his life without Amanda would be like. Not the vague fear of abandonment—that muted hollow terror he'd experienced before—but an actual conjuring of the days, some of them lonely, but all of them free of the tightness in his stomach, the creeping guilt of failure, the extra pair of eyes always on his work.

What he said was this: "Thank you. That should expedite things."

She rounded the screen and looked at him as though his face was new to her. "I thought you might react differently. I'm pleased that you're pleased."

She smiled, and in that smile Eddie read recognition: they both knew that something had changed between them.

Over the next several days, Amanda's willful defiance of his wishes—and her apparent disregard for his long-term best interests—cemented a transformation in Eddie's feelings toward his wife. He loved her as madly as ever, but what had once given him joy now gnawed and festered. He felt wronged by her.

She sensed it, he could tell, though he couldn't identify anything particular she said as specific evidence. But they no longer talked about books or music; they didn't even gossip about their friends and acquaintances. Indeed all of their conversations, which became increasingly brief, centered on money, publishing, and the necessary quotidian details of shopping and errands and mail. For the first two years of their marriage, their relationship itself had afforded them many happy conversations in which they reviewed moments of their days at Iowa, their courtship, their honeymoon, their late nights during Eddie's first book tour. Now their relationship was too dangerous to mention, as if naming it aloud would call forth its destruction. They had sex perhaps once every three weeks—a situation Eddie considered an abandonment of their vows.

Amanda was forever typing, typing, typing. When he finally reached the point where he had to confront her about it, in anguish accusing her of taking a cyber lover, she confessed that she was well into a novel—a fact Eddie knew should please him but instead frightened him. He fretted that her novel would be bad or would be very good—better than his—and he worried most of all that it would bring her enough money to buy her way out of not only their debts but their marriage. On the bleakest days, he told himself that would be for the best. He'd procure another copyediting position and marry a nice waitress with no materialistic tendencies or unbounded ambition.

While he waited for his agent to read *Conduct*, he idled away many of his days at the NYU library. Though he wasn't able to read with much concentration, he preferred sitting among strangers than under Amanda's resentful gaze or hearing her fingers clacking away on the keyboard. As he browsed the stacks, he began to think about writing some nonfiction—a magazine piece or a review, perhaps. Something to keep his name in circulation. Anything other than a novel. He started a piece on the phenomenon of being 'post cool,' thinking he might place it with one of the magazines marketed to men moving into and through their thirties. In a better mood, he could have written up the piece happily and easily, could have written with the light touch that had made his column in the University of Wisconsin paper such a hit. But pressure had ruined him; he belabored every word and abandoned the essay by the fourth paragraph like the sinking ship that it was.

It was that night, the very moment he crossed the threshold, that Amanda showed him Jackson Miller's new essay, which had just come out in *The Monthly*. Eddie dropped his backpack and sat at the dining-room table to flip through the magazine. The piece chronicled Jackson's brushes with famous authors, including the time he'd "borrowed" Denis Johnson's swim trunks and the time Norman Mailer extinguished a cigar on the toe of his shoe. The litany of literary misbehavior concluded by describing the drunken night Jackson had felt up the chunky wife of a Pulitzer-winning novelist in a diner booth and later had agreed to tackle Richard Ford for twenty dollars but had managed only to fall at his feet.

"I remember that guy's wife," Eddie said, hoping to catch Amanda's attention. "After her husband won the Pulitzer, she made him introduce her as 'also a novelist', though I don't think she ever wrote anything for adults. He even had to put it in his bios. Now that's whipped."

"Did I tell you about Jackson's piece in next Sunday's *The Times*?" Amanda asked. "He got hold of the iPod lists of well-known writers and analyzed them in relation to their work. He sent me an advance copy. It really is hilarious. You won't believe what some people listen to!"

"Greasing the wheels in anticipation of his publication date." Eddie heard the gloom in his tone and tried to lift it. "Actually, I'm working on an article, too. For a glossy, I should think. It's about being post-cool."

"I've been wondering what you've been up to."

"I figured you weren't interested. Why didn't you ask?"

"I was afraid to, Eddie. It would have seemed like reminding you that, well, you know."

"That we're still broke and facing another crisis? That I'm a failure as a provider?" He pushed back his chair with intentional drama, moved into the living room, and sank into the sofa. "At least you'd have appeared interested in me."

Amanda started to reply but waited. After she sat down, facing him across the coffee table, she asked, "Do you think you can place the piece? There was that book last year, you know, written by that journalist, on how you can't be cool after you have kids."

"Well, this is 'post-cool with no kids', not 'uncool with kids'. Different thing, and, anyway, it's not like things don't get published just because they're not thoroughly original in every way."

"Maybe Jackson could hook you up with Chuck Fadge, help you place something in *The Monthly*?"

"This isn't right for Fadge. And I'd rather do things on my own, without begging anyone for help."

"Jack's not 'anyone'. He's our friend. That's one of your problems, Eddie." Though her words cut, there was no edge to her voice. "Only the very strongest men are self-made. You should use any means of help possible."

"Because I'm weak."

"Don't be offended. That's not how I meant it." Exasperation tinged her words now, but, still, she didn't seem angry.

"You're right. I'm the sort of person who needs all the help I can get. But, really, this piece isn't right for *The Monthly*."

Amanda smiled a victor's smile and said, "Because it's unfinished or barely started?"

Eddie didn't want to answer. The article was barely begun and would never be finished, and they both knew it. He groped for another angle to direct their fight. "Amanda," he said at last. "Are you always regretting that I'm not more like Jackson? If I had his peculiar talent, we'd likely be coming into a lot more money, I don't doubt. But then I wouldn't have my talent. And, frankly, I wouldn't trade the one for the other."

"That's ridiculous. And just to prove it, I'll never mention Jackson Miller's name again."

"Now that really *is* ridiculous."

"Then let's just drop this whole subject. Anyway, my book is nearly done, so maybe I'll save us both."

"You say 'us both' instead of just 'us'. As though we aren't a unit, as though our fates are separate."

"Really, Eddie! I might as well have married a goddamn poet." Now obviously furious, she left the room.

Eddie knew that their union was chewing its own foundation, even that it was for the best, in the way that the inevitable often seems like it's for the best. Yet he also believed that money, if he was the one who earned it, could still save the marriage. He believed that if he could publish a successful book, he could win back Amanda's love. He gave up the short-lived idea of writing articles and began to consider ideas for a new novel. As much as Amanda would like to be rich, she valued prestige above wealth. She would choose Eddie over Jackson, even if Jackson's book was a bestseller, so long as Eddie had the more important reputation. If he could be short-listed for a major prize, Amanda's heart would be back on his side. Again he weighed a historical novel. Maybe the Hobbema book wasn't a bad idea. He vowed to read the literature from the Frick the next time Amanda was out of the apartment.

# Chapter twenty

A full week after the initial phone calls suggesting that his novel would soon be at the center of a bidding war, Jackson Miller still lacked a firm offer. He began to revise his expectations. His initial plan had been to pay off his debts, leave Doreen with a few extra months rent, and buy and furnish his own place. Perhaps also a home in the country or, better still, in Europe. After those interminable six days, he would have been relieved to just pay off most of his credit card debt, square things with Doreen, and buy some Italian shoes and a really good steak.

Even with his cell phone in his pocket and set to ring loudly as well as vibrate, he felt anxious away from his home phone and his email, which he checked hourly even though he knew that good book news always arrives by phone. He limited his calls to his agent to once a day, but this was not an easy discipline. For the first time in his life, his confidence felt brittle, like dry earth that could be washed downslope by sudden rain.

It was during the night of the fourth day of this misery that he re-read Margot's email about the sale of her book over and over. For a moment, a short but whole moment, he felt only happiness and respect for her. In the next moment, he felt angry that she still hadn't set a date for him to visit. Then he decided that what he wanted more than anything was to sell his book for stacks of money so that he could sweep Margot off her feet—her pedantic asshole of a father be damned—and take care of her so that she could write her little books and mother their children and keep him from becoming the awful person he knew he was capable of becoming.

"I'm worried about your mental health," Doreen told him on the fifth day.

After telling Doreen to go to hell, he phoned Amanda, who wasn't home. He told himself that was a good thing, that she would only get him into trouble with his friends, with himself, and with the world.

On day six, his agent sounded annoyed when she said, "There's no need to check in. You know that I'll call you the second I hear." Later that day, she offered to give the editors a deadline. "I can call this thing in," she said. "There's some risk, but the outcome will probably be the same either way. They either want the book or they don't."

Jackson asked her to hold off, promised to calm down, and drank himself nauseous. He didn't make any phone calls the next day, which he spent on the stained futon sofa, sipping ginger ale and nibbling saltines to cure his hangover and nourish his self-pity. On Monday, recovered fully from the hangover if not the self-pity, he phoned his agent. "Let's call it in, risk be damned."

"That's my boy. I'll set the deadline for Thursday. I'll call you Thursday at five with the good news."

That night he was back at the vodka when Margot phoned. "I'm having lunch with my editor and my agent tomorrow. I thought we might take a walk or something after." Her voice was still hesitant and girl-like, but Jackson thought he could hear something new: the lilting confidence of success.

"If you can squeeze me in," he said and heard her tinkling laugh.

"Doreen," he was saying even as he hung up. "You still dating that lawyer?"

"Must you call him 'that lawyer' every time? I might start thinking that you're jealous."

"My sincerest apologies. Of course he has a name. Calcium or Limestone or something, isn't it?"

"Dolomite. Mark Dolomite. I wasn't so sure at first—just thought it would be nice to go out with someone who has real furniture and new clothes and a job he goes to every morning. I thought it would be a refreshing change." She gave him a pointed look. "But now I quite like him. He's not witty, exactly. You know lawyers. Their brains are, well, specialized."

"The intellectual version of the tennis forearm on a scrawny body?"

"But he's sweet and really a lot of fun."

"You know me, I don't judge a person by looking into his heart but by looking at his bookshelves and CD collection."

"Gotcha. You'd approve of his music. He listens to a lot of the same awful music you do."

"What about his bookcase?"

Doreen sighed. "He doesn't have one. Why are you asking anyway?"

"Does he have books?"

She shook her head.

"Doesn't he even read books on the airplane?"

"Magazines, most likely. Why are you taking such an interest?"

Jackson stood behind the futon sofa and massaged his roommate's shoulders. "Well, dear, I was wondering if you might stay over there tomorrow night."

"You slut!" she exclaimed, but her relaxed shoulders suggested only feigned interest.

"Not like that, not this time. This is a nice girl, and I'm serious about her."

"You aren't still picking on that sweet pixie-looking girl from the bookstore, are you? Jackson, are you?"

"She has a name, too, just like your Dolomite. And I'm not picking on her. She's not helpless. She happens to be publishing a novel, I'll have you know. I admire the hell out of her. At least I'm a good enough person to recognize she's a much better person than I am. I should get some kind of credit for that." He squeezed the back of Doreen's neck, working his way up and down.

"You are serious, aren't you?" Doreen pulled forward, out of his grip, and turned to look at him. "I guess I'd better check the temperature in hell and the flight path for pigs."

Jackson took the vodka from the freezer and refilled his small tumbler. "I was serious about you, too, you know."

Doreen rolled her eyes. "I'll stay over at my beau's tomorrow if you promise not to have a hangover for your big date. And don't call your agent until she calls you."

"Of course, you're as right as ever." Jackson smiled at his pretty roommate, pleased to realize that he was no longer interested in anything other than her friendship. "Oh, and Doreen, ask Mr. Dolomite if he'd buy a book about cut-throat, bed-hopping, ecstasy-taking Wall Street types. Say if he saw it in an airport bookstore near the magazines and it was titled *Oink*. For instance."

"For instance," she repeated.

## Chapter twenty-one

The ringing phone annoyed Henry Baffler. He had tried to ignore it, but whoever it was kept calling back and Henry worried that the bell's rhythm would disrupt the cadence of his prose. Across the fall, he had pressed at his glacial pace, working with great patience and affection. It wouldn't be a terribly long novel, but it would be a book without a single discordant word choice. Every phrase, every punctuation mark would be essential. He believed he was making a perfect thing. And that's how he thought of it: as making something, rather than writing it. He was constructing a piece of visual art with words. It was a long poem, really, he sometimes thought. But on other days, he thought, no, it's a mosaic—and each word is a small colored tile.

"Yes," he said harshly into the receiver of the old phone.

"Yes, Henry, dear, is Patrick there?" It was the syrupy drawl of his absentee roommate's mother.

"I haven't seen him today," he said, and then caught himself. "Because I just got in. Should I have him return your call when he gets back?"

"That'd be lovely. You know how a mother worries."

Henry returned the phone to its cradle, then picked it back up, dialed the number of Patrick's girlfriend, and left the dutiful message. He could not afford to lose this living arrangement. He'd already cut back on the number of students he tutored so that he could give himself more fully to his book. To survive during this particularly lean stretch, he'd sold everything of value he had and was down to his last three CDs, his signed first-edition of *Naked Lunch*, and his grandfather's pocket watch, which his brother hadn't wanted. These might have to go, too—a sad conclusion he accepted as the price of art. Such was the life of the writer, now as much as ever in history. Burroughs would have understood, even if his grandfather wouldn't have forgiven him.

Henry knew that most people would have little sympathy for him, and he was keenly aware that those who passed him on the street—people in new clothes, people on their way to and from jobs and spouses and mistresses and stores—would view him as inert, weak, foolish, socially mutinous. They'd see him as an affront to every industrious person who bustles about, producing things people actually want to buy. They'd tell him that if he must write at all, he should take a page from Jackson Miller's book.

But Henry believed what his friend Eddie Renfros wanted to believe but doubted: the fact that his talent was incongruous with the circumstances into which he had been born made that talent no less valuable. Had he been born rich, his literary labors might have seemed noble to others. Because he was poor, he was more likely to be scorned. And his beautifully honed book would most likely go unpublished or, at best, be published in a small way, its few reviews deriding it as too quiet, perhaps even tedious.

Of course Henry would have preferred to take a job and buy back his CDs and get new clothes. He would like to eat well, go out for drinks, attend movies. But that was not his fate. He accepted his destiny as a starving artist with humility and a sense of responsibility. That was the hand he'd been dealt, and he would play it. If God or Harmony or DNA wanted in him a starving artist, he would be the finest one he could. And by doing justice to his noble bailiff, he would honor all the people out there leading their simple lives as best they could.

He had been at work for more than eight hours, interrupted only by the phone call, when he typed the hundred and twentieth page of *Bailiff.* More than halfway, he thought, and decided to reward himself by walking down to the market for a day-old bagel and a can of beer. When he returned, he would put in another two hours before allowing himself some sleep.

# Chapter twenty-two

Margot Yarborough shifted from foot to foot, using up a few minutes in front of the storefront that used to house The Shadow of the Valley of Books. She didn't want to arrive at the restaurant too early.

Because of her eye for color balance—and because she was smaller and more agile than anyone else who had worked there—it had been Margot who had composed the store's displays in the large plate-glass window. Working sometimes around a color and other times around a theme, she'd stack books, arrange them in fans, or space them like dominoes waiting to be felled. Once she'd built a playground of children's books, using a fan to send eight of them around like a merry-go-round. Another time she filled the window with books whose covers were every shade of blue, arranging them from a novel whose blue cover was so faint it looked white, through the azures and the ceruleans, the cobalts and the royals, the cyans and the navies, ending with a history of whaling in a midnight-blue wrap. The previous spring, over the weekend that launched daylight savings time, Margot had moved into the window every book in the store whose title contained the word 'time', from a horror novel titled *Killin' Time* to a romance called *Time of Destiny*.

Other than a poster educating consumers about shade-grown beans, the window was now empty, allowing passersby and patrons of the new coffeehouse branch to see and be seen by each other. Margot remembered that one of the other titles from the spring display had been *Time Changes Everything*, and she indulged in a moment of melancholy before spinning on the heel of her only pair of tall shoes and smiling at the sign across the street. Its letters were painted in an ornate floral calligraphy that belied the simplicity and homespun connotation of the word: GRUB.

Though she had made sure she was on time to the minute but not early, she was the first of her party to arrive. During her ten minutes under the watch of the maître d', who had handled her coat as though it were wet, Margot grew dissatisfied with what she was wearing. Surrounded by a sea of dark solid fabrics—black and gray and brown and olive—she felt like a schoolgirl in her print dress. At least she had worn her pumps. She rearranged her curls with her fingers and was just about to ask directions to the bathroom so that she could put on lipstick when two women pushed into the foyer. Both were tall, wearing slinky black slacks and muted silk blouses. One had darker hair than the other, but they had the same blunt-ended shoulder-length cut.

The darker-haired one walked straight over and said, "You can only be Margot! It's great to finally meet you."

Margot recognized the voice of her agent, Lana Thorpe, and offered her hand to the woman's cool grip.

"This is Lane Thompson."

The lighter-haired woman squeezed her hand in something slightly more feminine yet also far less committal than a handshake. "So good to finally meet you. We are thrilled to be bringing out your wonderful novel."

Both women gushed over her dress, calling it charming, quaintly chic, and ever so flattering to her slim frame. The maître d', smiling, reassured that she was not a waif or an aspiring waitress, showed them into the dining room. Lane and Lana insisted that

Margot take the booth seat so she could view the room. "We come here all the time," Lana said. "Besides, we know you fiction writers need to people-watch. Never gossip, I always say, because a writer might just be eavesdropping."

Like the lettering on the sign outside, the room also belied the restaurant's name: white tablecloths, Japanese flower arrangements in square black vases, and several small fountains spaced so that the sound of trickling water could be heard from every table. A handsome waiter with a Castilian accent brought them water and bread and a small dish of olive oil so green and viscous that it glowed. Next he delivered the bottles of white wine and still water that Lane requested.

Margot scanned the menu. The prices were all in whole dollars, in fancy script, and shockingly high. Before her mother had gone New Age and stopped dispensing practical advice in favor of spiritual platitudes, she'd told Margot never to order spaghetti, fried chicken, or anything laden with powdered sugar on a first or second date. Margot figured the same held true for a first meeting with your agent and editor. None of these options were on the menu, and Margot didn't know how to start eliminating anything else. Looking the menu down and then up, she decided that she would order neither the least nor the most expensive meal.

The waitress came before she had decided. In unison, Lane and Lana insisted that she order first. Stymied, Margot looked up to see Doreen smiling at her, hands clasped behind her back, ready to memorize her heart's culinary desires. Doreen cocked her head slightly in a way that revealed but didn't require recognition. Not knowing whether it was good or bad manners to acknowledge the acquaintanceship under the circumstances, Margot was further flummoxed. "It's good to see you," she said softly. She ordered the crab sandwich, which was the only thing she could remember from the menu.

"But what are you going to start with?" Lana asked.

"Start with," Margot repeated, fingering her menu and looking up to Doreen, who rescued her by recommending the roasted asparagus soup.

While they waited for the food, Lana and Lane praised the originality of Margot's novel.

"Your prose is hypnotic, absolutely gemlike," Lane said. "That's what drew me in."

"And the story," Lana took up. "Devastating."

As Doreen set cups of soup on the table, Lane murmured in agreement. "I wonder, though, whether it wouldn't be even more powerful if the Creole girl came back into the novel."

"Oh," said Margot, forgetting her social discomfort and finding her voice. "That's just it. She never leaves. She is always with Laird, always his inspiration. She's his better self."

"And that comes off marvelously. You really pulled that off. But I'm wondering if there's a way to embody that, by giving her an actual scene." Lane sipped her soup expertly from the almost flat cutlery.

Lana was not quite so skilled with her spoon, and Margot noticed other differences between the two women who had at first seemed almost clones of each other: Lana's jewelry was gold while Lane's was dainty and silver, and Lana spoke a little louder.

Lana said, "Exactly. Embody as in body. Maybe her body could re-enter the picture, if you see what I mean. Or does leprosy, you know, affect all areas of the body?"

Margot detected a patronizing sympathy as Lane paused from her soup to smile at her.

Lana continued. "I know. What if the beautiful Creole girl hears of Laird's sacrifice and comes to join him, even though she knows that she, too, will contract the disfiguring disease? I can't think of anything more romantic."

"But it's her absence, see, more than her presence. She's his ideal. He can only approximate her." Margot's voice locked as Doreen replaced her soup cup with the most frightening plate of food she had ever seen.

Sticking out from the two triangles of bread that purported to make the meal a sandwich were the grotesque legs of an extraordinarily large soft-shell crab. "You're not crab salad," Margot whispered to the gangly dead creature before her.

"I take Margot's point," Lane was saying. "And, let's be frank, leprous sex isn't, well, it isn't sexy. Frankly, it's disgusting. I'll grant you that there's probably a pervert or two in the world into it. No one else wants to read about that. No one." She paused as Doreen set before her a large plate containing three yam ravioli decorated with drizzles of brown butter and a bouquet of sage leaves. "But I do think the Creole woman could come to him. Maybe for a non-contact visit, like through the glass in prison scenes. Or maybe Laird turns her away. As drastically as he loves her and wants to see her, he won't risk her well being. Now *that* would be romantic."

Margot worked a fork and knife as inconspicuously as she could through one of the crab's legs, seeking a bite-size piece of food. The soup had awakened her appetite, but it would be difficult to lift the monstrous sandwich even if she didn't care how uncouth she looked. And in front of her editor and agent on what was supposed to be the best day of her life, it didn't seem possible. She put down her cutlery, deciding that soup and dessert would be plenty, would be just right. "Actually," she said, "leprosy isn't really that contagious. You generally have to live in close quarters with someone for a decade to contract it."

Lane and Lana relished their normal-looking food, saying "delicious" and "to die for." Margot's stomach rumbled as she saw Lana twirl linguine on the long tines of her fork. She caught whiffs of garlic, fennel, and something with a bit of fire to it.

Lane paused from eating. "I only ask that you give it some thought. You're the author, of course." She weighted the word 'author' as though to make sure Margot heard that she'd said author rather than writer. "But I *am* going to have to put my foot down about the title. I mean, if you really think about it, aren't all lepers reluctant? And besides, he's reluctant before he's a leper. Once he's a leper, he's more resigned, right?"

Margot retrieved her purse from the floor and withdrew a wrinkled square of paper. "I brought a list with some ideas."

"Excellent. Good girl," Lana exclaimed. "Didn't I tell you she'd be a dream to work with?"

Margot read the titles she had devised, feeling increasingly wretched as she realized that each and every one of them was much worse than terrible: *Laird the Leper, Under the Spanish Moss, The Unnatural History of Louisiana, Leper in Love,* and *Redemption.* The last made her choke down her own laugh. "They're terrible. I don't know what I was thinking."

Lana nodded. Lane smiled kindly and said, "We understand. You're a virgin."

"Virgin?"

"First-time author. Don't worry about it in the least, and that self-deprecating thing you do is really charming. I promise we'll come up with something."

"The thing of it is," Margot recovered, "the thing of it is that I think that *The Reluctant Leper* is the true title. You see, he's reluctant in his acceptance of his situation, but then he comes to identify with the lepers to such an extent that he becomes one."

Before she could explain Laird's multiple levels of reluctance and how they play out in his final choice, Lane cut her off. "Never you worry. I have every editor at the house on the job. They've all promised to bring me five titles by Friday. I'll let you know what we decide."

Seeming to notice that she was the only one still eating, Lana set down her fork even though it held an entire bite of food. "You mean you'll run your choices by her and see which ones she likes the most."

"You've got a good agent on your side, Margot. Of course we'll show her the title. She's the author."

The handsome assistant waiter cleared their dishes, and Doreen followed with a dessert tray. Margot's gaze shifted from a vanilla-raspberry roulade to a walnut-honey napoleon, from a sugar-crusted lemongrass crème brulee to a slice of chocolate cake decorated with thin curls of real gold. "We also have two soufflés," Doreen said directly to Margot, "chocolate with bitter orange and a really delicious key lime."

Lana pushed in her stomach. "I really shouldn't."

Transfixed by the pastries, Lane answered without looking up, "But you always do. And we can't leave our author underfed."

"Starvation is for the unpublished only," Lana added.

"We haven't time for the soufflés," Lane told Doreen, "but bring us one of everything else and three forks for each."

Fifty minutes and one-third of four desserts later, Margot rang the bell at Jackson's address and was buzzed in. She ascended the stairwell slowly, made anxious by all that sugar. She was also decidedly sore of foot from her grown-up shoes.

Jackson was standing at his open door when she stepped onto the fourth-floor landing. "Welcome, author." He smiled before adding in a more natural tone, "I'm glad you're here."

Though Margot was used to spending long hours alone and had never been the chatty type, she found herself leaning sideways into Jackson's sofa, telling him the details of her lunch, her breathing out of pace with her words.

"Are their names really Lane and Lana?" Jackson shook his head in exaggerated disbelief. "I'm sure they know what they're doing, but perhaps you and I will beat them to the perfect title."

"You couldn't do any worse than I did."

"I know we'd planned to stroll, but what would you think of staying here, sipping some wine? I had Doreen recommend a special bottle to toast your success."

Margot, without another pair of shoes, was relieved to avoid the walk. "That's nice, but we must toast your success first."

"Not yet, Margot. I've two more days of agony, and I'm bracing myself for bad news."

"It will be good news, I'm sure of it. If someone will publish a book about lepers in nineteenth-century Louisiana, they'll publish anything." She added hastily, "By which I don't mean to suggest that your book is just anything. I only meant that any topic has a chance."

"Your book sounds beautiful, Margot, and I love the few pages you've shown me. You're a master of the perfect word choice, that's clear."

Jackson rose and Margot's gaze followed him into the clean, almost professional looking kitchen. He pulled a bottle from a horizontal wine rack, carefully turning it upright before removing the foil with a small knife and the cork with the attached screw. "Your point about topic is good. I certainly take heart from a review I saw recently—get this—for a hundred-page novel—they're actually calling it a novel and not a novella—about the siege of Leningrad. Has no one heard of scale? Sounds awful, but the reviewer was nice about it and it certainly gives me hope."

Jackson Miller was closer to one of Henry James's urbane charmers than the men who populated Margot's fantasies: composites of Thomas Hardy's stolid, fate-battered heroes, Heathcliff, the Swann of the earliest volumes, and the occasional sincere-eyed European movie star. Yet as she watched the sure movements of his hands, she thought that she could love him if that's what he wanted from her.

Jackson put two glasses of the red wine on the chest that served as coffee table and sat on the sofa next to her. "Margot, I understand your father doesn't hold me in great affection, but I hope that's no reason that you and I can't continue our friendship."

"It's the same for me. The way I feel, I mean."

"Not that my friendship is any great prize. I am what I am, and I'll go on struggling for the good life that I've always wanted. But your friendship, well, it's worth a great deal. If I were sure of that friendship, I would at least be within sight of loftier ideals."

Margot accepted the wine he moved from the table to her hand, and they toasted the acceptance of her novel.

"Hey, I know. You can call it *Stumps*. You know, cypress knees and those literary leper parts." He held up his arm with his hand balled and twisted.

Margot swallowed her mouthful of wine quickly so that she wouldn't laugh it across the front of her dress.

"So you have a sense of humor." Jackson looked down into her eyes, smiling into his cheeks, his good looks boyish despite his height.

"Do I seem so very dull?" Margot tilted her head and tucked her curls behind the ear closest to Jackson, wondering if she was flirting well or poorly.

"Not dull, not at all. But smart and quiet and reticent. Serious. Those qualities are exactly what I like so much in you—and what I find so different from myself. But all the better that there's a generosity and sense of humor beneath it."

"And many of your qualities are attractive to me, because they're so foreign to who I am. You're self-confident and charming and determined to succeed." She felt a smile grow. "And tall."

As he took her glass from her hand, she noticed she'd drunk most of its contents. He set both glasses down and turned to her, wrapping her shoulders in his strong arm.

"I promise to be careful with you, Margot. I wouldn't hurt you for anything."

When he said that, his stature seemed more protective than intimidating, and she leaned into him. When he stroked her face with his free hand and kissed her mouth with just the right amount of pressure, she warmed with such pleasure that she thought the feeling might be love. It was like standing in a strong summer breeze, a welcome wind on a stagnant day. It was like the promise of change.

That night, lying in Jackson's bed listening to his slight snore, she believed that love might indeed be the word for what she felt.

# Chapter twenty-three

As winter stepped into the city, Amanda Renfros discovered something: she liked to write. Social by nature, she generally felt anxious by herself, with no one to react to, banter with, or enchant. Now though, she found that she didn't mind being alone at her computer, that actually, she wasn't quite solitary when she worked. She had for company a cast of attractive, witty, and highly promiscuous French aristocrats and their hangers-on. She befriended her heroine, Libertine, a buxom young woman of common birth who'd used her natural charm and ambition to wedge herself into a place at court. It helped, of course, that men found Libertine uncommonly pretty—all the more so because her humble background suggested that she might not be particularly skillful in deflecting the sexual advances of the well-born.

Amanda had begun *The Progress of Love* with an outline. She reminded herself to be open to the muse, though, and made some alterations along the way: folding two characters into one, twisting the plot an extra time or two, tucking in or eliminating scenes as she was moved to. Still, she stayed close to her plan, and it was a much more efficient way to work than the waiting-for-inspiration technique that everyone had espoused in graduate school. She'd heard interviews with novelists who spend a year or two "with their characters" before a four-year period of drafting and exploring, ever hoping to enter the "dream space" or be visited by some creative power from above or without. It was ridiculous, really, and it certainly explained why so many otherwise good books were thrown to the floor by readers hoping for a story. All a writer really needed was a good plot, a plan for its execution, a facility with sentences, a work ethic, and a copy-editor's eye. There was nothing magical about it. She even taped small signs to her computer to remind herself to stay on track: "Tell the story" and "No hocus pocus."

Once, while working on *Vapor*, Eddie had been nearly paralyzed, vexed by the vagaries of point-of-view: how close, how central, how reliable, whether temporal omniscience was cheating. "It's simple," Amanda had told him. "You're the writer. Tell the readers what you want them to know." Now she wrote her story of lust, longing, libido, and ambition among the eighteenth-century French aristocracy with an utterly unselfconscious omniscience.

At three in the afternoon on a Friday in early December, she typed her first novel's ultimate sentence. It was a line of dialogue mouthed by the comely Libertine: "All for love, and love for all."

Amanda planned to spend the next two weeks line editing, while waiting for her queries to agents to be answered. She had already decided she wouldn't even approach Eddie's agent. What she needed was a human piranha, a beast to be unleashed. What she needed was a bidding war.

She decided to celebrate the completion of the first draft by having a glass of wine somewhere posh and pleasant. Before leaving, she checked her email. First she accessed the dummy address she'd set up to submit "Bad Dog Séance." Among the spam was a message from the editor of *Swanky*, who said that he was holding a hundred fan emails and a dozen letters for Clarice Aames. He asked her if he could forward them to her, and he begged her for another story. Amanda grinned at the notion of being famous as two people, of having two names and two writing styles, of working two wardrobes. It could be almost like those people who have two separate families that never find out about each other. Already, she could see Clarice as a brunette: powdery skin, a bit goth, lots of bracelets, a husky voice comfortable with a sailor's vocabulary.

# Chapter twenty-four

Five weeks after his wife carried the draft of *Conduct* to his agent, Eddie Renfros received the response by telephone. After sleeping late and lingering in a steamy shower until the water ran cool, he was washing his cereal bowl when the call came.

Her voice modulated like a radio stock-market report, his agent said, "The prose isn't quite on par with that of *Sea Miss*, but you're writing well. I'm worried that the plot is a bit quiet, but there is a plot this time. Still, after the last disaster, we don't want to set ourselves up to be accused of being too quiet."

"Quiet?" Eddie asked. "There's a plane crash, death, adultery, bribery, surgery on a child's ear, a world premiere, a drunken cellist, and a beautiful shameless slut of a violin player."

"Eddie, I'm on your side. I want to sell this book even more than you do."

"I seriously doubt that."

"But you do believe I'm on your side, so let me finish. It's true that you have events in the book, and I'm going to emphasize them when I pitch the book. But your style does have a way of understating even the plane crash. It happens off the page, and the response of the violist to her lover's death is so muted."

"The plane crash can't be on the page. You can't kill off a point-of-view character. And the novel isn't about the plane crash; it's about what happens after the plane crash."

"I didn't say I couldn't sell the book. I think I can. I think a lot of educated women could want to read it. If nothing else, they'll think they're learning something about classical music. And the violin slut is good, particularly that one scene. Heterosexual sodomy is very in, after that dancer's memoir and all. And it's great that she's Scandinavian."

"So one plane crash is enough?" Eddie tried to suppress the sarcasm he felt surfacing like sweat.

"Is the music stuff accurate?"

"As far as it goes, yes."

"Eddie, I'm worried about you. You're starting to sound bitter. You're my writer, my artist, and I need you to stay calm. I do think I can sell this novel, but I don't want your expectations to be too high. This isn't an auction project. I want to send the manuscript one at a time to a few special editors—there aren't many editors who can really appreciate what you write."

"That could take forever. Can't you send it to those same editors simultaneously, like with *Sea Miss*?"

"Very young writers were in when I did that."

"They still are."

"But you're not twenty-three this time out, so it's not really the same situation, is it? Look, if I submit one at a time, the book will arrive with the patina of the exclusive. You're a boutique writer, and that's how I need to pitch this. I'm going to get you an advance, but I'm also going to let them know we aren't looking for body parts here. I know you're not in it for the money."

"I just want it published," Eddie said softly before adding, "but I do need some money."

"Of course. And this book is going to sell by word of mouth, by hand selling. I have a really good feeling about this one, Eddie. The only thing is, and this is important, if an interested editor wants to talk to you about creating a little more drama—around the events you already have, of course, I'm not talking a second plane crash—don't dismiss it out of hand."

"Right," said Eddie. "Don't bite the hand that feeds you."

The phone call left Eddie in a peculiar mood, jittery and a bit deflated. At least, he told himself, she was going to try to sell the book. After *Vapor*, that hadn't been a given. Still jumpy, he was unable to sit and read. The refrigerator held nothing much beyond Amanda's fat-free yogurt, fruit, skim milk, white wine, lettuce, and blueberries. It wasn't any great wonder that she was so goddamn thin.

He scanned the apartment, which evoked unpaid bills, and decided to take a long walk. What he needed was to see a friend who expected nothing from him. A few months ago, Jackson would have been his first choice, but he didn't have the energy for him now and wasn't certain he even liked his old pal. He sure as hell didn't want to be around when Jackson got the call Eddie knew was coming. He pictured the new, big-time Jackson, talking about his enormous advance and the foreign-rights deals and the film-option nibbles. Eddie didn't want to hear about the rewards soon to be heaped upon Jackson's so-many-pages-a-day, plot-before-all regimen. This conclusion was not guilt-free—he remembered that Jackson had cheered him through every bottle of champagne after *Sea Miss* was accepted—but they were older now, living grown-up lives, playing for more complicated stakes.

He grabbed his jacket and headed out into the overcast day, walking the long cross-town blocks toward Hell's Kitchen, stopping for a bag of bagels on his way. He lumbered through the theater streets, relatively still in mid-afternoon, except for a few waiters setting out the placards announcing prix fixe dinner specials and some out-of-costume performers carrying bags to their back-stage entrances. Eddie wondered if being in theater was as awful as trying to make it as a writer. This was likely, though no doubt that line of insanity held its own set of problems and annoyances: height taking precedence over talent in casting, temperamental associates, falling sick ahead of an audition. At least writers get to work alone, he concluded, and have their nights free for drinking.

After buzzing twice and hearing nothing, Eddie concluded that the ancient intercom in Henry's building was busted. He hollered up as he tried to throw a stone, then another, then a small stick, four stories up. After rather too long, Henry's shaggy head protruded from his window.

"I don't want to interrupt your work," Eddie called up.

He couldn't hear what Henry said, but whatever it was, he was buzzed in.

Henry met him at the door, as breathless as if he'd been the one to hoof up the four flights of banister-free stairs.

"I don't want to interrupt work on *Bailiff*," Eddie repeated.

"It's fine, fine. I'm due for a break. I've been working, well, working too hard. I am very close though, very, very close to having the first perfect New Realist novel."

"That's great Henry, just great." Eddie summoned his enthusiasm and set the bagels on the tiny table. "Here, I've brought food."

"Food," Henry said, as though it were a new-fangled concept, a curiosity that had yet to be tested by time.

From the looks of him, Eddie could believe that food was so far in Henry's past that he didn't remember it. Eddie wished that he'd thought to get cream cheese or had brought his friend a large sandwich or pizza or side of beef.

Spitting poppy seeds, Henry spoke as though he had not had companionship since his last substantial meal. "Great, great, yes, great. Except that now I have every reason to doubt the very foundation and premise on which my New Realism is based." He tossed Eddie the latest copy of *Swanky* and held up a cinnamon-raisin bagel. "Do you mind?"

"Knock yourself out," Eddie said.

On the cover of the magazine was the notorious picture of dogs playing poker, except that semi-human faces had been photoshopped onto the faces of the dogs. Eddie turned to the table of contents and then the letters page. "Your fan letter! Congratulations."

"But that's just it. That's the terrible thing. Reading that letter, enjoying it even, I realized that what I'm trying to do with fiction is utterly superficial. I'm right—but so what? I'm trite. I've said nothing more profound than if you mix red paint with yellow you get orange."

"Not following you, my friend."

Still chewing, Henry went on. "Don't you see? I've said what everyone already knows. Everyone smart who's thought about it, I mean. I've identified the symptoms of a problem evident to any reader. But I've done nothing to root out the problem. I have no solution. I'm nothing but an anodyne."

"But the person who wrote this letter admired, hell, she adored your essay, your ideas. Look here: she uses the word 'brilliant.' And I hope you caught the fact that she signed her name Nancy Horny."

"Exactly. One can spot an imposter by the absurdity of his fans." Henry shoved the last quarter of bagel into the pocket of his cheek.

"So a silly and apparently randy girl wants to feel smart by writing *Swanky* and saying she liked your essay. So what? Accept her flattery and get hold of her email address if they'll give it to you."

"It's not just the letter, Eddie. It's the fiction in this issue. There's a story by an emerging writer named Clarice Aames. It is, hands down, the most interesting piece of fiction I have read in a decade."

"How old are you, Henry?" Eddie cocked his head. "Oh, never mind. Is it really that good?"

"It's called 'Bad Dog Séance.' It does everything, in a dozen or so pages, that I'd hoped New Realism would do in my lifetime. Except that it's not at all like New Realism. It's a solution to the problems I merely name." He paused to let his breathing catch up to his words. "I've never heard of this Clarice Aames, but all I can think about now is throwing myself at her feet. If I could just follow her around, just so my eyesight could follow her gaze, see what she sees—"

"I believe that's called stalking. I take it she's good-looking, then, this Clarice?"

"I have no idea, nor do I care. Fat or thin, fair or pimpled, eighteen or eighty. I'm in love. Really in love."

Just as Eddie was about to explain to his friend that his absurd declaration was certainly the product of a famine of both stomach and heart, a rock hit the window hard enough to leave a thin, jagged fracture line in the glass.

Henry ignored the damage to his window and mumbled, "Could you buzz in whoever that is?"

What seemed like a good while later, Whelpdale heaved into the room. As if on cue, he said: "Whatever you do, never trust a woman. Stay away from them. Avoid them at all cost. If you must consort, make it an affair of the genitalia only. Guard your hearts, brothers!"

Hearing the word 'genitalia' issue from Whelpdale's fleshy mouth nauseated Eddie. It was also the case that he had never quite forgiven the fat writer for stealing his stage minutes at the Blue Ridge Writers' Conference. Not to mention the fact that Whelpdale's goals in life were to make a living as a fiction writer without actually writing any fiction, and to make himself the center of any conversation or situation he was peripheral to. Nevertheless, Whelpdale's voice held true pain. Eddie rationalized his reluctant sympathy this way: just because I eat steak doesn't mean I wouldn't pity the agony of some poor cow. He gave up his chair, the sole comfortable one in the place, and joined Henry on the piece of foam they pretended was a sofa.

Whelpdale wept—real tears and many of them—into his plump hands.

To help him along, help him get it out and then get out, Eddie said, "Girl from Birmingham broke your heart?"

Whelpdale nodded into his cupped palms, his crying still audible.

"Get a little bit of your money along the way?"

Eddie tried to say this in a soft tone that would imply that every man had trodden a few steps in those shoes. And though his own situation was not identical, Eddie's shoulders lowered at the thought that he could understand woman trouble all too well.

"I'm very sorry. You won't believe it just now, but you'll get over her soon and find a much better one."

Even as he passed along this masculine wisdom, he hated Amanda for being the most attractive woman he would ever have.

"I think I'm through with the softer sex this time." Whelpdale pulled a creased letter from his coat pocket. "I feel monstrously unlucky. She was my perfect woman. I should never have let her go back to Alabama, not for a week, not for a day. She got back together with an old boyfriend down there. If I had kept her near, captive audience and all, I believe I could have made her love me permanently." He unfolded the letter and pushed it toward Eddie and Henry. "Read it for yourself."

Eddie shook his head. "That's not a good idea. You should burn it so you never read it again."

"I just want you to see what she's like. She seems quite torn up about it herself. She blames only herself. Oh God, she's so gorgeous."

Eddie listened to him detail the beauty of an apparently ane-mic and austere-looking young woman with a hick twang. When Whelpdale started to describe her sexual tastes, Eddie held up his hand. "You'll be sorry later if you go on."

Henry displayed the new *Swanky*, not mentioning his own fan-mail but downright bubbling about the remarkable Clarice Aames. Whelpdale's crying diminished to sniffing, and he talked some about the new features of his website and his plans to compose a novel-writing manual. This cheered him up sufficiently to depart with a bit of dignity.

After he left, Henry asked, "Do you think it's possible that his girlfriend was actually decent in the first place? Or was it a scam all along?"

"Anything is possible in women," Eddie replied. "Speaking of which, are you getting out and about at all?"

Henry laughed. "Missed a chance not long ago. But as soon as the novel's done, I might just write a fan letter of my own."

"The mysterious and possibly lovely Clarice Aames?"

"I'm mostly just kidding, but I really would like to meet her. How many people are there in the world I can talk to about what I do?"

"Four?" Eddie said, pushing the rest of the bagels toward his friend. "Or is it three? Tell me, have you ever thought about doing something else?"

Henry's grin faded and he blinked slowly. "Something else?"

"Besides writing. It's all I ever wanted to do, but now I'm not sure why."

"Who was it who said that writers write because the poor bastards can't do anything else?" Henry poked through the bag and extracted an onion bagel. "Or did he say that writers write because the poor bastards can't help themselves?"

Eddie watched his friend. If he ignored Henry's Ramones tee-shirt and imagined a white smock instead, he could see an eighteenth-century poet: thin frame, pale cheeks, large, heavy-lashed eyes. "Do you think it was easier," he asked, "back in the days when artists had patrons?"

Henry shook his head. "Just the tyranny of a different kind of marketplace."

# Chapter twenty-five

On Thursday, Jackson Miller stayed close to his phone but tried to distract himself with work. He was writing a satirical article on "services" being offered to aspiring writers by those seeking to take financial advantage of them—themselves often writers more failed than aspiring. He debated whether to name Whelpdale specifically or merely describe him.

Writing such a piece, he felt like a "content provider" more than a writer. Yet the work was fun, and he hacked out a few pages with little effort. As the morning wore on, though, he found it difficult to concentrate. What he needed, he knew, was to master the art of unconscious composition—to write without thinking about it.

When Doreen emerged from her room at eleven, Jackson feigned irritation to mask his relief. He shoved back his chair with a great show and a loud sigh; in truth he was glad both for the company and for the excuse to take a break.

"Sorry," said his roommate from the doorjamb. "Don't mind me. Just grabbing a bite and a shower and heading to work."

"It's all right, sorry," he said. "I was in deep concentration is all. You know how I am when I write." He followed his roommate to the kitchen.

Doreen poured herself coffee.

"Dynamite date the other night with Mr. Dolomite?"

"I'm breaking it off. He's a nice guy, but I'm not in love."

"Not in love? You know I don't put much stock in love. I hardly know anyone who married for love. Eddie Renfros maybe, but not necessarily his wife, and no telling where that will get him. I think marriage is mostly based on mild preference, convenience, and advantage—made more interesting by sexual attraction. Almost anyone who isn't repulsive could fit the bill in the right circumstances."

Doreen rolled her pupils with deliberate exaggeration. "I'll agree with you that there isn't one right person out there for anyone. I could probably fall in love with any of a hundred men in the world. But not with anyone, and a hundred's not very many, really. How many people live in the world? And he'd have to fall in the right age range."

Jackson wasn't sure whether he believed his own argument, but he was having fun with it. He hoisted himself up next to the sink, knowing that it annoyed Doreen when he sat on the counter. "I think I object to the word 'love' generically, categorically. There probably is one woman out there who is perfectly fitted to me, and if there were any way to find out who she is and where she lives, I would probably make the effort and be blessed with decades of fantastic sex. But it's clear that most of us don't find that right person, and it's when people pretend they've found the ideal substitute that they act like the biggest asses."

"Are you saying you've never been in love?"

"Only with you, my dear, which makes my point."

"Thanks a lot." She swatted him with the dish towel, which she then folded in half and draped over the oven handle. "You're sweet on Margot, though, or did things not go so well the other night?"

"The other night was delightful. I'm extremely fond of Margot, very serious about her. But I'm not going to be so false as to say she's my destiny or the only woman out there for me. I do prefer her. I think we're compatible, and she's terrific, really terrific. Really cute and really sweet, and we got on well in bed." He paused for Doreen to make a face. "But I'm not going to lose my head over her or make bad decisions."

"You're waiting to marry money," she said triumphantly. "Please get off the counter."

"Not for money, but it's true that when I marry I want it to be a good match in every way—in circumstance as well as affection."

"My, isn't Margot a lucky girl to have found you!"

"No need for sarcasm. I've been very straightforward with Margot. She knows who I am."

"Well, Jackson, I'm not a good audience for this particular theory of yours. I've met someone, someone I'm really quite taken with. You'll laugh at this: he's a writer."

"Tell me he's not writing a book about a bailiff."

"Bailiff? I'm pretty sure not. At any rate, I wish I could see you fall madly in love and repent your cold analysis. Now, seriously, get off the counter. You know I hate that."

After Doreen left for work, Jackson managed to type out another two paragraphs and work in a very good line about the bull in front of the stock exchange. But soon enough his gaze darted to the telephone. His thoughts vacillated between bright fantasies of author tours and screenplay contracts and dark ones of alcoholic descents into obscurity.

At two, he allowed his mind to be diverted by his recent memories of Margot. Despite his cynical words to Doreen, the night Margot had spent with him had made him feel all the more tenderly toward her. If the worst news came, he believed that Margot's affections and goodness might save him from being too despairing. She really was a fine person.

By three, he was convinced that no news would be worse than bad news—and that no woman could console him in either event.

The phone rang at four, and he inflicted his full repertoire of obscenities on the hapless telemarketer on the other end of the line. When the phone rang again at four-thirty, he had just tossed back his second shot of vodka.

It was Chuck Fadge, editor of *The Monthly*. "Our readers love your stuff," he said in his mealy voice. "We want you to write a regular column. Do you have some more ideas like the iPod story?"

"I'm never out of ideas. I ooze them. They drip from my fingers. How about a piece on how famous writers who are dating other famous writers met?"

"Perfect," Fadge said across the crackling connection.

"It was a joke. I didn't plan to write anything that stupid. Next you'll be wanting a piece on the gym regimens of Pulitzer winners. If so, I have to tell you I may not be your man."

"Joke, yes. Stupid, sure. Perfect, you bet. Shall we say eight-hundred words by Friday after next? And don't rule out that workout story. I'm serious."

The second Jackson returned the phone to its cradle, he felt it vibrate in his hand. "Hello, Jackson Miller here," he said, practicing the confident tone of a regular columnist for one of the country's most recognizable literary publications.

"Jackson." It was his agent's voice. "Don't say anything, just listen to these words: six figures and page one in the catalogue." She paused, not without drama. "The lead book, Jackson! I told them to put the marketing budget in the contract. That's rare—they hate doing it—but they want to publish this book more than they want to breathe."

# Chapter twenty-six

Margot Yarborough expected the year between the acceptance and the publication of her novel to be a long agony, but time moved quickly and was punctuated by small pleasures.

Several times during the winter, Margot rode the train into the city to spend a night with Jackson, whose pieces now regularly appeared in *The Times* and—she knew but hoped her father did not—*The Monthly*.

When Jackson was with her, she felt the brightness of his full attention. He was always concerned that she get enough to eat. He solicited her views on various events and books. And he seemed to find it difficult to keep his hands off her. She enjoyed this—who wouldn't, she asked herself—but it was always a bit of a relief to leave the spotlight he shined on her, to no longer measure her words or worry that she had packed the wrong clothes when he wanted to take her out for a drink. And when she was at home, Jackson seemed much further away than an hour's commute. She thought of him, but it often seemed that he was separated from her by time rather than space, as though he belonged to her past rather than her present. Or, as in a fantastic film, that he existed in some alternate or imagined future that would never arrive in this life, that he lived in a parallel world that was visible, yet fully curtained off.

Between visits to the city, she worked. Among other projects, she wrote book reviews for a small trade journal. Though she received only forty dollars per review, she felt ethically bound to read every word of every book she was assigned. Often she was disheartened by the television thinness of the plots and the poor quality of the prose itself. She kept her mood from plummeting by reminding herself that many good books also make it into print. In her reviews, even of those books she did not admire, she was kind—sensitive to the truth that a real human being sat behind even the frailest effort.

During this time, she also proofread the galleys of both her book and her father's, going over each carefully and twice. Knowing she would be charged if she changed more than a certain percentage of lines, she chose her edits carefully, debating whether her use of the word 'night' in a description of the Creole girl's eyes was a cliché in need of repair, whether a particular pronoun was absolutely clear in its reference.

One afternoon, a courier hand-delivered an envelope from her publisher, and from the cardboard rectangle she pulled the proposed cover for her book. A beautiful woman with long curly black hair sat under a tree dripping with Spanish moss. Over the tree, in a looping script suggestive of French Quarter ironwork, curved the word *Pontchartrain*.

She was delighted for nearly an hour, walking around the house with light footsteps, humming, telling herself that, yes, her book really was being published. But the twelfth time she stared at the cover, it struck her that the design was all wrong. The composition was beautiful, but therein lay the problem. It should be the leper, not the Creole beauty, on the cover. Maybe a close up of a man's twisted face would work, or a blow up of the bacterium that causes leprosy. And if the book was to be called *Pontchartrain*—it still didn't sound right to her—then the letters should be solid and austere.

She checked her contract and pondered the meaning of the word 'consult': "The publisher shall consult with the author about the design of the book jacket." She spent the next half-hour drafting and revising a reasoned email to her editor. She argued that tricking romance readers into buying her book might do more harm than good in the long run. And she voiced her concern that those readers who might actually want to read her book, who might understand it, could be put off by the proposed jacket. "And so," she concluded, "while the last thing I want to be is a difficult author, I wonder if we might try out a different idea for the cover."

The following day, a day on which her father had gone into the city to have lunch with his friend Quarmbey, Margot finally talked to her mother about Jackson. "I guess I love him," she said.

Her mother hugged her and kissed her cheek. "That explains so much."

"I know that he was awful to you down at Blue Ridge. He's just, well, he's ambitious. He was trying to impress Dad."

"You know that I believe that grudges hurt only those who hold them. One of the very best things we can do for our own spiritual health is to forgive those who harm us. One day, everyone is going to practice this, and that will be the end of all war."

"Not while Dad's alive."

"Your father is another sort of animal altogether. At least he's unarmed. Tell you what, you know as well as I do that I haven't much sway with your father these days. But I do have a card or two left up my sleeve. I'll see what I can do to get your friend invited."

Before Margot could embrace her and thank her, her mother added, "If your stars line up. So to speak."

It took Margot more than an hour to complete the personality profiles for herself and for Jackson, and then she watched her mother spend forty minutes at the kitchen table, plotting her answers as locations on a nine-point star.

"Let's see," her mother said at last. "You are modest and quiet, while he is materialistic and brash. You are studious and introverted, while he is gregarious and power hungry. You are internally motivated, and he is externally motivated."

Margot sat, hunched, as her mother enumerated the myriad ways that she and Jackson were fundamental opposites.

"Well, my dear, it seems as though your friend Jackson's rather obnoxious personality may indeed be your true solace."

It took Margot a few moments to understand that her mother was condoning the match. She straightened. "True solace?"

"If only I'd known the significance of this system before I'd married your father! I could have saved myself decades of his toxicity."

"Then I wouldn't have been born."

"Well, yes, that's true, dear. Good point. And you know how I dote on you." Her mother crinkled her eyes and gave her a breast-squishing hug.

Later, at her computer, Margot read the response from her editor. "Of course you aren't a difficult author," Lane had typed, "and you know how we all adore you and your book. But we're certain that we've landed on the right title and the right cover to maximize your readership. After all, a writer writes to be read. It may seem odd to you, but you have to trust that we know what we are doing."

Margot tried to feel comforted; of course publishers hired professionals who knew what they were doing. But she was nagged by memories from her days at the bookstore, reminded particularly of a terrifically dark war novel whose cover—a cameo-like oval on a black background—had been ignored by browsers because it looked like a volume of contemplative poetry.

# Chapter twenty-seven

Amanda Renfros prepared for the holidays as though she and Eddie had no money problems, reasoning that their financial woes were near their end. She was hanging a plush wreath on the door to their apartment when her husband came home from the library one Wednesday evening.

"Only two people live above us," Eddie objected. "Who are you trying to impress?"

Amanda followed him inside. "I don't need to impress anyone but myself, and you should give me some credit for trying to pretend this is a home. I'm not going to just let things slide. You know aesthetics are important to me. Don't underestimate what dreary surroundings do to a person. Take poor Henry; he lives in that squalid place, and it follows naturally that he lets himself go to hell. I can only imagine that his book will necessarily be grim and ugly. That will, in turn define—and by define I mean limit—his readership. And that, in turn, will further dampen his outlook on life. And so on and so on, and I worry he'll wind up selling used books on the street."

Eddie emptied an ice tray and fixed himself a drink. "He's a better writer than I am. Want something?"

Amanda suspected that her husband was saying this so that she would protest, and there was a time when she would have jumped in to reassure him of his great talent. But she was tired of his pleas for ego stroking. Often his efforts to awaken her sympathy were followed by clumsy efforts to stir her desire, and she wondered if he knew her at all. There were women, she knew, prone to caretaking and attracted to weakness, but she wasn't one of them, and Eddie should know that by now.

"Look," she said. "If the wreath on the door cheers up the upstairs neighbors, it's been worth the effort."

"You're talking about the Levines, Amanda. I bet their December would be just fine without our Christmas wreath."

"Anyway," she continued, "we may decide to have some friends over for a bit of holiday cheer."

"Which friends?" The edge to his voice was unmistakable. "I really can't stomach Big Time Jack until I hear word on my book. Last chance on that drink."

"Don't be morbid, and don't be ridiculous." Amanda dragged a chair across the room so that she could reach the high closet that held their holiday ornaments. "Yes, pour me a glass of wine. I'm thinking all natural materials on the tree this year. You know, straw animals and raffia bows and the like. Maybe we have some trimmings from Christmas past that we can carry over, to save money."

She waited for Eddie to lend her a hand before climbing off the chair with the box in hand, gracefully, really, given the awkwardness of the maneuver. She started to make a comment about chivalry. But the sight of him slid halfway between sitting and laying on the sofa he had pretended to love when she bought it, combined with her certainty that at least one new book contract was in their very near future, swelled her generosity. There he was: the man she'd married, the author of the critically hailed *Sea Miss*, which couldn't have been completed without her.

She sat on the chair nearest him and thanked him as he handed her the wine. The tannins stung her tongue slightly, and the familiar pepper-and-cherry taste spread across her palate. "Eddie, as soon as Christmas has passed—the day after, even—let's go away somewhere warm, somewhere where we can gaze at water and dig our feet in the sand and you can start a book you can really be proud of."

"Amanda, if only I thought I could write such a book, I'd brave the creditors and fly south with you."

"But you could, Eddie, with a change of scenery. This just can't be your fate, after such a bright start. I won't believe it. You've got to make one more real effort. If you fail in literature—I mean give up on it—then what?"

"Amanda, do you love me? Say that you love me."

"Of course I do. That's why I'm proposing that we go away somewhere warm, somewhere you can work. I hate being poor, Eddie. I detest it. I promised myself that when I was an adult I would never be poor again. A person shouldn't have to be poor as a child and an adult."

"Grown-up poverty for rich kids?"

"Absolutely, let them take a turn. But it's not just that. It's the idea of you becoming an ordinary man."

"Even if I never write another line, that won't undo what I've done. I know I haven't been prolific, but you can't condemn my entire self."

"When I suggested the trip, I was being generous. I wanted to give you another chance to write a truly great book. I wanted to give us another chance."

"You say that as though the one is dependent on the other." Eddie roused himself from his slouch, knelt before her, and wrapped his arms around her waist. "I'm sorry. It's just that you've been so cool to me lately."

"I've been distracted, and busy. I have writing of my own now."

"Or course you do, and that makes me happy."

"Does it?" She urged a smile, stroked her husband's hair. "I believe that we're both going to be famous, at least a kind of famous. People will know our names if not our faces."

Eddie kissed her hair, her eyes, her mouth. As she imagined him as a three- and then four-book author, getting reviewed, giving readings, being photographed, she found that, for the first time in awhile, she desired her husband.

The mood was not dispelled by early morning, if only because she rose before he did. When she slid from bed, he slept on his side, his profile turned against the pillow. His breath was smooth, and he seemed composed in a way he rarely did when awake.

As was the case nearly every morning of late, Amanda found an email sent from the West Coast late the night before. It was from the editor of *Swanky*, begging Clarice Aames for anything. "Spit in a bag and we'll use it," he wrote.

When she searched the web for Clarice Aames, she found not only the link to the *Swanky* table of contents, but two websites with pages devoted to the mysterious author of "Bad Dog Séance." She typed out a reply to the editor, "I'll give you something better than spit. Un beso, Clarice." For the next three hours, while Eddie slept away the morning, Amanda wrote Clarice Aames' second story: "Sex Kitten Leaps from the Bleeding Edge."

When she was done, she checked her own messages—she was now using her maiden name, Amanda Yule, for correspondence—and saw that two of the agents she had queried wanted to read the entire manuscript of *The Progress of Love*. What she felt as her smile spread was not so much happiness as well being, the sense that things were right in the world, that she was at last living the life marked out for her.

# Chapter twenty-eight

Tere had been a time in his life when Andrew Yarborough considered himself an affluent man. That was before the literary world had gone to pot and before he had fathomed what the life he had grown accustomed to living would actually cost over time. Although at long last his wife was making some money with her goddamn healing workshops and assorted fru fra, she gave away more than she made to organizations buying cosmetics for war refugees and saving obscure species of invariably cute animals.

"Why don't you save a snake?" he'd asked her once, to which she'd replied, "Snakes are very potent symbols in our unconscious life, and I would be proud to help any species in danger. Certainly no snake is more venomous than you've become."

And, no great surprise, she spent even more than she gave away: a thousand dollars on the contraption that allowed her to bend upside down for hours on end—against gravity, she said—and who knew how much on her ridiculous clothing and the horrible things she hung on the walls of what was supposed to be his home.

They'd helped Margot with school some. Janelle had argued that they should give her a full ride, but Andrew had countered that it had been good for him to make it on his own and that he hoped his daughter could feel at least some of that pride. It was true—he'd admitted as much—that college cost a lot more now than in his day, but that was the reality of her times. His retirement fund held some money, but the stock market had seen to it that it wasn't as much as he had expected. There was the house, of course, which had cost five figures and was now worth close to seven. But they had to live somewhere, and he was too old to be thinking of moving. Plus, it was the only insurance he had against the nursing home should something happen to dear Margot. She'd take care of him, he knew, but he didn't trust her mother farther than he could smell her sandalwood perfume.

And so, as much as Andrew would have liked to launch a new literary publication, a journal that would be in every way superior to what Chuck Fadge had turned *The Monthly* into, it hadn't seemed possible before the sale of Margot's novel. Andrew was man enough to admit that it was a little humiliating that his daughter's modest advance was equal to his own, but that was the way of the publishing world—always insulting older talent in the pursuit of youth.

Eyeing Margot's advance, Andrew told himself he was not merely being selfish. No, Margot was young enough to take the financial risk that he could no longer afford, yet old enough that she should invest in her career rather than frittering away her money. It was in her best interest to use her bit of good fortune to start something worthy, something she could be proud of and eventually take over when he and Quarmbey retired.

Margot had always been a wonderful daughter—almost all a father could hope for despite the unfortunate DNA inherited from her mother—and he promised himself to be more obvious in his displays of paternal affection. And so, for several weeks after Margot finished proofing his galleys, he made a point of joining her at breakfast and of inquiring about her welfare and her work over dinner. He called her into his study several times a week to tell her a joke someone had sent him or to solicit her opinion on some book or other. Once, he asked her what she intended to do with her advance. She shrugged and said that she had put the money in the bank. She was pleased to know where it was, she said, and she'd be glad to have it when she was ready to take her next big step in life. Andrew took this to mean that she was at least agreeable to his proposition, though he worried when brochures for MFA programs began to arrive in the mail.

Taking advantage of the holidays as an excuse for entertaining, he invited Quarmbey over for some good cheer. "We must convince Margot that the time is ripe," he told his old friend over the phone. Next he called a younger man, Frank Hinks, who had published a novel that had met with mixed reviews but of which Andrew approved. Hinks was just the kind of writer Andrew hoped to publish in his new journal—and the sort despised by Chuck Fadge because of his solid, old-fashioned craftsmanship. Andrew believed that Hinks's presence would help Margot see the value of the undertaking. He also thought he'd be pelting two birds with a single stone if the young man happened to be good-looking enough to bump the horrid Jackson Miller from her affections.

Andrew instructed his wife to prepare some snacks and drinks but to stay out of the conversation beyond the initial pleasantries.

"What are you up to?" she asked.

"Nothing at all. I just don't want you frightening our guests with any of your psychobabble."

"If you knew me at all, you'd know that I believe that Freudian analysis has done the world far more harm than good. Women especially. Jung is a different matter, of course, but that's not psychobabble."

She would have continued ad nauseam, he was sure, had the saving doorbell not sounded.

"Would you be so gracious, dear," he said, "as to open our home to our guests?"

For the first time in years, his wife surprised him. She stuck out her tongue.

"The orator's last recourse?" He inserted a sneer in his tone, but what he was thinking was that his wife was still an attractive woman underneath the swirling prints and absurd earrings and layers of so-called natural cosmetics. He pressed this thought from his mind and mixed himself a Scotch and soda.

The smell of cigar smoke on wool moved with Quarmbey into the kitchen, where he made himself at home stirring vodka around a large tumbler of ice.

"What'll it be for you?" Andrew asked Frank Hinks.

"Wine, I think," said the younger man, who hurriedly added, "or beer is fine."

Andrew worked the corkscrew into a bottle of red wine while he took stock of Hinks. Though nondescript, his face was not unattractive. The nose was all right, and he had a decent jaw on him. But Andrew's hopes shrank to nothing when Hinks removed his blazer, revealing sloped shoulders and womanly hips. The young man had a severely inclined neck, making his face jut far out in front of his body; it was clear that he would look more and more like a turtle as the years went by. He doubted that Margot would go for such a fellow, nor could he wish on himself an old age surrounded by terrapin-like grandchildren. He pulled out the cork with a loud thwop and consoled himself that Hinks could still serve the primary function of convincing Margot to finance the journal.

The three men sat in the living room and talked about the state of literature, Quarmbey arguing that the relegation of literary fiction to university writing programs had drained the vitality from the short story and Hinks arguing that the academy was as good a home and patron to literature as any other arrangement.

"Margot!" Andrew bellowed. "Do pour yourself something and join us."

When she finally entered the living room, Margot was wearing a simply cut black dress and sipping half a glass of wine.

"What's your view, Margot," Quarmbey asked. "Should the country have a fiction laureate in addition to a poet laureate?"

Hinks, who was sitting in the room's most comfortable chair, huddled himself up and offered the seat he had been occupying to Margot.

She sat and tucked a curl behind her ear. "I think it might lead to more literary quarrelling, and we have quite enough of that as it is."

Quarmbey and Hinks laughed, murmuring "True, true,"

and Andrew produced a smile before steering the conversation to periodicals.

"There's really no journal or magazine that publishes uniformly fine short stories. The problem with the university-based journals is that it's always decision-by-committee, or student readers who don't know what the hell they're doing, or else editors trying to boost their meager circulations by including the drawer-leavings of anyone with a name bigger than their own. It's the usual suspects, but it's the stories *The City* didn't want."

"And of course," chimed in Hinks, "they all publish their friends."

"And each other," Quarmbey agreed. "You publish me, and I'll publish you, and we'll all get tenure."

"But the magazines outside the university are just as bad in their own way. Hopping on trends, half of them, or surviving by bilking aspiring writers with contest after contest with ever-higher entry fees and ever-smaller prizes."

"I've spent hundreds of dollars this year," Hinks said, "and I don't mean to sound immodest when I say that the winning stories are worse than what I submitted."

Quarmbey nodded. "The judges often pick the work of their friends or former students. Or else the readers screen out everything that's actually interesting, leaving the poor judge to try to pick something from among the bland leftovers."

"The other day," Hinks said, his neck curved, his head jutting from his tortoise body, "I received a rejection letter from a journal that was considering two of my stories. The editor wrote that she couldn't decide whether to publish one or both of the stories, so she was going to opt for neither."

"That's terrible," Margot said sympathetically. "I once received my self-addressed stamped envelope back from a journal, and they hadn't even bothered to put in the form rejection letter. They just sent the empty envelope."

Hinks pumped his head. "I once received a lovely rejection letter that went on and on about the story's wonderful control of tone, vivid characterization, and all. Then I realized that it wasn't even about my story and that some other writer had received my rejection letter."

"Terrible," Margot agreed. "And the rejection letters are getting smaller and smaller, have you noticed? I'm all for saving natural resources, but it is disheartening to receive a sentence on one-sixteenth of a piece of paper in exchange for a thirty-page short story."

"Thirty pages?" Quarmbey asked. "I don't want to offend you, sweetheart, but that might be the problem right there."

"There are the glossies, of course," Andrew put in quickly. "But they're hodgepodges, and it's rare for any of them to publish more than one decent story amid their general clap-trap. What this country needs is a good quarterly publication that publishes the highest quality fiction with a few good critical essays."

"It wouldn't take a lot of start-up money, either," Quarmbey added, "and the thing would likely pay for itself in no time, with grant money and such."

"I think it would be downright successful just in subscriptions. It would take its place between those academy-based annuals and Fadge's horrendous monthly. It would publish only the finest stories, without taking the pulse of the trendy set. Solid craftsmanship, strong imagery, vivid characterization, classic plot arcs. The kind of stories you write." Andrew paused and turned to Margot. "Did you know that Mr. Hinks, one of our finest short story writers, has trouble placing his work?"

"That's terrible," she said. "Especially since there are so many journals these days."

"But not of the right kind! Hardly one of them is worth its salt," Andrew spouted.

"I ran across one the other day," said Quarmbey, "that actually bragged about publishing no realism whatsoever, while claiming to be socially and politically relevant. How can you pretend to be socially and politically relevant if you don't publish representations of the times in which you live?"

Hinks shook his head, and the three men proceeded to discuss their imaginary journal as though they were its editorial committee and the first issue was about to go to print.

A good half an hour had passed when Margot, who had finished her drink and was not participating in their conversation, rose to leave. "Can I get anyone another drink before I retire?" she asked, collecting Quarmbey's empty glass as he nodded.

"Yourself," Andrew said. "Get yourself another drink."

His daughter lifted the back of her hand to cover her yawn.

"We very much wanted you to be part of this discussion. I'm thinking about your wellbeing, financial as well as intellectual, and I think the opportunity to launch a really quality literary journal would prepare your way."

Margot's gaze held his steadily, yet he could not read it.

"I'd hate to see you squander your literary gains when you could be ensuring not just your literary future but indeed that of your country."

"Don't exaggerate, Dad. It's just so clear to me that there are more journals than there are good stories. Most of them fold. And it seems as though soon more than half of them will be online only. If we start a journal, no one will notice, and what little money I have will be gone."

Anger rose in Andrew's chest, but he stayed seated and kept his mouth clamped.

"Besides, my paltry advance would cover you for all of six months."

Quarmbey countered: "But by then we'd be fundraising, applying for grants, putting on some events, and of course building circulation all the while."

"I don't want to be the arbiter of taste," Margot said. "I just want to write some stories and then maybe another novel."

Now Andrew rose and in his lowest growl said, "About what? Syphilitics in Alabama? That's what the world needs, not a quality journal, no indeed, but a very quiet novel about syphilitics in Alabama written by an upper-middle-class white girl from Annandale-on-Hudson."

Quarmbey looked down and shook his head. Hinks rose, placing a physical obstacle between father and daughter.

"You've always been bellicose and pig-headed and basically

selfish. But I didn't realize until just now that you are a cruel man."
Margot did not cry before leaving the room.

"It's time for you to leave," Andrew told the two men. "My
wife will drive you to the train."

Later, he sat in the dark in his study and pictured himself walking
down the hall, tapping softly on his daughter's door, asking if he
could read her a story. He knew he should go and apologize, but he
could not translate the thought into action, could not lift himself to
stand. He pushed the skin of his face, using his fingertips to smooth
it up and out, trying to remember the names of the books he'd read
to Margot when she was a child. Some of them he must have read a
hundred times, forcing himself to repeat them over and over while
she listened raptly, fighting sleep, as though the ending might be different each time.

# Chapter twenty-nine

On Christmas Eve, Jackson Miller was enjoying Amanda's saffron-laced seafood stew. Amanda and Eddie had toasted Jackson's publishing contract at the beginning of the meal, and Amanda had inquired about every detail of the sale except for the size of his advance, which was, no doubt, the piece of information that most interested her.

Jackson talked some about his publisher's plans for the book: the pre-publication publicity lunch, the publication soiree, the plot for media infiltration, the advertising budget, the corporate sales. It was clear by the way he concentrated on his utensils that Eddie was not enjoying the conversation. Jackson wasn't even sure that his friend was happy for him.

When Eddie's book had sold, Jackson had faced down his own jealousy and cheered on his friend. He had told himself: I wish it were me; I'm glad it's Eddie; I look forward to the day when it's me. And so now he felt a bit dented by the lack of reciprocal enthusiasm. After all, Eddie had already published a book—and he had Amanda.

It rankled Jackson, too, that underlying Eddie's lukewarm congratulations was the belief that Jackson's success was undeserved, that he wasn't a good writer. Still, Jack sympathized with Eddie's failure to follow up on his early success, even if the misery was largely self-inflicted, and understood that disappointment fuels bitterness. Jackson could now afford to be magnanimous, and he'd always been affable if not particularly loyal. He always wished others well, all the more so if it didn't cost him anything.

Directing the conversation away from his contract for Eddie's sake, he said, "So fill me in on the doings of Whelpdale."

Eddie lightened. "He's offering a local workshop called 'how to write and sell a novel in ten weeks,' if you can believe it. He claims to have invented something called the 'crystal method' of novel writing, which he promises will generate a publishable novel through a series of easy-to-follow steps. All you need to start is one idea for a character."

"At least he's trying to succeed," Amanda met Jackson's eyes as she poured more Pinot Gris into his glass.

"At what?" Eddie's tone echoed the contempt in his wife's.

"That's funny," Jackson said, stepping around the palpable tension between his married friends. "Doreen had a copy of a pamphlet called *The Crystal Method of Novel Writing*. I hope that means she's going to write some romances or children's books so she can quit her godawful job."

"What's most scandalous," added Amanda, "is that the advertisements for Whelpdale's workshops suggest that he can help his victims get their dreadful little novels published. The ads have lines like 'instructor has extensive contacts in the publishing world' and 'instructor will evaluate completed novels for suitable agents.'"

Jackson set his spoon down in his empty bowl and sipped the wine. "Speaking of literary enterprises," he continued, "what's up with Henry? Any news?"

"He says he's close to finishing his novel. He read some pages to me. He really is a first-rate writer. It will be unfair if he can't find a publisher."

"I, for one, will be quite disappointed if I never get to read it." Amanda spoke with such charm that it was unclear whether she was serious or making fun of Henry.

"I'm not sure it's your cup of tea, Amanda," Eddie said. "You'd likely call it too quiet."

"The hero's actually a bailiff, right?" Jackson said, amused. "What does Henry call him? The decently ignoble or the ignobly decent? Something like that."

"No doubt your sales will dwarf his, but he's like me," Eddie said. "He's not in it for the money."

"Art and money are not antonyms," Jackson replied, "but I freely admit that money does motivate me. I'm not a martyr for literature like you. I plan to develop an extravagant lifestyle and lead it into deep old age."

"Did you tell your family about your book?" Amanda asked him.

Jackson saw his father compulsively touching the tops of his sailing trophies, counting them forwards and backwards. He shook his head. "When it's published, I'll send a copy to my mother. She can tell my father or not. I don't give a damn."

"Really?" She paused for his answer but quickly moved on when he didn't respond. "Are you dedicating it to anyone?"

Again he shook his head, thinking that he had no one he could dedicate his first novel to. "No one helped me write it," he said, his voice buoyant. "I'm taking all the credit."

Two bottles of wine later, Amanda excused herself to go to bed. "Merry Christmas, Jackson," she said as she hugged him. "I'm glad you still have time for your ordinary friends."

"There's nothing ordinary about you, my dear," he said, holding the embrace for what felt like a few seconds too long, his hands spanning her shoulder blades, his fingertips only a layer of angora from her skin.

The two men finished another bottle of wine. Jackson felt remarkably even and fresh, but clearly Eddie was feeling the wine's effect; he was beginning to slur his words and was now pacing the room erratically.

"You know," Eddie said, "it's all well and good for you to worship Mammon, but you should at least try to notice what it costs me when you're always praising success in front of someone else." He emphasized the final two words.

"Oh, Eddie, let's skip this and talk about anything else you wish."

"Your way of talking isn't much to my taste just now. It comes with a price tag, you know."

"Price tag? What do you mean?" Jackson watched his once-easygoing friend.

Eddie thrust his hands deep into his pockets and leaned forward at the waist, as though observing something on the floor. He straightened and said, in a thick voice, "Your way of talking glorifies success at the expense of quality—as though success is the only goal. If you'd talked this way in front of just me, we could have just argued and it wouldn't have mattered. But you know as well as I do that there's usually someone else in earshot. Frankly, I'm guessing she's your real audience, so you'll be glad to hear that your words have had their effect. Where Amanda once saw talent, now she sees only failure."

Jackson summoned his anger for a protest, but Eddie looked so wretched that he could muster little emotion other than pity. "That's an astonishing thing to say, Eddie. I have no idea what's going on with you and Amanda, but I assure you that it's more about you than me."

"Your words, your words have turned Amanda against me. I shouldn't have implied that that's what you intended. Maybe it's just my bad luck." Eddie looked up and finally made eye contact. "She can hardly stand to look at me, Jack, and we almost never have sex anymore."

"I always figured you two were after each other like rabbits." Jackson smiled, hoping to turn the conversation. Seeing that his attempt at levity failed, he said, "Look, Eddie, you shouldn't tell me about that. But do you remember what I told you when you got engaged? That your success would make her happy?"

"So you've always guessed that Amanda wasn't a for-better-or-worse kind of girl. You think she married me just because my book was being published?"

"I'm not going to answer that. Look, I'm your friend, but if we can't talk like friends, we'd better not talk about this sort of thing at all." Jackson paused. "I will say this: what you're thinking isn't true. My words don't have that kind of influence on her. If you two are really having serious trouble, maybe you should see a counselor or something."

Both men concentrated more on drinking than talking for the next half hour. Jackson mentally replayed his meeting with Amanda at the Frick, their talk about Hobbema, the drink after, imagining how Eddie would view that encounter. Jackson knew that he sometimes said things to Amanda when they were alone in a room that he wouldn't say in Eddie's earshot, things wrong in tone more than in the words themselves. It stemmed from his vanity, from his own form of weakness. Yet he was convinced that any troubles in the Renfros marriage had little to do with him and likely much to do with Eddie himself. If a marriage can't withstand a little harmless outside flirting, it isn't much of a union in the first place.

Finally Jackson said, "If you love her, talk to her. Work it out."

"Work it out," Eddie repeated dully.

It took only one more glass of wine to put Eddie to sleep in his chair, granting Jackson his chance to escape.

# Chapter thirty

Late on New Years Eve, Henry Baffler was a single paragraph away from completing *Bailiff*. He toyed with the idea of waiting until morning to finish. Or perhaps he should take the entire day to get the final few sentences just right. Ultimately, he told himself that would be silly—he'd planned the paragraph for weeks now—and he was quite fond of the idea of finishing the novel in the same year he had started it.

And so he composed the last paragraph, noticing that the ink was growing pale, that he needed a new ribbon. He typed *The End.* He took pleasure in the fact that the novel concluded essentially where it began: his bailiff, unchanged despite his brief love affair, still fed pigeons on his lunch hour while contemplating the ways in which the stout birds represented the human types that made their way through petty-claims court.

Life had proved art and theory right. Henry's real-world bailiff had illustrated a key tenet of New Realism, which debunked the popular attitude that novels were stories of character change. Henry believed that novels should reflect human character. And people rarely change; they only become more themselves. In his final paragraph, his bailiff was precisely the same as he was in the opening sentence—only more so.

Henry hit return and rolled the final page off the cannister. He placed it face down on the stack of its predecessors, lifted the whole manuscript, and carefully tapped its four sides against the tabletop. He made a mental note to be on the lookout for a large rubber band or a clean, manuscript-sized box.

He was hungry as well as anxious to celebrate his accomplishment and toast New Realism. Though he knew his refrigerator was empty, he opened the door anyway and pondered the bare shelves. He didn't have to examine his money either—he knew exactly how much he had—but he counted and tabulated the same figure: two dollars and sixty-eight cents. There was an all-night market about nine blocks up that sold single bottles of beer, tax included, for a dollar and sixty-nine cents. Six blocks in the other direction, toward Chelsea, he could buy a bag of day-old rolls for a dollar flat. He threw off the sofa cushions and, as if fate rewarded art, found a single shiny penny. He shouldered his way into the corduroy jacket that had been too warm in the fall but was now only thick enough keep him from freezing, setting out quickly, as the store that sold the rolls would soon close. One floor down, he had to step around his only English-speaking neighbor, Martin Briggs, who sat on the landing next to a half-gone bottle of gin, wearing a filthy tuxedo jacket and jeans and using one cigarette to light the next.

"I wish I were dead," the man said. "I mean, you don't dump someone on New Year's Eve. It's just not done. It's just not right."

Henry navigated around him, dropping two steps at a time to get by on the narrow staircase. Despite his growling stomach and the cold snapping through his thin jacket, Henry's stride was springy as he made his way through clots of Dominican revelers and then past the trendy couples on Tenth Avenue. A new year was moving in, his book was done, and he was about to drink the first beer he had allowed himself in weeks.

The owner of the bodega was just lowering the window armor, but the old man opened the door to Henry and sold him the dollar bag of torta rolls. Half an hour later, Henry was on his way home with a bottle of beer and his bread, thinking about how he might submit his manuscript. He could use the library computer to query agents and editors by email and then hand-deliver the manuscript to the first person who seemed interested. But he'd eventually need to make a copy or two. He shouldn't have bought the beer, but he told himself that since he had, he shouldn't let regret spoil the taste.

Two blocks away from his apartment, the sidewalks grew heavier with people. He heard sirens close by. At the smell of smoke, he broke into a run. "Let me get through!" he shouted, looking for gaps in the crowd and shooting narrowly through.

Smoke billowed from several windows on the upper floors of his building. Henry sliced his skinny body between two policemen and raced up the steps of the burning tenement.

"Hey you! Stop there!" called one of the cops, but he made no move to chase or restrain him.

"I live here! I've got to get something!" Henry called behind him, dropping bread and beer as he ascended the exterior steps three at a time. At the entrance, he had to push by Martin Briggs, who was exiting the building gripping the pack of cigarettes that had likely set the fire. Inside the building, the smoke swarmed the stairwell, but Henry pushed up, holding his jacket sleeve over his mouth and nose and closing his eyes for as long as possible. He was desperate with the dread of losing *Bailiff*—his great work and reason for waking each morning. On the verge of unconsciousness, he pushed his key into his lock and tumbled forward into the fresher air of his apartment. His manuscript lay on the table, where he had left it. Despite the fire raging above and below his flat, the realist felt relief, even joy, as he rested his hand on the undamaged stack of pages. He removed his jacket and used it to wrap the manuscript, bundling it to his chest like a baby.

Now that he had his manuscript in hand, Henry's courage receded. Watching the flames now engulfing the door to his apartment, he contemplated death by fire—the ultimate melodrama—with a nauseous mind. He had no choice but to climb through his little window and onto the ledge. There should be a fire escape, he thought, and wondered why he had never noticed its absence until now. He looked down the five stories to the street. A crowd looked up, cheering in a mix of Spanish and English.

Two fire engines had arrived, and a man in yellow slickers called to him on a megaphone. "You need to jump. Just push off and point your feet toward the trampoline."

Henry looked down at the inflatable pad, grasping his novel to his chest. Already pinned to the wall by vertigo, he was sickened further by the nightmarish fantasy of the hundreds of pages of his pure example of New Realism fluttering through the neighborhood, white rectangles scattered the length and breadth of Hell's Kitchen to be stepped on, snowed on, picked up for scrap. His ideas could be pilfered or mocked. Lines could be read out of context and misunderstood.

The front of his body was cold, but his back was hot from the heat mounting in the building. Spotlights scanned his face in bright flashes as the crowd chanted for him to escape. Holding the manuscript gently against one forearm, he worked to better secure it with the jacket, the shouts of "Jump, jump, jump!" and *"Saltese, saltese, saltese!"* pounding in the canals and drums of his ears. He grasped *Bailiff* tightly and leaped, willing his legs toward the trampoline. At the instant he jumped, he heard a firefighter call out: "I think he's got a baby!"

He opened his eyes before he stopped bouncing up and back into the embrace of the plastic, taking in the swarm of faces and cameras and flaring light as images from an Ezra Pound poem.

"The brave man saved a cat!" a child called.

A woman firefighter with a beautiful face leaned over him and lifted her hand toward his bundle. "Is it all right? Is it a baby? A pet? It was a crazy thing for you to do, but it was courageous to run in."

A television crew filming the scene still pointed its camera at Henry. He grinned at them and unwrapped *Bailiff.* "I saved my manuscript," he said. "It's a novel of New Realism."

The look on the beautiful firefighter's face sharpened, and she crinkled her nose in what even Henry could not mistake for anything but disgust. "You risked your life for an unpublished novel?"

"I guess I do it every day," he muttered, wondering if something was wrong with him and, if so, whether a doctor could treat it.

# Chapter thirty-one

With the exception of the horrible night her father got drunk with Quarmbey and Frank Hinks, Margot had found his demeanor greatly improved since they'd turned in his book. Everyone in the house had been relieved when his editor accepted the manuscript. No doubt her father's pride was hurt because it had taken the woman two months to get around to reading it and because she'd told him that the modest advance initially mentioned had been further reduced after in-house discussions. The editor had promised her father, though, that they "would make money."

Margot was unsure whether it was a sign of softening or weakening that her father had agreed to this. He even said that it was better this way, better to have some of the money up front and the bulk of it later. She didn't doubt that the speedy publication schedule was keeping him in better humor than he might have been in otherwise, and she'd smiled when he told her that the book needed only the lightest of copyedits, that it was virtually without error. In her work on the galleys, Margot found only three small mistakes, and one of those had been introduced by the editor.

Since that awful night with Quarmbey and Hinks, her father

had been reasonably nice around the house, even to her mother, and one Sunday after reading the ongoing dispute over Quarmbey's review and Fadge's response in the letters page of *The Times*, he apologized, in his way, for his comments about Margot's writing.

"Of course I know you wouldn't really write a novel about syphilis sufferers in Birmingham," he said.

"Actually, Dad, it's not such a bad idea."

Such extreme alarm overtook his face that Margot immediately admitted that she was kidding. "No, actually, I've started a novel set on the coast of Maine. There are only three characters: an elderly man, a boy, and a seagull." She watched her father carefully to see if he was remorseful enough over his cruel remarks to let this opportunity for sarcasm pass.

"Margot, there's something I haven't wanted to mention but which you will eventually need to know." He folded his paper and removed his reading glasses.

"What is it, Dad?"

"I'm beginning to forget things."

"You've always been forgetful."

"No, Margot, I haven't."

"Well, eventually one's brain is so full of facts that a few of them have to go." Margot lifted the corners of her mouth, tried to lighten her words. "But you should go see a doctor, just to reassure yourself."

"Do you think I could have saved more money over the years? I mean, in one way I might have been able to, but it's hard when you're self-employed. I've had to buy our health insurance, save for my retirement, pay for your college."

Margot flinched at his suggestion that he had paid for her education. She'd won and kept a full academic scholarship in her undergraduate years and had had a research assistantship while getting her Master's. Throughout, she'd paid most of her living expenses—all but a few hundred dollars here and there when her father remembered—by working, likely at the expense of her learning. Because of this, there were holes in her education—books she should have read but had not.

"We haven't much but this house," her father continued his lament, "and it would kill your mother to leave it."

"Dad, I honestly don't think it would. She often talks about moving into a place that requires less work. She says she's planted enough flowers and cooked enough meals for the rest of her life. She'd like to move to the southwest, the harmonic convergence place or somewhere like that."

"I assure you that that would kill me. Besides, your mother just says that. Despite all her crystals and what-not crap, she couldn't stand to live more than an hour from New York. Just tell her she'll wrinkle up in the dry desert air, and I guarantee she'll never mention New Mexico or Arizona again. Anyway, my point is that I don't know what will happen to us if I'm no longer able to make a living with my pen. And that's why I want you to think long and hard about the journal we discussed."

"Oh, Dad, it's just that there are so many of them." Margot heard new maturity in her voice—she was talking not as adolescent to parent but as adult to adult, writer to writer. Fatigue tinged her even tone.

"Not one of them worth its salt, though, not one of them with the right editorial vision."

Margot stood behind her father, wrapped her arms around his thickening neck, and kissed his cheek, smelling his most recent cigar and the one before that. "I promise I'll think about it." Again her voice sounded older to her, older and a little tired.

"That's all I ask, and I appreciate it. I know that I've made you something of a martyr, but I want you to know that much of my literary life has been drudgery, scribbling words to make ends meet. It's not something I can keep doing, and it's not a life I want for you. A writer should only have to write when he feels like it, when he actually has something to say. And I'm ready to really edit. If it goes well, we can add a small press, so we can publish our friends."

Since her father had passed up the chance to make a crack about her work, she refrained from saying, "But I thought people publishing their friends was part of the problem."

Over the days that followed, her father continued to be

solicitous, and even kind. Margot was not so stupid or naïve as to believe he was a changed man, but she did think his recent knocks had softened him, and certainly she enjoyed their more harmonious domestic life. If she could launch the journal he wanted and if it could succeed, then perhaps the tranquility would continue. And so she did as she had promised: she considered the proposal. Setting aside the Maine novel, which was causing her trouble because she could not figure out how to account for the presence of a solitary orphan boy on the rocky island, she researched the world of literary journals and magazines. From website to website, she saw the usual writing-program suspects everywhere represented. And she read the appalling web-published efforts in flash fiction side by side with the desperate appeals for donations. The cross-breeding of editors, writers, journals, and links sickened her in the same way as would staring at the progeny resulting from long inbreeding.

She emailed Jackson about her quandary, which elicited the speediest response she'd ever received from him: "Save your money. Just write your next book. Let them publish you and not the other way around. And come see me soon. I'm surrounded by idiots. I'm lonely for you. I'm becoming someone I don't even like."

They weren't right for each other on paper, no matter what her mother's charts proclaimed, but she knew Jackson was fond of her. Margot pictured herself at his side, imagining both of them with money in the bank and books on the shelves. Yet each time she tried to still the image, to hold it in her mind and see it clearly, it went grainy and faded out.

She approached her mother, who advised her to go ahead and extend the invitation for Jackson to visit. "I'm playing my cards with your father, and he's unlikely to ever be in this good a mood again. He certainly won't be after he reads his reviews."

It was a good idea, Margot decided, to see Jackson in another setting, to determine if their affection was transferable or belonged only to the city. She had never seen him anywhere else.

# Chapter thirty-two

Henry Baffler had saved his manuscript from the fire, but he had lost everything else beyond the clothes he was wearing and his cash-empty wallet. In the confusion, he had even lost track of the beer and bread that had occasioned his excursion. Faced with seeking a shelter cot, he phoned Eddie Renfros.

Henry had worried that Eddie had invited him to stay without first asking his wife, and Amanda's greeting had been a little cool, even as she'd fluffed guest pillows into clean cases. Yet she seemed genuinely enthusiastic when they saw the story on several television news shows: "Local writer risks life for novel", and "Would-be novelist risks all for book".

"I'm not a would-be novelist," Henry objected, but he laughed at the footage of him pulling his manuscript from its corduroy swaddling as the firefighter's smile smeared into disapproval.

Even *The Times* covered the event, including with the story a photo of Henry, flat on his back on the inflatable trampoline, manuscript lifted triumphantly toward the camera. The three writers laughed themselves hysterical.

For two days, Henry enjoyed the Renfros' hospitality, which

included the sizeable pleasures of sweetened coffee, good water pressure, and hearing Amanda pad around in bare feet. The sofa pulled out into a bed more comfortable than Henry's own, and he realized that a clean apartment with hardcover books and CDs and nice things on the wall calmed his mind. New stories tickled his brain, exciting but soft like feathers. On the third day, however, when Henry remembered to phone his absentee roommate, he found out that he was planning to tell his Southern Baptist family he was living with his girlfriend. Henry realized the dire nature of his situation.

"I've lost everything!" he said to Eddie that morning. "I'll never find such a cheap and easy living arrangement. My clothes weren't much, but they were my clothes. And my books—and the years of handwritten margin notes. And my copies of *Swanky*."

"Henry," Eddie said kindly. "Is there anyone you can email or call? Family that could help out?"

The last time Henry had seen his brother, he'd just lost the condo flanked by stone lions, lost their grandparent's furniture store, and relapsed after thirty days in rehab. "I'd rather starve," he told Eddie.

"People always say they'd rather starve, but as soon as their stomachs growl, well, the call doesn't seem as hard to make."

"That's people, but you may have noticed there's something wrong with me. I actually would rather starve than speak to my brother. He can't help me anyway. There's no one I can call."

"The starvation outcome seems increasingly likely, Henry, unless you can find a job quick. You and I are alike in one sense: no one warned us that writing is now a gentleman's profession, an occupation only for those who don't need to make money."

A series of images of himself at work blinked across Henry's mind, clicking in and out as in a child's viewfinder: screwing in the grounds holder of an espresso machine, spreading mayonnaise on a slice of white bread, handing ticket stubs back to cinema goers, netting goldfish to transfer into a portable plastic bag.

"Maybe now that the book is done I can spare the time," he said.

Amanda, who had been watching the street from the window,

chimed in. "Is your novel completely finished? Yes? It's obvious then: you saved your bailiff and now maybe he can save you. You've got to query agents right away. I'll help you research some." Just before the doorbell sounded, she added, "Jackson's here."

"I'm sorry to come over uninvited," Jackson said as he entered the room. "But I wanted to talk to Henry. I think he's got to strike while the iron is hot."

"Precisely what I was just saying," said Amanda.

Jackson and Amanda helped Henry compose a query letter on Amanda's computer, while Eddie, drinking in the living room, shouted occasional comments across the blue shoji screen.

"Should I say much about the nature of the book? Maybe hint—only hint—that it deals with the ignobly decent?" Henry asked his friends.

Eddie called out, "Maybe you should just say that it's a realist novel about a court worker in New York. You know, keep it simple."

"You need to make it sound even more interesting than I'm sure it is," advised Amanda.

"I know. I'll just say that I'd like them to consider a novel of modern life, the scope of which is in some degree suggested by the title." He paused, liking the idea. "I wish I could tell them how close the manuscript came to conflagration, plead with them to save from obscurity the book I saved from oblivion."

"That's exactly what you have to do," Jackson said. "Include clippings, for godsakes. Name the TV stations that covered you."

"Wouldn't that be tacky? I couldn't do that." As he contemplated the idea, Henry's neck heated, the warmth spreading up each side and climbing over his jaw and into his cheeks.

"Oh, hell." Clearly exasperated, Jackson asked Amanda for the phone and took it around the screen.

While he was gone and Amanda rummaged for scissors to cut out *The Times* report, Henry searched the internet for Clarice Aames. There were several websites paying her homage, but Henry was disappointed to discover that none of her fiction was available online. He would have to write to the editor of *Swanky* and get his copies replaced.

"What are you doing?" Jackson asked when he returned.

Henry closed the browser.

"Never mind," Jackson said. "I just got off the phone with my agent and asked her if she'd heard about the writer who saved his book from the fire on New Year's Eve. She actually saw your jump on late-night news."

Henry shrugged.

"She loves the story."

"But she hasn't read it," Henry said.

"Not the book, the story. She loves the story. Fantastic publicity, she said. Anyway, she wants to read your manuscript. Right away—an exclusive. We can take it over so she can read it while you're waiting on the other queries, which you are going to let Amanda write for you. No ignobly decent crap, and we're certainly not going to call extra attention to the title."

Henry smiled at the idea of an exclusive; he wouldn't need to borrow the money to copy the manuscript.

Jackson walked him through the cold, sunny day to a large office building in midtown, joking that he should take an ad out, à la Whelpdale, as "fiction security" or "the novel guard". Jackson laughed at his own tag line: "Call him when it's your only copy."

After Jackson delivered his name to the security desk, they were issued clip-on badges and allowed to cross the shiny-floored lobby and board the elevator for the eleventh floor.

Though the building was grand, the office had been sub-divided with cheap screens to accommodate all four agents who formed the agency. Jackson introduced Henry to Suzanne Reznick, a middle-aged woman dressed in the print skirt and tinkling silver-and-bead earrings of a younger woman. She had interesting eyes, somewhere between green and hazel. Henry tried to invent a word for the color.

"Call me Suze," she said, shaking his hand. She wrote down the Renfros' telephone number and Henry's email address and told him she'd be in touch.

She hugged Jackson, kissed him on both cheeks, and told him to phone the next day. "We have so much to talk about. First serial rights, for starters, and our foreign rights person is working on the Asian markets now."

"Can you find your way back to Casa Renfros?" Jackson asked when they were back outside.

Henry grinned. "You know me, man on the street."

That night, Jackson returned with pizzas and bottles of Chianti. His high spirits infected everyone but Eddie.

"I just can't believe," Eddie said to Henry, "that you have had to struggle so hard and in such squalor only to lose everything."

Amanda glared at her husband. "But of course, to every man of mettle comes an opportunity, and Henry's has arrived. I have a superstitious faith in *Bailiff.* Henry, I only hope you won't forget us when you're famous."

"I'll never forget my friends," Henry said, enjoying the pleasant sting of young wine on his tongue.

Jackson set down his third piece of pizza crust, refilled his glass, and crossed his legs. "So then, Amanda, you've read about the days and joys of our bailiff?"

Amanda smoothed her hair and held her smile. "I haven't yet had the pleasure. I'm sure that when I do my faith will no longer be superstitious."

"Well, Henry," said Eddie, "I hope that your success will be long lasting. That's what I wish for you, that your book will stay on the shelves. To have had even a small reputation and to have outlived it, that's the worst. It's like anticipating your own death."

"Slow down on the grape juice." Amanda spoke sharply to her husband.

"Thinking about my recent adventure," Henry said, "I find it funny as hell to picture you guys at the morgue identifying my charred body. Imagine the news stories then: 'Deluded and poverty-stricken writer overestimates the value of his unpublished novel' and so on."

"That's horrible," Amanda said, but she laughed.

"You'd have even ranked a cartoon in *The City* and been memorialized on the ULCER website," said Jackson.

"What's ULCER?" Henry asked.

"A bunch of bad writers who've chosen to blame the literary

establishment rather than their own shoddy prose for the fact that they're unpublished. Their name stands for the Underground Literary Coalition for the Elimination of Revision or Reification or some such."

"It is true, you know," Eddie meted out his words, "that many very fine books go unpublished. It's not always a function of shoddy prose. It's the market. The chain stores control everything now."

"I hope it isn't Realism that they want to eliminate," said Henry, "unless they mean Realism in the old sense of the word."

"Anyway," Jackson continued, "these ULCER guys—and it is mostly guys, surprise, surprise—did put me on to a terrific short story by someone I've never heard of. Clarice something."

"Clarice Aames," Henry said. "Is there a new story?"

"You like her, too?" Amanda removed the empty pizza boxes to the kitchen.

It struck Henry that her smile carried some sort of riddle. He'd enjoyed the domestic calm her ordering of the apartment had yielded, and it had been long enough since his last girlfriend that her presence aroused him. But she most definitely wasn't his type. In her enigmatic smile, though, she seemed more interesting than the glossy what-you-see-is-what-you-get female he'd always taken her to be. She still wasn't his romantic type, but he suspected there was something more under the surface. He suspected that she might be worth writing about.

# Chapter thirty-three

Amanda Renfros enjoyed having Henry Baffler in their home for a few weeks, in part because she was touched by his blind devotion to her alter ego. It was also a relief—she could admit this to herself, though of course she would never say it aloud—to have a writer in the house who was an even greater failure than Eddie. She had worried, though, that they might be stuck with Henry forever, but as it turned out, his little news splash did indeed bring salvation. Not only had Jackson's agent taken on and quickly sold his novel for a modest advance, but someone had anonymously donated a year's rent on a decent apartment on Lennox near 110th.

"Maybe your anonymous donor is some reclusive genius," Amanda suggested, "moved by memories of his own lean early days."

Henry rubbed his hands together and asked if they thought it could be Salinger.

Eddie, dishrag that he'd become, lectured Henry on why that was unlikely and why it was much more likely that his benefactor was a hack thriller or horror writer who describes his characters in terms of television and movie personalities.

But Amanda saw no harm in letting Henry believe that the reclusive author of "For Esme, with Love and Squalor" was taking a personal interest in saving him from squalor and furthering his literary career. "Sure," she'd told him. "It very well could be Salinger. He's using you to try out the New Harlem. I'd almost be surprised if it wasn't the kind of thing he'd do."

The day after Henry moved out, Eddie's agent called. Even across the room, Amanda could hear her voice, nearly breathless, streaming from the receiver. She'd called to tell Eddie that the editor-in-chief of a large house loved his book and saw it as the perfect novel for her assistant, newly promoted to editor, to cut his teeth on. "They may ask you about the autobiographical angle."

"But my narrator's a woman and a musician. She has a deaf child. Her lover died in a plane crash."

The agent's voice rasped through their living room. "A client of mine wrote a novel about a battered wife. The publisher assumed it was autobiographical. When she refused to go on a talk show and talk about her nonexistent experiences as a battered wife, they killed her marketing."

"So what am I supposed to say?"

"Something vague maybe, a hint of a great loss that you don't like to talk about. A mention of your long-suffering wife."

That call was followed, an hour later, by a long call with Dan, the up-and-comer. Eddie was in a fully manic state by the time he hung up, talking rapidly, going back and forth on whether this was a sure thing. He repeated the young editor's phrases: 'mainstream crossover' and 'commercial potential.' "That means it's a question of how much, not if? Right?"

Amanda nodded. "Sounds like it."

"Why do you say that?" he demanded.

"It's going to be hard, Eddie, but you're just going to have to wait this one out."

All evening he bounced and paced, sitting with a book or magazine only to abandon it minutes later, opening and closing the refrigerator a dozen times without taking out anything to eat, lying on the rug to do a few sit-ups then popping up to check his email.

Amanda felt more sympathy for him than she had in months, and she was comforted by the probability of a happy ending. Unless publishers had devised new methods of tormenting writers, then surely a book deal was the certain outcome.

"They don't call you if they don't want the book. That would be beyond the pale even for them." Amanda tried to knead his tense shoulders, but he kept looking over his shoulders asking "Really?"

Amanda waited for him to go out the next day before phoning her agent, Patrice, for a second opinion.

"Funny," her agent said, "because Dan still answers her phones. Still, sounds like a sure thing, a question of how much and not if."

When the bad news came seventeen torturous days later, Eddie, who by that point was never more than a few feet from the phone, fielded the call. "How can they do that to me?" he asked over and over. "Couldn't they have just kicked my teeth out? Why'd they have to set me up? What did I ever do to them?"

Amanda watched her husband, wanting to help but knowing there was nothing she could say to change the horrible, hard fact. From behind, she wrapped her arms around his neck and chest, kissed the back of his head. She said that she was sorry and promised that someone else would buy his novel. What she did not tell him was that she had given notice at work—and in language that ruled out ever asking for her job back.

She wondered if Eddie was supposed to have slept with someone—the editor-in-chief, or maybe Dan—and had missed the hint. She didn't think it worked like that, not in publishing, where transactions are done at a distance and anyone can be made to look good in an author photo, but there had to be some explanation. Something had to have gone wrong.

"This is all I found out," Patrice told her the next day. "The editor-in-chief says it was never a done deal. She claims that it's great for a writer to come close, to at least talk to an editor interested in his work, that lots of writers would think that's an honor. She actually said that the next best thing to having serious mainstream crossover appeal it to be *told* that you might have serious mainstream crossover appeal, though perhaps only in another life."

As Patrice paused, Amanda could hear her own husky breathing. She leaned against the brick exterior of an apartment building down the street from her own, the cold spreading across the seat of her jeans and her upper back. She said, "Only someone who has never written would ever say such a thing."

"Bingo," her agent said. "And likely never worked a job she couldn't afford to quit. Daddy's loaded, big surprise, and so's hubby."

Though Amanda could no longer say she loved Eddie, he was her husband and he was a writer. You don't get to treat us like that, she thought. She made her agent promise never to send her work to that house.

"Smart anyway," Patrice said. "They don't publish fiction well at all. They really botched that antebellum mystery. What a fiasco."

"But really," Amanda said. "I'd rather not publish anywhere than publish there."

"Honey, that doesn't sound like you at all. But no matter, it's not even going to come close to that."

The publishing near-miss sunk Eddie into a new psychological trough from which Amanda worried he would never emerge. He drank more and more, night after night, and rarely left the apartment unless they were out of liquor. He slept on the sofa significant portions of most days.

"Start a new book," Amanda instructed him with no effect. "Remember that your book is out with other editors," she pleaded softly.

She herself wrote a great deal while she awaited word on *The Progress of Love*, trying to keep up with the requests for Clarice Aames stories. On her first day of unemployment, she told Eddie that she had called in sick. Using the morning and half the afternoon, she wrote three Clarice pieces: a second-person story about a deformed girl living on a garbage barge, an omniscient narration describing a world-ending apocalypse that no one notices, and a love story told from the point of view of a female sadist. She received acceptances by email the next day, placing "Cauliflower Girl" in *Swanky*, "End Zone" in *The Bleeding Edge*, and "Assume the Position" in *Virus*, which was the publishing organ of ULCER.

When she walked into the living room brimming with the secret good news, Eddie roused from his half-sleep and sat up on the sofa. "How can you smile while our books are out there and your husband is in pain?"

"Today could be the day. Good news in publishing always comes on Thursday or Friday. You should be glad you made it through Wednesday. Do you want a sandwich?"

"No, I don't want a sandwich. I want a publishing contract and a wife who loves me."

Amanda made two cheese-and-tomato sandwiches, and Eddie ate the one she handed him.

"Don't we have any chips?" he asked. "It's not the same without chips."

Often the small sums up the large, and it was that statement, as much as anything else, that started Amanda thinking through the logistics of divorce.

Later that day, Eddie perked up when he received a letter informing him that *Vapor* had been second runner-up in a manuscript competition. His prize was a coupon waiving the entry fee in the same competition next year.

"What have you come to that you consider this good news?" Amanda asked.

"Well, if I don't place the new book, I can enter it next year for free."

"Even if you win, what's the prize? A print-run of eight hundred and a thousand dollars?"

"Five hundred," Eddie said. "Print run and prize money."

Amanda knew they were on the verge of the argument that might end their marriage when the first call came. It was Eddie's agent phoning with the news that she had sold *Conduct* to a mid-size publisher with a good reputation. The advance was fifteen thousand dollars for world rights, but his agent believed they would "make more money" on sales.

Eddie lifted Amanda and spun her twice, so fast that her hair whipped around, releasing the citrus smell that she considered part of herself. He set her down and kissed her on the mouth. "Finally!"

"This is fabulous news!" she said. "You needed to get one across the finish line and now you have! Now you can take the time to write a really good book."

"Thanks, honey," Eddie said. "You know I love sports analogies."

She was about to ask him whether he was engaging the sarcasm center of his brain when he lifted and spun her again.

"You're beautiful," he said, cupping her cheekbone, "and I'm taking you out for dinner."

The second call came while she was dressing. This time is was Amanda's agent, and the size of the advance for the Fragonard book surprised even Amanda.

"Oh," Eddie said when she told him. "Then let's get drunk, too."

Ignoring the deflation in his tone, Amanda said, "For once I agree with you, but we're getting drunk on the best champagne. If I can get a reservation, we're eating dinner at Grub. What's Jackson's roommate's name again? Maybe she can get us a good table. I'll phone while you shower."

Amanda was glad to have this reason to call Jackson. Though she was annoyed that Eddie seemed less than happy that she'd also sold a book, she couldn't rub her advance in his face—not on the day he'd finally sold another book. But Jackson could share in her exultation. She was disappointed to hear Jackson's recorded voice when she called.

"Me too," she said to the answering machine. "Six figures, that is."

# Chapter thirty-four

The train braked for and jerked away from one absurd stop after another, depositing doughy men to stomp across filthy snow to drive their generic cars home to overweight, practically-shod wives in soul-deadening subdivisions and characterless towns. Jackson Miller promised himself that he would never live anywhere but New York, except, perhaps, Paris.

As he stepped off the train at the Annandale-on-Hudson station, he spotted Margot on the platform. It had been only a couple of weeks since he had last seen her, but she looked smaller than he remembered—shorter and, in pale jeans and a black turtleneck, thinner than ever. She smiled when she saw him, but glanced away when he made eye contact.

"Everything all right?" Jackson put an arm around her narrow shoulders.

"Of course. I'm just happy to see you. And I'm a little nervous." She hooked a curl with her index finger and tucked it away from her eye, a small gesture which endeared her to Jackson all over again. "Especially now that you're on the verge of fame," she said. "And my father's not the nicest host in the world."

"Let's face it, even the most famous novelist is hardly mobbed on the street. People may know his name but not his face. Anyway, I'm here to see you and not your father, so never mind about that. We'll get through the best we can, and we know that you can always come to me."

The Yarborough house sat on a pretty hill overlooking the wide river, but the Cape Cod itself was smaller and plainer than Jackson had anticipated. Jackson knew little about architecture and construction, but the roof bowed and it was obvious that the clapboard needed a fresh coat of white paint. It probably looked better in the spring; against the snow and bare trees, the house looked dingy.

"It's a great place, isn't it?" Margot said. "I'm afraid the day is coming when Dad will have to sell it, though no doubt he'll hold out as long as possible. My mother would actually like the change."

"I suppose real estate up here is worth a lot, regardless of the condition of the house itself. Being a train ride from the city and overlooking the Hudson and all."

"Yes. My parents bought it a long time ago. Only rich people can move here now."

Jackson laughed. "What's that joke about middle-aged men? They talk about sex but think about real estate?"

"We're not middle-aged."

"Exactly, so perhaps we're doing the opposite." Jackson slithered an arm around her small waist and pulled her momentarily closer to him.

Margot, whose cheeks were already pink from the cold, blushed hard, and Jackson felt refreshed. There weren't many girls who'd lived in the city and still blushed at so mild a comment.

Margot led him into the house and introduced him to her mother as though they had never met. He was relieved he hadn't made a pass at her at the Blue Ridge Writers' Conference, which of course was the only thing that would have been worse than what he *had* done. She was attractive, though, in that way that aging women with leisure and some financial resources can be when they make appearance a priority.

She was gracious as well, taking his hand between both of hers. "Call me Janelle. I'm glad you're here."

"It's my pleasure to finally be here. I think the world of Margot, and I've been working very hard at learning to be well behaved." Jackson made sure his voice was loud and even, that his hint of apology was in no way servile or obsequious.

After they were seated in the living room with drinks, Andrew Yarborough stomped in. For a moment he looked as though he would retreat, but, caught, he came in and took a seat. Jackson stood and nodded, and the old fellow offered a grunt.

They fumbled their way through the relatively safe subject of sports, and Jackson refrained from making his usual comment that Ivy League football is not actually a sport. After touching on movies and politics, they dipped into an uncomfortable silence.

"I've been hearing the highest praise for your new work, sir." Jackson knew that flattery, even if transparent, was his safest course. "And I think it's high time for just the sort of measured synthesis you've attempted."

"Attempted? It's finished, and it's not an attempt at anything. And, mind you, it's no mere synthesis either. I take some real stands."

"Of course, sir, I merely used the word 'synthesis' to allude to the comprehensive nature of your project."

"Buttering me up," Andrew grumbled even as his body language softened. "Fix me a drink, Janelle. Scotch and soda, I think."

Margot was seated on a large chair, and her toes barely grazed the floor. "Dad's career certainly doesn't need a crown. This will be a jewel in it."

"That's an absurd metaphor, my darling, and another reason I think your real future lies in editing rather than writing."

Jackson wanted to weigh the advantages of defending his girlfriend or siding with her father, but he knew that a quick reaction was likely the best. "Of course I adore Margot's lyrical prose—and her dedication—but she does strike me as someone with a fine editorial eye. There's no reason, is there, that she can't practice both literary activities?"

"Dad wants me to start a journal. He'll be the editorial board, and I'll be the editor."

"Well, that's a capital idea. Except, of course, there's a lot of competition, and much of that competition can claim institutional financing."

"Yes," honked Andrew, "and institutional kowtowing and tastes. Even the newest, supposedly independent reviews are clamoring to publish Adam Richards so he'll review the editors' books on his radio show. Even those without books always assume they'll write one soon, so they'll pass up four great short stories to publish some egomaniacal ninety-page monstrosity by Richards. Or else they'll publish Don Darlington or some other usual suspect just because."

"I don't disagree with you, sir. In fact that's why I was so relieved the other day to read something really interesting in *Putrid City*. It was by a new writer named Clarice Aames."

"I haven't read it, but *Putrid City* only publishes New York stories. You know, you can be so avant-garde as to be old-fashioned. Besides, that name. It's ridiculous."

They skirmished over the relative merits of a few other journals, Jackson cautious not to mention any publication related to Chuck Fadge.

"Oh," Margot said as though she'd been stuck with a pin, "I saw that Hinks finally placed that story he was having trouble placing. It's in the new issue of the *MidMichigan Review*."

"It's harder and harder for him to publish, though," Andrew said.

As the alcohol and the conversation relaxed Jackson, he felt his guard lowering and relished the edge of excitement, the hint of social danger, that accompanied it. "Speaking of old fashioned," he commented. "Hinks has trouble placing his stories because they're bland. Well-crafted pieces of nothing. Nothing at stake. Nothing new to say."

Margot sank down in her chair as Andrew sat up straighter to more fully inhabit his.

"Then name me a journal publishing stories with something at stake, stories with something to say."

Jackson knew that he should back down, but he also saw no reason why he should have to suffer an old fool, a man of yesteryear, when the codger couldn't even trouble himself to be civil. And so he spoke: "*Putrid City* for one, though, yes, its focus is the city—and not without cause. *Swanky*'s great, and, unlike the *MidMichigan Review*, people actually read it." Jackson ignored the eye contact that Margot sought. "By people, I mean of course young people. And then there's *The Monthly*. I've got a regular gig with them, not because I need it, but because I respect what they do."

"*The Monthly*? *The Monthly*!" Andrew stood up, his face florid, his cheeks inflating. He looked as though he might, quite literally, explode. "You write for Chuck Fadge? That goddamn fucking, conniving, gay, piss ant?"

Jackson knew he should restrain himself, but he was tired of biting his tongue in deference to the old blow-hard. Something about Yarborough pissed him off so thoroughly that he couldn't stop himself from pushing back, consequences be damned. "Now, let me get this straight: Which adjective there gives you the most trouble? That he gets laid, that he's as clever as you wish you were? Or is it that he's a damned homosexual?"

Margot stood and said, her voice a tremolo, "Please." The word trailed off, and she lifted her hand in a stop gesture.

"Get out of my house!" boomed the old man.

Pleasantly flushed with liquor and feeling more triumphant than sorry, Jackson apologized to Margot and said farewell to Janelle.

"Let me drive you to the train station," Margot said.

"Not in my car!" commanded her father.

"Fine," Margot whispered. "We'll walk." Her voice restored to its normal volume, she said, "And I'm not funding your journal, Dad, and I plan to leave home as soon as possible."

She followed Jackson outside, apologizing.

"Please, don't," Jackson said, smoothing her hair, patting her shoulder. "You have nothing to be sorry for. It was all him and me. You know men and their pissing contests."

"But now, well, it's all so impossible."

"Walk with me, okay? Let's talk." They headed down the hill, stepping around patches of ice, toward the road that paralleled the river. Jackson continued, "I don't want to damage your relationship with your father. I'd hate to make you choose between your father and me, but do I flatter myself to think you might choose me? You see, I'm old-fashioned enough to believe that a woman worthy of a man's love is better than he is, that she condescends in giving herself to him—and thus that you might love me in a way that's better than the way I love you."

"Your love for me is a bad thing? A low thing?"

"Well, a man's love is both peculiar and astonishingly common. You're everything I should want. You're sweet and cute and smart and kind. It's that I know that I'm vulgar in comparison, and of course there's no new way to express love. That's part of why I didn't speak of love sooner."

He felt Margot stiffen each time he said the word 'love.'

"Jackson," she asked, loosening herself from his arm and pulling back, "what do you want from life?"

"I'll be honest with you. I want what money can buy. I want a place in society and culture. I want to live among beautiful things and never be troubled by material want. I want to travel and interact as an equal with interesting people. I want season tickets to the Knicks and invitations to black-tie fundraisers at the Guggenheim. I want people to look at me when I enter a room and wish they were me." He looked at her steadily.

"And nothing more?"

"That's a lot, Margot. It will mean that I made it on my own merits, so, yes, I admit it: I want what money can buy."

"And yet you used the word 'love' to me."

"Suppose I said that my only goal in life was to win your love? Would you believe me?" He paused to give his words gravity. "I hope not. But I can honestly say to you that everything I desire will be even more satisfying if I can share it with a woman who loves me. With you, Margot."

"I'm not wearing a coat. I should turn around." Her voice was tight.

"Don't you care for me? I know that I've offended you, but don't you love me?" Jackson blocked her path, wrapped his arms around her small frame, kissed the middle of her forehead.

"Do you really love me?" she whispered.

"I think so, and too much to croon exaggerations in your ear. But, well, you're perfect." Jackson pulled his fingers through her curls.

She pressed the side of her face into his chest. "I've been thinking of growing out my hair."

"It's perfect like it is, Margot. Every other hairstyle looks ridiculous next to yours."

He felt her small weight against him, felt her face against his chest.

"Please don't fret about the row today." He lifted her chin. "You'll just have to visit me instead of the other way around. Maybe you can make an honest man of me, now that I can afford it. Trust me on this one: your father will want to be around to criticize any grandchildren he might have." He kissed the top of her head. "I'd better get hoofing. Call me later, if you can, or send me an email. And don't worry. We'll figure something out. We'll see each other soon."

Lulled by the slight back-and-forth stutter of the train as it returned him to the city he never wanted to leave again, Jackson replayed the afternoon's brief dispute. It might be fun, he decided, to write a piece about literary journals and writers' efforts to publish stories in them. He remembered poor Henry Baffler's tale of a journal that sat on one of his stories for nearly a year. After considering a few angles, he had the perfect idea: he'd slap a fake name on an impeccable story by a master fiction writer—Chekhov or Babel or Welty or someone—and submit it to a dozen journals to see what would happen.

Arriving home to find Doreen out, he checked his answering machine, hearing Amanda's big news before falling into a stuporous sleep.

# Chapter thirty-five

Margot Yarborough was not deluded about the sort of person Jackson Miller was, and she knew his talk of love was certainly overblown. But it was clear he was genuinely enamored of her. In the weeks that followed the nasty contretemps between Jackson and her father, she avoided her father almost completely and spent her time weighing various contingencies. Sometimes she imagined that her book would earn a lot of money—she entertained vague ideas about book-club sales or a film option—or that Jackson would invite her to live with him soon. In the absence of either of these life-changing events, her options were more limited. She sent copies of her résumé to the several area colleges that hired adjunct composition instructors, and, once in awhile, she browsed the New York apartment listings. She read the brochures sent by MFA programs around the country and looked at their websites showing some combination of natural splendor and intellectually engaged twenty-somethings, pencils in hand. She pictured herself among them, drawing inspiration from the surrounding mountains or the shimmering Pacific and sustenance from peers more interested in the writing than the publishing.

Punctuating her holding-pattern of a life were contacts from her editor about the approaching release date of her book. Margot pressed herself to relish every step and task: writing the acknowledgements page (on which she thanked her mother and Jackson and her beloved third-grade teacher but not her father); hearing that foreign rights had been sold in Portugal with other languages still possible; receiving an endorsement from a mid-list writer whose work she admired as solid and who termed hers as "heartfelt" and "quietly moving"; sending her editor a list of her institutional connections (a list limited to her alma maters and the writers' union she'd had to join to publish book reviews in the *Hudson Valley Free Weekly*). This is really happening to me, she told herself.

She also tried to savor her times with Jackson, the night or two she spent at his place every couple of weeks. But the disturbing truth was this: it was the *idea* of him that made her happy. While she was with him, she fretted over saying the wrong thing or sounding stupid, about talking too much or too little, about the time passing too quickly or too slowly. And sometimes—she needed to face this—his rants were repetitive. He espoused the same ideas over and over; they never seemed to develop or move toward any deeper truth.

She was happiest, perhaps, when looking forward to their next meeting or reflecting on an earlier encounter. She would go over each weekend spent together as if shuffling photos from a nice vacation to a country you don't necessarily want to visit again once you remember the details—the cold water or mosquitoes or unsettling food—that aren't visible in the snapshots.

Yet each time she started to draw the obvious conclusion—that she probably wasn't in love—she stepped back from the line. She wanted to be in love. And she didn't like the idea of being post-Jackson, of not having him as her boyfriend, of not celebrating their twin publications. Such were her thoughts one morning when the phone rang while she was alone in the house. She gulped a small breath and readied to hear Jackson's voice.

"It's Lane," said the voice. "I need you to steel yourself. There's nothing to worry about, mind you. *Circus* reviews are always first and commonly negative, even vicious. Just remember that it was written by some thirty-five-year-old loser still living in his mother's basement and picking his zits."

"That's not a very kind characterization," Margot said, processing what Lane was trying to break to her.

"Believe me, sweetheart, you're going to have worse things to say about him after you read the review."

Her stomach clenched. "Review of my book?"

"Can I fax it to your father's number?"

It took Margot a moment to realize that she was nodding rather than answering Lane's question in an audible manner. "Sure," she croaked.

"Remember, now: first and worst. The good reviews will follow in short order."

Margot's hands trembled just a little as she lifted the sheet from the fax machine in her father's office. Her intestines churned as her eyes skimmed phrases like "term-paper-like," "curiously unmoving," and "childishly romantic."

Only when the urge to spit had safely passed did she try to call Jackson. She hung up on his answering machine once before calling back and leaving a message: "I really need a friend to talk to. Please call me."

Later she checked her email and found a message from her ex-boyfriend the guitar player saying he'd learned to appreciate a soft-spoken woman. She laughed and felt a little better.

# Chapter thirty-six

When people asked her if she was excited about the impending publication of *The Progress of Love*, Amanda Renfros said "I'm very happy about my book." What she felt was not the excitement of striking gold or matching lottery-ticket numbers but the pleasurable satisfaction of settling into destined success after a cosmic foul-up that had threatened to snatch it away but in fact had only delayed it. She felt as though she had been born to lead the life she was about to lead.

"Just wear a black turtleneck," Eddie told her when she'd returned to their place with several bags of a mix-and-match wardrobe, selected to last the duration of her twenty-city author tour without repeat combinations.

"I'm not that kind of writer," she said, clipping price tags with her manicure scissors. "And I hope that's not what you're planning to wear to your own publication party."

"It's hardly a party, Amanda," Eddie said. "Just a cordoned-off corner of a bar so my editor can repay a few vodka-and-tonic debts and not be accused of having done nothing at all for my book. It's right next to nothing at all."

"I suppose they're all sensitive after that poor young woman—what was her name?—was in that plane crash. Remember? Her parents chartered the plane because her publisher cancelled her author tour after the editor who acquired her changed houses. And then it crashed right after her second stop. Her dad had just learned to fly. She hardly sold any books at all."

"Yes, my ever-supportive wife, that's likely why they're at least bothering to liquor me up."

"Perhaps they've noticed that you don't need much help in that area."

After that bleak connubial conversation, Amanda made Jackson her confidante in all publication-related matters. In Jackson, she recognized a kindred spirit with whom she could discuss those details she knew would only demoralize her husband.

"I understand," Jackson said when she'd explained this over coffee one afternoon. "It's the same with me and Margot. She's elated her book is being published, and I don't want to tell her anything that will make it small to her."

Amanda looked around the diner, noting the plastic vines wrapping the coat racks, the brown-rimmed translucent plates supporting white toast and eggs, the Eastern European servers whose beauty was quickly fading now that they'd become waitresses instead of models. In them she saw herself as she might have been if she hadn't noticed the boat pulling away, or hadn't leaped across the widening gap of water and landed safely on deck. "You're not really still seeing her, are you? She works in a bookstore, right?"

"Worse. She's living at home for awhile, with her insufferable father."

"Is Andrew Yarborough insufferable? He looks so, well, avuncular."

"Trust me. He's an oaf."

"Regardless, he's certainly last year's model, soon to be obsolete. He's like a car without air conditioning."

"You do have a way with words," Jackson said. "At any rate, I've been crossing my fingers that Margot's book will do really well. I don't have the heart to tell her everything my publisher is doing for me. She doesn't write for the kind of audience we aim for, of course, but she's really very good. Gorgeous sentences."

"Well, that's enough to keep someone like Eddie or Henry Baffler reading a book, but let's face the fact that most people aren't much like those two." Amanda tried for an inscrutable smile.

"Her first review was a massacre. I mean out-and-out mean spirited. Worse than if it had been written by an ex-boyfriend. I don't understand why any reviewer would pick on someone like her. Someone like me, sure, and it would only help my cause. But it has decimated Margot."

"Where's the review?"

"Just *Circus*, but it might be one of the only reviews the poor girl gets."

"But your own prospects continue to brighten, I have no doubt."

"Of course, but I had hoped that Margot and I could be something of a literary couple—two big books out at once."

"My, Jack, are you that serious about her? I always figured you'd opt to marry for money or at least operate as a gigolo. A sweet little crafter of fine sentences with curly hair? This throws new light upon your character. I thought you were more ambitious in every way."

"Do you think me so desperately scheming and ice-veined that I could never marry for love?"

"Sorry, Jack, I didn't mean it that way. And for all I know, your Margot may be perfectly suited to you. I certainly hope she is."

"In ways that I wouldn't have imagined, yes, she is. Of course she is a much better person than I am."

"Terrific. I take it she's witty and gracious to boot?" Amanda hated her catty tone and didn't understand why she sometimes reverted into the unhappy teenager she had been in Wilkes-Barre. She sipped the weak coffee, reminding herself that she could afford to be generous to other people, that she wanted to be generous, that it was a better way to be.

"I believe you've already asked me that. I hope you aren't slipping? Anyway, those aren't the exact words I would use first. She's soft-spoken and sincere. She appreciates a good sense of humor, but she's more sweet than witty."

"So you're giving up your old social ambitions for love. I admire that."

"Just like you did." Jackson held her gaze steadily in his own.

Amanda held still and was careful to give nothing away. She waited for Jackson to speak first.

"Just like you," he continued, "I am at last claiming the success that is mine, and I want to share it with someone who can appreciate what it means."

Amanda ran a section of her hair repeatedly through her thumbs and forefingers, bicycling her hands as she smoothed the width of hair. She dropped her hands when she realized what she was doing. "Sorry, old habit."

"I remember it from workshop, but I never knew if it was a calculation or a compulsion."

"Sometimes one becomes the other, doesn't it?" She smiled, feeling back in control as her cup was refilled by a dyed-blonde poured into black stretch pants and a sweatshirt.

"You'll like this," Jackson said when the waitress had moved on. "I submitted one of Chekhov's finest stories to twenty literary journals under the name Anthony Chernesky. It's for a piece for *The Monthly*."

"You're a very bad boy."

"I've only got a few responses back so far, but I can already tell it'll be a hoot. *The City* and the other glossy I submitted to sent immediate form rejections. *The Adirondack Gazette*, which must have a circulation smaller than its contributors list, sent a handwritten rejection saying that the editors did see some merit in the story but were concerned that the characterization was a bit thin and the characters' motivations didn't seem rooted in their back stories."

"And no one has recognized the story?"

"Not yet. Not one. I'm dying for some editor to say that it's too Chekhovian."

"Will you name names in your piece?"

"Of course." Jackson pulled a small spiral notebook from his bag.

"Don't tell me you've become a note taker or—worse—a journal person."

"Not at all," he said. "I thought we might compare cities."

As they finished their coffee, they mapped out the crisscrossing flights of their author tours.

"We're bad," Jackson said, drumming rhythm and blues on the formica with both hands. "We're nationwide."

"I wonder why you're being sent to Cleveland but not Kansas City," Amanda said as a long-haired girl in tight jeans passed their table. Amanda watched to see if Jackson's eyes would follow her.

Still looking directly at Amanda, he said, "Who knows. But most of our cities are the same. You're going to look great in L.A."

"Next time we meet," Amanda said, "I pick the restaurant."

# Chapter thirty-seven

During the year between the acceptance and publication of *Sea Miss*, Eddie Renfros had savored the process as if each event were a course in a long, delicious meal. Early on, there were days on which he would forget he was on the verge of authorship. Then he'd remember, smile mid-street and think author, authority, authorship, my ship has come in. Calls from his adoring editor were like fine chocolate in his mouth. The week the check came, he'd drunk the most expensive wine of his life: a 1982 Croizet-Bages Pauillac he may have been too young to appreciate.

The author-photo session had taken place in the studio of a Tribeca photographer, whom his publisher had paid to shoot seven rolls of color and black-and-white film. "We want you to look accessible yet mysterious," his editor had cooed. "Friendly but foxy." He still remembered the photographer's dog: a Rhodesian Ridgeback named Chester.

After the emotional ransacking of submitting *Vapor* serially and without success, Eddie looked forward to having the new book in production regardless of his ambivalence about the novel's worth. He also saw the impending publication as a chance to renew his marriage and his friendship with Jackson: three graduate school friends all with books coming out around the same time. Even if he didn't quite approve of the kinds of books Amanda and Jackson had chosen to write, they were capable writers. And if their advances dwarfed his own, he could take comfort from the thought that the critics were more likely to give him the nod. And if he didn't always like the way that Amanda peered at Jack sideways, he could tell himself that a little outside flirtation only brought energy to a monogamous relationship.

And yet, despite his honest efforts, the months ahead did not hold the pleasures that the year of *Sea Miss*'s production had. *You're only as good as your next book*—a phrase whose origin he couldn't place—played over and over like some one-track eight-track in his head. There was no Tribeca shoot this time, either; the editor argued for "brand consistency" and bought extended rights to his old author photo. Eddie worried that people would think he hadn't updated it because he was trying to look younger than he was.

Still, other steps in the process did offer small pleasures. The assistant art director came up with a terrific cover on which the body of a faceless woman and the body of her viola mirrored each other's shapes in ways that suggested the story's sensuality. The presence of a small shell in the corner hinted at the themes of sound and hearing, and of the pivotal conflict over the daughter's deafness, in a manner that would be obvious only after the book was read. The flap copy was pretty good, given that it was flap copy. It made the book sound interesting to a general readership without pandering, and the editor had agreed to Eddie's few small changes, agreed to change the word 'promiscuous' to 'adventurous' in describing the slutty Scandinavian violinist and the word 'tragic' to 'disturbing' in mentioning the lover's demise by air accident.

Eddie had heard the horror stories of books orphaned by editors' mid-life-crisis trips to the Amazonian rainforest. He'd heard about psychotic jacket designers and illiterate copyeditors, and so he was pleased with the production of his book—so long as he didn't think about the advertising or marketing plans. Perhaps it was this repressed concern that made him sulk. Because, despite his real attempts, he just couldn't be as wildly happy as Amanda and Jack appeared to be.

"It's like sex with a condom," he told Jack one day as they walked through the park on their way back from a movie Amanda had had no interest in seeing. "It's better than nothing, but it doesn't feel the same."

"It's just that you're no virgin," Jack overextended the metaphor. "You know what it's like to wake up with the girl morning after morning, watch her turn to soap operas and donuts and trade in those tight jeans for sweat pants."

"Charming," Eddie said. "I don't know if I'd be madder if I thought you were talking about my novel or my wife."

"Neither of course. I hold Amanda and *Sea Miss* in the highest regard. I'm just trying to show you how absurd you're being. I doubt either of us will ever see Amanda don sweat pants—not unless the fashion mavens dictate it a must and then we know she'll look fantastic in them."

"You can stop right there." Eddie stopped walking as he said it, light snowflakes cooling tiny circles of his nose and cheeks. Those that touched the ground melted with the contact. Eddie didn't think the snow would stick.

"Sorry, just stating the obvious," Jackson said, still in motion.

"A particular talent of yours, it would seem."

By a coincidence that seemed nearly perverse, the three friends' publication dates were within a few weeks of each other. Jackson's and Amanda's were at the beginning of April. Eddie's book would be released later in the month, after the other two were off on their tours. So Amanda arranged an early celebration, reserving a good table in one of Grub's private rooms. Jackson asked Doreen to ensure they would have one of the restaurant's best servers, someone who would take good care of them.

"Promise not to even peek at the check," Amanda had instructed, and Eddie decided to obey. He ordered up and celebrated with those he had long thought of as his two favorite people.

Like many people who drink a lot, Eddie was generally

unhappy sober, in great spirits during his first and second drink, either extremely happy or getting edgy by the end of the third drink, and turning sour fast after that. On that night, he decided to let himself feel important—more important than Amanda and Jack because of the quality of his writing. He chose to believe that quality would lead him to a longer and more prestigious career than the splashier flash-in-the-pan stuff written by his companions. As if to bolster his temporarily inflated self-worth, Amanda and Jackson steered the conversation to less successful writers: not one but two of their fellow alumni had recently killed themselves over failed writing careers.

Jackson shrugged. "But one of them was a poet."

"Still have it in for poets?" Amanda asked.

"Until the day I die," Jackson said.

A group of poets at Iowa had abandoned a reading at the intermission—after a fellow poet had read, but before Jackson had taken the podium to give his first-ever public reading—and had then showed up at the after-party to feel each other up in the jacuzzi. Jackson had never forgiven them and chose to scorn all poets from that moment on.

Almost keeping pace with Eddie, Jackson drained the last of a bottle of champagne into his flute and called for the wine list. "How's Baffler holding up? Has he awakened to the smell of money and the bell of his publicist's voice?"

"I doubt it. He told me he was glad that *Bailiff* was being published but that he was through with the book. 'Once it's written, it's over for me.' That's what he said. And he's developed serious reservations about his theories, says New Realism may not be all he'd hoped."

"Still obsessed with that bleeding-edge girl? Clarice something?"

Amanda chimed in. "I think Henry's sweet, and we would all do well to begin thinking about our next books."

Unable to help himself, Eddie said, "I suppose that comment was for my benefit."

"Not at all." Amanda gave him a china-cold look. "I was chastising myself, if you must know. I think the ideal is to have the next book finished before the last one hits the stores. I wasted too much time this go round, but that's my plan from here on out."

Eddie worked on his fillet and horseradish mashed potatoes and had to admit that the food at Grub was nothing short of very good.

"Oh, I have news," Jackson said, tapping his water glass with his fork. "I'm appalled, of course, but happy for her. My former girlfriend cum former roommate has betrothed herself to Whelpdale."

Amanda laughed so hard she choked on her water.

"He became a regular customer here and apparently was quite smitten by her complete disinterest in all matters literary. He's going to marry her and put her through cooking school. She says he's the perfect eater."

"He's going to put her through cooking school with what?" said Amanda, now recovered from the skirmish with her water glass.

Jackson's bangs fell across his eyes as he shook his head, laughing. "I would have been annoyed if my own lot hadn't improved so much since the Blue Ridge Writers' Conference, but Whelpdale's non-writing writing career is going very well. He's making a lot of money as a 'manuscript doctor' and gets scores of referrals from an unscrupulous agent he's befriended. The agent hints to the authors of the lackluster novels that populate his slush pile that their work has real promise and that he might take them on with a bit of restructuring. He includes in these rejection letters a flyer touting Whelpdale's services. Great racket, no?"

"That's criminal," Eddie said, glad he wasn't one of the unfortunate souls.

"It would be," Jackson agreed, "if it preyed on anyone who wasn't completely lacking in both intelligence and talent. Anyway, Whelpdale's fishing deeper waters now. He read some book about getting rich by hanging out around rich people, and, sure enough, he found some wealthy literary-wannabe to finance a publication. He's calling it *ProProse*. Every story in the thing will be a contest winner, meaning he'll clean up with entry fees. It's like vanity publishing for the short story, but he's also including interviews with real writers and what amounts to a literary gossip column—who's publishing where, which prize judges are selecting their friends, that sort of thing. That will give the magazine some legitimacy and no doubt boost circulation."

"Not so unlike what Fadge has done with *The Monthly*," Eddie said and then wished he hadn't.

"Well, I've got to hand it to him," Amanda said quickly. "If he pays for Doreen's culinary training while removing some of those horrid stories from the desks of real journals, then maybe he's actually doing the world some good. Speaking of real journals, how's the Chekhov project coming along?"

"Speaking of literary gossip columns for the vain?" Jackson gave Eddie a pointed look, but smiled it away. "You're not going to believe this: I actually did receive a rejection that accused the story of being too Chekhovian and another suggesting that Anthony Chernesky would benefit from reading more Chekhov. Eighteen of the twenty journals rejected the story, and the rejections contradict each other all over the place. Not enough setting. Too much setting. Not character-driven. Flimsy plot. Of course, the form letters all say the same thing."

"What about the other two?"

"One journal still hasn't responded. The last—some tiny magazine I've never heard of that publishes out of some woman's house in Idaho—actually recognized the story. The editor sent a long letter about the evils of plagiarism but conceded that my choice was, at least, in good taste. She's the one person I'll allow to come off looking good in the piece I write."

They finished with Stilton and port, and Eddie experienced as a warm swell the satisfaction he'd been missing. At that moment, he felt right with the world because he again felt a part of it. He sipped just a little more port, listening to the sounds of conversation and eating from the open dining room behind him, and set his gaze on his lovely wife, who—flushed from her wine and softly lit—seemed to glow from within.

It was a few weeks later, after Amanda left on her tour, that the sourness arrived and lingered, helped along at regular intervals by whiskey and its morning-after aftermath. Eddie knew he was turning feral and promised himself a return to structured living as soon as

Amanda was back home. But for now, he needed to survive the four weeks alone. He told himself not to watch the calendar; instead he watched the clock.

At first twice a day and then giving way to hourly counts, Eddie checked the Amazon sales rankings of *The Progress of Love*, *Oink*, and *Conduct*. His book had not yet been officially published, so it was unsurprising albeit disappointing that his number was over a million while Amanda's and Jackson's ranked in the thousands, then hundreds.

Two weeks later, though, his book was in the stores and had been reviewed in a few places, including an in-brief review in *The Times*. He'd expected a full review, but any review in *The Times* was good. Beside, the in-brief reviews were almost always neutral or slightly positive, whereas the full reviews could be vicious, as Chuck Fadge had found out the hard way. The West Coast papers had ignored him so far, but *Conduct* had been reviewed in the Chicago, Philly, and Minneapolis papers. The reviews were guardedly mixed, but he hadn't been savaged. Most reviewers ended with some variant of "We'll look forward to seeing what the author of *Sea Miss* writes next" or by suggesting that any sophomore book by a talented writer is expected to be a tad disappointing, a small letdown between the charming debut and the break-out third book.

Still, Eddie's Amazon numbers hardly budged once publication pushed him into the high six figures. Occasionally, what he presumed was the sale of a single book spiked *Conduct* into five-figure territory, but it always dropped back into the hundreds of thousands within a few hours. Eddie's misery only increased, against his best efforts at magnanimity and high-mindedness, when Amanda and Jackson both entered bestselling territory: Amazon numbers under one hundred and reviews in *America Today*, not to mention everywhere else. His and hers bestsellers, Eddie thought, king and queen of the prom. What they wouldn't understand is that his sourness wasn't simple envy. He craved bigger reviews and higher sales—yes, it was true—but he didn't envy them authorship of their books. He did not want to be the person who had written *Oink*.

Amanda phoned in regularly with news of large crowds,

successful signings, radio interviews, wining and dining. "I'm going to be on national television!" she exclaimed into the receiver one night.

"It's three hours later here," Eddie said.

"Need that beauty rest?" she'd asked sharply.

"No," Eddie lied. "I've been getting up early. I'm working on a new book—something I'm really excited about, something that feels important."

"Fantastic," Amanda said, compounding his guilt with what sounded like genuine enthusiasm. "That's great! Now we can all be on TV."

"All?" Eddie asked, but she'd already signed off with a smooch sound that barely simulated a real kiss.

Eddie slept in the middle of the bed that night, clutching Amanda's lemony pillow, able to smell but not touch her. His sleep made shallow by the alcohol that wore off just after midnight and rendered him insomniac, he rearranged himself and the pillow, reviewing Amanda's words and telling himself that he would moderate his drinking as soon as she returned. At four he rose and did something that surprised him: he wrote a poem. It struck him as a good poem, though he knew it would be awful if read in the morning light. He pressed himself into a few more hours of sleep.

Shortly after he got up the next morning, he understood what Amanda had meant on the phone: she had one national morning show; Jackson, the other. In a moment of panic, Eddie pictured them both in Los Angeles, leaving their television studios, walking tan arm in tan arm to the beach. But, no, Jackson had been in a Chicago studio; only Amanda was in California. Still, Eddie wished that she'd invited him to go on tour with her and worried about what it meant that she hadn't. And it wasn't lost on him that his wife had known about Jackson's television appearance even though they were separated by numerous states. They'd been comparing notes, if nothing else.

Eddie poured himself his earliest drink to date. After he drained it, he poured more whiskey into a flask. Sensing that Henry Baffler might make him feel better about his life, he headed out and caught the subway to the 125th Street station.

# Chapter thirty-eight

Rather than riding all the way into Grand Central, Andrew Yarborough disembarked the commuter train at the 125$^{th}$ Street station. Most people he knew did not, and in fact would not, get off or on the train in Harlem no matter how many artists or former presidents set up lofts or offices in the neighborhood. And so he was surprised when he saw a familiar face on the platform. Andrew tried to place the young man but could not, and so was more relieved than irritated that the fellow strode past, looking too preoccupied by anger or dyspepsia to recognize the man of letters.

It was unlike Andrew to forget a name, but lately he had forgotten more than names. He'd missed more than one appointment and sometimes found himself standing in the market unable to remember what he had come to buy. Throughout his career, he'd often failed to meet deadlines due to procrastination or even malice, and many times he had *claimed* that a deadline had slipped his mind. But that had never actually been the case—not until this week, when he'd received a phone call asking for a book review he could not for the life of him remember agreeing to write. There on his desk sat the book—a meta-fictional detective story narrated by a deaf-mute pro-tagonist—but he couldn't remember how it had landed there.

It was this episode that had convinced him, finally, to see a doctor, which is how he came to be standing on 125th Street, buying a bag of boiled peanuts while fending off a vocal young woman hell bent on selling him a pair of ostentatious knock-off sunglasses.

He hailed a taxi with little trouble and closed the door as the woman screamed, "you rich fuck."

As he ascended in the Upper East Side elevator, he thought how ironic it was that he had just been called a rich fuck; he wished he had spent some of his earnings on better health insurance. During his hour in the plush waiting room he tried to ignore the other waiting patient: a drooling elderly man with blank eyes who was accompanied by a sad-looking, overweight daughter. To distract himself, he read the available magazines, including *The City* and some woman's maga-zine with an attractive redhead on the cover. Finally, grudgingly, he lifted *The Monthly* from a glass side table and felt his blood pressure rise as he saw Chuck Fadge's name on the masthead. He scanned the table of contents and saw Jackson Miller credited with a story about the travel destinations of well-known writers, as though any idiot couldn't figure out that the Amalfi coast was a nice place to be if you could afford to stay above the crowds. Perhaps, he thought, a faulty memory was more blessing than curse.

The doctor was small and bespectacled. His head was as smooth as an egg, unblemished by lines, pocks, or even, Andrew noticed with small alarm, eyebrows. Andrew completed the series of word games, picture-grams, and jigsaws with which the doctor tried to puzzle him. The man nodded and took notes with a small pencil, but his face was inscrutable.

"That all I'm getting for my money?" Andrew joked.

"Follow me."

The doctor led him through another door, which opened into what appeared to be a fully furnished, uninhabited apartment. Had it been a real residence, it would have rented by the month for tens of thousands of dollars. Andrew felt his anxiety grow: the doctor's bill was going to dwarf his wife's wardrobe budget.

The doctor handed him a hat, a ring of keys, and a book. "Pretend you've just arrived home. Put your things where you would if you lived here and then sit down to read."

"This is absurd."

"Perhaps, but like so many of life's absurdities, necessary."

Andrew placed the hat on a shelf and his keys in a drawer in the model kitchen, before sitting in a recliner with the book.

"Have you read it yet? My wife's book club loved it."

The doctor left, and Andrew soon found himself absorbed by a depiction of the sexual antics of the French court. It wasn't the kind of book he would ordinarily open, but the prose was competent and, despite himself, he was caught up in the romantic quandaries of the main character. He closed his eyes and conjured up the buxom Libertine in a tightly laced corset, batting her eyelashes at him and whispering provocations, practically begging to be spanked for her saucy behavior.

He woke up when the doctor opened the door. "All right, Mister Yarborough. Please collect your hat and keys and return to my office."

Andrew stood in the center of the faux apartment. He was sure he was in New York, but where and when he had no idea.

"Where am I? Where's Felice?" he asked, looking around for his college sweetheart, a lovely girl from Lyon.

"Do you remember where you put the keys, Mister Yarborough?"

Andrew looked helplessly around the room.

# Chapter thirty-nine

Henry Baffler settled happily into the Harlem apartment given to him, for a luxurious year, by the mysterious benefactor he still hoped might be J.D. Salinger. Though the size of the place made the possessions he'd acquired with the book advance seem all the more sparse, Henry believed that the airiness and light from the apartment's nine large windows would do wonders for his writing. He was formulating the idea of an open book. Though he had yet to discover precisely what 'open' meant, or how it would translate into a literary form, he was certain that he'd found his next direction.

His concern was that the hunger he had loathed for all the months it had taken him to compose *Bailiff* was actually a creative necessity. Now that his pantry was reasonably well stocked, he worried that he would lose his momentum, that his edges would be blunted, that he'd become soft and corn-fed, fit for little more than hacking out legal thrillers or sea adventures. It was good to be eating well, but he vowed to restrict his calories should he find his sentences growing flabby.

Such were his thoughts when his doorbell sounded for the first time since he'd moved in. Despite promises of visits, none of his acquaintances had trekked up to Harlem, not even when the Museo del Barrio hosted an exhibit of Rivera, Kahlo, and Seranno—an event that lured quite a few lower Manhattanites into higher street numbers than they tended to frequent.

Eddie's voice penetrated the intercom, and Henry buzzed him up.

Enjoying the novelty of having both a guest and something to serve him, Henry boiled water for tea and spiraled windmill cookies onto a plate. "I'm turning bourgeois," he said over his shoulder.

"Henry, there's no crime in a little caffeine and nourishment. You're not exactly pigging out like Balzac, and even his sharpest critic was known to eat, drink, smoke, and fuck." Eddie paused for Henry to catch the reference. "But for godsake don't start devoting whole paragraphs to describing the corners of your apartment and the slant of your blinds."

"Curtains," Henry said. "I don't have blinds. I have curtains."

"I was just making a Robbe-Grillet joke. What's this, The New Literalism?"

Henry laughed. "Never fear. Something else. Something, well, something open." He lifted his arms over his head, then spread them wide. "Yet contained," he added, pulling his arms closer a fraction of an inch.

"Open, yet contained." Eddie eyed him, then walked over to claim a cup of the tea and three biscuits. "Sounds tricky."

Henry felt a delicious panic. "Maybe," he called out, "maybe the solution lies in variation." He played Ravel's piano trio, one of his several new CDs, on the cheap, portable player he'd bought. He listened standing, eyes closed, mentally book-marking the different treatments of the seventh note. By the time Henry opened his eyes, Eddie had finished the cookies and drained his tea.

"Terribly sorry," Henry said.

"Don't sweat it," his friend smiled. "It's part of your charm, and it beats staring at the blank screen."

"I'm terribly sorry, but I've got a book to start."

"I came all the way up from Murray Hill," Eddie said. "I just got here."

Henry felt like a heel. "I appreciate it, I really do, and you can hang out if you want, but I need to work. You know how it is."

"I used to," Eddie said. "I remember feeling how you feel."

"Why don't you stay and hang out?" Henry asked, sensing that his friend was in some sort of writerly crisis, some version of what people mean by the generic term 'writers' block.' "I like the idea of working with someone else in the room. That's a neat idea actually: a series of stories all written with other people around. Could be very interesting to see the subtle effects of that, see if the presence of different sorts of people would influence tone and style."

"You're starting to sound like a poet," Eddie said, adding quickly, "which I mean as a compliment, not how Jack means it."

"What's your opinion of the word 'splay'?" Henry clamped a clean sheet of paper onto his typewriter and turned the canister, comforted by its familiar clicks. "Is that a word we can still use?"

# Chapter forty

It didn't take long for Jackson Miller to become accustomed not merely to success but to having his opinion solicited. While he had not enjoyed the travel itself, he had relished the long lines of people wanting his signature on *Oink*, the laughter his puns elicited, the attractive women who lingered at the end of the evening. Now that he was back home, it was a rare day when he wasn't contacted by a journalist or editor or nonprofit group asking for his thoughts on the new head of the National Endowment for the Arts, the quality of Adam Richards' radio book reviews, or, for that matter, the best sushi in New York or the political landscape in Afghanistan. National Public Radio interviewed him about his adventure submitting the Chekhov story, and, as he'd promised Amanda, he named the editors who'd not only failed to recognize but had deigned to criticize one of the finest short stories ever crafted.

After his triumphant book tour and swift rise up *The Times'* list of bestsellers, he increasingly associated with a circle of other writers—men in their thirties, all possessed of some version of Jackson's own name: Jack, Jake, Johnson, John, and Jonathan. These Jonathans often dined at Grub, in combinations of two or three, or occasionally the whole council. Jackson was gratified to observe that they were noticed, watched, eavesdropped upon.

Jackson had become who he'd planned to become on his ninth birthday—a vow he had renewed looking over the North Carolina mountains—and he never wanted to give it up. And so, with Amanda's encouragement, which was often flirtatious but sometimes quite strict, Jackson began in earnest to write about Meindert Hobbema's abandoned life of art. In mind of the small human forms the artist tucked into his landscapes, Jackson tentatively titled the new book *Hide and Seek*.

"Don't read too much, just the basics," Amanda had advised. "The important thing is to stack up some pages."

He wondered if Amanda was making him her project because she'd given up on Eddie ever being the great man she could be the great woman behind. He knew better than to vocalize this thought, and the truth was that he was glad for the extra guidance and motivation. Amanda wouldn't let him fail; he believed that.

Elegant variation was effortless work for Jackson, and, as always, the sentences came easily. He soon realized, though, that the sardonic tone that came to him more naturally than intentionally, and had worked so perfectly in *Oink*, was inappropriate for the new book. So he worked more conscientiously with his ideas, creating full-blown on the page the beautiful female main character for whom his artist-protagonist forsakes art for a desk job, and then used the events of his plot to blame her for the world's loss in paintings. Jackson presumed this was a much better story than Hobbema's actual biography. More than likely, the man had lacked artistic commitment from the get-go, was lazy, or had succumbed to the dull pressure of a new father-in-law or small-pursed uncle. Some people needed schedules dictated by others, or maybe the man hadn't really cared for the smell of paint. Whatever the historical truth was, Jackson penned a romantic tragedy, delivered with a droll cynicism moderated by empathetic diction.

After turning down several invitations because he was busy with the book and with the Jonathans, Jackson at last agreed to have dinner with Doreen and her abominable fiancé. He figured he owed it to Doreen, and Whelpdale's doings might provide fodder for an article and, possibly, a bit of amusement. Besides, even without formal training, Doreen was a great cook.

His former roommate did not disappoint: she served a first-rate Insalata Caprese, pepper-encrusted lamb shanks with a mint salsa, perfectly roasted potatoes and parsnips, and a simple custard-filled cake studded with pine nuts.

Jackson was struck by the genuine fondness Whelpdale exhibited for Doreen. He would quickly hoist up his large body whenever she approached or rose from the table.

"Southern upbringing," he said apologetically.

"It's charming," Jackson said, as he considered recovering his own manners. "But aren't you from Toledo?"

He briefly considered a column about the table habits and general levels of politeness of well-known authors—who's a gentleman at dinner and who's a real boor, that sort of thing—but dismissed it because it would likely get him in trouble with the Jonathans, one of whom had never encountered an entrée he didn't consider finger food, and another who guarded his plate with his forearm as though he'd spent long years in maximum-security lockup. Instead, he offered the idea to Whelpdale, who pulled a small stack of index cards and a pen from his inside coat pocket and jotted down a note.

"Yes," said the large young man, "it might be a good topic for my publication's 'Right Writing' column. I'll see if there's someone I can assign it to." He returned the cards and pen to his jacket pocket. "Say, Jackson, I don't suppose you'd be interested in writing for me?"

Doreen set down a forkful of lamb and watched Jackson, fearful, no doubt, that he'd say something rude. As she made eye contact with him he was overwhelmed by fraternal love for this gold-hearted girl.

"I'd love to, naturally," he said, "but my plate is full just now. So to speak, no pun intended. But I hear *ProProse* is a tremendous success."

Whelpdale's already formidable chest expanded as his posture straightened. "Well, I just hope that it's helpful. That's my mission in life: to help us poor sots who pick up the pen for our livelihood."

Jackson couldn't help himself. "So, you're still writing fiction? Got anything coming out?"

Whelpdale was not flapped. "You know me; I've always got my irons in the fire."

"Caff or decaff with dessert?" Doreen injected into the small pause. "And I hope you both left room."

"Leaded," Whelpdale said. "I don't plan to retire early, and I always have room for your desserts."

Pushing away the appalling thought of Whelpdale coupling with the pretty Doreen, Jackson asked him if he'd read Henry Baffler's book.

"A work of genius," Whelpdale exclaimed. "It's wonderful."

"Can I borrow it?" Doreen asked.

Whelpdale shook his head.

"You're right," Jackson said. "Poor Henry needs every sale he can get. I'm not going to loan mine out either."

"Oh, it's not that," Whelpdale said quickly. "It's just not the sort of thing Doreen would like reading."

"Surely you don't imagine me so feeble-minded that I'm capable of reading only beach novels and chick lit? If it's a work of genius, I should read it."

"Of course not. You have a perfect mind! It's just that by work of genius, I meant that it's impenetrable. Literally almost nothing happens in four hundred pages. And I can't stand the thought of you associated with what Baffler calls the ignobly decent—not even on the page."

Despite Whelpdale's blatant flattery and the affectation of his manners and gestures—he's no more a gentleman than I am, Jackson thought—his tone evinced sincere affection for Doreen.

"I'm afraid," Jackson said, "that the reviewers are with you there."

"Except for the anonymous reviewer in *The Monthly*," Whelpdale said.

Jackson wondered if Whelpdale knew that it was he who had written the review. He hoped not. Real charity is anonymous, but, more important, Jackson wanted Henry to believe a neutral reviewer had really admired and tried to understand *Bailiff*. "Yes," he said, "now *that* fellow understood the literary importance of what our friend is up to."

"Or else," said Whelpdale slyly, "he's good to his friends."

"Let's hope the occasional good deed goes unpunished," Jackson said, filling his mouth with pastry.

# Chapter forty-one

Between her uncertainty about her feelings toward Jackson and her trepidation in the face of pending reviews, Margot Yarborough couldn't say she was happy. No matter which angle she came at the problem of Jackson from, she could not commit to the idea of a future with him. But neither could she determine to give him up.

She decided to take some sort of action about the review journals though, and made a study of their respective styles in order to armor herself. Her editor had been right: about half of the *Circus* reviews were downright spiteful, and the other half, possibly written by friends of authors or publicists, were kind enough but said next to nothing. *The Monthly* rarely offered blanket praise or condemnation and, in fact, often said little about the book supposedly under the microscope, instead using the review to launch a more general discussion of some literary passion or pet peeve. *The Times* was fairly even-handed. It seemed to save its harsh reviews for well-known writers with disappointing new books while reviewing only those debuts that it could praise.

There was a glaring exception to this generality, though. *The Times* had eviscerated a new book by a first-time author named Henry

Baffler. Its comments nauseated Margot: "Let Mr. Baffler remember that a novelist's first responsibility is to tell a story"; "A reader must want to finish reading the book"; "A pretentious book guilty of the intentional fallacy. Just because one writes about ennui does not mean one should induce it in the reader"; "Here is another of those intolerable objects that prove the sheer wrong-headedness of what Baffler would have us call the New Realism. This book is never interesting, never profitable, never insightful, and hardly ever readable." The reviewer paraphrased Mickey Spillane's assertion that no one ever reads a book to get to the middle.

Another publication that had reviewed Baffler's novel included the sensational story of the young author rescuing his book from flames, noting that it was the news coverage of the rescue that had led to its publication. "We can only wish," the piece concluded, "that the fire had consumed the manuscript rather than spitting it out into the world." Others had their fun with Henry's name, as though describing his book or its publication as baffling was the height of original wordplay.

Feeling devastated for the poor fellow who had written the book, Margot vowed to buy a copy, read it, and write a fan letter to Henry Baffler.

That night she dreamed she was naked in a room, surrounded by crumpled sheets of paper: all viciously negative reviews of *Pontchartrain*. "It's not my title!" she tried to scream, choked by newsprint. "They made me call it that!"

But the reviewers were much kinder to Margot than they had been to the unfortunate Henry Baffler. A half-page review in *The Times*, no less, argued that her novel was a brilliant pastiche of the eighteenth-century American naturalist novel and applauded Margot's satirical use of the present tense as the cleverest of anachronisms.

Upon her initial read of the review, Margot smiled, nervous but pleased. Lane and Lana both called her, effusive with their congratulations. Yet after successive readings of the review—three and then four—Margot was seized by self-doubt, by the fear of being uncovered as a poser, an imposter. Margot knew that her book was not so much a pastiche as written in the tradition of—even in imitation of—the old-fashioned novels she loved. She had chosen the present tense not as an act of subversive genius but simply because it made the book, with its cumbersome back story, easier to write. It had allowed her to write the lengthy flashbacks in simple past tense, thereby avoiding all those messy participles.

Margot's lack of confidence in her own good fortune was soon validated. One Friday, exactly a week before her regional book tour was to commence, Lane phoned.

"There's nothing to worry about," her editor said. "But one of the large chain stores—I won't say which one—says it over-ordered first fiction for the spring. They're cutting quite a few books, and unfortunately yours is one of them."

"Why mine?"

"Capricious, arbitrary decision on their part. Maybe it's the southern setting, or maybe some buyer doesn't like the name Margot."

"Is it an unpopular name?" Margot asked, trying to understand what the conversation meant.

"It's a lovely name. I'm just saying that you can't take it personally." Lane paused, then went on when Margot didn't say anything. "I won't pretend it's not bad news. At least one copy of your book was slated to go to every one of their stores, and they'd ordered half a dozen copies for a good number of stores in the south and some larger cities."

"How many are they taking now? Will it still be in most stores?"

"Darling, you don't understand. They cut your title."

"Cut?"

"They aren't ordering any."

"But the review in *The Times* was so good."

"All of your reviews have glowed, and that's wonderful. It's not only wonderful, it's deserved. If only reviews translated into sales, you'd be a wealthy young woman, but that's just not the case any longer."

"People don't want to read good books?"

Margot realized how naïve she sounded, but she couldn't

believe that her good reviews—however much she doubted their wisdom—didn't mean anything.

"Don't worry; all is not lost. We're still sending you to Vermont next week, and Renate booked you into the fiction series at the CIA Bar. You'll be reading before someone named Clarice Aames. She doesn't have a book out yet, but she's gathered quite a following. The turnout should be great."

Margot had been to a reading at the CIA once, and her stomach shifted at the idea of reading to a large, inebriated crowd.

"I believe in your book. The indies are going to hand-sell, and word will get out."

After she put the phone down, Margot continued what she'd been doing: heating tomato soup and melting butter in a skillet to grill a cheese sandwich. But when she sat down with the meal that had constituted her winter comfort food since childhood, her appetite was gone. She chided herself for being disappointed by expectations she had never held. It's not as though she'd ever thought she was writing a bestseller; she was happy just to be publishing a book and garnering a few readers and reviews. It was still a dream come true. Pushing away the image of books stacked high in large, well-lit bookstores, she dipped a corner of sandwich into the scarlet soup.

# Chapter forty-two

Amanda Yule's novel parked on every bestseller list in the country. It was hailed as a literary crossover book—a book club favorite praised by critics for the magic realist elements that so captured the mood of the paintings on which it was based. At the same time, Amanda's alternative career as Clarice Aames soared, with more stories published and more websites devoted to her work appearing online.

Amanda kept a color-coded calendar, using blue to mark her publicity appearances for *The Progress of Love* and red for Clarice Aames's readings. Her even script crowded the calendar, blurring into purple. When Amanda was scheduled for a television appearance in Los Angeles, Clarice gave a surprise reading at an Orange County community college. When Amanda signed books at A Clean Well-Lighted Place for Books, Clarice read at an art bar in Oakland. When Amanda appeared in Denver or Minneapolis, Clarice showed up in Boulder or St. Paul. They drew different constituencies, and no one picked up on the pattern. Yet Amanda was careful to keep her two authorial identities distinct, and Clarice always appeared in disguise—a face powdered white, too much black eyeliner, and a long black wig with bangs covering her forehead. Amanda also limited Clarice's appearances in New York, though she had finally succumbed to pressure and vanity, agreeing to appear at the CIA Bar.

Her biggest problem in maintaining her double identity was her husband, who asked detailed questions about her itineraries and hotel room changes. In the spring, when she changed her drink of choice from red wine to white and from Irish whiskey with a splash of soda to a salty dog, Eddie grilled her. They'd once figured out that a friend of theirs was having an affair with their professor because the friend, out of the blue, had started ordering Makers Mark. And she'd heard of a man whose infidelity was discovered after he acquired his mistress's mispronunciation of the word *macadam*, a verbal tick whose origin was not lost on his wife. Amanda confronted Eddie one morning as he was busy not-writing. "You think I'm having an affair."

He stayed hunched over his computer, eyes on the blank screen. "Are you?"

"No," said Amanda, "I'm not. You have no appreciation for how hard I am working. And despite all the publicity and phone calls for quotes and travel, I'm a lot further along on my new book than you are."

"That's a cruel thing to say."

"The truth hurts."

Eddie pushed out his chair and swiveled sideways. "You're really not seeing someone else?"

"Not yet." She softened even as she said it. "Really, Eddie, I'm not having an affair. It's all work. And I always change my drinks with the weather, you know that."

Amanda came close to telling Eddie about her black-wearing alter ego, but she stopped herself. She could not articulate why—she wasn't sure whether she was trying to protect herself or Eddie or perhaps even Clarice—but she didn't want him to know. It was a secret she wanted to hold close, a marvelous thing that was all her own and didn't have to be shared. Some people, she knew, only enjoyed good things—from sexual relationships to compliments at work—if and when they could tell someone else. She wasn't like that, and she wondered if it meant she was self-sufficient or that there was something askew about her, something related to her childhood, that made her comfortable with complete privacy.

"And now I must get back to work." She paused, spinning Eddie's chair back toward his computer. "Perhaps you'd feel better if you did the same."

For the next four hours, Amanda typed away on her new book: an increasingly autobiographical novel about a pretty young girl reared in poverty who marries an aspiring writing whose star seems to be rising.

As she was taking a break to fix dinner, Henry Baffler phoned.

"How's Harlem?" Amanda asked.

"I like having an apartment, but I hope it won't corrupt my work."

Amanda laughed: at least she hadn't married Henry. "Impossible," she said. "And Henry, I want you to know how much we love *Bailiff*. It's terrific." She eyed the book on the coffee table, vowing to move the bookmark further along before Henry's next visit. Perhaps she could memorize a few key lines and make him think she'd studied the whole thing.

"Thank you, Amanda." Henry sounded moved. "That means a lot to me. A lot."

She noticed that he said nothing about her book. Maybe he couldn't afford it, and she knew it was tough to borrow—all the public libraries had waiting lists.

"I just found out that one of the best writers in the country will be reading at the CIA Bar. Clarice Aames. I thought you and Eddie might want to go hear her."

"Terrific." Amanda thought quickly. "When is it?"

When he told her the date, she said, "Rats, I'm going to be out of town."

"That's a shame. It's really amazing what she does with non-realism. I'm rethinking my whole aesthetic. I already got tickets. Maybe Jackson will want to go with me and Eddie."

Amanda realized that she was going to have to improve her

disguise or, perhaps, cancel the event. Maybe Clarice should only make surprise, unadvertised appearances in New York.

"Amanda, can I ask you something?"

"Of course."

"The word *copse*. How many times can it be used in one book?"

"Once every hundred pages," she said without hesitation.

"Yes, I think that's the right answer." He paused, then asked, "What about *splay*?"

"Just once," Amanda said.

"Even in a very long book?"

"Yes," Amanda answered with the confidence of the popular. "Just once per book."

"Damn it all to hell!" Henry exclaimed before apologizing. "Of course you're right. It's just that I was hoping to use it a few times. I'm writing an open book."

"I almost understand what that might mean, and I certainly look forward to reading it."

"Goodbye, Amanda."

"Nice chatting with you, Henry."

She dropped the receiver into its cradle, knowing she should cancel Clarice's appearance but already imagining how it would feel to have her friends there listening to her read, even her husband, none of them guessing her secret.

# Chapter forty-three

Jackson Miller strode across the room and opened the door to Margot's light knock.

"Let me take that." He shook water droplets from her dark umbrella and slid it into the frog-shaped holder that Doreen had given him as a housewarming present.

As Margot arranged her short curls with her fingers, Jackson was smitten all over again by the elegant shape of her head, her lithe arms, her slender waist.

"Your apartment is beautiful," she said.

"Albeit still nearly empty." He gestured to his first piece of real furniture: a lone leather sofa.

"So," she asked after she'd perched on the sofa. "How are your friends the Renfroses?"

Jackson felt peculiar for having told Margot about his friends, about having linked the two spheres of his life, yet he valued her opinion—not necessarily as one he would follow but as one to consider as the most ethical if not the most practical route. That was one role Margot could play in his life: the voice of duty, of how he should act.

"Well, they're certainly happier now that they have more money," he said. "Amanda wasn't cut out to be the supportive wife of a struggling novelist."

"You don't have a very high opinion of her?" Margot looked quizzical.

"On the contrary. And even the fact that Eddie and I quarreled over her hasn't changed that."

"Quarreled over her?" Margot held her voice steady, but it was tight, and Jackson recognized concern, perhaps jealousy.

"It's nothing really. It's that Eddie—before his book sold, mind you—blamed me in part for Amanda's unhappiness with him."

Margot did not speak and did not lift her eyes.

"It's funny really. My fault was supposed to have been glorifying worldly success and so contributing to Amanda's discontent with their lot. Ridiculous, no?"

Margot nodded.

"The thing of it was that Eddie was as serious as a boat taking on water with no way to bail it out."

Again she nodded, giving away nothing but earnestness in her expression. "But you don't think your talk had a negative effect?"

"Who knows? I certainly didn't mean it to."

"Well," said Margot, "if it did, then Amanda can't be very strong minded."

"You mean if she was influenced by so insignificant a fellow as me?" Jackson smiled, touched her damp hair.

But Margot didn't take his flirtatious bait. "To be influenced by anyone in such a way, to accept someone else's values as her own," she said.

"You think the worse of me now?" Jackson pictured the conversation as something solid, slipping into a place both unknown and unpleasant and himself helpless to right it.

"Of course not, but I don't quite understand it. What was the tone of your conversation with her?" Margot's tone was matter-of-fact, but she folded her arms.

"Same as always. You've heard me say it before. Unless you're a genius, then the goal of writing is to make money and gain a reputation. If that's scandalous, I'm sorry." He paused, at once hurt and rankled at Margot's response to what he'd brought up only in passing. "It's possible that Amanda was a little too vigorous in agreeing with me. She saw that in my case my writing was leading to solid results at the same time that she was frustrated with Eddie for not working so practically."

"That's a shame." Her head tilted, she stared across the room.

"You think it's my fault?" He heard his own tone tightening, as though the key to his vocal chords had been turned by an unsympathetic hand. He didn't understand why Margot, who had always seemed supportive, even adoring, was now critical. It's not like he hadn't been up front about who and what he was.

"I'm sure you were only speaking in your natural way and didn't mean to cause your friend trouble. I think you're probably a very good friend so long as it doesn't inconvenience you. Didn't you once tell me something like that?"

Jackson pushed back in his seat, thinking that he'd been too open with Margot. She'd always been so agreeable, so anxious to please him, that he'd assumed he could be frank with her. Before, he had only to speak when he wanted assurance of her devotion. Now she seemed changed, seemed much more self-possessed, even aloof.

"You have doubts about me? Because I recognize the necessity of making money at writing in order to keep writing?"

"You resign yourself quite happily to the necessity."

Her gaze felt more clinical than adoring as he searched her face, looking for the sweet, insecure girl who could barely pump her own gas.

"You would rather have me bemoan my fate in not being able to devote my life to nobly unremunerative work?"

"That you never do does give me pause," she said, "but I don't mean to be harsh."

"I suppose you think I don't care about the quality of my work, or that I'm not capable of writing literature?"

A small smile clung to Margot's lips and she fiddled with her hands, small in her lap.

"I know that some people don't have a high opinion of me,

but I don't want you to be one of them. You're one of the few people whose opinion of me matters. Do you think I'm even capable of generous feelings?"

"Of course. There aren't many people who aren't *capable* of generous feelings." She met his gaze, her small chin lifted with a defiance he had not noticed before.

"Well, that's good news. I'm a rung up from the lowest of the low." Jackson's disbelief in Margot's changed demeanor gave ground to his rising anger. "Tell me this, then: what do you think of my book?"

"You already know that I like your book."

"Well that's a relief. You like my book and don't think I'm headed straight for hell. High praise from the author of *Pontchartrain*, who would never let worldly ambitions enter her gemlike sentences."

He regretted his line as soon as he saw her chin lower and her eyes go gauzy. She got up and moved toward the door unsteadily, like a bird with a wing injury, and tried to rescue her umbrella, which was caught on the others.

"I'm sorry, Margot."

"If I need someone to make fun of my book, there's no reason for me to leave the house."

"It hurts, doesn't it? Having someone you care about disrespect your work."

"Oh, just forget it." She gave up on trying to disentangle the umbrella and grabbed the doorknob.

"If you insist on running away, let me at least help you with that." He took the umbrella's handle and worked to untangle its spokes.

"Like I care about a little rain when my whole life is falling apart."

"You consider me your whole life?" Jackson asked, softening to her small presence.

"Of course not." She yelled at him for the first time. "It's my book. And my father. And, yes, you. I came here for comfort, but it seems that I can never say the right thing to you."

"I'm sorry, here, come sit."

"First, one question. Are you in love with me?"

"Oh, Margot, you know I'm crazy for you. You're pretty and good and talented and sweet."

"Are you in love with me?"

He held his forehead. "Margot, I don't even know what it means to be in love. You find me an accurate definition, and I'll let you know if that's what I feel. But I do know that if it's in my power to make you happy, I'd like to. You deserve to be happy."

"Deserve? I don't want you to be with me as some kind of reward for good behavior. Do you love me?"

Whether out of perverseness or the belief that he was doing her a favor—most likely from a jumbled combination of these motives—he merely shrugged.

"But I guess that's not a fair question, is it?" she said, looking down, her voice dropping. "Because the real problem is that I don't love you."

Leaving her broken umbrella in the joke of a frog stand, she pushed out of his apartment and into the rainy city. From his window, Jackson watched her make her way through the heavy storm, running in spurts from tree to tree, awning to awning, getting completely drenched.

"Yes," he said to his streaming window pane. "I do love you. God, I do love you."

But he understood now that she didn't love him, and his ego wanted to resist that knowledge. Already he was altering the memory of what his relationship with Margot had been, protecting himself with the story of a match not fated, of his generous concern for a girl who was better off without him.

Late that night, sulking in a deep rut, yet warm with good single malt, he wrote his farewell email:

Allow me to help you remember me with indifference. Remember me as a man who was reckless with the affections of a fine and pretty girl, a man who wanted to make himself proud among fools and idiots. Remember, too, that you are the one who broke things off with me—and wisely so. I have always been too much at the mercy of vulgar ambition to make any kind-hearted girl happy. Soon you would have despised me thoroughly, and, even though I would have known that I deserved your disapproval, I would have revolted against it. It's the kind of man I am. I'm sending you a new umbrella, and it will be my loss, not yours, that I will never share it with you.

There was no quick reply from Annandale-on-Hudson, and Jackson fell asleep telling himself this new story of failed love.

# Chapter forty-four

It was like a sore Eddie Renfros couldn't resist picking. But at least he set limits: Amazon checks no more than twice per hour, internet review searches no more than twice per day, and attempts to infiltrate his wife's email accounts—she seemed to keep several—only when he knew she was out of town or, at a minimum, out of the apartment for at least several hours. He came to see the latter as a test: if he couldn't crack her password, how well could he claim to know her? He was certain that Amanda was the sort of person who would choose her own password as she determined her own life; she would never accept a random combination of letters issued by someone else.

He had tried various combinations of her name (first, last, married, maiden, middle) and important dates. He'd tried his own name and, in one of his most pathetic moments, Jackson's, as well as the name of the professor he was sure she'd slept with at Iowa. He'd tried various words associated with her novel, including anagrams of its title, the name *Fragonard*, and the word *Frick*.

Frick had come to him in the middle of the night and seemed so perfect that it was difficult to wait for his wife to leave the house so that he could try it. It was so very Amanda in its bridging of high and low, its innocently crude innuendo, that he was stunned to receive the "incorrect password/please retype your password" message in the annoying red triangle.

This was one of the ways he passed the time in which he was supposed to be writing. He had alternatives: he had taken up baking and computer solitaire and was doing his utmost to keep up his prodigious and growing tolerance for alcohol in several of its varieties. In response to the expanding waistline that accompanied his increased consumption of homemade baked goods and cocktails, he assigned himself a hundred crunches and two longs walks daily. He was much less likely to give himself permission to forego the crunches than the page-a-day minimum he had also set for himself. A long paragraph covering the better part of a page could easily be rounded up, and sometimes a single sentence could be considered a good day's work if it promised momentum for the next day. And, of course, sometimes Eddie wrote nothing at all.

"How can I be expected to write a book I wouldn't want to read?" he had asked when Henry Baffler called to confirm their plans to see Clarice Aames at the CIA Bar.

"Do you think that matters?" Henry had asked. "If it's a book you really want to write, does it matter if anyone wants to read it?"

So Eddie had begun to ponder the meaning of writing a book he wouldn't want to read. He'd written one already, but not on purpose. *Conduct* hadn't been the book he'd hoped, but it wasn't a book he'd hurl into the fireplace. Now he imagined following his wife's advice: he would write just the sort of novel he always cursed for its very popularity.

After checking the Amazon ranking numbers for his book, Jackson's, and Amanda's one more time, he ordered a copy of Whelpdale's *How to Write a Novel*. He perused the "customers who bought this title also bought" list and added to his shopping cart *Give the People What They Want*, *How to Write a Damn Good Book*, and *Scribble Yourself to Wealth*. Maybe he'd gather the wisdom in these jewels and hack out a bestseller. Probably not—he wasn't that desperate yet—but it was important to know what the enemy was up to.

He shut down his computer and contemplated the liquor cabinet, wondering how much Irish whiskey he'd have to drink to actually vomit.

*Chapter forty-five*

Margot Yarborough drove her mother's sedan upstate toward the first reading of her author tour, skirting the Adirondacks as the area awakened to economic life after a winter's hibernation. The car's CD folder contained a large selection of non-classical instrumental music and assorted people singing or chanting in Gaelic, Native American languages, Vietnamese, Tibetan, Butanese, and Hungarian. There was not a single English-language lyric in the lot, and Margot decided that it might be a good thing that her drive would not be intruded upon by other people's words—at least not by any that she could understand.

She could be alone with thoughts, could figure out what had happened with Jackson. The story she wanted to tell herself was that she was nursing a broken heart and it would make her a real writer, would infuse her future work with depth of feeling, with pain. But it wasn't true. She hadn't loved Jackson, though she'd wanted to and he'd wanted her to. For whatever reason, he'd convinced himself that she could give him some form of authenticity, that she could make him a better person, a more serious writer. That meant, of course, that he'd idealized her, saw in her something that wasn't there. When she asked herself why she hadn't been able to fall in love with Jackson, she had no answer, and worried that she was missing some capacity she was supposed to have. She hadn't been in love with the guitar player either. She'd never really been in love, unless she could count the overwhelming crush she'd had on her eleventh-grade literature teacher, which she knew she couldn't. She always wound up with boy-friends she liked. Maybe that was supposed to be enough—maybe that's what people called love—but her definitions of love came from novels, and real-life had never come close.

At Keeseville, the snow-cone stand was still locked up. A wooden shingle hanging over the road to the boat that Margot had assumed would ferry her across Lake Champlain read "CLOSED FOR SEASON." If she headed back south and went around, she'd likely be late for her reading in Burlington. If she soldiered on, she might be able to catch the northernmost ferry, which the map indicated led to an island in the middle of the lake, from which there was a bridge to the Vermont side. But if that ferry wasn't operating, she'd have to double back or cross into Canada, circumvent the lake, and reenter the country at the Vermont border-crossing.

Despite her predicament, what Margot felt was resignation more than anxiety. She'd come to expect that anything pertaining to her book would not go her way. Her decision to forge ahead was based on a single criterion: she didn't like the idea of turning back the way she'd come. She pointed the car toward Plattsburgh and continued to the northernmost portion of New York. Wind pushed at the car, and the sky grayed as French appeared more frequently on the road signs.

She took the last U.S. exit and followed the narrow road as it curved around the lake's flank. She imagined living on its banks, in one of the houses that somehow stood against odds and sense and against the relentless wind. The idea of living somewhere remote and even harsh had always appealed to Margot—it was a notion that had helped her infuse her Louisiana setting with romance—but she'd always imagined her life as a hermit in a warm climate—desert rather than arctic harshness. Now, though, questioning the substance of her heart and feeling mostly alone in the world, the idea of holing up on some bitterly cold lake and writing about its hardy inhabitants had its appeal. She wondered how one might write about a group of people who rarely interact with each other, picturing each person segregated in his or her own chapter, each chapter like a closed house.

Given her state of mind, she was surprised to find the ferry in service and further surprised to get a space on it, even though she was last in a line of what looked to be more cars than would fit. Perhaps this was a sign that her luck would change if she lived in such a place, a place where men didn't throw themselves away on the world. As she rode the ferry, Margot tried to reconstruct Eudora Welty's story of a man and woman who meet at a luncheon in New Orleans and drive practically off the map. There was a ferry ride in that story, she was sure of it, but she remembered only the lush language—and the fact that the two characters failed to ever really connect, departed without knowing one another, and yet were profoundly changed. She wondered if she had changed Jackson, and how she might now be different for knowing him.

Margot had no time to shower, but she made her reading. Like the rest of Burlington, the bookstore sat on a steep hill that rose from the lake and was battered by its cold wind. She was at once disappointed and relieved to find an audience of only six. An elderly man punctuated her reading with demands that she speak more loudly, but otherwise, the reading went well. Three of the six people bought her book and asked her to sign it. She'd practiced her signature, developing a more interesting capital 'M', and a 'Y' with some flourish, but she was stumped by what to write in the books. In two she wrote "with appreciation," and in the other she simply wrote the location and date under her signature. She was then left alone with the hard-of-hearing man, who thrust a manuscript into her hands.

"Politics and poetry," he said, running an index finger over an eyebrow grown long. "Combined. Show it to your editor and then I'll call her."

Margot smiled what she hoped was a kind smile. "I wish I had that kind of clout, but I don't. And my editor doesn't handle poetry."

"But it's politics, too. She'll love it."

Margot shook her head. "I'm really not the person to help you, and I'd hate for you to waste a copy. You should get one of those writer's market books and query some agents who handle your sort of book."

"Oh, they never write back!" the man growled at her. "Look, I drove for two hours and I listened to your reading—you need to learn to speak up—just to give this to you to give to your editor. Take it."

"But how would I get it back to you?"

"You won't need to, because you're going to get it published." He poked her repeatedly with the shaggy manuscript. "Take it. Take it."

At last, the bookstore owner rescued her by telling the man the shop was closing.

"You probably want dinner," the middle-aged woman said to Margot as she let her out on the street. "You might try the Mexican place right up the street. Or if your publisher's paying, there's a good restaurant at the cooking school. Expensive, though. Really nice reading, by the way. Really nice." And with that, the woman let the glass door fall heavily between them, leaving Margot on the frigid street gripping hundreds of pages of the old man's poems and musings.

She'd heard a story once, about a writer who had violently destroyed a manuscript sent to him by an unwanted admirer. She couldn't remember who the writer was—maybe Richard Ford or Denis Johnson or Jonathan Warbury—but she could picture the image of him leaping up and down, gorilla-like, on the offending stack of pages and then jumping in the dumpster after it to finish the job. She walked to the public trash can in the center of the block, but once she got there, she found she just couldn't drop the manuscript. Maybe her father would get a kick out of it, or at least she'd mail it back to the man, being sure to leave off her return address.

After Burlington, the so-called book tour got worse, and Margot could feel something sour expand in her stomach with every stop. In Montpelier, she read to an audience of two: both bookstore employees who had been called in on their day off under threat of dismissal. In Stockbridge, she read to an audience of one: a very tall woman who, unlike most Vermonters, wore a full face of makeup. Margot offered to skip the reading and instead take the woman to coffee and discuss the book.

"I like readings." The woman folded her arms. "The flyer said it would be a reading. I'm here for a reading. Read."

When Margot halted after twenty minutes, the woman said, "More. A reading is supposed to be at least thirty minutes. I want you to read for thirty or forty minutes. That's what a reading is."

At a small college in Rutland, her reading got off to a more auspicious start. It was held in a room that looked like a chapel, and the audience grew to more than a handful, then to over a dozen. The setting sun shone through a round stained-glass window and washed Margot in red and blue light. Though exhausted, she read well, and it seemed that the jewel-colored light lent extra depth to her sentences.

At the reception after the reading, a buxom redhead with a tilted glass of wine cornered her. "It must be awesome to be a writer. I think it would be really cool." The girl guzzled the wine, getting most but not all of her gulp in her mouth and wiping away the rest with the back of her hand. "I've got three books in my head. All I've got to do is write them down."

"That's the hard part." Margot heard something new and sharp in her voice.

The young woman shrugged and said, "Maybe next summer."

Margot arrived in Shaftsbury to find that the bookstore that invited her had gone out of business the day before. Its glass door was papered over—blank white except for a sign reading, "Sorry, but you'll have to buy your books online like everyone else."

In Bennington, Margot was again handed a manuscript at the end of her reading, this time by a young man who claimed to have been a leper in Louisiana in one of his past lives.

"But my book is about a different life," he explained. "It's about one of my female lives. I was Louis the Fourteenth's lover for twenty years."

"My editor is handling less and less fiction," Margot explained.

"It's non-fiction," said the young man. "I know that memoir is where the money is these days."

By the time Margot crossed the southern state line into Massachusetts, she was glad to be leaving her book tour behind. She drove through the Berkshires exhausted but proud of herself for surviving the appearances. What had been demoralizing—the slow death of her first novel—had turned comic. And she was pleased to observe that she thought of Jackson less and less. Let him have his fame, she thought, because that's what he wants.

Fame wasn't what she wanted. What she wanted was to rise after ten straight hours of sleep in her own bed and write a short story while sipping a hot cup of tea. That, and to hand off to her father the manuscript by the old man with the horrible eyebrows, so she didn't have to look at it anymore.

# Chapter forty-six

Andrew Yarborough did not divulge the details of the doctor's diagnosis to his wife or daughter. Knowing that he would have to depend upon them for money as well as any kindness, that he would all too soon be reduced to playing with teddy bears, his dignity subject to their mercy, he could not bring himself to treat them with anything but disdain. While secretly hoping for its financial success, he continued to deride Janelle's launch of a line of New Age gift books. Each book was only three-by-four inches large and contained a short story illustrating some dumb-ass Buddhist or Taoist saying. They had names such as *Be Here Now*, *Light a Lamp for Another*, *The Strongest Man*, *One Moon/Many Pools*, and *What You Already Have*.

"You'd be better off selling hypochondriacs those hypoallergenic blankets," he said. "Those jacket colors are appalling. And if you're going to hand out inane advice, give the people what they already know. You know: *This is the First Day of the Rest of your Life* and *Nothing Tastes as Good as Thin Feels*. People want to be told what they already think. First rule of publishing."

"That's half the point of *Being Unto Yourself*," Janelle said in her pseudo-benevolent voice. "Besides, sometimes the strongest man is invisible and when you light a lamp for another, your own path is lit."

Stricken by the idea that all speech would eventually sound as incomprehensible to him as his wife's mumbo jumbo, Andrew screamed.

When his daughter returned with horror stories from her book tour, he was unable to muster more than a few versions of I told you so. If only she'd have started up the journal, they could have worked together as father and daughter. He would have had a chance to make one more mark before descending into his pathetic future. But now he could only view his daughter with the loathing of the dependent. It would be she, he knew, who would wipe the drool from his chin and change his soiled linens. For a man who valued dignity above most things, it was too awful to think about.

A few weeks after her return, Andrew found Margot crying at the kitchen table.

"Forget him," he said. "What kind of man wears those sweaters anyway?"

Margot shook her head. "I don't cry over Jackson. It's this obituary." She lifted a finger toward the paper she had pushed away. "You remember Hinks?"

"Hinks is dead?"

His daughter nodded. "By his own hand."

"Jesus! That's awful." Andrew picked up the phone and called Quarmbey.

His friend confirmed the news. "And what's really horrible is that he did it for literature."

"How do you mean?" Andrew asked.

"Before he shot himself, he wrote me a letter saying that he couldn't get his novel published. He'd read about that kid who sold that godawful novel about a bailiff based on the publicity he got for risking his life to save the manuscript from a fire. And he talked about how John Kennedy Toole's suicide helped get *Confederacy of Dunces* sold. His letter said that he was killing himself so that *The Great Adirondack Novel* would find a wide readership."

"Jesus," Andrew said, this time in a whisper, remembering poor Hinks with his turtle shape and solidly crafted short stories.

"I've asked a couple of the editors I know to take another look at the book now."

"Then maybe his suicide wasn't such a bad idea. Maybe it will work."

After he hung up, Andrew sat in his yard, smoking a cigar and watching the Hudson drowse its way downriver. Even as he pondered suicide as a solution to his own problems, he knew he'd never do it.

# Chapter forty-seven

Sipping Grub's fennel bisque from an absurdly large spoon, Jackson Miller listened to his agent for ten minutes without interjecting. While Suzanne spoke her predictable words, he analyzed her face, trying to guess her age from the depth of the horizontal lines across her forehead. Passing for thirty, he figured, but pushing forty in a business that was increasingly controlled by the young. Her long silver-and-blue earrings shimmied as she spoke, and she drank water before swallowing the food in her mouth.

Finally she concluded her lecture: "It's a dangerous game you're playing."

"I'm not going on the show," he said, reaffirming his decision to decline an appearance on the country's most popular talk show.

"Publicity is a good thing, Jackson."

He waited for the server to clear their first course and scrape the bread crumbs from the table with a silver level. "The book is number two in the country. I don't have to pander."

They paused the conversation again when the server set down their entrees.

Jackson pulled a long spear of fried sweet potato from a tall stack of shrimp and vegetables. "Is it just me, or is the trend toward stacked food getting ridiculous?"

"You should never order the napoleon if you don't like that sort of thing."

It was at precisely that moment that he decided to fire her. He certainly didn't need someone who would undermine his opinions and criticize his order skimming fifteen percent of his earnings.

"Trust me, I will gain far more publicity by refusing the show than by going on."

"I'm trying to trust you, but, contrary to what they say, any publicity isn't good publicity."

"What about Stegner? As soon as it was alleged that he plagiarized *Angle of Repose* from Mary Hallet Foote, what was the publishing world's response?"

His agent looked around the room, but Jackson kept his gaze steadily on her weirdly small eyes. "Well?"

"A box-set of both works."

"Released in early December. Just in time for Christmas."

"Look, it was a service to literature to package those two books together so readers could draw their own conclusions. Anyway, it didn't sell very well. And, besides, they're both dead. What I'm saying is that if the public perceives you as arrogant, they won't buy your books."

"I'm well aware who buys books and who does not." Mentally composing a letter breaking off their professional relationship, Jackson said, "And everyone who buys books has already bought mine."

An hour later, he was on the phone to his editor. "Brilliant!" she cooed. "You made the news. The on-line sales spike is unbelievable."

Two hours later, he completed his revision of *Hide and Seek.*

# Chapter forty-eight

Henry Baffler returned to a grueling schedule, writing his "open and circular" novel from six until noon each morning, breaking for a small lunch, and then writing until his stomach could wait for dinner no longer. If he ate dinner in his apartment, he usually went straight to bed afterwards. If he went out, the stimulation was enough to allow him to work a few more hours upon his return. Even when he wrote deep into the night, he never failed to rise at six to begin the next day's work. If pressed, he couldn't have said what day of the week it was; he worked all seven.

His only distraction was Clarice Aames. As the date of her public reading neared, his excitement grew and his work ethic eroded. To the best of his knowledge, no picture of Clarice Aames had been published. Sometimes he imagined her as a dominatrix—tall, dark, wrapped in tight black clothes—but sweet-natured. Other times he fantasized about the opposite combination: pretty and petite and innocent-looking, but with a mouth full of biting sarcasm. He knew that speaking to her was a long shot, but he prepared lines anyway. Just in case he got the chance, he wanted to make sure that he didn't sound like some obsessed or groveling fan. No, he'd speak to her as an equal, only less so, and get her ideas on the triangular relationship between her work, anti-realism, and the *nouveau roman*. He had no doubt, none whatsoever, that she'd read Robbe-Grillet, but preferred Sarraute. He wondered if he would sound immature or mystical if he mentioned that his birthday was the same as Sarraute's: July 18.

On the appointed day, he took the subway down to Murray Hill to meet up with Eddie and Jackson at Eddie's place. He made his way past the miniature police post that had sat outside the Cuban embassy in this WASP and East Indian neighborhood since Castro's bell-bottom-era visit, and waited with Eddie for Jackson to show up.

"My book's reviewed in there?" Henry reached for the paper folded on the Renfros' coffee table before Eddie could snatch it away.

Not only had he not been reading his reviews, it hadn't even occurred to him that his book was being reviewed until he saw his name on the newsprint.

"Don't read it, Henry. It's better not to read your reviews ever, even when they're good."

"So it's a good review?" Henry asked.

Eddie shook his head as Henry read:

This poor creature was so deluded as to the quality of his novel that he risked his life to save the manuscript. Anyone who has managed to read a hundred pages of it—it is impossible, I assure you, to read much more—wishes that this young writer would take fewer chances with his life.

"I certainly didn't mean to risk my life," Henry said. "What a way to die: in a fire started by some mawkish drunk. That's not how I want to go."

"How would you like to go? Not like that poor writer Hinks, I hope?"

As a man who owned neither television nor computer, Henry was accustomed to not understanding cultural references, and continued, "At home, I think. I mean a real home. A cabin in the woods. That's what I'd like to have, and then die there."

"Is that where you'd be living if you'd never come to New York?"

Henry tried to recall his mother's face while avoiding the image of his brother's. "Yeah, maybe. Maybe I could have taught school somewhere—maybe on Lake Superior or somewhere like that. Just teach and write by the fire. What about you?"

Eddie scratched the stubble on his cheeks. "I should have lived a quiet life, working some day job and married to some unambitious girl who'd never even been to New York. But I made the mistake so many of us make. We think we're writers and so we have to live in New York. The art, the libraries, the concerts, the museums, the plays. The truth is that I never go anywhere but the bar. Hell, I might as well live in Idaho or somewhere. I mean if I wrote specifically about New York, it might matter. Otherwise it's a disaster. Writers come here to be degraded or to perish. It would make a lot more sense to live somewhere remote if you want to write."

Henry nodded. "And somewhere cheaper."

"We should go be expatriate writers somewhere."

"The Midwest?"

"No, a real other country. Hemingway in Paris. But somewhere less expensive and warmer. We should all move to Greece!"

Henry was about to ask Eddie if he'd already started drinking, when Jackson's voice boomed through the intercom.

"Get your asses down here and let's get that curry in a hurry."

By the time they'd eaten Afghan food and made their way down to the CIA Bar, a young, black-clad, and mostly bespectacled crowd had gathered.

"Don't worry." Jackson patted Henry on the back.

In a few minutes, he returned with the manager, who led them to a table near the front and took their drink orders.

"You slip him a hundred?" Eddie asked.

Jackson shook his head, his bangs flopping to the side. "Much higher price. I have to read here next month."

Eddie folded his arms and looked over his shoulder at the bar.

The three writers sipped their way through a few rounds of drinks as the room filled, seemingly past capacity, and grew loud with conversation. Several people came to the table to introduce themselves to Jackson, praise *Oink*, or solicit an opinion about this or that agent. All of them made comments about the bar's Cold-War-era spy décor. Jackson consistently introduced his friends and plugged their books, a gesture that Henry appreciated but seemed to annoy Eddie.

"They aren't here to schmooze about *Conduct*," Eddie snarled, "so just leave me out of it."

"Oh no," Jackson whispered as a slight girl with hair like a cap wisped by the table. He watched her as she moved away, toward the podium and microphone.

Butterflies rose in Henry's stomach. "That's not Clarice Aames?"

Jackson shook his head. "Warm-up act, I guess."

The manager slid behind the microphone and thanked the crowd for coming. "Welcome, welcome to this great line-up. Yes, it's true, we do have Clarice Aames, and I guarantee she'll flatten this room."

The crowd whistled and clapped. The atmosphere was like that of a rock concert. Henry realized that Clarice would never even make eye contact with him, that he certainly wouldn't get to talk to her.

"But first, first, I've got a terrific new novelist for you to hear. Any writer here would die for the reviews she's been getting."

The crowd stayed noisy, but its sounds returned to conversation.

"Reading from her novel *Pontchartrain*—Margot Yarborough."

A few people, including Jackson but not Eddie, offered subdued applause, but most continued talking, drinking, and bustling to the bar for more drinks.

The writer was small, her face barely clearing the podium, and Henry strained to hear her over the crowd and the feedback from the microphone. He couldn't make out all her words, but she seemed to be reading about a man confined to a leper colony somewhere in the deep south.

"So am I to understand that leprosy isn't too quiet?" Eddie said under his breath.

Jackson kept his gaze on the writer, who didn't look up from the book she was reading from.

Henry closed his eyes. Unable to hear whole sentences, he concentrated on picking out words. Even the shortest ones seemed rare and faceted, like poems unto themselves: moss, glide, muskrat, pirogue, heartache.

Her reading lasted only fifteen minutes and was followed by brief, polite clapping. The young woman, who was quite pretty, slipped through the crowd. As the crowd grew restless waiting for the very tardy Clarice Aames, Henry glanced around to see where Margot Yarborough was sitting, but he never saw her again.

# Chapter forty-nine

Jackson Miller, in the middle of one of the strangest nights of his life, felt nothing short of fractured. In a room full of aspiring writers—who the hell else attends a fiction reading—he was a celebrity. But this seemed to elicit only disdain from his friends, or at least from Eddie. Eddie acted pissed off that he'd bargained a reading in order to get them a table, and Jackson was tempted to tell him to grow the fuck up and realize that he'd done it not to show off but for Henry's sake. Instead he tried to appease Eddie by talking up his book to fans, but those efforts also met with disapproval. All he seemed to be able to do for his once-best-friend was to give him yet another excuse to drink too much.

And then, watching Margot read, Jackson was overwhelmed by tenderness. He toyed with the idea of begging her to marry him but was also taken with the notion that Margot and Henry might be hapless soul mates. Mostly, he worried that he would never be able to have real friends again. As he clapped loudly after Margot's mostly inaudible reading, he realized anew what she must have known all along: she was better off without him.

What he needed was a woman like himself. He wanted a

woman who was successful and good-looking so could he be sure he was truly desired rather than seen as a good trade-up, an opportunity, an object of bragging rights. What he needed was the female equivalent of the Jonathans. He stared at Eddie, whose posture already sagged with the liquor he was knocking back, and resisted the urge to hit him as hard as he could. Eddie had no idea what to do with a woman like Amanda. Jackson should have stopped him from marrying her in the first place.

Whether or not he really would have decked his friend, he would never know. Several women shrieked, and the room seemed to roar. A tall woman in a long, black wig and white cat-suit stalked through the CIA Bar. Jackson measured the perfect but familiar line of arm, the bottom shaped like an inverted heart, the long curve of slender calf. The woman grabbed the microphone.

"I don't want an introduction," she said loudly, surveying the crowd. "I *am* an introduction."

All she needed was a guitar to convince anyone she was a rock star. She even sang her first story: a short-short told from the point of view of a politician's penis. Her falsetto was confident, and she swayed her ribcage in a snake-like move.

"That one's titled 'Little One Eye,'" she said to the raucous room. "And now for something serious."

She read from a pristine manuscript in an unnaturally low voice. Jackson concentrated on her features, imaging her without the wig and makeup. He glanced at Henry, to his right, whose hands fell to his lap as he leaned forward, staring. To his left, Eddie was scanning the room as he swirled melting ice cubes around his almost-empty drink. Even when he looked toward the podium, his stare was vague.

Clarice Aames continued to read her story about a movie star trapped by her own fame who hires a ghostwriter to pen a fake autobiography. Toward the end of the story, the narrator puts her ghostwriter in his place by calling him an amanuensis. Jackson had not seen nor heard the word since Iowa, when the workshop had argued that Amanda couldn't use it, that it was too pretentious for fiction. Amanda had been furious, in her subdued way, arguing over post-class drinks that nothing was too pretentious for fiction, that she could use the word if she damn well pleased.

And so it was the theme of the story and that single ridiculous word, even more than the hints of Amanda's silky voice leaking through Clarice's low husk, that convinced Jackson that he had been right at first sight. Clarice Aames was Amanda Renfros. Barely hearing the story now, he watched her mouth open and close over her words. He adored her more than ever.

Jackson studied Eddie's face again and decided that his friend was too far gone, was beyond contempt, if he couldn't even recognize his own wife's fabulous limbs under the skin-tight white spandex, her hand in its glove, the shape of her eye under the thick black liner and purple contact lenses. Eddie was a ruined man if he didn't remember how badly she had wanted to get away with using the word *amanuensis* to distinguish someone who merely copies from someone who writes.

He no longer wanted to punch his friend. As he watched Amanda frenzy the room with rhyming couplets, he wanted to kill him.

As Amanda pushed herself through the rising swarm of fans, Jackson stood and kicked Eddie's chair out from under him. He grinned, feeling strong. But pity overcame his rage at the sight of his old friend inebriated, knocked back on his can, oblivious to the life he could have claimed for himself. Too drunk to realize why he was ass to the floor, Eddie reached up a hand for help and was pulled to his feet by Jackson's old basketball hoist.

# Chapter fifty

Back at home, Margot Yarborough contemplated the fate of intelligent good girls throughout history: teaching. She accessed the job lists of the Modern Language Association and the Association of Departments of English. Without a terminal degree, she could not hope for a tenure-track professorship, but there were instructorships and lectureships for which a Master's degree and a published book were sufficient credentials.

One morning, while she was tailoring her application letter to a women's college in upstate New York and a liberal arts school in Virginia, the phone rang. It was her father's friend, Mr. Quarmbey.

"I'm afraid he's not in," said Margot, realizing that her father had again failed to return from what was supposed to have been a short walk. "Can I take a message?"

"I just wanted to let him know about poor Hinks's novel."

"Wasn't it terrible about his death!" Margot said. "He was a nice man and a very good writer."

In truth, she felt more than a little guilt over not starting the journal that her father, Quarmbey, and Hinks had advocated. It would have been an economic failure, she knew that, but it would have been no worse than how things had turned out. Hinks might still be alive, and her father would be a happier person.

"I've done my best to place *The Great Adirondack Novel* so that his death won't be a complete waste."

"That's a nice thing to do."

"I'm afraid I've had no luck. I thought maybe the publicity angle would help—man dies in service of literature and all that—but the few editors willing to take a second look haven't changed their minds since they rejected it the first time."

"It just doesn't seem fair. I suppose the novel is too well-written and too quiet? Maybe too rural?"

"Apparently the novel is actually quite awful. So many writers of the literary short story write plotless novels, but Hinks overcompensated. Too melodramatic is what I'm hearing back. Not quiet enough. Not literary enough. And his effort to write in a female point of view was apparently dreadful. Lots of talk of menstruation and that sort of thing. I always did view Hinks as a short story writer. Some writers have their form, their length, and that's that. I should have warned him away from the novel. Anyway, let your father know I tried."

"It was a good thing to do. Thanks for letting us know." Margot paused to switch ears. "You should come see us sometime. We miss having you around."

She was aware that no one came to visit them anymore, not even Quarmbey, and that her father's notorious irascibility could not be the lone reason. Wondering if her mother had figured out what she had observed, she slipped out to help her ailing father find his way home.

# Chapter fifty-one

Sitting only a few blocks away from the Frick and the painting that had sparked her wealth and fame, Amanda Renfros stared at the tall case of tortes and tarts in the Café Sabarsky. She made a mental note to ask her copyeditor if it was proper to say ladyfingers or ladies-finger as she gazed at the Walderbeere torte buried under small, wild strawberries. But the chocolates vied for her attention: the simple, dense sachertorte, the flourless chocolate-walnut cake, the chocolate-rum cake, the German chocolate roulade. That was the problem, really, with Grub—no proper pastry chef. She was glad Jackson had picked this up-town location for their meeting. The world of women read-ers that could forgive her for being attractive and successful might be less generous about her ability to eat desserts without putting on weight. They might not see it as she did: compensation for living for her first eighteen years with poverty, anxiety, and weirdly colored boxes of generic cake mix.

"I'll wait to order," she told the obsequious waiter, "but bring some champagne."

"Celebrating the end of summer?"

"I'm celebrating everything." She held her smile as Jackson filled the entryway.

As they neared the end of their first bottle of sparkling wine and waited for her spatzle and his liverwurst and onion confit, Jackson got to the point. "I'm here to blackmail you. I know your secret."

With Eddie, Amanda always felt a step ahead, in charge, the grown up, on top of the game. Part of the excitement of being around Jackson was that he was capable of one-upmanship, the trickier line, the ambush. He could pull her strings.

"I have no secrets from you, Jack." She pulled back her smile, worked an expression of mild astonishment and light concern.

"From me? Not anymore. But you do have a secret."

Jackson emptied the last of the champagne into her flute, paused as the waiter set down their food, and nodded that they did indeed want another bottle. As the waiter backed away, Jackson whispered, "Clarice."

"Oh. That." Amanda ducked her shoulder under her hair as she speared a piece of wild mushroom with a silver tine. She looked up, lifting her eyebrows, "But you said blackmail?"

"Surely you don't want Amanda Yule's legions of women fans to know that she dresses like catgirl and reads to liquored-up irony boys in the West Village? And isn't Amanda Yule everything that Clarice Aames's fans find repellent?" He concentrated on his food again, mumbling about the high quality of the liverwurst before saying in a way that sounded at once planned and off-hand, "And then, of course, there's Eddie."

Amanda continued to make her way through the mound of spatzle and sweet corn. "But you're only supposed to blackmail people who are richer than you are. I don't have anything you don't."

"Yes you do." Jackson's stare bore through her. "You have exactly what I want."

Neither of them wanted to flatten the electricity with a long cab ride or spoil the romance with a bed one of them had shared with someone else. And so twenty minutes found them not at Jackson's apartment but in the lobby of a newly opened East Side luxury hotel.

"Just one night?" the young woman at the desk asked.

"About four hours ought to do."

"You'll have to pay for a whole night," the clerk said flatly, without looking up.

Jackson pushed a credit card across the counter. "Charge me for a week if you want. I intend to get my money's worth."

Feeling momentarily shy, Amanda concentrated on the elevator's paisley carpet as they ascended to the eleventh floor, but Jackson caught her gaze and locked it. As she returned his stare, she felt more vulnerable than she had in years. But unlike in those early years, the vulnerability felt good. She was tired of always being strong.

Everything in their room was pale blue or glass, and Amanda felt as though she were floating in cool light as Jackson kissed her. Eddie's lips were shallow, and sometimes with him Amanda had felt as though she were kissing his skull. And it had been months and months since Eddie's mouth hadn't tasted sour with Jim Beam or the cheapest of Highland malts.

Jackson's lips were soft and full, the good champagne on his breath had a pleasing mineral taste, and their mouths fit together perfectly. As they stretched out on the king-sized bed in front of mirrored closet doors, Amanda realized that she was finally with the right person. Jackson pulled back from kissing her, stroked her cheek, and then swatted her hard on the rear.

"You're going to do whatever you want to me, aren't you?"

"You made me wait a long time," he answered. "I've had a long time to think about it."

The feeling that she wasn't in control—that she wasn't the responsible one, that she would do whatever he wanted—thrilled her. She was at his mercy, and her throat trembled.

At first Jackson's moves were gentle and smooth. He touched her face, her hair, undressed her slowly, ran his hands down her sides, kissed her more, made love to her with real tenderness. But by the time the room was lit with only the faded, slanted light of dusk, she had, at Jackson's bidding, submitted to nearly every act she could imagine even the most degraded of courtesans committing. She felt used, exhausted, and happier than she'd ever been.

"Maybe next time I'll come as Clarice," Amanda said as she dressed, pleasantly shaky on her feet. "And then we can really have some fun."

"I love you," Jackson told her as he put her into a cab. "For years now, I think."

Traffic was fierce, and Amanda was happy for the long ride. She replayed the afternoon in her mind, holding her hands to her face to breathe in Jackson's lingering smell.

As the taxi neared her block, though, she felt unsure of herself and embarrassed at the thought of being seen by Eddie. Relieved when she found he wasn't home, she showered and set to work. By the time her husband had returned to drink and read in their living room, Amanda had complicated the plot of her new novel.

Her protagonist, Amelia—the female writer married to a marginally successful writer—launches an affair with an ambitious writer named Jaspar, who becomes wildly successful after writing a book about a moderately-known painter, an idea he gets from Amelia. His reputation further skyrockets when he refuses to appear on a popular television book club. The talented lovers meet over tiramisu. Unable to resist each other's fabulous good looks and irresistible charm any longer, they romp in the good linens and over the chairs and ottomans of a near-by luxury hotel. Discussion of the Proustian madeleine ensues. It needed refining, Amanda knew, but the draft read:

> Jaspar traced the conspicuous yet feminine vertebrae that delineated Amelia's perfect back. "Whenever I taste espresso-soaked ladyfingers/ladiesfinger," he said, "I will be permeated by the tender nostalgia that so overwhelmed Marcel Proust's narrator, Swann, when his lips tasted the petite madeleine."
>
> "Oh yes," replied Amelia, nearly purring, "that famous literary pastry of fond memory."

Amanda's warm sense of wellbeing drained as she thought about Eddie, and she put on a cardigan against the chill. There was ugliness and hurt ahead—it couldn't be avoided—and she wished she was already on the other side of it, already leading the life that would permit no further stain.

# Chapter fifty-two

After reading the how-to books he'd ordered, most of them written by marginally successful literary agents or blatantly unsuccessful novelists, Eddie Renfros decided that he might as well make the final stop before he hit rock bottom and try his hand at poetry.

Thanks to Amanda's out-of-control success, they no longer needed what money his fiction might bring in, and it was clear to Eddie that he had lost his wife's respect for him as a novelist. He assumed that he was going to lose her fully, in feeling, probably in deed, but he harbored a small hope that he could win back her affection with the very thing that had driven her away: his commitment to language rather than the literary marketplace. Besides, he reasoned, he might more easily manage verse since his concentration was too soggy to sustain an entire novel. It would be good for him, too, to move away from the computer screen and work again in pencil. He'd always loved the sound of soft graphite moving across paper.

He waited for Amanda to inquire, or at least to notice what he was doing, but it had been weeks since she had last asked him about his work. What had once seemed like aggressive nagging, he now yearned for as evidence of wifely interest. Amanda was always coming in or going out—rarely in the apartment except to sleep and write. More and more, though, she left each morning with her new laptop, saying it was easier for her to write in public than at home.

One Saturday afternoon she breezed in with several shopping bags. Eddie recognized the names of expensive department stores, women's boutiques, and a lingerie retailer. It had been months since he'd seen Amanda in anything other than full street clothes or her oversized bathrobe and hair towel. It seemed as though a decade had passed since the early days of their marriage, when she would rush in from shopping and then materialize in the living room wearing a corset and garters, or adorable panties and ankle socks, or something cake-like with layers of white lace.

He wanted to ask her to model whatever it was that she'd just bought, and he hated her because he could not. "You're spending a lot of money lately," he said instead. "The advance may not last forever."

"I've got another one and it's going to last a long time."

"Another advance? I didn't know you'd even finished the new book."

"Yep," said Amanda from the bedroom. Eddie could hear the rustling of bags and tissue paper. "Last week. Sorry, I should have told you."

Eddie walked slowly to their bedroom. "You weren't going to have me read it?"

"I'll give it to you when I get the galleys. You've seemed busy—writing letters or whatever it is that you've been up to with all that pencil sharpening."

"Not letters. Poetry."

She turned and cocked her head, her smile not unkind. "Poetry?"

"I'd really like to read your new book." He moved behind her and stroked her back tentatively, wincing as her body tensed against his touch.

"Capital," she said. "I'll print you a copy. Meanwhile, can I see a poem?"

Eddie sat across the room on the sofa while his wife read three of his poems at the dining room table.

She looked straight at him when she finished. "These are good. Especially the sonnet."

"Really?" he asked.

She nodded. "Really good. You might consider applying for a fellowship or grant of some kind."

"The kind where I go away for a few months and leave you alone?"

She pushed the pages away and stood. "No, Eddie, for once I wasn't thinking of myself. These are really good poems, and I'd like something good to happen for you."

Two days later, working through a blunt headache and a slow breakfast of coffee and toast, Eddie realized that Amanda still hadn't given him a copy of her new manuscript.

"Print me a copy right now," he said to his wife as she checked her purse to go out. "Or don't you want me to read it?"

"The truth is that I do and I don't. I haven't quite recovered from your remarks about the point-of-view scheme in *The Progress of Love*." In jeans and a white turtleneck and no make-up, she looked very much like the graduate student he'd courted and married.

"May I remind you that your responses to my work have occasionally been less than sensitive?" he said.

Amanda sat down across from him, nodding slowly. "Fair enough, and I'm sorry for that. I guess I understand better now how it smarts. But I really can't bear to field any snide comments about what's literary and what's commercial. I write what I write, and frankly that's what pays the bills."

"I'm sure that if I forget that, you'll remind me."

"It's just that you make me feel like I'm a bad writer, and I'm not. I've just made a decision to try to write things that people are interested in reading."

"Then let me read your new book. I'll bite my tongue about that other stuff."

"The truth is that I kind of wish I hadn't written this new book, that I'd written about something else instead." She chewed her bottom lip a little, her face clouded by a rare shadow of uncertainty.

"I'm sure it's really good, Amanda. Really, I'd like a copy to read—just as a reader. You know I've always admired your prose, the way you can end a paragraph with a punch that doesn't feel like a gimmick."

She walked around behind the sofa and folded her arms around his neck. Her sleek hair slid against his cheek, and he breathed in the clean, sharp smell of citrus.

"I don't know how we ever let things get so difficult," she said in a tone he couldn't parse.

"It's not too late, don't you think?" He tried to turn his head to face her, but he didn't want to break the embrace. "I hope it's not too late."

She pulled over and went to the counter to retrieve her purse. "If you really want to read the book, ask me next week, and I'll print you a copy. But remember that it's not what I wanted to write. I wish I could have written something else." She sought his eyes and gave several small, earnest nods before leaving.

By the time Eddie remembered to ask her where she was going, she was already out the door. At the window, he watched for her to appear on the sidewalk below, saw her step into the street and hail a taxi to wherever it was that she was heading.

# Chapter fifty-three

Standing by one of his nine windows as night sank into Harlem, Henry Baffler argued with Eddie over the difference between flash fiction and prose poetry. His inebriated friend claimed that the two were synonymous and could be used interchangeably, only that poets were more likely to use the term prose poem, while fiction writers and most readers tended to say short-shorts or flash fiction.

"That may be the case, but it shouldn't be the case," Henry insisted and laid out the case for flash fiction as a distinct form.

"Fine," Eddie said, with a stretched sigh. "To go on debating this might lead you to believe that I actually care about this particular issue."

"How can you not care?" Henry asked, more bewildered than indignant.

On the other side of the glass fell a slow, steady snow—distinct flakes visible against the lighted store signs and streetlights.

"The art of living is the art of compromise or, in my case, of not giving a damn, which amounts to compromise. Who are we to foster our precious sensibilities and act like the world gives a rat's ass about our petty ideals? Ideals lead to misery for others and ourselves. That's true in politics, so why shouldn't it be true in literature and in life? You and I need to learn to cultivate genial vulgarity—that's what we need—if we're to get anywhere at all in life. What right do we have to make ourselves and others miserable for the sake of our stubborn idealism? We must make the best of circumstances. Why cut bread with a sharp razor when a serviceable bread knife is at hand?"

"Where'd you get that line? And what are you talking about?" Henry asked. Still he watched the snow, falling harder now.

"Oh my God. I sound like Jackson now, heaven help me."

"It's impossible to really describe all the kinds of snow in words, isn't it?"

"Unless you speak Inuit or Norwegian or one of those languages with three hundred words for snow."

"That's not really true about those languages," Henry said. "Nowhere near three hundred, and a lot of them are just compound words. You know, like wet-snow. Anyway, I think maybe our highest calling would be to develop and write in an entirely new language. Pure invention."

"Highest calling? Ask yourself what the coarsest man would do, and do that. That's the only safe way to live."

A shift in wind changed the pattern of the snow against the street lights. Ice-edge, Henry thought, were words that paired nicely. Icedge, a word like a blade scraping on ice. He grabbed a notebook and wrote it down. Later he would find a way to build a paragraph around it. Further down the page he wrote wetsnow, wets-now, wet-snow. He was on the brink of something, he could feel it, though he didn't know what.

*Chapter fifty-four*

The first time Jackson had slept with Amanda, the event was as emotionally rich as he thought it would be. The next time, later that same blue afternoon, had been as deliciously depraved as he had hoped it would be.

It was true that Amanda lacked Margot's girlish quality. On the contrary, she looked a little older than she was. But hers was a beauty independent of age, and it was clear that even at forty, at fifty, at sixty, she would be attractive and elegant, even regal. Every lilting line she uttered suggested just enough deliberation to give it the value of considered opinion without sounding either opinionated or, worse, indecisive. Her smile was at once playful and intelligent, and her glance suggested that no subtlety would slip past her unnoticed.

And all this, despite the fact that her origins were humble in the extreme. She was a self-made woman, and if it happened that the occasional smutty word or trailer-inflected phrase rolled off her tongue in bed, then so much the luckier was the man who possessed her. In the living room, at parties, during her television appearances, she sounded as though she'd been born and raised by Ivy-educated, martini-drinking, Connecticut Episcopalians.

It was as he had expected: she was the perfect woman, and she belonged at his side. So Jackson continued the affair with no thought to morality and little to the unpleasantness of being caught and confronted by her husband, his once best friend. The sooner, the better, really, though he realized he could not appear to seek that eventuality. Amanda was not a woman to be pushed, and, besides, the deception and danger would provide them with an exotic memory of how they got together.

At any rate, it could be only a matter of time before Eddie read her book, and only an idiot could read her book and not come up with four for two-plus-two. Eddie wasn't stupid. Even without reading the book, he must already know. After all, Amanda spent three afternoons a week with Jackson and sometimes attended dinners and parties at his side. A snapped photograph at one such dinner had appeared in the society page of *The Times*. Another showed up on the party-poop page of a glossy.

"What happened with that sweet girl you were dating?" Amanda asked one day as they rested after making love.

"Are you jealous?"

"Jealousy isn't a productive emotion," she said, "but I am curious. You were quite keen on her. I wonder if I seem shallow in comparison."

"There's nothing second-place about you, Amanda. You're my blue ribbon."

"Did you love her?"

"I guess I was most of the way there. The truth is this: I would have made her a terrible husband. With you, I'm not such a detestable guy."

"Watch out, or I might decide to take that the wrong way." Amanda stroked his arm with cool fingers.

"Happiness is the nurse of virtue. I read that once."

"And who was it who said that independence is the root of happiness?"

"I don't know, Amanda, but the world is ours." Jackson rolled to his side so he could kiss her with his hand on her waist.

Their affair continued through the winter and into early spring. As Jackson had long imagined, Amanda was willing to try anything in bed, and their adventures kept him content while he waited to have her on paper and forever. If she had the upper hand in their relationship, he held power in the bedroom. It was an arrangement that pleased them, an arrangement that worked.

Now a year after the release of their first novels, their publication dates were again with weeks of each other. "Better than simultaneous orgasm" is how Amanda put it when they were alone.

One evening, shortly before the publication of *Hide and Seek* and *The Writers*, Amanda phoned.

"Eddie got hold of an advanced reading copy from a friend. He's reading it now."

"Come over," Jackson said.

"No." Amanda's voice was remarkably even. "It's time to finish up here. I have to do this myself—I owe him that. I am his wife. I'll let you know when it's over."

Jackson worried that Eddie would trick her into a reconciliation, that he would forgive her and convince her to stay married. But even as he fretted, he didn't believe in the unpleasant scenario. He and Amanda were too perfect a couple not to come true.

# Chapter fifty-five

For months, Henry Baffler struggled with his "open" novel, refusing to admit, even as page stacked upon page, that the book was going nowhere. With *Bailiff,* he'd *intended* the plot to go nowhere, for the book to circle back around to where it began and leave his plump protagonist unchanged. But that was not a formula he wanted to repeat. Repetition was death to art—that is what he'd read and what he believed. Besides, while he wanted this novel to unfurl rather than to move linearly, he certainly did not want it to be circular or static. The winter months were elasticized agony, as the very meaning of *open* raced away from him each time he pursued it.

When the phone call came, he had not yet conceded defeat, had not yet admitted that this might be the novel that he would always want to write but never would. The call was from a curator at MUCA, the Museum of Ultra-Contemporary Art, who wanted to gage his interest in being part of an exhibit on living novelists.

"Exhibit of living novelists," the man corrected himself.

Three novelists were being invited to live in the museum—on display—for one month, during which time they were each to compose a novel of at least fifty thousand words. The idea that this event might attract the attention of Clarice Aames, or at least the officers of ULCER, occurred to Henry, and he agreed to the small stipend and other terms.

"Let us know what you need in terms of typewriter or computer. To prevent the emailing or downloading of work-in-progress, there will be no internet access. You can bring no notes or books, only yourself, a few changes of clothes, and your toiletries."

"Even better," said Henry. "I won't even come with an idea."

"Perfect!" the curator said, with a glee that was either genuine or convincingly faked.

Two weeks later, Henry arrived at MUCA with a small suitcase boxing all his clothes and bathroom items. The other two novelists waiting in the museum foyer were not such light packers. The first was a woman of about fifty, wearing silk parachute pants tucked into some sort of cross between a sneaker and a knee-length boot. Her white tee shirt was weighed down with a dozen silver necklaces, and she was standing next to three very large suitcases. "It looks like a lot," she said, "but I have to carry my own bedding and towels. Chemical sensitivities."

The other novelist was a much younger woman, probably not even twenty-five. She was so drained of color that Henry inspected her to determine whether she was actually albino, but he discerned a trace of blue in her irises and the occasional blonde hair in her white eyelashes. She was as thin as Henry and her cowboy boots looked enormous under cinched up jeans and a man's dress shirt.

"They don't exist," she said. "Those New Age magazines try to get you to obsess about gluten and dust mites and simplicity so that you won't notice that the corporations who publish them are destroying our culture."

"Hmm." The older woman quivered a smile and fingered one of the silver medallions on her sternum.

Henry backed away a few steps and was relieved to see a man approaching. Though dressed like someone in his twenties, he looked to be in his late thirties. He tucked his hair behind his ears before shaking Henry's hand.

"Pete," he said, "I'm the curator of the exhibit."

"The exhibit," Henry repeated.

The writers were, indeed, an exhibit, though not an especially popular one—and considerably less popular than the fecal art show whose patrons they could hear through the temporary wall separating the two sections of the museum. Each writer had a platform with a twin bed, dresser, desk, and chair. Henry had asked for a computer, since it was free. The women had opted for manual typewriters—Maia on the grounds that metal was less allergenic than plastic and Rhiannon because typewriters used fewer of the world's dwindling petrochemical resources.

They were not allowed to leave the museum, though they were given regular food and bathroom breaks during the day. After hours they were allowed to use the employee areas, including the showers and lounge, but their contracts required them to sleep in the exhibit.

"I know that writers often sleep late," said Pete, "and there's no reason for you to get up before the museum opens. In fact, I think some of our patrons might find sleeping novelists more interesting than novelists-at-work."

Maia lasted three days before breaking her contract on the grounds of eye strain due to florescent lighting and the presence of more artificial materials in her living space than had been represented to her.

"I guess it's just you and me now," Henry said to Rhiannon that evening.

"What page are you on?" she snapped.

"We have the whole month," Henry replied. "I don't think it's a competition."

"When your parents name you after a shitty pop song, everything's a competition." Her pale eyes glared at him through the black eyeliner.

Unsure how to respond, he tried: "Do you like Clarice Aames?"

The brightening effect was immediate. "I love her. Have you read 'Lethal' yet?"

Later that night, over the millet and tempeh that Rhiannon had requested for their dinner, she told him the story of her childhood guinea pig. "If you don't breed a female guinea pig before she's about seven or so months old, you should never breed her, because her pelvic bones fuse."

Henry nodded, noticing that her nose was perfectly straight, evenly dividing her not unpleasant face.

"We didn't know, and I let the male into the pen one day. Evangeline got pregnant and I was all excited about the cute babies she would have. But her bones wouldn't open and the babies couldn't get out and she died." Rhiannon grinned. "Leave it to Clarice to top that guinea-pig story. 'Lethal' was incredible."

"That's a terrible story. Yours, I mean." He added that he was sorry, but it sounded like a question.

She shrugged. "My parents gave the male to a pet store, which probably sold him to some snake owner. We kept cats after that."

"Do you write about your family?"

She shook her head grimly. "Autobiographical fiction should be killed if it's not dead already."

"I agree." Henry resisted the compulsion to touch her colorless hair.

Their friendship grew across the weeks, though Rhiannon remained competitive about page counts and wouldn't tell him what she was working on. "It's kind of a labor novel," was the most she would say.

Henry worked away on his tale of a blind child—probably a boy though he refrained from using a gendered name or pronoun—living near a landfill with an alcoholic, deaf parent, probably the mother. He thought of it as meta-fiction: a comment on the state of the contemporary novel.

While the exhibit was not popular, it drew a handful of viewers, including a repeat visitor who never took off his Yankees cap and tried to taunt the writers into talking to him, which they were forbidden to do.

"I feel like a zoo animal," Rhiannon said to Henry one night.

"No," said Henry. "We're museum pieces. The novel itself is

a museum piece. How can we deign to write long narratives in this fractured world? It's fitting that we are an exhibit. We're history. Long live the death of the novel."

"I have a confession," she said after a pause. "I'm writing a novel-in-flash-fictions."

"That's a brilliant idea." Henry reached for her bony hand.

"Except," she smiled, "they don't really go together. It's really not a novel at all."

That night they made love in both of the twin beds they'd been issued. Rhiannon was bone and joint and fiber and hair with no fat and not much muscle. Lightly, with just his fingerpads, Henry touched her jutting hipbones, traced her ribs, thinking how like him she was. He was struck by the idea of a series of erotic flash fictions, each piece dedicated to an angle of the skinny body during sex.

"I suppose Pete would like us to do that during museum hours," he said after they finished.

"Would that be a bigger draw?" his new lover asked, "Novelists fucking instead of novelists-at-work?"

Henry winced at the verb. "Making love," he offered.

"Making love is dead," Rhiannon answered, but she backed closer into him and pulled his arm over her while she fell asleep.

Henry watched her from that angle, thanking fate for bringing him together with a literary girl with a serrated edge.

# Chapter fifty-six

Margot Yarborough had earned four interviews at that winter's MLA conference, where the nation's institutions of higher learning conducted their preliminary interviews for the following year's hires. She reviewed her interview schedule, together with the questions and answers she had typed up for each of the schools that might change her life with a job offer. Two of the interviews were to be held in hotel suites—a sign that the colleges had some money—but the other two were in the notorious cattle call room where forty interviews occurred simultaneously, many within earshot of one another.

She still had the one suit she had owned since graduating from college, though it now hung loose on her. She'd lost weight over the years plus a few more pounds as her father's illness had progressed and the waxing dementia exaggerated the selfish streak he'd always shown. He guarded his dinner plate as though his wife and daughter plotted to steal his war-time rations, and he often took food from Margot's plate as well as her mother's, grumbling that they had never appreciated everything he'd done for them. Once, as Margot reached for a dinner roll, he stabbed the back of her hand with his fork, saying

"That'll show you." She wore the four small, closely spaced bruises for a week.

Margot looked sideways at the full-length mirror on her closet door. Even with the shirt bunched into the waistband, the skirt slid to her hips, but she hated the idea of going to the mall with its bright lights and noisy people. More and more she lived in the literary past. Using two large safety pins, she tightened the skirt around her waist, telling herself that the jacket would hide the fashion wasteland. That thought carried her mind to Elliot, which—curiously or maybe not—brought her to Wallace Stevens. She grabbed *The Palm at the End of the Mind*, thinking it would make fine train reading.

Two hours later, she sat in the lobby of the Wellington Hotel, which swelled with suit-wearing young academics acting out various states of confidence and terror. Their one or maybe six interviews would be their sole chance at landing the coveted academic jobs that would elude, forever, slightly more than half of them. Like the breast man who never looks a woman in the eye, these nervous would-be intellectuals avoided each other's gaze and searched only for the university affiliations listed on name tags. Where the University of Nevada-Reno brought relief, Virginia sparked envy and Princeton inspired despair.

Because she had been outside the halls of academia for a couple of years, Margot had felt that it would be improper to claim her institution and had typed "No affiliation" onto her on-line registration form. The computer had taken her at her word, and her name tag read: "Margot Yarborough. No affiliation."

A tall man who looked to be in his twenties approached her. He had a long, blond ponytail, wore jeans, and carried a camera. "I'm making a documentary about the MLA convention. Are you here to get a job?"

Margot nodded.

"Can I ask you a few questions on film?"

Margot half shrugged, and the man smiled and switched on his camera.

"How many interviews do you have today?"

Looking into the lens, Margot told him four.

"Are you feeling ground down and humiliated yet? Any horror stories?"

She shook her head. "No, I'm feeling hopeful. If nothing else, it's a chance to talk about literature with intelligent and interesting people."

The young man flicked the switch and lowered the camera. "Sorry, love, but that's not what I'm after at all. Maybe I'll catch you at the end of the day and see what you have to say then." He stalked toward another job-seeker.

Margot had read all the interview advice she could find, and she watched the small bank of lobby phones carefully. It was considered impolite to phone up to the room more than ten minutes prior to the interview, because an earlier interview could still be going on. Yet to wait longer was to risk having to stand in a long line for a phone and then be made late by the overworked elevators at the conference hotels.

At twelve minutes before the hour, she moved toward the phones, lurking with a couple of dozen other men and women, most of them young and clutching new but inexpensive briefcases. She got to a phone, and a woman with a pleasant southern accent granted her the room number. Despite a wait for the elevator, she knocked on the hotel-room door at an ideal one minute past the hour, pleased at the perfection of her timing.

The door opened, and a head popped through the crack. "Just a minute," said a man with a chin-length bob and a red tie. "We're running a bit behind schedule."

Margot waited, her eyes tracing the swirls of paisley in the carpet. She was unsure whether it was more seemly to wait by the door or linger back by the elevator bank until the previous interviewee passed her. As minutes elapsed, she fretted about whether she could complete the interview in time to make it to her next appointment, in the group-interview area at a hotel several long blocks away. At last, a young man emerged and brushed past her, visibly trembling in his black suit, his feet leaving no impression in the loudly patterned carpet.

The man with chin-length hair popped out at her. "We're ready for you now."

The room smelled of people—too many of them too close for too long. The bobbed head introduced himself as Professor Smith, and two other men stood and introduced themselves as Dr. or Professor something. The lone woman shook Margot's hand with a lighter grip and introduced herself by first and last name.

"So," said the man in the red tie, "which job are you interviewing for?"

"Creative writing," Margot answered, clearing her voice. "Fiction."

"Oh, right, I'm in charge of that one."

"We're an expanding campus," the woman explained. "We're hoping to fill twelve positions."

"Twelve?" Margot knew that each school interviewed ten or so candidates for each job. "I suppose you aren't getting out of this room much."

"No," said one of the men. "We haven't seen a thing of New York."

The man with the red tie found her vita, and the interview proceeded well enough, if a bit stiffly.

When it was time for her to leave, the search committee chair said, "I only have one final question. Are you willing to live in rural Missouri?"

Margot nodded. "I'm willing to live anywhere."

She arrived at the cattle-call waiting area just in time to be ushered to the right table. Two very young men welcomed her and began their rapid-fire questions, mostly answering each other. Both seemed to have drunk too much coffee, and Margot didn't have to say much.

At this interview, the final question was: "Why would you even consider a job with a 4/4 teaching load that won't pay you enough to live within a hundred miles of our college?"

Margot smiled at them, seeking eye contact with first one and then the other interviewer, trying to make them remember her when they discussed candidates later. "I like to work hard," she said, "and I live frugally."

She had two hours before her next interview and so she toured the publishers' displays in the exhibits hall of the convention center, looking at the glossy covers of the intellectual biographies published by larger publishing houses and written by those few academic celebrities. She also examined the matte covers of the literary studies texts and poetry volumes of the university presses. The literary journals and magazines were there, too, so Margot paged through a few in the hopes of finding an appropriate one to submit a story she was contemplating. Thumbing through a journal with an austere brown front and no art, she found Frank Hinks' last story, published posthumously. Margot dug through her purse until she found a ten-dollar bill and four rumpled ones.

"Thank you," said the older man with the cashbox, seeming surprised by the sale.

At another table, a periodical with Kandinsky-like art on the cover caught her eye. Thumbing through, she recognized the name of the woman she'd been billed with at the CIA Bar: Clarice Aames. Her story, titled "The Lethal," opened with a child's pet guinea pig giving birth to offspring with no eyes. Margot set down the magazine and went to freshen up.

For her third interview—for a tenure-track job at a public university in the deep South—the timing of her knock was fine, and Margot was ushered into the room by a skinny man with a goatee, who introduced himself as the department's poet. She was also introduced to "the Shakespeare guy" and a woman whose specialty was Caribbean literature.

They occupied the only chairs in the room, leaving her to sit on the high bed, her feet dangling several inches above the floor. Their questions were straightforward, ranging from what she would do if a student turned in a truly wretched piece of writing to queries as to her literary influences. They agreed with Margot that reading was the first and best training for any young writer.

Margot nodded and continued, "While I'm not suggesting that writers should be trained as critics—"

"Why the hell not?!" The poet leaped from his chair. "The entire problem with literature is that young writers don't think enough about what they're doing."

Margot tried to explain her point of view. "I agree with you completely that young writers should be trained in literature, probably before they try to write."

The poet slammed his leg with his fist. "How am I supposed to know whether you're agreeing with me because you agree with me or because you want the job?" He looked furiously, left to right, right to left, left to right.

"It's both," Margot said. "I want the job, but I wouldn't misrepresent my views."

"What? I can't hear you. If I can't hear you in this small room, how are students supposed to hear you?"

Margot swallowed hard.

"Now I suppose you're going to cry. Look, you seem like a nice young woman, and I admire you for writing about leprosy—brave choice that—but we can't have you crying in the classroom."

With nothing any longer at stake, Margot stood. "I can think of no better words to leave you with than these, from the final paragraph of *The Return of the Native*: 'He left alone creeds and systems of philosophy, finding enough and more than enough to occupy his tongue in the opinions and actions common to all good men. Some believed him, and some believed not; some said that his words were commonplace, others complained of his want of doctrine; while others again remarked that it was well enough of a man to take to preaching who could not see to do anything else. But everywhere he was kindly received.'" She sucked in a large but silent breath. "It's difficult to imagine that our world might actually be crueler than that of Mr. Hardy."

The poet nodded vigorously and laughed. "But remember this: those folks tolerated Yeobright because 'the story of his life had become generally known.' We don't know you from Adam. Now, however, I'm a bit impressed."

Realizing that all might not be lost and that indeed this poet who could quote one of her favorite novels might actually be a kindred soul, Margot slipped her hand tentatively out to shake his good-bye. As she turned to the Shakespearean, though, the safety pin holding up her skirt popped open, and it fell nearly to her hips. She clutched at her waistband and backed from the room, bent over her briefcase and thinking *you won't call me, I won't call you.*

As had been the case during her book tour in Vermont, Margot was able to disassociate herself from what was happening to her, to see herself as though she were a character in a novel she was writing or reading. And again, as in Vermont, the book she was living was a minor comi-tragedy. She walked in her increasingly uncomfortable shoes back to the cattle-call area. In the closest bathroom, sardined between women busily brushing hair, blowing noses, and reapplying makeup, she double checked the security of her safety pins, patted her face with cool water, and put on a little lipstick. Get this job, she told herself, and wished she were indeed a character in a novel so that she could write her own ending.

There were three interviewers at the table, two men and a woman, all small and somewhat nebbishy, and she felt more comfortable with them than she had with any group of people in a long while. They actually discussed literature, and Margot grew hopeful as they told her about their library and bragged about their small Illinois town's farmers market.

"It gives us something to do as well as something to buy," said the older of the two men, smiling at her in a way that felt more paternal than anything she remembered from home.

# Chapter fifty-seven

When Eddie Renfros read the galley of his wife's book, he'd known at once that his suspicions had been well-founded. Just as he had always assumed might happen, Amanda was having an affair with Jackson. Worse, she was writing about it for the whole world, which would now know him as the lazy, underachieving, alcoholic spouse of celebrity novelist Amanda Renfros.

Still, he'd been prepared to forgive her, provided that she agreed never to see, speak to, or mention Jackson Miller again. But not only was she uninterested in his forgiveness, she seemed relieved that her adultery had been discovered.

"I'm sorry I didn't tell you myself, and I'm sorry if you're hurt," she'd said, her face composed.

"You're going to stop it right now."

She shook her head. "No, Eddie. It's really a question now of who will live where. You're welcome to the apartment, if you can afford it. You should certainly be the one to stay here for now."

Calmly, her eyes clear and her hair perfectly shiny, she packed a single suitcase, kissed him on the cheek, and thanked him for those months of their marriage that had been good. "I did love you, Eddie, and I kind of wish that we had never let it get past the point of no return. Probably we were never right for each other, but I don't think I would have written *The Progress of Love* if it weren't for you."

"You're welcome," Eddie spat out, but he no longer had the energy for real venom.

It was this listlessness that prevented him from taking scissors to the clothes Amanda had left behind, an idea he relished right up to the moment he pulled the scissors from the drawer, replaced them, and reached for a shot glass instead.

He remembered what Jackson had told him at his bachelor party: "Keep in mind that if you marry a head-turner, she's going to turn heads." That night he slept shallowly, jerking fitfully, with dreams that centered on the words 'head-turner' and 'page-turner,' 'page-turner' and 'head-turner.' He awoke thinking that he'd write a poem around the wordplay, but he went the day without lifting a pencil.

After wallowing in self-pity and vodka across the spring and summer, Eddie stacked the bills, checked his Amazon ranking, and realized that he should get a job. He was relieved; for the first time in a long time, he knew what to do with himself.

Eddie might not have interviewed at the MLA had the convention been held anywhere other than New York. That would have been too much effort, and his vigor waned rapidly after the initial burst of application-letter writing and vita printing. But the conference was in New York that year, and it seemed easy enough to move through the process.

Despite his dearth of teaching experience, Eddie held an MFA from one of the most prestigious fiction programs in the country, and he'd published two books—one of them critically acclaimed and the second, if not acclaimed, at least recent. While none of this had made him a success in his wife's sharp eyes, it served him well in a job market with a glut of one-book writers, many of whom had published nothing in years. He had ten MLA interviews for creative writing jobs, which led to three campus interviews, for which he sobered up long enough to receive two job offers. He turned down what many writers covet: a 2/1 teaching load at a large research-oriented university. He accepted instead a position at a small liberal arts college, where he would be expected to pamper the not-Harvard-material children of the wealthy, but could earn tenure without publishing another novel.

He moved to the central part of the state as soon as he was hired, identified the small town's least expensive liquor store, and settled into a nice old house and his new life while he waited for the students to return, the fall semester to commence, and the leaves to turn fabulous colors.

It was, he told himself, the life he would have chosen had he not married Amanda and her ambitions. Though it would take years to complete the revision in his head, he began to tell himself a different story of their relationship. In this new story, he cast himself as a somewhat roguish but very fine literary writer, who briefly slummed with a shallow writer of slick fiction for the usual reasons that men marry down: beauty and sex.

# Chapter fifty-eight

After their second criss-crossing book tours, Amanda Renfros settled happily into near-married life with Jackson. His decision to turn down the talk show had proved a brilliant publicity move. There was no other way to explain how a novel about the rather mundane life of a not-particularly-well-known Dutch artist could top the fiction bestseller list.

"Do you mind," Jackson had asked, "being number two?"

"Not as long as I'm your number one," she'd said in the voice she'd perfected for delivering sweet clichés in a way that made them sound at once ironic and genuine.

And, indeed, it was true that she did not mind. After years of marriage to Eddie, it was a relief to feel that she was finally wedding up.

Their apartment, located behind the locked gates of Sniffen Court, so perfectly suited her taste that she suspected Jackson had had her in mind when he bought it.

She kept busy conforming the interior of the apartment to her tastes—adding a grand piano, selecting window coverings, choosing colors for their guest room. She grew busier still planning a wedding likely to be covered in the society page of *The Times* and at least mentioned in *The Fair* or *Monde*.

Still, ever mindful of the disastrous fate of the has-been, she typed away at a new novel every morning. Titled *True Story*, the book told the story of a woman whose marriage destructs after she publishes a thinly disguised novel about her own adultery.

Occasionally, when Jackson went out to a party that didn't interest her, she coughed up a Clarice Aames story. She toyed with the idea of killing Clarice dramatically—perhaps in the line of fictional duty—but she loved and perhaps even needed her alter ego. She enjoyed having two different fan bases; she certainly didn't want to write only for women. But it was more than that. The truth she admitted to herself was that she liked Clarice's fiction more than her own. Clarice's stories seemed more important, telling the awful world into which she'd been born not what it wanted to hear, but what was wrong with it. She even liked the idea that she didn't get paid for most of Clarice's work, and so her bleeding-edge stories formed a kind of penance or tithe to literature, in exchange for the money she earned under her own name.

About two months before their own nuptials, Amanda and Jackson attended the wedding of Doreen to the insufferable Whelpdale. As Amanda expected, the ceremony—held in Grub's banquet room—was a rather appalling affair of interdenominational hoo-ha and weak floral artistry. Still, Doreen looked like the sweet girl that she was in a simple ivory satin dress. Amanda and Jackson were seated at the bridal table, together with two of the Jonathans. She had to hand it to Whelpdale; he'd put together a fairly impressive literary guest list.

"I have news." Doreen sounded slightly manic.

"Do tell," replied Jackson, ever charming and on cue.

"She's signed a book contract!" said her groom, pride visible in his smile and expanded chest.

"Oh my, my!" answered Jackson. "And this, after I had to sit through your little everyone-doesn't-need-to-be-a-writer speeches. What happened to culinary training?"

Doreen blushed and popped her shoulders up and down twice.

"I admit it. I was wrong. Besides, we want to start a family, so I can't be working long restaurant nights."

"A children's book?" Amanda asked, scooting backwards as the waiter set down a plate of goat-cheese manicotti before her.

Whelpdale continued to beam.

"Let me guess," said Jackson, pausing as though really thinking. "A chick-lit novel."

"Close," answered Doreen, eating gingerly across the satin of her bodice. "Two. Well, they're really two versions of the same book, geared at different audiences."

"Brilliant, isn't it?" said Whelpdale, his mouth not quite closed around his food.

Doreen turned back to Jackson. "One is for that adult chick-lit line, "Thong," and then I'm toning it down and younging it up for their new teen chick-lit series, which will be called "Kiss and Tell." My book will be the first in the series, and they've got some other writers lined up."

Other writers, Amanda thought, knowing those words would have elicited angry laughter from Eddie.

Jackson raised his glass. "To the author, on her wedding day!"

# Chapter fifty-nine

As the edges of his mind frayed, Andrew Yarborough often remembered how he'd felt before his bitterness had turned him into the self- and others-loathing version of himself that he had become. Related to this reawakening of his more likable self was his new life's work: the cleaning of his office and ordering of his papers and mementoes. This work would take months, perhaps even his remaining lifespan, but already he was reaping the rewards of less clutter and pleasing rediscoveries. He'd re-read letters from the best and brightest novelists from the generation after his, thanking him for reviews, recommendations, behind-the-scenes help. He had been someone, damn it; he had been known and respected.

One morning he tried to explain to Janelle this remembered sense of being someone, of mattering, of needing to be reckoned with. She'd set his breakfast before him—he might need her to cook, but he could still feed himself—and suggested that perhaps he'd been most powerful when he had concentrated on helping others. "It's when we focus on our own ambitions that they begin to outpace us."

Sharp come-backs were harder and harder for him, so he just muttered, "Mumbo-jumbo, write it up in a gift book."

But what he was thinking was that Janelle had held up remarkably well. He reached up and grabbed at her breasts before she backed away. Maybe there was something to that upside-down crap. And the gift books had saved their finances, he had to admit. She wasn't getting rich, but she was pulling in the money that he used to. They would be able to keep up with the property taxes and stay out of the poor house, particularly now that Margot was leaving home.

He could never have forced a real apology to Margot, but he made amends as best he could. They played the games they had played together when she was that cute, sweet little girl: checkers, jacks, twenty questions, guess the word.

He still had ill-tempered days when he grumbled at the women in his house. These usually came on his sharpest days, when he was closer to the man he had most recently been and could muster only rage at the prospect of his future. But more often than not, he gave way to the softening of his mind and enjoyed the declining responsibilities that accompanied his growing professional obscurity.

"Just don't ever let me be undignified," he said to Margot before she drove away. "When I die, don't let them bang my head on the floor of the morgue."

"I'm going to miss you, Dad." His daughter looked up at him with the same wide eyes she'd opened the day she was born.

"I was there when you were born, you know. I at least did that."

He stood in the driveway, feeling a sudden weakness in his left knee, as though he were standing on a slope and not level concrete. He lifted his hand, more in salute than in a wave.

# Chapter sixty

It was a phone call from Chuck Fadge that had Jackson Miller fuming. Fadge had proposed yet another inane writing story, something about which writers were dog people and which cat people, and was it true that one or more of the Jonathans had some sort of reptile for a pet. Except for the money, Jackson could see little difference between writing for Fadge's paper and writing for Whelpdale's ridiculous rag.

"He thinks I'm some hack," Jackson bellowed. "After *Oink*, it was one thing to write those pieces—I needed a platform, a way to get my name bandied about—but not now. Now people want to know what I think about actual issues."

"You're the man of letters," Amanda said, with no audible trace of sarcasm. "Tell him to go to hell."

"Really?"

He eyed his beautiful new wife, watched her hands as she scrolled out her perfect script on the engraved thank-you cards.

She set down the fountain pen and looked right at him. "Absolutely, straight to hell. You don't need him any more."

"Every man should have such a supportive wife."

"Every woman should have a husband short-listed for the National Novel Award." She resumed, then paused from her note writing. "Guess what I've done?"

"Should I be frightened?"

"No, it's something nice. I finished *Bailiff.* I even kind of liked it, so Clarice wrote a review and sent it to *Swanky.* I thought it might make Henry happy—if he's still sweet on Clarice."

"Are you going soft on me?"

She laughed and said, "Never fear."

In the living room, Jackson read his way through a couple of dozen pages of the book that had beat out *Hide and Seek* for the prize. It was a relief, really, to find the situation as he had expected. As more than one commentator had noted: the winning book was arty to a fault, written in what the author called "juxtaposed fragments," and by a woman. No doubt he'd never stood a chance with this year's panel of judges, and he'd been wise to be "previously engaged" the night of the award ceremony, photo op or no.

According to what his editor had been able to find out, the winning volume had sold only two thousand copies, even after the award announcement. Yet it was also true that he found the book's language oddly hypnotic, and he continued to read until he heard the squeak of Amanda's chair suggest that she was done with her note-writing and might be willing to retire to the bedroom.

A scant few weeks later the call came. He found out not from the Pulitzer committee but from a reporter from *The Times*, calling for his reaction to the good news. He fielded calls all day.

"I think we're going to have to change our number again," he told Amanda.

"People don't realize how hard our lives can be," she grinned.

"And now we'll be expected to go out and celebrate in style."

"Of course," she said, "but not at Grub. The quality of the food just isn't what it used to be. I felt sorry for Doreen when I had that manicotti. I read about a new place. I'll see if I can get us in tonight."

Jackson nodded. "Amanda?"

She reached for his hand.

"What should I write next?"

"Anything you want," she answered. "Anything you write will be capital."

# Chapter sixty-one

He couldn't remember asking her to, not exactly, but Rhiannon more or less followed him home after they left the exhibit. Despite her growing jealousy of anything he happened to be reading and their near-constant bickering, despite the relegation of his writing area to an office made from a kitchen closet, and Rhiannon's constant pronouncements that everything "is dead," Henry grew used to living with another body. With Rhiannon, he was not alone with his poverty and ideals; he shared them with her.

And so everything was both bad and good on the evening that they opened their door to find a somewhat stout man, wearing a suit with faux gold buttons and nervously smoothing back his thinning red hair.

"My apartment," the man explained, spreading his hands as though displaying his empire.

To Henry's great dismay, his anonymous benefactor was not in fact J.D. Salinger, John Fowles, John Berger, or some other reclusive genius, but simply a businessman named John Young, who had been overcome by eggnog-inspired good will after seeing Henry's on-camera leap on television. After a year of rent-free property ownership however, he remembered his disdain for skinny, poorly dressed young men who turned out to be living in sin with consumptive-looking girls in baggy pants. He was evicting Henry and Rhiannon from his Harlem apartment.

"I'm sorry," said Mr. Young to the unhappy couple, "but I've decided to steer my voluntary donations toward a public sports program for the boys up here."

"Voluntary and donation are redundant," said Rhiannon before Henry could stop her.

"What? At any rate, I am sorry, but I don't think I've done you young people a service by putting you on the dole. From the looks of you, I would have done better by you if I'd given you a gym membership. You've got to exercise the body first, then worry about the mind."

Henry eyed the bulging stomach on the man and recognized, from his middle-school nightmares, the football shoulders and chest. He had been first saved and then evicted by a man who had probably never read a real book.

Recognizing the foolishness of arguing, Henry said quietly to his girlfriend: "Back to Hell's Kitchen."

"If we can afford it." Rhiannon crossed her arms and issued a snort. "I saw the other day that another gallery has gone in by that old French restaurant with the jigsaw-puzzle portrait of Edith Piaff."

"Did you know that Edith Piaff was born blind in a whorehouse?"

"Then maybe your girlfriend Clarice Aames can write a story about her."

John Young interrupted. "I have no idea what you all are talking about, but I'm a decent man and so I'm going to give you two months' notice instead of one. No need to clean, because a sledgehammer's the next tenant. Just take all your stuff, lock the door behind you, and throw away the keys." He strode a few feet down the hall before turning back and handing Henry a letter. "Found this on the landing. Postman must have butterfingers."

Rhiannon snatched the envelope from Henry's hands and opened the letter. "Looks like you've got a girly fan. Margot something.

Before you know it you'll have quite a harem. You should remember this, though: polygamy is dead."

"I did buy your book, by the way, and I really did like the first few pages. Nice to see an author writing about a regular guy." John Young took only one more step before turning again. "Do throw away those keys when you leave, now, because they'll do you no good. The locks will be changed the very first thing."

## Chapter sixty-two

There hadn't even been a campus interview—just the one in the cattle-call pit and then the small surprise of the telephoned job offer, not tenure track, but permanent so long as she held up in the classroom. So Margot saw Rebuke, Illinois, for the first time when she arrived with a car full of her belongings. Driving in, she had been disheartened by the dreary two lane highway peppered with sex shops, hunting stores, and a single behemoth club grocery. Yet the town itself sat on a river, and there was a charm to the old albeit cheaply constructed houses. Rebuke could be walked end to end easily. There would be little, other than her students, to distract her from her work. The teaching load would be heavy, she understood this well, and her nights would be filled reading uninspired compositions about capital punishment and cigarettes and the electoral college and the virtues of sunscreen. She realized already, though, that it would be better to feel as though she had too little time than too much of it.

She taught sincerely and well. She drank coffee with her colleagues and occasionally tested a romance with a nice man in another department. She wrote and she published, sometimes in relatively obscure periodicals, but not infrequently in the country's most prestigious literary magazines. She did not read the other stories in these journals, though, and instead retreated to the eighteenth- and nineteenth-century novels she had always loved. Not only did she not attempt to write another novel, she determined that she would never write another book.

But the day came when she was contacted without warning by an editor at a university press. He had seen and loved some of her stories and wanted to collect her work into a volume. She agreed after he promised that she wouldn't have to give any readings and that she would have veto power over the cover art and title. As it turned out, she liked the jacket design presented to her: a simple black and gray graphic with the words *Bend, River, Bend.*

Encouraged by her colleagues, including the kind souls who had interviewed her and recognized her as one of their own, Margot earned her MFA through a low-residency program. She paid her tuition, submitted via email stories that had already been anthologized in *Best Midwestern Short Stories*, and endured wrong-headed suggestions for revisions offered by the energetic, barely published writer assigned as her mentor. With the terminal degree in hand and a new book in print, Margot was promoted to a professorship and awarded the tenure that would allow her to spend the rest of her career at Rebuke College.

Still a person who loved, perhaps above all else, reading and working with words, Margot was content. On those rare nights when she drank a little too much sherry, she sat in her bay window, listened to the passing river, and imagined herself as the heroine of one of the novels she loved: beautiful, well-spoken, and happily chaste.

# Chapter sixty-three

As a final payment, and to secure the consequence-less evacuation of his contract with *The Monthly*, Jackson penned a loving tribute to Chuck Fadge, praising his balanced encouragement of aspiring young writers, crediting him with far more influence than he in fact commanded, and lauding his silly compendium.

As a final effort to help good-hearted Doreen, he fervently argued, via phone and email, that she publish under the name she had been born into. But, alas, her incomprehensible love and respect for Whelpdale overpowered her slightly feminist upbringing. Both of her books were to be published under the name Doreen Whelpdale.

"It will help sell his how-to books," she explained. "You of all people should understand the financial component of my decision."

Despite his good effort to do the right thing by Doreen, Jackson no longer much cared. He realized, albeit somewhat sadly, that friends such as these were of the past. There were a few people in every life who were original casts. Amanda was one, and he could admit that there would never in his life be a replacement for Margot Yarborough or for his crusty old friend Eddie Renfros. Other people were, no matter how pleasant, interchangeable. Perhaps when he and

Amanda started a family they would hire a down-to-earth nanny who thought ill of no one and whose eyelashes had a girlish flutter. She would be their new Doreen. But the real Doreen wasn't worth the price of being linked to Whelpdale's how-to industry, which preyed on the hopes of aspiring writers. Jackson could have endured a connection to the "Thong" imprint, but not that. He had to let the association fade.

No doubt the organizers of the Blue Ridge Writers' Conference had sent him the invitation in some vain hope for generosity and nostalgia—past participant wins major literary prize—and indeed the director sounded disbelieving as Jackson mentioned possible dates for his short layover.

"We appreciate this so much!" she said, in a way that forced him to think of a word every writer loathes as much as utilize: enthuse. "Really, any day works for us. Any day at all."

"Awesome," he said. "Your conference rocks." He had no idea if the woman knew he was insulting her.

He'd planned to bring Amanda, to return with her as his wife and not Eddie's, and yet he found himself relieved when she was called away to Los Angeles. Though her agent had warned that calls from the West Coast meant less than any other calls in publishing, the film option for *The Progress of Love* had come to fruition. It was unlikely that the director would actually use the screenplay Amanda was working on, but she would in any case be paid handsomely for the effort.

"I'll join you on Saturday," Jackson had promised, booking a coast-to-coast flight from Charlotte. The New South, he thought, the inkling of a new novel crawling across his inner eye.

The Outlook Bar had been packed for his reading, drawing regional residents and tourists as well as the conference goers. Abiding by his publisher's sound advice, he'd read only early sections from his most recent book. He'd smiled widely during the signing and offered encouragement and occasionally suggestions of tangible assistance to the most attractive female conference participants. He was pleased to see, though, that not one of the women could compete with Amanda for more than an hour or two. The place was lucky she'd ever stood in the room.

It was much later, out on the deck, that Eddie Renfros approached him. The co-ed Eddie had trotted out to the conference was more young than pretty. She looked eager during the introductions but then, perhaps knowing her place, stepped away to look out at the view.

The two former friends started with small talk. Jackson knew that he shouldn't, but he couldn't help asking Eddie what he was working on.

"I'm dead as a novelist, and I'm happy enough to attend my own funeral. No, it's poetry, wine, and young women for me from here on out. The youngest I can get away with, anyway." His laugh was good natured, but the edge of one drink too many serrated the surface of his voice. "And I read more these days. To wit: 'We are such stuff / As dreams are made of, and our little life / Is rounded with a sleep.' There was a time when a way with words was enough, you know. Anyway, I've got a chapbook coming out with a publisher who's doing some really interesting things. And a real volume, too, with a university press."

Jackson tried his weight against the rail as the evening moon passed behind a cloud. "If you've found your calling, then I'm happy for you."

"And what of our old friend Baffler? Has he found his calling?" Eddie asked.

Jackson almost said *Amanda saw him* but caught himself and replied, "He's been spotted on the streets of Hell's Kitchen. Seems he's hooked up with an anorexic punk writer and lives even further west than he used to. Anyway, they tromp east toward the stagies every morning with those huge over-the-shoulder newspaper carriers filled with self-produced pamphlets. They're called something like *Flash One, Flash Two, Flash Three,* and so on. Dedicated to Clarice Aames, one suspects."

Eddie smirked as though amused, but underneath the smile, he looked fundamentally sad. "He eking out a living from that?"

Jackson shook his head. "I don't think so, but they also sell used books and make some bit off of that."

"He's the purest novelist I've ever met," said Eddie, gesturing back his girlfriend with a wave.

"You're a lucky man, Eddie." Jackson winked. "Be sure," he said in an exaggerated aside to the young woman, "be sure he tells you the story of how the *Sea Miss* emerged from the mist."

"Oh yes," she replied with an enthusiasm that already sounded forced. "That's a great story."

"Tuck him in tight." Jackson turned to embrace his friend, who held the grasp a bit too long.

"No hard feelings," said Eddie.

"None at all," Jackson whispered, more or less to himself.

After Eddie and the girl tottered off, Jackson stood in the spot where he'd promised himself success. He surveyed the vista he'd tried to describe five years earlier.

"The backs of the mountains curve like those of sleeping monsters," he tested, "benevolent in that they mean no one real harm—yet dangerous all the same."

# Acknowledgments

*G*rub is an updating of George Gissing's satire of the Victorian literary marketplace (*New Grub Street*, 1891). It draws on it, borrows from it, and could never have been written without it. I am indebted, also, to those friends who told me their stories of writing triumph and humiliation. Thank you.

# About the Author

CREDIT PHOTO TO:
Keith McGraw, University of South Carolina

*Elise Blackwell*

Elise Blackwell is the author of *Hunger* and *The Unnatural History of Cypress Parish*. She teaches at the University of South Carolina, in Columbia, where she lives with her husband, writer David Bajo, and their daughter Esme.

*The fonts used in this book are from the Garamond family*

*The* Toby Press publishes fine writing,
available at leading bookstores everywhere. For more
information, please visit www.tobypress.com